Praise for *Now That I've Found You* and Ciara Geraghty

'My favourite author does it again in this superbly written perceptive, poignant novel that makes you laugh and cry! Oh, I envy you the read of this. Treat yourself to a brilliant book!'
Patricia Scanlan

'Ciara Geraghty is a superb writer . . . Her books are meticulously researched, beautifully written, and infused with warmth, humour and human understanding.'
Irish Examiner

'With this witty and poignant novel, Ciara Geraghty continues to earn her well-deserved place among the best women writers in romantic fiction working in Ireland today'
Irish Independent on *Now That I've Found You*

'Heart-breaking and funny, poignant and life affirming.'
www.novelicious.com on *Lifesaving for Beginners*

'A beautifully written, somewhat whimsical and very encouraging tale about grabbing hold of life's reins, breaking away from the monotony of a dull routine and following your dreams . . . emotional, joyous . . . I adored it.'
Daily Mail on *Finding Mr Flood*

'Sad, funny and wise' *Marie Claire* on *Finding Mr Flood*

'Certain to appeal to fans of chick-lit supreme Marian Keyes'
Herald Sun, Australia on *Becoming Scarlett*

'A perfect mix of romance and comedy. Witty, sharp and intelligent' *RTE Guide* on *Becoming Scarlett*

'Move over Marian, it's Ciara' *Irish Independent* on *Saving Grace*

Also by Ciara Geraghty

CIARA GERAGHTY

now that I've found you

HACHETTE
BOOKS
IRELAND

First published in Ireland in 2014 by Hachette Books Ireland
An Hachette UK company

First published in paperback in 2015

1

Copyright © Ciara Geraghty 2014

The right of Ciara Geraghty to be identified as the Author of the
Work has been asserted by her in accordance with the Copyright,
Designs and Patents Act 1988.

A CIP catalogue record for this title is available from the British Library

B format paperback ISBN 978 1 444 725 865

Printed and bound by CPI Group (UK) Ltd, Croydon, CR0 4YY

Hachette Books Ireland policy is to use papers that are natural, renewable
and recyclable products and made from wood grown in sustainable forests.
The logging and manufacturing processes are expected to conform to the
environmental regulations of the country of origin.

Hachette Books Ireland
8 Castlecourt Centre, Castleknock, Dublin 15, Ireland

A division of Hachette UK Ltd
338 Euston Road
London NW1 3BH

www.hachette.ie

For Sadhbh MacLochlainn,
who showed me how to be a mother.

Dear Neil,

Dr Deery says I'm going through the anger phase. Apparently, bargaining is next. For example, I might find myself saying, if you come back, I'll . . . I don't know . . . give up cigarettes or something.

I said I won't make any bargains. Certainly nothing about cigarettes.

She says it's because I'm angry.

I preferred when she said I was in denial. Something soothing about denial. And compelling. It's true, you should never underestimate the power of denial. You could make yourself believe anything. Anything! Like when the buzzer went that afternoon in the apartment. I was watching the telly. One of those tragic daytime shows where the male and female presenters wear outfits that match the set and one of them reads the autocue and the other smiles and nods, against a backdrop of pseudo-sexual tension. Someone should research depression and possible links to daytime television.

Anyway, the buzzer went and I ignored it because I'm not expecting Mum til later. It went again. On and on, like someone had their finger pressed against it and everyone always said you were persistent. You'd keep worrying at something til you got what you wanted. That's how you got me to marry you, remember? I said no the first time.

And the second time.

I became convinced it was you at the door. You'd come back. You'd found out where I'd moved to even though I've told no one except Electric Ireland. That's it. Electric Ireland. Any other post goes to the clinic. Colm doesn't mind. He forwards it. Colm

1

knows I've moved. And Mum. But that's it. No one else. Colm still phones the odd time. Asks me to meet him at that café a couple of doors up from the clinic. The one you and me had a coffee at, the first day we looked at the premises. Seafood pie. That was the special that day, remember? We said we'd have lunch there, every Friday, after we bought the business. Another thing we never managed. Six times maybe. In five years. Didn't even notice at the time. Too busy, I suppose. It's only now, looking back.

Anyway, Colm still rings the odd time and asks me to meet him there. Says he wants to be able to 'bounce ideas off me'. I tell him he doesn't need me. He has lots of ideas for the clinic. He loves being in charge. Running the place. Reminds me of us at the beginning.

Third time lucky, you said. You had a ring that time. Booked a restaurant. Got down on one knee. You knew I'd be mortified. Everyone staring. You knew I'd say yes, just to get you back on the chair.

The buzzer rang another couple of times and then it stopped. That's how I knew it wasn't you.

It stopped.

Dr Deery says it's 'OK' to be angry. I didn't tell her I was writing to you. She might not think that's 'OK'.

If I'd done my residency at Crumlin instead of the Mater, I wouldn't have met you. Or if I'd studied something else. Art, maybe. I loved art at school. Still life. My mother smiled when I talked about studying art, like I'd said something amusing. Three generations of doctors. It was always assumed.

Or if my locker hadn't been beside yours at the hospital. All the things that might have happened. Might not have happened. All the ways that things might have been different.

Apparently, this is a form of bargaining. Dr Deery's always got something to say for herself. She says someone's got to do *some talking. Still, the insurance company insisted on counsel-ling. Or their doctor did. Said it was 'pertinent in the circum-stances', which is another way of saying they won't pay out unless I do as I'm told.*

Nearly time for the news at one. Then lunch, even though I'm not hungry. Still, it's important to maintain some kind of routine. That's what Mum says. I haven't seen this much of her since before I went to boarding school.

We've got a sort of a routine now. She brings food, I micro-wave it, we eat and watch telly and talk about random things, like the difference between raisins and currants and sultanas. It's size, mostly. That's the conclusion we reached. She brought scones that day. She had no raisins so she put sultanas in instead. Her first time making scones. That's how that conversa-tion started.

Sometimes we just talk about whatever programme happens to be on the telly. She watches Home *and* Away *with me, then declares it a dreadful waste of time.*

Meals on wheels. That's what she calls herself. We laughed the first time she said it. We have the same laugh. I never noticed that before. We laugh exactly the same way.

Friday today. Pretty busy, by my revised standards. The taxi will arrive at three to take me to the weekly physio appointment with the torturously cheerful Duncan. Still, at least that's one day I'll miss that afternoon show. I'd watch it otherwise. Confirmation and reassurance, Dr Deery might say. I need to watch it to reassure myself that it's as dreadful as I think it is.

A telly addict, I suppose. That's what I've become. I never had time before. And it's not like I'm all that interested. It's more like punctuation. That sounds pathetic, doesn't it? Maybe I want you to feel sorry for me? To see what you've reduced me to? Dr Deery says nobody has reduced me to anything. That I am responsible for myself. My own life. I swear, years and years in university and this is the shit she comes out with. I could have got that advice from a Good Housekeeping *problem page.*

Although I suppose she could be right about the anger stage. I never used to curse. Remember?

Ellen

One

I get the first pain at eleven o'clock in the morning. It's nothing, really. A twinge is all. I don't take much notice of it.

I'm in the taxi again. I'd say, if you added it up, I spend more time here than anywhere else. It's not that bad. It's quiet in here. Tidy. Not like the house. Like a bomb hit it most of the time. You could nearly call it a refuge, the taxi. Except when the punters get in. People tell taxi drivers things. The confessional, Kenny calls it. Could be the quiet. The worst are the ones who sit in the front. Men, mostly.

'Busy tonight?'

'Town's packed.'

'Big scrap on Westmoreland Street.'

'What time d'ya start?'

'Graveyard shift?'

'Red eye shift?'

'Fuckin' recession.'

Drive you scatty, some of them.

I'd say it's a bit of indigestion. Wolfed the breakfast down, standing at the kitchen counter, making Finn's lunch. Kerry didn't want lunch. She's on a diet now. That's the latest.

'You're not.'

'I am.'

'You're too young to be on a diet.'

'I'm nearly fifteen.'

'Nearly fifteen is fourteen. That's too young to be on a diet.'

'Says who?'

'Says me.'

'What would you know?'

'Put something on your head, it's freezin' out.'

When she slams the front door, every window in the house rattles.

The windows. Could do with being replaced. Should have done it before the winter set in. Draughty as hell. I found a bit of mould on the wall in Finn's bedroom the other day.

I eat lunch on the rank. Sitting on the bonnet, stretching the legs.

'Howeya, Vinnie.' Kenny pulls up behind me, picks himself and his packed lunch out of his taxi. He takes a large handkerchief out of his pocket and arranges it on the bonnet before sitting on it.

'What do you think of my new threads?'

'What, the trousers?'

'These duds? I've had these vintage Sta-Prests for several seasons. Although, you're right, the dogtooth check keeps them fresh.'

I open the tinfoil I've wrapped my sandwich in.

'It's the jacket, obviously,' says Kenny, doing a 360-degree turn.

'It doesn't look new,' I tell him.

'Reclaimed leather, comrade.'

'Reclaimed from where? A ditch?'

'Vinnie, Vinnie, Vinnie,' he sighs, shaking his head. He picks black olives and celery out of his tuna salad. I hope I'm not still making lunches for the kids when they're Kenny's age. Still, his ma puts a good feed together, all the same.

'What ails you, comrade?' he says. 'You're lookin' a bit peaky.'

I put the sandwich back in the tinfoil. The bread is soggy now. And pink, where the jam has seeped through. I'd used up the ham. Gave the last slice to Archibald. I thought there was another pack in the fridge. No wonder the dog's so fat. A vast giant of a yoke, he is. Still, he's a harmless auldfella. Had him since he was a pup. There's something comforting about the dog. He hasn't changed in all the years, apart from the size of him. Like a house, he is.

'A bit tired is all. Did an airport run first thing.' I don't mind the early mornings. Gives me a chance to clock up a few quid before the kids wake up. Without having to do nights too often. You'd never let your kids out the door if you did nights on a regular basis.

'Beverage later?' Kenny takes a comb out of his back pocket, runs it through his black hair, then teases the ends of his thick moustache with it.

'When are you going to shave that yoke off? You look like Freddie Mercury.'

'You really think so?' He bends to examine himself in the wing mirror.

'I didn't mean it as a compliment.'

'What about that pint?'

'I dunno. I think there's a meeting tonight at the school for Finn's Holy Communion.'

'Another one?'

'Or a mass or something. I have to check.'

'You should have sent him to the Educate Together.'

'Yeah.'

'You can come for a bevvie after. Kerry can watch him.'

'She's in a strop.'

'Again?'

'Yeah.'

'Or your mother. She could watch the pair of them, couldn't she? We'll just go for the one. Watch the match.'

'We're gettin' relegated.'

'Nothing new there, comrade.'

'Ma's got something on tonight.'

'A social butterfly, your mother.'

'The Nifty Fifties. They're going kayaking.'

'Kayaking?'

'Yeah.'

'A bit cold for that caper, no?'

'She borrowed a wetsuit from Fr Murphy's housekeeper, she says.'

'Would Mrs Boland not be a tad . . . mature for the Nifty Fifties? No offence or anything.'

'I'd say she might, alright.'

'Fair dues to her.'

'Yeah.'

'Kayaking.'

'It's like canoeing.'

'She's got the legs for it.'

'What do you mean?'

'Sea legs, comrade. D'ya remember? When we went to Ireland's Eye last summer with the kids. We all got sick except for your ma.'

'Oh, yeah.'

Kenny stands up and brushes crumbs off his trousers. He picks his handkerchief off the bonnet and uses it to shine the buckle on his crocodile skin Chelsea boots.

The March day is raw, with the white glare of a persistent winter. Traffic is heavy. Traffic is always heavy around town on a Friday. People going places. Me taking them there. Heuston Station. Busáras. Dublin airport. People coming and going. Long lines of them, always moving. Like ants, they are.

I pick Ma up from the parish hall, when she finishes her meals on wheels shift, and drop her at the school with three minutes to spare before Finn gets out. Her motor's in for a service.

'Do you want T-bone steaks for dinner tonight, Vincent? They're on special in Brady's,' says Ma, squeezing herself into the taxi. 'They're lovely big ones, so they are. I'll fry them for you and the kids for a treat. Chips as well. Will you make sure there's fresh oil in the deep-fat fryer?'

'There's no need for you to make dinner for us, Ma. We're grand.'

'It's no trouble, son. I've just enough time, before I've to go home and change for the seminar.'

'What seminar?'

'At the old folks' home. It's about Healthy Living. I'm doing a talk on diet. Salads and that sort of nonsense.'

'I thought you were going kayaking.'

'That's tomorrow.'

'Right.' Hard to keep up with her, being honest.

I shake my head. 'It's fine, Ma. I already have the dinner sorted for today. But thanks.' I don't want to get into Kerry's latest dieting fad. An embargo on red meat. And sausages, apparently. No more sausages. Finn ate hers yesterday evening. She managed a few of the carrots and picked at the mash.

'Are you alright, Vincent?'

'Yeah. Not a bother.'

'You look a bit pale.'

'I'm grand.'

'Did you take that tonic I got you in the chemist?'

'Yeah.' It's still in the box on the hall table.

'I wouldn't say you're gettin' your five fruit and veg a day, with that pallor on your mush.'

'Jaysus, Ma.'

'Watch your language. You're not too old for a clip around the ear.'

'I'm forty-two.'

'Exactly.'

It takes her a while to get out of the taxi. I have to put my hands on the small of her back in the end. Give her a bit of momentum.

I don't know how she's going to negotiate herself into a kayak. Or a wetsuit.

A headache now. And the pain is still there. In my chest. You couldn't really call it a twinge any more.

A good night's sleep is what I need. A proper eight hours, uninterrupted. Finn was into me again last night. Half asleep he was, standing beside my bed and his pyjama bottoms soaked.

Sheets. I need more sheets. I'll go to Guineys on Saturday. If they haven't closed down yet.

Bloody recession.

I get the call after lunch.

'Calamity Jane rang. The usual run.'

'Would you stop calling her that.'

'It's not like I say it to her face, Vinnie.'

'Still . . .'

'Fine, then. Ellen rang. Ellen Woods. The usual run. That do ya?' There's a pop and then the sound of Janine peeling the burst bubble of chewing gum off her face.

'Can you not get someone else to do it? I'm on the quays. It'll take me ages to get to Clontarf with the traffic.'

'She asked for you so get your lanky arse over there pronto.' Janine takes exception to thin people. She's been on a diet since I started in the business. She hates when she sees me eating bread. Or buns. Cakes. Anything like that. Goes spare, she does.

I hang up. Indicate. Inch into the right-hand lane, stop at the red light. Ages it'll take me, at this rate.

Ellen Woods. No idea why she asks for me every Friday afternoon. I pick her up in Clontarf, take her to some physiotherapy clinic in Portmarnock. Same run, every week. She doesn't say much. Apart from the usual 'hello', 'goodbye', 'how are you?', 'fine, thanks', 'desperate weather', 'keep the change'.

She's standing where she always stands, on the path outside a block of flats. An apartment complex, you'd call it. Lovely looking place. Plush. She's a back-seat passenger, thank God. She gets in, says hello, I say hello and then I say something about the weather, I think. Something about it being a bitter day. She nods and I start driving and that's that. I pull up outside the clinic, she gets out. Takes her a while, with the crutches, but I know she doesn't want my help. Eight years in the taxi game and you get to know a thing or two about people. Hard to believe it's eight years since the business went under. I still miss it. Being my own boss. Being a carpenter. Try not to think about it, mostly.

I wait in the car, listen to Sean Moncrieff talking about films I haven't seen and beers I've never heard of. She's usually back in half an hour. Forty minutes tops.

It's a grand fare, all the same. Gettin' paid to sit in the car and do nothing.

'If it weren't for her face, she'd be very attractive,' Kenny said, when he did the run a few weeks ago. I had that meeting with the principal of Kerry's school. Another bloody meeting. This is her second warning, Miss Pratchett said.

'That's charming, that is,' I say.

'I'm only sayin'. She's a bit Al Pacino, with the scar an' tha'. It's distracting.'

'We can't all be as gorgeous as you.'

'That's true, comrade,' says Kenny, forlorn, like he wishes things could be fairer.

I've never really thought about her like that. Being attractive, I mean. Short, dark hair. Pale. Sunglasses usually, even on the dull days. Somewhere in her thirties. Hard to tell with some women. Skin and bone, though, not a pick on her. Janine wouldn't be best pleased. And there's ... I don't know ...

something derelict about her face. And it's not because of her scar. I see her face sometimes, in the rear-view mirror, when the green silk scarf she wears around her head slips.

I take out my iPhone while I'm waiting and check Kerry's Facebook page. That was the condition, when I found out she was on Facebook. She had to accept my 'friend' request. So we're friends. On Facebook at least. *Wake me up at the end of Irish.* That's her status update. Ten o'clock this morning, she put that up. She's not even supposed to have her phone switched on at school. That'll be another argument. I can't even muster up annoyance. Weary. That's how I feel. And uncomfortable, with that pain in my chest. It feels sharper now. Need to buy a box of Rennie.

She's out in thirty-five minutes today. Looks tired now. She puts the crutches in the car first, lies them on the floor. Then she lowers herself onto the back seat, careful as a box of eggs, closes the door and I drive off. Same routine every week.

She's cold. I see it in the way she folds her arms around her body. I turn the heat up and drive through Portmarnock and Malahide, head towards town. Janine radios in to say there's been an accident on the Malahide road. The traffic is backed up from the Artane roundabout all the way to Clare Hall. I indicate left at Balgriffin, think about Da as I pass the cemetery there, and take the back road to Raheny, drive down the Howth Road.

That's when it happens. At the bottom of Vernon Avenue, with the grey expanse of Dublin Bay laid out in front of me, like a corpse at a wake. The heat of the car wraps around me. I slip my fingers inside the collar of my shirt, pulling it away from my neck, encourage a bit of air down. I take a deep breath but it's like I can't get enough air inside me. I'm sweating too. On my forehead, down my back, my fingers slippery on the wheel. And the pain. Expanding through my chest. Reaching down my arm.

I don't think it's indigestion after all. Haven't eaten much. A tightening sensation now inside my chest. Pins and needles down my arm, right down to the fingers that are wrapped tight around the wheel.

The lights turn green. I don't move. A car behind beeps. I need to take the handbrake off. Put the thing in Drive. Turn right, the sea on my left. I sit there. Look at the sea. At the dirty grey of the water. Dublin Bay. I concentrate on it. The water.

Think about the city. Where I grew up. The sounds and the smells and the dirt and the comfort of its familiarity. My back-yard it was, growing up, this city, the ridges of my runners smooth with all the running I did, up and down the streets and lanes of North Strand.

I make myself think about these things. The city. The bay. Cardiff playing tonight. Possibility of relegation. Nothing new there.

I don't think about Finn and Kerry. Don't let myself. The scene in front of me blackens around the edges, like a singed photograph. I have a curious sensation now. Like I'm falling.

But I can't be falling.

Can I?

Two

'Are you alright?' Her voice is low and hesitant, like she's testing it out. Like she hasn't used it in a while.

'Are you alright?' She says it again, louder this time. I open my mouth but no words come out. It's like I've been winded by one of Kenny's fouls at the Wednesday night five-a-side.

I hear the back door opening, and then a surge of air as my door opens. She props the crutches against the door, leans in, using the dashboard and the back of my seat to support herself. I'm gulping now. Gasping. Like a fish out of water. Those small yokes me and Joey used to catch in the canal. Wriggling and twitching at the end of the line. I would have thrown them back in. Joey showed me how to gut them. We never ate them. But he said I should know how to gut one, all the same. My brother is four years older than me and he always took those four years seriously.

Her eyes are a curious colour. A sort of yellowy-brown. Amber. I think that's what you call it. Close up, the scar is more a curve than a line, deep enough, the skin around it puckered and pink.

I can't remember her name. I've been picking her up every Friday for a few months now and I can't remember her name. It's gone. She leans across me, puts on the hazard lights, looks at me. 'Try to relax,' she says. 'Concentrate on your breathing, in and out, that's it.' She lays a hand across my forehead. Freezing, her hand. She reaches for the top button of my shirt. Undoes it.

Her hands move to the next button. And the next. 'You're hot,' she says. I nod but I don't feel hot. I feel cold. Clammy.

My breathing sounds like gasping. I can't seem to get it under control.

'Breathe into this,' she says, reaching into her handbag, fishing out a paper bag and emptying it. A pharmacy bag, I think it is. 'Close your eyes and concentrate on breathing in and out.'

I try to do what she says. She seems to know what she's about. It's hard, though. Feels like someone has their hands around my neck.

Freezing air against the skin of my chest. She reaches for my wrist, holds it between her fingers. I look at her face. She's calm. It's a comfort, her calmness. I breathe into the bag. She cocks her head to one side. Concentrating. A silver Claddagh ring wrapped around her little finger. Heart pointing out. I try to remember the significance of that. There's something significant about the way you wear a Claddagh ring, isn't there? Paula told me once. We were sharing a bag of chips sitting on the pier at Howth. Her mouth tasted hot and salty when I kissed her. She closed her eyes when she laughed. Threw her head back and closed her eyes.

The woman leans across me again. I smell soap. Sweet. Dove, maybe. What am I like? Thinking about soap. A navy and white box it comes in, as far as I remember. I swear to God. Dove. That's what I'm thinking about. She undoes my seat belt. 'Can you move?' she says, nodding towards the passenger seat.

She has to prise the fingers of my other hand away from the wheel. It's like I have locked-in syndrome. I saw a programme about it once. That's what it feels like. Like I'm frozen. Not just frozen with the cold. But frozen through. Like a packet of fish fingers.

The woman – what is her name? – puts both hands on my shoulder, leans the weight of her body against me, tries to move me. In the end, I think she asks someone to help her. She must have. I don't know how she would have got me into the passenger seat otherwise. I don't remember that bit. I really don't.

She gets into the driver's seat, lifts her crutches in, drops them into the back.

She tells me to reach for the seat belt. I can't. She reaches across. Grabs the belt. Fastens it around me, then fastens her own. She scans the dashboard, puts her hands on the wheel real slow, like she's not sure what it's for. I wonder if she's ever driven an automatic. If she even knows how to drive. The pain in my chest tightens so I close my eyes and soon I feel the car moving and I concentrate on breathing in and out of the bag and try not to think about anything at all.

When I open my eyes, we're parked outside the front entrance of Beaumont Hospital and the woman has the car door open, shouting at a porter to help her. I look at my hand, wrapped around the paper bag. It seems like somebody else's hand. That's strange. Everything is strange. I'm not myself.

My door opens. I'm hauled out. I'm on a trolley. The wheels bump against the ground, sending vibrations through me. An oxygen mask is put over my face. A blanket is thrown over me. I'm pinned under the weight of it. The heat of it. I could let myself go now. I could loosen my grip on the rails of the trolley and just let go. Part of me thinks that that would be the easiest thing in the world to do. Let go.

I tighten my grip.

Now I'm thinking about my father. Except he never made it to the hospital. He shouted out. Once. I heard the shout. I was in the kitchen making a sandwich for my school lunch. It was more like a scream than a shout. High-pitched. By the time I got out to the garden and ran to the vegetable patch where he'd been digging for worms, that was it. He was already gone. I knew it without touching him. That he wasn't there any more. He'd never go fishing again. A massive coronary, they said. Massive. That seemed fitting for him. He was a mountain of a man. He could put me on one shoulder and Joey on the other and hold us like that for the whole St Patrick's Day parade. We could see everything from up there.

The next thing I know, I'm in a cubicle with the curtains pulled and wires attaching me to a monitor that beeps every so often. My hands grip the rails of the trolley.

The doctor looks about nineteen with his fluffy little tache and the dark shadow of blackheads across the bridge of his nose.

'There you are,' he says. His scrubs are green. The colours are significant. Is green for the surgery fellas? Is he going to open me up?

'Did I pass out?'

He looks at the monitor and writes something down on a clipboard, shaking his head. 'You fell asleep.'

'Are you going to operate on me?'

When he smiles, he looks not much older than Kerry. 'Not today, Mr Boland.'

'Did I have a heart attack?'

He picks up my arm, wraps a black band around it, starts squeezing a rubber tube and I feel the band swell and tighten around my skin. He releases the tube and the band loosens as the air seeps away. He concentrates on the dial and I study his face for bad news.

He scribbles something on the clipboard, then takes his stethoscope from around his neck, puts the ends in his ears and places the disc against my chest.

'Does the machine not do all that stuff?' I ask, nodding at the monitor.

'I'm old-fashioned,' he says.

'You don't look old enough to be old-fashioned.'

The cold of the disc is shocking. The buttons of my shirt are still undone. He looks out the window as he listens to my chest.

His face is impassive. Doctors are probably trained to have faces like that.

More scribbling on the clipboard. Then he stops and looks at me.

'Go ahead, Doc, tell me what it is. What's wrong with me?' I sound braver than I feel.

'Your blood pressure is perfect.'

'What about my ticker?'

'Not a bother.'

'And I wasn't unconscious?'

'Sleeping like a baby.'

'So what happened to me, then?'

'I'd say you had a panic attack.'

'A panic attack?'

'Yes.'

I've heard of panic attacks. Of course I have. Someone got one on *Grey's Anatomy* once. A woman. Highly strung. She was on IVF. Trying to have a baby. I remember thinking, Jaysus, if she's having panic attacks now, what'll she be like when the kid comes along?

'Mr Boland?'

I try to remember what I'd been thinking about in the cab before I . . . before the thing. Nothing panicky there. Just a few thoughts about the woman, how cold she looked. I might have been thinking about what to cook for the kids' tea. Chicken burgers, I thought. They like them. Curly fries maybe. Pick up a pack of Bundys on the way home. A tin of peas. The rest is in the freezer.

Just stuff like that. Nothing major.

'Mr Boland?'

I look at the doctor. He looks worried now. I want to tell him there's nothing to worry about. Just the usual. I look at my wrist before I remember that the watch is still in the jeweller's. I forgot to pick it up again. 'What time is it, Doc?'

'Just gone ten.'

'Ten!' I was supposed to pick Finn up from my ma's house. Get the kids their tea. And I had a job at seven. In the limo. I struggle to sit up, without disturbing any of the wires. Don't want the machine to start screeching.

'You need to take it easy, Mr Boland.'

'I have to go.' I pull the sheet off me and try to work out how to collapse the rails along the sides of the trolley.

The doctor shakes his head as if I've just asked him a question and the answer is no.

I didn't ask him a question. Did I?

'You can't go,' he says. 'Not on your own. You can't drive.'

'Of course I can drive. That's what I do. I'm a taxi driver.'

'Ms Woods rang your office. She said that someone will pick you up when you're discharged.'

'Ms Woods?'

'The woman who brought you in, remember?'

Ellen Woods. That's it. That's her name. 'She's a fare,' I say. Janine's always on at me to call them clients.

'Did she tell them what happened?' I ask.

'I don't know. I suppose she did.'

'Did she mention a panic attack?'

'I really couldn't say.'

'Why does someone have to pick me up?'

'Because you've had an episode and you need to rest.' He takes a pad out of his pocket and scribbles something on it. Then he rips the page off and hands it to me. 'Here's a prescription for Valium.'

'Valium?' Fuck sake.

'And the name of someone I'd like you to talk to.'

'A shrink?'

'He's a therapist. A very good one.'

'I'm not losing me marbles, Doctor. Just a bit short of breath is all.'

'Nobody is suggesting you're losing your marbles.'

'What if I don't go?'

He's writing something else now. On another page. Hands it to me. 'Here's a medical certificate excusing you from work for two weeks.'

'Two weeks? Jaysus, Doc, there's no need for . . .'

'I can't make you see a therapist. But you've had a panic attack, which is not something you should take lightly, especially in your line of work. What if you'd been driving at the time? Instead of stopped at traffic lights?'

'I would have pulled over.' Would I? The thing happened so suddenly. Took me by surprise. It's hard to know what I might have done.

'Take some time off, Mr Boland. Get some rest. Take up yoga, perhaps. Meditation. Do you exercise at all?'

'Five-a-side.'

Yoga! I'd never hear the end of it.

'Do you drink?'

'Couple of pints.'

'Do you smoke?'

'About three times a day.' Morning, noon and night.

'And what about your diet?'

'What about it?'

'Are you eating well? Getting your five-a-day and all that?'

'You sound like me ma.'

'These things are important.' He nods at the gold band around my finger. 'Tell your wife you need taking care of, alright? A bit of TLC.' He smiles like he's just told a joke.

I wait for Kenny in the reception area. There's no sign of the woman. Ellen Woods. I wonder briefly how she got home. I'll have to thank her, I suppose. Janine has her number in the office.

The first thing Kenny says to me is, 'Don't panic! I'm here.' Then he laughs at his own little joke and everybody stares at us and I say, 'Give over,' and he says, 'Did you have your sense of humour removed while you were here?'

I stand up and head towards the door. Can't wait to get out of this place.

Three

Kenny opens the back door of his motor and gently places his hat on the seat. 'Are you going to belt it in?' I ask.

'It's not just a hat, Vinnie,' he says, shaking his head. 'It's a fedora. Fur felt. Soft as cashmere. Here, feel it.'

'I'll take your word for it.'

Kenny drives the way he always does: a combination of speeding and emergency stops, so that you're always getting thrown against the window, straining against the seat belt.

Usually, I can handle it but today it's making me feel a bit nauseous. I think it's something to do with the smell of the hospital. I've always hated that smell.

He speeds towards a red light and I brace myself for the emergency stop by pressing my hands against the dashboard. 'Take it easy, will you?'

'You're not going to have another panic attack, are you?'

'Fuck off.'

'I'm only slaggin'.'

'It's not funny.'

'I knew you were a little under par this morning.'

'I was just a bit tired.'

'Just goes to show you, doesn't it?'

'What?'

He shrugs.

It's weird being a passenger.

Kenny jerks to a stop outside the house. He turns the key in the ignition. The engine ticks as it quietens. From the outside, the house looks solid. Dependable. Me and Paula bought it before the boom. Before the bust. Before everything went arseways. Mrs O'Neill owned it before us. She said she'd be carried out of the place in a wooden box and she was right. The house was overrun with her cats. The smell off them. Months it took us, to get rid of the smell. Weekends spent painting. We didn't have the money to do much else in those days. The fights we had about the colours. Spatters of paint in her hair. The pair of us in the bath with the shampoo and the soap. Water all over the floor afterwards.

Kenny nods towards the house. 'The place could do with a lick of paint.'

'You're not wrong.'

'I'll give you a dig out with it. When it gets a bit warmer.'

'Thanks, Kenny.'

When I open the car door, the cold wraps around me like a damp blanket. I rub my hands together. 'I wish you hadn't said anything to Ma.'

'I had to. She rang me when she couldn't reach you. She was worried.'

'You coulda said I had to go somewhere.'

'Like where?' He's right. I'm usually in the house or out in the cab.

I put both hands on the frame of the door and pull myself out of the car. I stand up, put a hand on the lamp-post, steady myself. I'm not one hundred per cent. Not yet. A good night's sleep. That's all I need.

'And don't worry about your motor. I'll get Janine to drop me at the hospital in the morning to pick it up. I'll drive it back to the depot, OK?'

I hand him my car keys. 'Appreciate that, Kenny.'

'I've a limo run tomorrow but I'll call in after. See how you're faring.' He screeches away from the kerb, leaving scorch marks on the tarmac. He drives a hundred yards up the road, slams on the brakes and reverses the car into his driveway.

The garden gate creaks when I open it. Needs a bit of WD40.

I stop in the garden. Take a cigarette out of the packet. No way am I taking two weeks off. But a couple of days, all the same. A bit of time to get things sorted. The grass, for example. Could do with a mow. The pear tree I planted when Finn was born. A bit of pruning there. Borrow Kenny's ladder and take the leaves out of the gutters. Do a job on the drains. A funny smell coming up from the kitchen sink lately. Maybe buy Finn a suit for his big day. He told me all the fellas are getting suits for their First Holy Communion.

The front door opens and the light from the hall spills into the garden, blinding me.

'Jesus, Mary and Holy Saint Joseph and all the saints, preserve us, you frightened the life out of me, skulking around the garden like a thug. And that better not be a cigarette between your fingers, Vincent Patrick Boland, after the scare you gave us all today. And have you never heard of a mobile phone? You could have used it to ring your poor old mother and not have her worrying herself into an early grave, like your unfortunate father, God rest his soul.' She blesses herself, as she always does when she mentions Da. She's been a widow for as long as anyone can remember. Twenty-six years it'll be this September. I tuck the unlit cigarette behind my ear and move towards her. 'Sorry, Ma. I didn't want to be worrying you. Are the kids in bed?'

'Of course they are, isn't it nearly eleven o'clock at night?' Ma backs down the hall so I can get in the door. I'm tired. All of a sudden. The glare of the hall light presses against my eyes. I switch off the light, turn on the lamp instead, rub my eyes with the backs of my fingers.

'Did Kerry study? She's a maths exam tomorrow.'

'That madam.' She raises her eyes and turns towards the kitchen. I follow her. The kitchen is cramped and worn and full of the smell of frying. 'Wouldn't eat any of her dinner. Said that red meat was bad for your heart. How in the name of the Archangel Gabriel could red meat be bad for your heart, I ask you?'

I shake my head. I could fall asleep now, here, on a kitchen chair.

'I offered to fry her an egg and she said I was to use this spray stuff on the pan instead of butter.' She shakes her head, folds her arms across her chest. 'Would you mind tellin' me how a person can fry an egg without butter or a bit of suet? Well? Vincent? Are you listening to me at all?'

'She's on a diet.'

'There's more meat on a butcher's apron.'

'It's just a phase.'

'Anorexia. That'll be the next thing.'

'I'll speak to her.'

'Or what's that other yoke? Bulimia.'

'It's just a teenage thing. I'll have a word with her.'

'You always say that and you never do.'

'I will. In the morning. I'll talk to her.'

'For whatever good that'll do you.'

'You didn't tell her, did you? Or Finn? Where I was?'

'I said you were doing a limo run.'

'Thanks, Ma.'

'Kenny said it was a panic attack.'

'Yeah. Just a small one. Nothing to worry about. The doctor gave me some tablets. Right as rain, I am now.'

'It'll be a heart attack next. With the hours you're working. You're spreading yourself much too thin, Vincent, in that taxi all hours and trying to take care of those children in between.'

'I have you, don't I? You're a great help to me.'

She shakes her head. 'A heart attack,' she says again. 'With your genes and those cigarettes. Mark my words.'

'I'm grand now. Just need a good night's sleep.'

'Mrs O'Toole in number fifty-eight was on her nerves too. And look what happened to her. Dead in the chair and the curlers still in her hair from the night before. May the good Lord defend me from an end like that.' There she goes, blessing herself again.

'The doctor checked my ticker. Said it was fine.'

She looks at me, shakes her head. 'I could stay. You look like leftovers. I could help with Finn in the morning. You could have a lie-in.'

'No. But thanks. We'll be fine.'

'Overdoing it. I told ya. Takin' on too much after that wan . . . with her midnight flit . . .'

'Ah, Ma, don't start that.'

'You're too soft, Vincent. You'll kill yourself one of these days.'

'I'll ring you in the morning.' I've got her as far as the front door. I have her handbag in my hand. I'm giving it to her. Her keys are in there. I've checked. They're in the zip section. She's about to step out into the night when she stops, puts the bag on the floor, grabs my head and pulls it towards her, squashing my face against the coarse wool of the winter coat she's had for years. Decades.

'I was up the walls, worrying about you, son.'

'I'm fine.' A hair from her coat is trapped between my teeth. I prise my face away from the terrible coat with its insistent smell of meals on wheels. She cups my face in her soft, fleshy hands. Shakes her head. 'I had high hopes for you, Vincent.'

'I know you did, Ma.'

'High hopes.' She's still standing there, shaking her head. She wasn't mad about me doing the carpentry apprenticeship. But then she saw how much I enjoyed it. The shape of the grain beneath my hands. The smell of the wood. That dense, sweet smell. And when people were pleased with the work. She liked that. They'd tell her about the cabinets and the wardrobes and the shelves and the tables. She loved that. Accepted the compliments like she'd gone into St Anne's Park and cut the tree down herself. Gas. But yeah, I wasn't bad. People said I wasn't bad. In demand, back in the day.

'I'll walk you home.'

'Do I look like someone who needs a chaperone, Vincent?'

OK, then, but I'll stay here til you're in the door.' I have my hand on her back now, just short of pushing her into the garden.

'Don't worry, I'm going. And one of these days I'll be gone for good and then you'll be sorry.'

'You'll never be gone, Ma.' Chance would be a fine thing.

'I'm in my sixties, Vincent. Don't forget it.'

She must be seventy-five. At least. I don't mention it. More than my life is worth.

Dear Neil,

Got the letter from your solicitor the other day. They sent it to the clinic. Colm came by to drop it off. Rang the buzzer. Countdown was on so it must have been after three o'clock. I asked him to leave it in my postbox. Said I had gastroenteritis.

The apartment's not exactly ready for visitors.

The solicitor described it as a 'miracle'. Getting such a good offer for the house in the current market. It's funny, thinking about the solicitor typing out the word. Or dictating it, I suppose. Miracle. It doesn't seem an appropriate sort of word for a solicitor to use.

I've been in the apartment for six months now, but it still feels strange to think of our house being viewed by other people. I hope it goes to good owners. Not like us. A couple with a family, perhaps. And domestic animals. A gerbil, maybe. A hamster. Hutches in the garden. Dog hairs all over the Chesterfield in the study.

We were never there. Were we? In the house? We were always at the clinic. We looked after that clinic like it was a child. Our child. We would have brought it home if we could. At the end of the day. Wouldn't we? Put it to bed, rocked it to sleep.

Dr Deery told me to think of two good things in my life:

1. *There's an offer on the house;*
2. *The clinic is sold;*
3. *It's Saturday so that dreadful afternoon programme isn't on.*

See? I managed to come up with three!

Mum's just left – chicken tikka masala and a tub of vanilla ice cream today. We watched a nature programme instead of the news. I'm being serious. I've no idea what's happening in the world but I can tell you anything you need to know about giant otters. Only one out of every three of their cubs survives. For a moment, I thought I might cry. Over giant otter cubs. I know you don't believe me.

We ate dinner on the couch, trays on our laps. Mum gave me the last piece of naan bread – like she knew I was sad about the cubs – and we finished our dinner and watched the telly and drank glasses of milk. In a way, I feel like a child again except that Mum would never have allowed me to eat my dinner on the couch in front of the telly when I was a kid.

I drove the other day. I drove a car. I didn't think I'd remember how. It's been eight months. Still, it was only an automatic. Like driving a bumper car, really. It was a taxi. A few people tried to hail me. The driver – the one who takes me to the physio clinic in Portmarnock every Friday – had a panic attack except of course he thought it was a heart attack. He always looks like he could do with a haircut and a square meal and a good night's sleep. He was quiet. He's always quiet, mind. But he was pale and sweaty too, when he picked me up. I found myself diagnosing him in my head. It's hard to stop being a doctor sometimes. Flu, I was thinking. Paracetamol and hot drinks. Bedrest. I nearly said, 'That'll be fifty euros, please.'

All these months of him driving me, and we've never had a conversation. Not a proper one. I get in and he says, 'Portmarnock?' and I nod and off we go. It would have been nice if I'd been able to get a physio nearer the apartment. Like Dr Deery, two minutes' walk away. But Duncan specialises in my type of injuries and he doesn't do house calls. I asked him.

The taxi driver doesn't gawk at my face like everyone else. Doesn't ask about my leg. We're two people, together but separate. Does that sound familiar? Sorry, Dr Deery says bitterness *is a waste of time. But so is decaffeinated coffee and people still drink it.*

I got him to breathe into a paper bag I found in my handbag. I had to go into the hospital with him. He had a death grip on my hand. I was terrified I'd see someone we used to know. They medicated him and he calmed down and I was able to get away. I had to hail a random cab at the hospital. The cabbie nearly fell over himself in his hurry to open the door for me. 'I can manage,' I say, but they never listen.

'You've been in the wars, love,' he said, getting into the car and nodding at my face in the rear-view mirror. I left my scarf at the hospital. He made it sound like a question, with that strained tone of sympathy.

I wanted to nod at his face and say, 'What's your excuse?' Instead, I gave him my address. Perhaps Dr Deery is right. The next step is acceptance, she says. She seems to think it's just a matter of time.

Driving, though. That was strange. I used to love driving. Duncan says there's no physical reason why I can't drive. Turns out, he's right.

I felt tired afterwards. Spent, like I'd used myself up. I hope Vinnie – that's the taxi driver's name – will be back to work by next week. Get things back to normal.

I just said normal.

Isn't that strange?

Ellen

Four

Monday morning. Business as usual.

'I need a tenner, Da.'

'I gave you a tenner yesterday.'

'I need another one.'

'What for?'

'A hardback notebook. Science.'

'They couldn't be a tenner.'

'I need two.'

Jaysus.

I open my wallet. Hand over the note. Kerry takes it, slips it into the pocket of her school skirt. She catches me looking, and scowls.

'What?'

Her green eyes are ringed with thick black pencil, her face is paler than usual and her mouth is a garish red. I don't have the stomach for an argument. The Valium has left me heavy-limbed and drowsy, although it's good that I slept. I didn't wake up at four the last few mornings. I slept through.

'Clean that stuff off your face before you go to school.'

'Everyone else wears make-up.'

'I don't care what everyone else does.'

'I look like a freak with no make-up on.'

'I bought those wipes you wanted. You can use those. They're in the bathroom.'

The kitchen door shudders in its frame when she slams it. Then the pounding of her feet on the stairs. I haven't talked to her about the diet thing yet. I'll do it tonight. Or tomorrow maybe.

Coffee. I take the beans out of the press, put them in the grinder. I love the noise of it. Guttural. And the smell. That smell can bring me back to one of a hundred memories. The most powerful of all of the five senses. Smell. Finn told me that the other day. He's learning about senses at school.

I put the coffee pot on the hob, add the ground beans and the water and turn the flame on underneath it. It brings me right back to our first day in the house after the honeymoon. Unwrapping the presents. Paula wasn't impressed with the coffee pot, being more of a tea person. Her favourite present was the Budget Travel vouchers. 'We can see the world, Vinnie. You and me and the open road.' We spent the vouchers on a trip to Paris and when we got back, she was pregnant with Kerry. 'You got me pregnant.' That's what she said, when I got home from work that day.

I go upstairs to see what's keeping Finn. His bedroom door is ajar and there he is, kneeling at the edge of the bed, his hands joined across his chest and his eyes closed. He's taking this First Holy Communion thing seriously.

'Dear God, Please help me not to spit in the school pond any more cos one of the fish died yesterday and me and Callam think they might be allergic to the spits. Miss Cronin said she didn't think there was a fish heaven so I suppose he must have gone to ordinary heaven where you live. I hope you like him but don't try to pick him up or you might squeeze him to death by accident, like Maximillian in Mrs Lynch's class did to one of them last week. Fr Murphy told us we've to be good as gold for our First Holy Communion so I'm not going to stare at the hairs growing out of Mrs Finnegan's wart on her chin any more cos Granny says someday I'll be old and I might have a hairy wart and I wouldn't like it if a young fella was staring at me, would I?

And I won't eat sweets cos Dad says they're bad for your teeth and it must be true because my teeth keep falling out.

'God bless Dad and Kerry and Granny and Mam and Uncle Joey and all my friends, especially Callam, and my enemies, even Declan O'Toole, and all the dead people, especially Grandad Boland and Spanish Granny and Auntie Maureen and the two goldfish. And God bless Papa Spain and make sure he doesn't get sunburned again like he did that time when it was a hundred degrees. In the name of the Father. And of the Son. And of the Holy. Spirit. Ahhhh-men.'

When he turns around and sees me, he smiles, revealing two lines of pink gum. 'Can I have pancakes for breakfast?'

'Thought you weren't going to eat rubbish?'

'I said I'm not going to eat sweets. Pancakes aren't sweets.'

'Fair enough.' Everything about my son and his room is neat as a pin, except for his hair, which stands on his head in a shocking mass of brown curls. Like mine at that age.

Kerry is still in the bathroom. I knock on the door. 'Hurry up. You'll be late for school.'

No answer.

I toast two pancakes, spread them with strawberry jam and hand them to Finn. He makes a sandwich out of them and the thing is gone in three bites. He washes it down with milk.

'Don't forget you have basketball after school.'

'I won't.'

'Did you put your lunch in your bag?'

'Yeah.'

'Is Callam's mam walking you to school?'

'Yeah.'

He kisses me before he leaves, leaving a sticky residue of jam on the side of my face. He kisses Kerry too, when she eventually appears downstairs. She lets him. In fact, she wraps her arms around him, hugs him. Then she straightens, grabs her bag and heads for the door without so much as a glance at me. Without her make-up, she looks smaller somehow. Younger. The spit of Paula. Everyone always said so. Cut out of her.

It's quiet in the house with the kids gone. Only Archibald's snores nudge at the silence, and even these are not the roar they once were. A gentle rumbling now.

I'm thinking about death. Swear to God. Not death, exactly. But a will. I'm thinking about the fact that I don't have a will.

It must be the Valium has me so maudlin. A side-effect maybe. Although I've only been on them a couple of days. A week's worth, I have. Don't think I fancy feeling like this for much longer than that. Everything seems muffled. Distant. Good for night-time, though. The pills have me asleep in minutes, instead of lying there trying to remember what's what for the next day.

My estate. Ha! Not much to leave behind, bein' honest. The motor, I suppose. Neither of them can drive, of course, but they could sell it, couldn't they? Get the few bob for it.

My watch. That's what I can do later. Pick it up from the jeweller's. It's an ancient yoke, been in the family for generations. Both wars, it's been in. Ma's father never came back from the second one but the watch did, a crack down the face but still ticking away. That'll have to be left to Finn. Kerry can have Paula's rings. She left the three of them on the kitchen table. The wedding ring, the engagement ring and the eternity ring I bought after she'd had Kerry. I meant to get her one after Finn but I never got around to it. She could wear them on a chain around her neck, Kerry could. If she wanted to. A keepsake, I suppose.

If we hadn't remortgaged after Finn was born, we'd be home and dry by now. The banks were throwing money around and Paula had plans. She always had plans. A fitted kitchen, the wooden floorboards, a new fireplace, a power shower, the little extension at the back. The sunroom, she called it. Things would be better after this job. After that one. She'd feel better. Home improvements. A few home improvements and we'd live happily ever after. Part of me believed it. That's what desperation does to you. I would have done just about anything to get things back to normal.

I'll ask Ailbhe and Grainne across the road about a will. The bisexual barristers, Kenny calls them. 'They're not bisexual,' I tell him. 'They're gay.'

'They'd be bisexual after a stint with Kenneth Byrne, wha'?'

I'll ask them about a will.

Janine rings again. 'How are you feeling today?'

'Grand.'

'The boss wants to know if you're going to sue.'

'Sue?'

'Yeah. For stress an' tha'.'

'No.'

'I'll let him know.'

Mr Cunningham. That's the boss. He rarely shows his face in the place. No need, with Janine at the helm. He plays golf. Wears those tartan trousers and a little peaked cap. Skinny little man. His wife is the size of a double-decker. You'd wonder how they manage.

'So . . .' Janine says, and I can hear the smack of her chewing gum against her teeth. 'When are you coming back to work?'

'Couple of days, I'd say.' I can't afford to be off the road for any longer than that. Not with Finn's big day coming up.

'You can get a few quid off the social. Sick leave. Leave it with me. I'll get the form for you. Give it to Kenny. He'll drop it in to you.'

'Thanks, Janine. You're great.'

'I have two ex-husbands who mightn't agree with you.'

'What would they know?'

'Not as much as I'd hoped.'

My mobile rings. It's Kerry's year head. She wants me to come in to the school.

'What's she done this time?'

'She's vandalised school property.'

'What do you mean?'

'Graffiti.'

'Graffiti?'

'And lewd graffiti at that. I don't think she'll be able to avoid a suspension this time. The principal wants to see you.'

'I'm on my way.'

It's only when I get outside the door, I remember the car's at the depot. Meant to pick it up at the weekend. I was a bit knackered after Friday. A bit preoccupied after what happened. I glance down the road towards Kenny's house and I see the limo's there now, parked in his driveway, a good third of it sticking out the drive and across the footpath.

'Morning, comrade. Glad to see you're on your uppers.' Kenny's coming out his front door with a bucket and a cloth, and his mother's apron over his chauffeur threads, which is a black tuxedo. 'I look like a bouncer in this get-up,' I said to Kenny when I started in the place.

He sets the bucket on the ground beside the limo, and uses a chamois to wipe a drop of water off his shoes. His Stretch Shoes, he calls them. Black patent with a toe so pointy, it could go through the eye of a needle.

Mrs Byrne pokes her head out of her bedroom window. 'Don't you get any suds in them flowerbeds like last time, Kenny Byrne. My rhododendrons haven't been the same since.'

'Your rhododendrons are in safe hands, Mother. Don't be annoyin' yourself.' He turns to me, smiles indulgently. 'How can I be of assistance to you on this fine morning, my good man?'

'I need a lift.'

He nods at the bucket of water, shakes his head.

'I've to wash her before I pick Mr Redmond up. He goes spare if there's a speck on her when he's picking his fancy piece up.'

'It's Kerry. She's in trouble at school.'

'Ah, no. Again?'

'Graffiti. Her year head said it was lewd.'

'Lewd?'

'Dirty.'

'I know what lewd means, thanks very much.'

'So will you give me a lift?'

'Go on,' he says.

'Thanks, Kenny. I owe you one.'

Kenny gets behind the wheel and I walk out the driveway, towards Ailbhe and Grainne's house across the road. The road where we live – where we grew up – is narrow. Built before there were any such things as stretch limousines. Certain . . . *adjustments* . . . have to be made. Kenny reverses as far as the fence in front of the women's house, then hops out of the car, leaving it idling in the road. I grab one end of the fence, he takes the other. We mouth, *one, two, three*, and lift the fence out of its foundations. Took us ages the first time, back when the boss decided we were going into the stretch limo business. We walk up the path a bit, carrying the fence between us, then set it down. Kenny gets back behind the wheel and reverses the limo across the road and up into Ailbhe and Grainne's garden. He backs it all the way up to their front door. It's the only way he can turn it.

I rarely park the stretch at the house. Mrs Finnegan across the road from my house has a concrete wall across the front of her garden. No budge in that.

When Kenny has the car out on the road and facing the right way, he hops out again and we return the fence. The whole operation takes less than two minutes and in all these years, Ailbhe and Grainne have never caught us. They're usually in the Four Courts or their office, or at some dinner party or on the Vincent Browne show. I don't think they'd mind though. If they knew. They're high-flyers, alright. But neighbourly, all the same.

Kenny drives with his white gloves on. And the apron. He thinks he's Morgan Freeman with those white gloves. I'd say he's forgotten about the apron.

Five

The smell of the school hasn't changed since I was a lad. That same smell of damp anoraks and cheap polish. It's quiet. The sound of my shoes against the tiles echoes up and down the corridor, bounces off the walls. I pass the canteen where me and Paula ate our lunch a million times, holding hands underneath the table. It's not easy, unwrapping corned-beef sandwiches with one hand. I worried about my hand gettin' sweaty. I'd let go, let on I was looking at my grandad's watch, then slip my hand back under the table, rub it on my trousers, reach across, push my fingers through hers again.

Gas. The things you do when you're young.

'Hello, Vinnie.' The receptionist pulls the glass partition across the hatch and smiles. She knows me well at this stage. She has a skinny body and enormous breasts so she looks a little unstable. She folds her arms under them, pushes them up.

'I'm back again.' I know her name but I can't remember it. It's the Valium. It's turned my head into a sieve. Things are slipping out.

'Sign here.' She slides a book towards me, tapping a blank line with a pointy red nail. Without her arms for support, her breasts spill onto the counter between us, like overturned drinks. I concentrate on the page. She hands me a pen, brushing her fingers against mine. She always does that. She never opens her mouth when she smiles. Buck teeth, maybe? I keep my head down and write my name.

'They're waiting for you in Miss Pratchett's office.'

I move down the corridor. Fran. That's the receptionist's name. Short for Frances, she said. Too late now.

No problem remembering where the office is. Not that I was all that wild when I was here. The usual stuff. Scrappin' and the odd bit of mitching. Shoplifting in H Williams with Kenny. Of course we got caught. Kenny stuffed the pack of Mikados up his bomber jacket and they fell out. Landed in front of the security guard. A week's detention and a whack across the back of the knees with a damp tea towel. Ma was always a dab hand with a tea towel.

I knock on the door.

'Come in.' Thick Cork accent.

The principal is a hawk of a woman. Long, hooked nose. Beady eyes. Dark hair with streaks of grey through it. Long, thin hands topped with thick yellow nails like talons. 'Take a seat, Mr Boland.' She points to a chair beside the door.

Kerry is sitting beside her year head. Miss Watson. Or Wallis, is it? It'll come to me. The kid's got her head down, hiding behind her hair, which hangs like curtains around her face. She's sitting on her hands, like she's trying to keep them from doing something rash.

I cross the room and sit on the chair beside her. She doesn't look at me but she raises her head a little so her hair falls back and her eyes appear, ringed with fresh pencil and mascara. Her fringe could do with a cut.

The principal supervises my progress across the room with those beady eyes, then nods at the other woman. 'Miss Wallis, would you like to begin?'

Miss Wallis. That's it. I look at her. She's only a youngone. Her face is flushed, like she's been sitting in a sauna. She clears her throat. Here we go.

'Kerry has defiled the wall of the bicycle shed.'

'I didn't defile it. It's art,' Kerry says, not looking at anyone.

The principal eyeballs her. 'That's enough, Kerry. You'll get an opportunity to respond when Miss Wallis has finished speaking, is that understood?'

Kerry rolls her eyes, slumps in her chair. I think I'm more afraid of the principal than she is. I don't think she's afraid at all.

'I noticed it this morning when I was parking my bike. I brought the art teacher – Mrs Clancy – down to have a look at it. She knew immediately it was Kerry's work. And Kerry doesn't deny it.'

The principal looks at Kerry again. 'When did you do this, Kerry?'

Kerry shrugs, her shoulders narrow in the school jumper.

'It must have been after hours. Was it? When the school was closed? That means you were trespassing too. And let me tell you, that's a criminal offence, young lady.'

That's a bit strong. She's a kid. Hardly a criminal. Still, it's done the trick. Kerry looks scared. I want to do something. Let her know I'm on her side. In her corner. I can't think of anything.

'Well?' the principal says, leaning forward so the shadow of her nose on the desk becomes a long, thin line.

Kerry lifts her head. Looks at the woman. 'I did it on Friday night,' she says. She turns to me. 'When you were out.'

'I had to work.' I look at the principal. No way I'm saying anything about the hospital. Don't want to give them more fuel for their fire. 'Her granny was in the house. She stayed til I got home.'

Miss Pratchett acknowledges me with a slight movement of her head. I turn back to Kerry. 'I can't believe you snuck out of the house like that. Your granny would have been up the walls if she'd known. Anything could have happened to you.'

Kerry shrugs.

Miss Wallis folds her arms, performs a little cough, gets ready to throw in her tuppence worth. 'And then there's the . . . pornographic nature of the picture. That has to be taken into consideration.' She looks at the principal, who nods.

'It's not pornography,' says Kerry. 'That's just ignorant. It's a nude.'

'It's two women with no clothes on. And how dare you call me ignorant.'

'I didn't call you ignorant. I just said it was ignorant to call art pornography. Or graffiti. That's all.'

'Well, I . . .' Miss Wallis begins, then stops, like she's run out of words.

'You will not be disrespectful to members of my staff, Kerry Boland.' The tip of the principal's nose is a bloodless white now.

I stand up. All of a sudden. I don't know why. Everyone looks at me. Even Kerry. The office is static with silence. Then I say, 'So what happens now?' I wish I hadn't stood up. Now that I'm up, I can't very well sit back down and the meeting isn't over yet. But here I am, on my pins and everyone gawking.

The principal sighs. She looks normal when she does that. A normal person having your average bad day at work. I get that. 'You should take Kerry home, Mr Boland.'

'I will.' Best to get her out of here pronto, before she does any more damage.

'She's suspended for two days,' she goes on.

'Including today?' I ask.

She shakes her head. It could be worse, I suppose.

'And there's the graffiti, of course.' She pauses there, as if daring Kerry to contradict her. 'It'll have to be taken off and I'm making Kerry responsible for this.' I want to say, *Good luck to you.* Almost impossible to get Kerry to do a tap at home. I rarely ask her any more. Not worth the hassle.

'It won't wash off,' Kerry says.

'Well, then, you'll have to paint over it.'

'Don't worry,' I say, moving towards the door. 'She will. I'll make sure of that.' I open the door. Think about the next two days. The house'll be like a boxing ring, her in one corner, me in the other.

It's a depressing thought. Especially after that carry-on on Friday, in the taxi. All that waitin' around the hospital. I didn't tell Kerry or Finn what happened. Finn's questions. And Kerry shrugging like she couldn't care less. I wouldn't be able for it.

I nearly make it out the door when I hear, 'Mr Boland?'

I turn around. 'Yes?' Impatient, like I'm a person with places to get to.

'I have no choice but to put this on Kerry's official school record. She's had enough warnings. Next time, we'll have to seriously consider our position, in relation to Kerry's attendance at this school.'

I nod. I know. 'There won't be a next time,' I say, with more conviction than I feel. 'Come on, Kerry,' I say, ushering her through the office door and closing it behind me.

We walk down the corridor. A bell goes off and immediately, all you can hear is the scraping of chairs and the din of a thousand kids talking at the same time. It sounds ominous, like thunder. I hurry up. Don't want to get caught up in the crowd. I keep my head down on the way past the reception hatch. I'm sure they all know by now. Give them something to talk about. Something else.

Outside, Kerry stops walking. 'Dad?'

'Not a word.'

'But I just—'

'We'll discuss it at home.' I don't want to discuss it at home. Or anywhere. I just want a bit of peace and quiet, to be honest. That never happens.

Kenny's blocking the school gates with the Stretch.

'Where's your car?' Kerry says, looking at the limo.

'In for a service.'

'It had a service last month.'

'Willya get in?'

'How's Picasso?' Kenny winks at Kerry in the rear-view mirror. Kerry shrugs and slots her earphones into her ears. Next thing, all you can hear is the thud, thud, thud of that desperate music she likes. Swedish House Mafia or something. I know I should probably confiscate her iPod after what's happened but I'm relieved that she's got it. It means I don't have to say anything. Not yet anyway. Never put off til tomorrow what you can do the day after. That's what Ma says my motto is. All I want is a strong cup of coffee and a fag and maybe a bit of a read of the paper and a Valium. That's not a lot to ask, is it?

It's only when Kenny drops us at the house and speeds off down the road that I realise I've no fags. And no paper.

A coffee and a Valium, so.

Dear Neil,

Monday. Not fond of Mondays. Nothing great on the telly. Film4 is doing some Hitchcock tribute thing but it's not starting til tomorrow. No appointments on Mondays. I found myself looking at my watch this morning and wondering what time Mum would be here.

I used to phone her once a week. Sunday evening, after dinner, I phoned her. I suppose it was a sense of duty, back then. An item on my To Do list. It's not like we didn't get on. We were just . . . busy with our lives. She was always an independent woman. Even after my father left, I don't remember anything changing. I went back to boarding school and she went back to work and David went back to university. And five years later, at his funeral, she didn't cry. She sat near the back of the church, as if she were a glancing acquaintance rather than the woman who used to be his wife. The mother of his children. She was stoic. And strong. Still is.

She charges into the apartment, flinging open windows and beating cushions, filling the kettle and clearing the crumbs off the table with the curve of her hand. She's stopped trying to get me to turn the telly off but she insists on opening the curtains. 'A bit of natural light will do you the world of good,' she says, when I shield my eyes against the stab of sun. Same goes for vine tomatoes, exercise and putting on make-up. Do you the world of good, she says.

She's doing a good job of pretending her knees aren't hurting her. I see the telltale swell of arthritis in both of them. I ask her about it but she waves her hand at the question, shakes her head and that's that. She puts my dinner into the microwave.

Beef Stroganoff from Marks & Spencer's today. She used to be so anti-microwave. She wrote a paper on it once. Years ago. The health implications of using electromagnetic radiation to cook food.

We watch Neighbours *and eat the beef and it's only when the credits roll and the theme music plays at the end, she realises it's not* Home and Away. *'I'm getting old,' she says.*

'They're pretty much the same thing,' I tell her. 'Neighbours *and* Home and Away.'

I don't think I've ever heard her refer to her age in a negative way. It gave me a jolt, made me notice other things. Like the lines around her eyes, deeper and longer than I remember, the slackening of her jawline, the slight slope of her shoulders. Even her hair, steel grey for years, is thinning in places to reveal the vulnerable pink of her scalp.

You used to flirt with her. You used to flirt with everybody, mind. I asked you not to, remember? I didn't think Mum would approve. But she liked it. She'd get coquettish, giggling with her hand cupped over her mouth. You'd never think she'd been the Master at Holles Street when she did that.

I tell her there's no need to come over so often. She arrives anyway. With our dinner in her Bag for Life shopping bag. She's so energetic. It's like being run over by a truck sometimes. It's quite the impact.

Dr Deery says she's a positive force in my life. I say, 'Force is an apt word,' but she doesn't laugh or even smile. Just writes something into her notebook, as usual.

Still, Mum seems a little subdued after her declaration of age. I distract her with enquiries. Get her to tell me about her volunteer work. How the pottery classes are going. What book her book club is reading this month. If she's managed to lower her handicap again.

Over coffee, she perks up. Asks her usual questions.

'How's the physio coming along?'
'Good.'
'How's the counselling coming along?'
'Good.'
'Good,' she says. 'That's good.'
She never mentions my face.
Or you.

Ellen

Six

Kerry's in bed with her clothes on when I go to check on her later. She's reading. 'What are you reading?' I say, when I poke my head in the door. I've practised the conversation in my head. Going to start nice and easy.

'A book.' She doesn't look up.

I should take the book off her. Unplug the laptop. Tell her to get out of the bed and straighten up her room. It's like a bomb site. A carpet of clothes on the floor and make-up all over the desk where she's supposed to do her homework. The lamp is on. It's always on. I don't think she ever turns it off.

'Look, can you just try and get through the rest of the school year without any more hassle, yeah? It's your Junior Cert year. You need to, you know, focus. On your schoolwork and that. No more messin'.'

She turns a page. Shrugs.

'What did you say?'

'I didn't say anything.'

There was a time – not even that long ago, a couple of years, maybe – when I could have sat on the edge of the bed and talked to her. She'd have told me everything. She wore her hair in plaits then. Two long plaits down her back. Like Laura from *Little House on the Prairie*, she was, with those plaits.

'I'll get some paint from Edges. For the wall, at the school. The principal said the caretaker has put something over it for the moment. A sheet or something. But it's to be done before next week. Are you listening to me?'

She looks at me suspiciously then. 'Why are you not at work?'

'Have to keep an eye on you, don't I?'

She returns to her book.

'But that's an end to it now, do you hear me? I don't want to be getting any more calls from that school, OK? I've enough to be worrying about.'

'Yeah.' Doesn't even bother glancing at me. It wasn't always like this.

'An apology would be nice.'

'Sorry.'

'And a thank you.'

'Thank you.'

This wasn't the conversation I'd planned. The one I'd practised. I leave the room.

'Can you close the door?' she says.

I don't slam it. I think about it. But I don't.

I pull the duvet off Finn's bed. Put my hand on the sheet. Damp. I take it off the bed. Roll it in a ball and throw it towards the top of the stairs. The only sheet in the hot press is a double one. I fold it in half and tuck it around the plastic cover on top of his mattress. He has the pull-ups but he won't wear them. He says he's too old for pull-ups. I've tried everything. No drinks in the evening, not even milk on the cereal he has for supper. Sometimes, when I'm going to bed, I wake him. Sit him on the jacks. He hates that. He cries when I do that, even though he's half-asleep. I hate when he cries. He asks for her when he cries. Fifteen months and he still asks for her when he cries.

I put the sheet in the washing machine and a load of other stuff that's mostly white-ish. Turn it on. It rattles a bit, the machine. Especially when it's spinning. I happen to like the noise of it. And the smell of the clothes when I take them out.

Fresh. You feel you've done something good, with a smell like that.

I look in the freezer. There isn't much. I need to do a shop. Near the back of the bottom drawer, there's a tray of mince. Spaghetti Bolognese. Finn loves spaghetti Bolognese. I tell him it's because of my secret ingredient but I never tell him what the secret ingredient is. Drives him spare, it does. I have everything I need for it. The mince, the jar of Dolmio, the packet of pasta. And of course, the tomato ketchup. That's it. The secret ingredient. You wouldn't think it would make that much of a difference.

I like the walk to Finn's school. Even before, I'd nip home from work at lunchtime, drop the car at the house and stroll around to get him. Not always. But sometimes. His little face'd light up like a Christmas tree when he'd spot me and he'd hurl himself at me, like he hadn't seen me for days. Once a week, I'd say. Sometimes twice. Give Paula a bit of a break. She was tired a lot. Even though they were good kids, when they were little. Slept all night and that. But I know it's tiring, being home all day with them. That's all I thought it was, at first. Tiredness.

The day has warmed itself up since this morning. The sun struggles out from a bank of cloud. I walk up the road. I know everyone on the street, even the blow-ins who came during the boom. We have all sorts here now. Yer man from *Fair City* lives in number twenty-five. Jonathon. I've seen him on the show a couple of times. He looks smaller in real life. Younger. He lives with the youngone who does the kids' programmes in the mornings. Deborah. Nice girl. She helped me find Finn that time. He said he was going to run away but I didn't pay a blind bit of notice. He was only six. Ended up hiding in that overgrown bush in Ma's front garden. Deborah O'Sullivan. That's her name. She copped it. Smart, she is. Smarter than Jonathon anyway. He never puts the bins out on the right day. They end up overflowing in his front garden. Asking for trouble with bins like that. The rats from the canal are only too delighted to pay a visit, with bins like that.

There's the architect in number thirty-two. Benjamin something-or-other. You'd think, with a name like Benjamin, people'd call you Ben but no-one does. Unemployed now, of course. He did a lovely job on the front of the house, though. Imported the stone from Wicklow, he said. Back in the day. You don't see him as much any more. The blinds are often down, even in the middle of the afternoon.

A couple of journos. Like the columnist from *The Irish Times* around the corner. Smiley. Wears a helmet when she cycles her bike. A few artists. Like the sculptor at the top of the road. Or she could be a potter. Always has dried clay on her clothes and under her fingernails. Her front garden's full of junk. Or it could be some of her pieces. That's what she calls her stuff. Pieces.

Mostly, though, it's us lot. A lot of them are like me. Lived here all our lives. Second generation, third generation, some of them go all the way back. I could walk around the place with a blindfold on and I'd still get around. It's the smells and sounds as much as what you see. The smell of detergent and the blast of heat when you're passing the dry-cleaner's. The bells of St Mary's ringing on the hour. That's where Finn is making his Communion. Where I made mine. And my Confirmation. I got married in there. The kids got baptised in there. Huge church. Draughty as hell. Hard to fill. Except when there's a funeral on and then it's up to the rafters. That's the thing here. We all know each other. Whether we like it or not.

Around the corner, on the next street, is where Paula's parents used to live. Before they upped sticks and moved to Spain. After what happened to Maureen. You couldn't blame them, I suppose. Everyone talking about it. Coming up with their theories. All the reasons. The fella who dumped her. The redundancy, maybe.

The projects she started and never finished. She wanted to be a dancer. When she was a kid. Always lepping and twirling around the hall, any time I called for Paula. Then she did the exam for the civil service and that was that. She forgot all about the dancing. Except the odd time down the pub when she had the few jars on. She'd put Bruce on the jukebox and go spare.

But there aren't any reasons for something like that. Not as far as I can see.

Their mother is dead too. Cancer. Just before Finn was born. Her auldfella stayed on. Nerja, their place is. Costa del Sol. He took up golf. Paula was convinced he was playing away. 'He's a widower. How can he be playing away?' I said.

'She's not dead a year. That's playing away.' I had my doubts. A pompous git with a bulbous nose and a passion for tellin' long jokes with no punchline. How can a fella like that play away?

He's the first person I rang. After Paula left. I waited for a couple of days before I rang. I was convinced she'd be back. She'd gone before. A few times. And then she'd come back. Sweets for the kids, her hair glossy and bouncy from a blow-dry. 'Sorry,' she said, when she came back that first time. I noticed how thin she'd gotten. Her jumper sliding off her shoulders and the waist of her jeans tightened with a belt. 'Come here,' I said, and she walked over to me. I lifted her and she wrapped her legs around me. Light as a feather, she was. I carried her up the stairs. Into our bedroom. She cried when she came. 'I don't deserve you, Vinnie.'

'Will you go 'way.'

'I'm a terrible mother.'

'You just needed a break. A few days was all.'

'I wasn't sure I'd come back.'

'Ssshhh. You're here now, aren't you? You came back. We're grand. Aren't we?' I moved over in the bed and pulled her towards me, into my warm spot. She was always cold. It was hard to get the heat into her. I wrapped my arms around her. Held her tight. I thought that'd be enough. Just hold her tight and close my eyes and everything would be alright.

A bad patch. That's all it was. That's what I thought anyway. At the time.

Past McCarthy's now. The cigarette smoke curling around the front door. Inside, in the little foyer, are Jimmy and Jackie Stowe. Brothers. I know they're there before I see them. They're always there. First thing in the morning. Ten o'clock. Whenever the pub opens. Eleven maybe. They share a corpo house a few roads over. They used to work. Back when everyone had a job. A bit of labouring. Now, nothing, so it's into the pub for their pints and their chasers and they don't leave until Mary calls time. Harmless enough. Throw the few shapes the odd time but there's no muscle in it.

Already I see kids coming from the direction of the school. I pull up the cuff of my jacket before I remember about the watch. I didn't think I was late. I must have been dawdling. Thinking about Christ knows what. I start to run but I'm out of puff real quick and it makes me think about the panic attack, and that worries me. The thought of having another one. The doctor said I wasn't to worry. He said loads of stuff. Yoga. Fuck sake.

I stop running and walk instead, but brisk now. I see Callam, on the other side of the street, being pulled along behind his ma. He sees me and smiles, the same gappy smile that Finn has. 'Finn is crying, so he is.'

Dammit.

'He thinks you've forgotten to collect him.' He says this at full volume so everyone can hear him, even over the roar of the traffic.

Callam's mother, Monica, yanks his arm and hisses at him to be quiet. She looks at me and smiles, shaking her head.

I run the last bit. I've taken the Valium so I'd say I'll be grand. My breath wheezes in and out of my chest. I used to be in better shape. I'm sure I was.

Finn's standing in the yard beside his teacher. Miss . . . something beginning with a C. Crosbie, maybe? Or Curtin. This is the second year he's had her. I should remember. Cronin. That's it. Cronin. I'm positive. Pretty sure.

She's holding his hand. There's another kid beside her, waiting. I'm not the only one who's late. But it's Finn's hand she's holding.

'Dad!' When he sees me, his face breaks into a smile and he slips his hand out of his teacher's and wipes his nose with the sleeve of his jacket.

'Hey, son, sorry I'm a bit late.' I try to catch Miss Cronin's eye but she's bending towards Finn, slipping his arms through the straps of his schoolbag.

'Finn,' she says, straightening. 'Would you do me a favour and get my hat? It's on a hook in the cloakroom.'

'What colour is it?'

'Red.' She smiles at him, her hand on the top of his head.

'Back in a minute, Dad.' He flashes his gummy smile and sets off at a dart across the yard.

The teacher watches Finn disappear through the front door of the school and then she turns to me. No smile now.

I get in first. 'I'm not that late, am I?'

Miss Cronin studies my face. She's taking it all in. The stubble, the red-veined eyes, the hair that could do with a wash. A brush even. Should have worn the hat. It's cold enough.

She looks at her watch. 'I know you're only a couple of minutes late and usually I wouldn't say anything. It's just that Finn gets very . . . he becomes a little distressed when you aren't here on the dot.'

'Which one is it?'

'Pardon?'

'Very distressed? Or a little distressed?'

I see her filing me under D for Difficult. But fuck it, they'd make you feel like you were some kind of scumbag abuser or something. I'm doin' my best here. Amn't I?

'You saw him there. He tried to hide it but he's been crying. You saw that. Didn't you?'

I nod. 'He can be a bit highly strung.'

'He's a lovely child.'

'I know that.' I smile after I say that. Take the edge off the words. Defensive, I sound.

It works because she sort of smiles back. 'Is that your mother who usually picks him up?'

I nod. 'Yeah. I don't suppose she's ever late, is she?'

Miss Cronin smiles, shakes her head. 'Look, as I say, I wouldn't have mentioned it. It's just that Finn can be a little—'

'Distressed. Yeah, you said.' Distressed. It seems like too big a word to use on a seven-year-old. Seven-year-olds shouldn't be distressed. They should be playing football and licking ice-cream cones. That's it. That's all I did when I was seven. I can't remember Ma ever being late picking me up from school. But I'm sure she was. A couple of times, at least. Everyone is. Once in a while.

'If you ever need to discuss anything with me, please don't hesitate. Alright?' She's eyeballing me now. They all know, of course. I had to tell them. Had to take Finn out of school for a few days, he was that . . . distressed, I suppose. They would have found out in jig time anyway, with the young fella asking everyone he met if they knew where his mammy was. When she'd be back.

Finn arrives back, thank Christ. He's got the hat, fair dues to him. He hands it to her, chuffed with himself.

'Come on, son.' I nod at the teacher and Finn slips his hand into mine and we move away.

Once we're back on the street, I squeeze his hand. Look down at him. He's getting tall. His school trousers are flapping around his ankles, the ends a bit frayed from all the washing and ironing and the bit of horseplay in the yard. I'll pick up a pair in Dunnes later. A longer pair.

'Sorry I was late.'

'Doesn't matter,' he says, kicking a stone along the path. The tips of his shoes are a bit scuffed. A lick of polish. That should do the trick.

'You were a bit upset, though.'

'Did Miss Cronin say that?'

'No.'

'Do you think Mam will come home for my First Holy Communion? The mams and dads have a special seat in the church where they're supposed to sit.'

'I . . .'

'I'd say she will cos she wouldn't want to miss the party, wouldn't she not?'

'Well . . .'

'And seein' me in my outfit.'

'I made spaghetti Bolognese for your dinner.'

'With the secret ingredient?'

'Course.'

'Cool.'

We walk home and he doesn't mention her again.

Seven

Kenny persuades me to go to the local for a pint. 'Doctor's orders,' he says. 'Besides, I want to fill you in on my latest date.' Kenny is always going on dates. First dates, mostly.

We walk to McCarthy's, Kenny with some difficulty as he's breaking in a new pair of blue suede Chelsea boots. He stops at the chip shop on the way. 'My mother's gone to visit me auntie Doreen for the night,' he says, by way of explanation.

'It's weird. How you're not overweight.'

'Jane Fonda,' he says. 'Every night, no exceptions.'

Chips. That's what he fed the kids when Paula was in the hospital that first time. Chips from the chip shop. Ma was on her annual pilgrimage to Knock. I'd visit in the evening. Finn was only a nipper then. Just gone two, I think. Kerry would have been eight. Even the kids were sick of chips after a week.

'Carol.'

'Wha'?'

'That's her name. Carol. There's something a bit regal about it, isn't there?'

'Kenny, there's nothing regal about the name Carol.'

'She's a fine-looking woman.'

I take a long draught from my pint. I wince at the dark, sour taste. Put the pint down. Lick the cream that gathers along the top of my mouth. Sweet. I sit at the bar with both hands wrapped around the glass like it's warming me.

'A surgery.'

'What are you talking about?'

'That's her occupation. She works in a doctor's surgery. Front desk management. She's got her own apartment.' Kenny would love an apartment. A bachelor pad, he'd probably call it. Wouldn't say it's going to happen now. He was one of the unfortunates who bought the taxi plate before deregulation. A hundred grand he paid for it. Three months before deregulation. Thought it would be his nest egg. Fairly worthless now. Still, he has his health. That's what he says. 'I'm in fine fettle.' He's right there.

'Near the Grand Canal. Lovely spacious apartments.'

'You've been inside her apartment?'

'Not yet. I heard they were spacious, though.'

'Where'd you meet her?'

'At one of the charity shops in Dún Laoghaire. I was mooching around the shoes – they had a lovely pair of Spats but they were too small for me – and she was at the counter, discussing prices. She ended up paying two euros for an Orla Kiely scarf. Beautiful piece of fabric, it was. She has a great eye, Carol.'

'Is it not bad form, haggling in a charity shop?'

'Negotiating, comrade.' Kenny touches the side of his nose with the tip of his finger, lowers his head, busies himself with his pint. Then he settles back on his stool, winds his fingers around the ends of his ronnie. 'You could be right, Vincent. She could be the one.'

'I never said that.'

'No, but you were thinking it.'

Kenny is an optimist. His pint of Guinness is always half-full, except when it's my round.

'I might take her out in the Stretch. Not immediately. I'll give it a couple of weeks. See what's what.'

'Ah, Kenny, don't. Remember what happened last time? There were ructions.'

'There was no way for me to know that that woman was going to turn into a psychopath.'

'She told us.'

'She only said she was out on bail.'

'She was bein' tried for murder!'

'Manslaughter.'

I shake my head. Take a drink of my pint.

'Anyway, the insurance coughed up for the damage,' he says.

'Eventually.'

He brightens. 'Well, Carol's no psycho, I guarantee you. She plays bridge. Bet you can't name one psychopathic bridge player.'

'The only bridge player I know is my mother.'

'There you are, then.' He twists on the stool, reaching his hand into his back pocket for his wallet. 'One for the ditch, comrade?'

'I'd better hit the road. I've to get milk and bread on the way home.'

'Always with the milk and bread.'

'The kids. They're like locusts.' I stand up.

Mary behind the bar clocks me. 'You're not headin' already, are you, gorgeous?'

'Early start,' I say, picking my weather-beaten leather jacket off the stool.

Kenny raises his eyes. He can't understand why I don't go for it. 'I would,' he says.

'You'd go for a Rottweiler in a skirt,' I remind him. That shuts him up.

Near the door is a crowd of women in a circle, talking. The screech of them. I'm surprised there's any glass left in the windows. One of them sees me, stands up. It's Trish. Paula's best friend. Joined at the hip, they were, when they were youngones. Trish wasn't mad about me, to be honest. When I first started going out with Paula. Things settled down when she got her own bloke. Her own set of troubles.

'Howeya, handsome,' she says. Her breath smells of wine and crisps.

I nod at her, buttoning my jacket. 'Howeya, Trish.'

She sways a little, puts her hand on my shoulder to steady herself, pushes the other hand through her hair. 'How's things?'

'Yeah, grand, the usual. You?'

She nods. The slow nod of someone who should have said no to the last drink. She looks the same, really. Trish. You could pick her out from her school photo. A little heavier, yeah. The mouth a bit harder, the hair longer and a different colour altogether.

'Same shite, different day,' she says, taking a tube of bright red lipstick out of the pocket of her denim skirt. She slides the lipstick from one side of her bottom lip to the other, then smacks her lips together so they're both the same garish red. The colour makes her teeth look yellow.

'Well, it was nice seeing you, Trish. I better head. I've to get a few bits from the garage before it closes.'

'How are the kids?'

'Grand, not a bother.'

'God love them.'

'They're happy enough.' I take a cigarette out of the pack. Tuck it behind my ear. For when I manage to get outside.

Trish leans towards me. 'Have you heard from her?'

I shake my head. 'She sent the kids a postcard. Couple of weeks ago.' Postcards. That's what she sends now. Like she's on her holidays.

Trish laughs like I've said something funny. 'Great that she got the job at the salon. And so close to her da's apartment. Handy.'

60

'Yeah.' It's strange how things turn out. Paula and her auld-fella. Living together. She couldn't stick him when she was growing up.

'Let's hope her cutting technique has improved. Remember the fringe she gave you that time? She kept hacking at it til it was on the top of your head. Remember?'

'That was a long time ago.'

Trish stops laughing. Looks me up and down. 'Time you got yourself back out there,' she says. She leans over and brushes the shoulder of my jacket with the tips of her fingers, like there's a bit of dust there or something.

'Ah, sure, I'm still hitched, amn't I?' I step back, and for a moment her hand is suspended in the air, the bitten nails exposed and sore in the flickering light of last orders.

She pulls her hand back, stuffs it into the pocket of her skirt.

I smile to take the sting out of it but it's too late because she pulls her mouth into a sneer and says, 'That never stopped Paula, did it?'

Eight

Promiscuous.

There's a word.

But Paula wasn't like that before. She wasn't promiscuous. A bit flirty sometimes. Dr McDaid said it could have been the medication. A side-effect, maybe.

Dr McDaid should have retired by now. He's been at it since I was a kid with chickenpox.

'Sure what would I do with myself if I retired?' he says, when I mentioned it years ago.

'You could take up a sport. Golf, maybe.'

'Golf?' He looks like he's swallowed cod liver oil. I hand him the prescription from the hospital. 'They put me on this stuff, would you believe? And insisted I come in to you for a check-up this week. No wonder the health service is so clogged.'

He looks at the prescription, pulling at the long, coarse hairs sprouting from his nostrils. Paula gave me a little hand-held gadget for dealing with those. Does the trick. The doctor leans back in his chair and the thing reclines til he's almost horizontal. Tucks his massive hands behind his head. The tips of his fingers poke out on either side, like wings.

'I heard about your little drama.'

'The town crier, I presume?' Kenny's mother is basically where yer man, whatshisface, Mark Zuckerberg, got the idea for Facebook. Status updates every minute, whether you want one or not. And she's one of the surgery's regulars, in spite of the fact that there's not much wrong with her, other than her insatiable appetite for other people's misfortunes.

Dr McDaid doesn't answer. He doesn't need to. 'And I need a letter from you as well. For the boss man. Just letting him know I'm fit for purpose.'

'A panic attack shouldn't be taken lightly.' Dr McDaid nods like he's agreeing with himself. Closes his eyes. It wouldn't surprise me if he started snoring. 'And you've a lot on your plate, Vinnie.' The doctor knows all about it.

He thought it was post-natal depression at first. After Kerry. He said it wouldn't last. After Finn, he called it severe. Severe post-natal depression. He didn't say anything about it not lasting. It was a relief in one way. Having a name for it. Still, it would have been better if it had been something else. Something you could take antibiotics for.

'So,' he says, 'what happened?'

'I thought Mrs Byrne filled you in.'

'Her details were sketchy. Not up to her usual standard.' He allows himself a small smile. I shift in my chair. 'It was nothing, really. I was a bit short of breath was all. These help.' I nod towards the prescription.

He shakes his head. 'I'm not mad about those yokes,' he says. For a doctor, he can be a bit funny about medication.

'I'm not taking the full monty. Just when I go to bed, mostly. Helps me sleep. Another few courses of them and I'll be grand.'

He pulls himself off the chair, using my shoulder as leverage. 'I'm going to check your heart and your blood pressure and get you to give me a sample.'

'Everything's grand, Doc.'

'When did you get your medical degree?'

I take off my jacket and roll up my sleeve.

'Any word from Paula?' he says, when he has the band around my arm.

I nod. 'She's grand.'

Kerry was unimpressed when she opened the parcel Paula sent her at Christmas. 'Now That's What I Call Music! 83'. A few strange-looking sweets. Spanish ones. A key ring with a donkey in a straw hat hanging off it. She ate the sweets, alright. The CD is in her room. Unopened. Never saw the donkey again.

Finn cried. He thought she'd come home for Christmas. I hate that about Christmas, I really do. The things people hope for.

'How about the kids? How are they doing?'

'They're fine.' I mentioned the bedwetting before but Dr McDaid just said it'll stop eventually. That was a year ago. I don't know if 'eventually' is supposed to take this long. I don't mention it now.

'Your Kerry's growing up quick. I saw her the other day. The spit of her mother.' Dr McDaid puts his great paw of a hand on my shoulder. A fatherly gesture. He was the one who came. That time in the garden with Da. He put his hand on my shoulder that time too. 'I'll give you one more prescription of that stuff, and then we'll see, alright?'

'We'll see?' I'm not loving the sound of that.

Dr McDaid bends towards his prescription pad. Licks the nib of the pen before he starts to write. No idea what that's about. He tears off the page, waves it in front of my face. 'After these, it's drastic measures, Vinnie.' He eyeballs me then, to demonstrate his resolve.

'What kind of drastic measures?' I'm thinking about me, in a hospital gown with my arse hanging out the back, getting prodded and poked by doctors and nurses and what have you. Getting tested for Christ knows what.

'Counselling, maybe. A bit of yoga. Diet. Giving up those cancer sticks. There's lots you could be doing for yourself.'

'Yoga?' Jaysus, I'm getting fired on from all sides. Nobody will be happy until I'm sitting cross-legged on a mat, with my eyes closed, humming to myself.

'And I'm not happy about you going back to work so soon.'

'I need the rent, Doc.'

He nods, hands me the prescription.

'I know, Vinnie. But you're to take it easy. No overtime. Your body has sent you a message. It's like getting a parcel in the post. You should open it.'

I found the dreamcatcher the other day. She sent it for Kerry's birthday. Last year.

'What's it for?' Kerry asked. I didn't know.

I saw it under her bed. A few weeks ago, when I was hoovering. Dust catcher more like. I took it out. Googled it. It's supposed to protect you from nightmares. You hang it over your bed.

I put it in her wardrobe. I'll tell her what it's for. Some day. When she's in better form.

Dear Neil,

Dr Deery wants to know what my friends thought of you. Of us.

I said I was never all that good at making friends. I had my work colleagues, and your friends, of course, who allowed me to join their ranks when we were together. I haven't seen them in months. And then there's Faye, who I sat beside every day from junior infants to university, who was my bridesmaid at our wedding, as I was at hers. She was the first person I told about you.

She stopped ringing a while ago. Can't say I blame her. I've declined every suggestion, every invitation. I never called her my best friend. But that's how I thought of her. How I think of her still.

Faye said you were too old for me. 'When you're fifty-five, he'll be seventy. Seventy!'

At least we won't have to worry about that particular scenario. Dr Deery would probably describe it as a 'positive'.

In the end, it was me who grew too old for you. How old was she? Twenty-seven? Twenty-eight? She wasn't the first, was she? Just the first I found out about.

It was nothing, you said. It meant nothing. One of those things. Shouldn't have happened. Too much to drink. Oh, the clichés you trotted out. Like lines learned from a script.

You were too polite to deny it. Or to ask how I found out. Carol, of course. Our receptionist. Except she was always your receptionist, really, following you everywhere with those big, limpid eyes, bringing you whatever you needed before you knew that you needed it.

You were charming. A charming man. Distinguished.
Mannerly. Funny. Authoritative.
Faye loved you in the end.
That's what I told Dr Deery. Everyone loved you in the end.

Ellen

Nine

It's finally Wednesday. After a bit of haggling, Dr McDaid agreed that I could go back to work today. I promised him I'd do those breathing exercises he showed me. I can do them in the motor. I'm not cut out for sitting around, doing nothing. Nothing to do but think. I'm better off keeping busy, getting on with things.

Ma nearly went spare when I told her.

'You can't go back so soon, Vincent. You could have *died*.'

'You don't die from a panic attack.'

'How do you know? I suppose you Googled it?'

'The doctor told me.'

'Doctors. They think they know it all.'

'Well, they know a good bit about medical stuff, to be fair.'

'They couldn't save your poor father, Lord have mercy on him' – she does a swift sign of the cross – 'could they?'

'Dr McDaid had told him to stop eating fry-ups and butter and cakes. Exercise a bit. Remember?'

She dismisses this reminder with a shake of her head. 'A fry-up? That's hardly going to kill you, is it?' She grabs the cushion behind my back and beats the dust out of it with her fist. She's strong for an auldone. 'Seven years in medical school and that's the best they can come up with? Stop eating fries?' Bashing the cushion all the while. The stuffing will be out of it if she doesn't let up.

'Could you pick Finn up after school for me?'

'You've been working much too hard. You should be taking it easy.'

The thought of getting behind the wheel again makes me nervous. But I have to. The mortgage isn't going to pay itself. 'I need the dough. Finn's big day.'

'I told you I'd get him his little outfit.'

'I want to do it.' I'm not even good at clothes shopping. Paula used to get the few threads for me. I couldn't even tell you what size I am, in shirts or jeans.

Ma looks appalled. 'You wouldn't even know where to bring him.'

'Arnotts,' I say, loud and clear. That stops her in her tracks. She can't argue with Arnotts. I don't know why I don't let her do it. It's just . . . I want to do it. Finn reckons it's important. An important day, I mean. It should be me buying him the suit and that. Navy, I think. Navy would be nice on him. I think. I'll check with Janine. Janine is good with colours.

'How come madam's not up yet?'

'She's got a day off school.'

'I didn't come down in the last shower, Vincent Patrick Boland.'

'I have to go.' I put Finn's lunchbox and drink into his schoolbag. 'Seeya, Finn,' I shout up the stairs.

He runs down, his mouth full of toothpaste. 'You weren't going to go without kissing me goodbye, were you?' he asks. The toothpaste leaks out of his mouth and down his chin in shaky lines.

I wish he was a bit tougher, Finn.

I get the bus to the depot. I could have asked Kenny for a lift but his bedroom blind was down.

Janine agrees with me. Navy. She says Arnotts is grand, like it's no big deal, but I can tell she's impressed, all the same. I don't have a clue what a navy suit for a kid will cost in Arnotts, but I'd better start earning.

It's only been a few days but it feels more like a week. The car could do with a wash. I'll do that first.

'You're still a bit peaky looking, Vinnie,' says Janine. 'Have you lost weight?'

'No,' I say quickly. Janine goes mad if people lose weight. Especially if they're not on a diet.

'Where's Kenny?' I say, to distract her.

'Not on til tonight.' That explains the blinds and the offer of a third pint last night. I avoid the night shift as much as I can. If I have to do it, I get Ma to stay over, but I worry. About Finn, mostly. Waking up and I'm not there. Ma finds it tricky to calm him.

Janine sits on a high stool beside the car while I wash it. I roll up my sleeves and get stuck in.

She lifts her head from her mug of tea. Sighs.

'What's wrong?' I say.

'Watched *Titanic* last night.'

'Again?'

'I never complain when you and Kenny watch the Ireland–Romania penalty shoot-out in Genoa over and over again, do I?'

'You do.'

'That's because it happened twenty-four years ago.'

'So?'

'So build a bridge and get over it.'

'You shouldn't watch that film. It puts you in bad form.'

'It's just that it's so romantic. I can't remember the last time I had a bit of romance in my life.'

'Did you not get a bellyful with yer man, whatshisface? Brendan?'

She rolls her eyes. 'That eejit.'

'Eloping at eighteen. That was fairly romantic.'

'The idea of it was romantic. The reality was different. Puked my ring up on the ferry over. Bren had the runs. Dodgy kebabs and a rough crossing. The ceremony was nice enough. I still have the white miniskirt and the matching halter-neck. Two years with Bren in that smelly bedsit in Peckham before I rang my mother and told her she could say it now.'

'Say what?'

'I told you so.'

'And did she?'

'Course she did. Still does.'

I pour the warm, sudsy water over the body of the car and scrub it with a sponge.

'Calamity Jane saved your life, you know. That's pretty romantic.' Janine reaches inside her top and pulls her bra straps, poking out the ends of her sleeves, back onto her shoulders.

'You're worse than Ma, with the drama.'

'Still.'

'Still, wha'?'

'You should get her something. To say thanks.'

I dip the cloth into the bucket of hot water and rinse it. Start on the windscreen. 'What kind of something?'

Janine gets up from the stool, pulls at the end of her skirt. I don't know why she doesn't buy longer skirts. Save all that reefing. She walks towards the kettle, shaking her head again. 'I don't know how you managed to get a woman to marry you, Vinnie. You haven't got a clue.'

'Enlighten me.' I lift a wiper and run a cloth along its length.

'Flowers. Chocolates. Hand cream. Bath bombs.' She intones this list in the bored monotone of a woman discovering – yet again – how useless men are.

'She mightn't have a bathtub.'

'She sounds like the type of woman who has a bathtub.' Janine can create entire lives and personas based on the tone of a voice over the phone.

'What are bath bombs anyway?'

'Ah, here.' She hands me a cup of coffee – instant, but still – and heads back towards her office, leaving a fug of industrial-strength perfume in her wake.

Flowers, I suppose. Women like flowers. Carnations maybe. Not roses. They could be misconstrued. Not that I think she'll read anything into it. But still. Carnations. Just to be safe. I don't even have to drive over. I'll have them delivered. Along with a thank you note. That'll do the job.

The Interflora man I phone says it'll cost fifty euros for a bunch of flowers to be delivered. He recommends a spring bouquet. Tulips and daisies. Pink and white, he reckons. Nothing says thank you like pink and white tulips and daisies, he says. I cancel the order and hang up. Fifty euros! I'll drive round.

My arms ache when I'm finished but the car looks like new. Janine wants me to pick up a punter from Google, drop him to the airport. I can swing by Clontarf on my way back. Sorted.

'Don't buy flowers from a garage,' Janine shouts after me as I drive out of the depot. I don't know what women have against flowers from a garage. But I know enough not to buy them. More than your life is worth, garage flowers.

The Google fare is a doddle. Just sits in the back of the cab and fiddles with his phone. Grand job. It's nice being back at work, with fares like this one.

The day is chilly but bright. I drive over the Liffey on the Samuel Beckett Bridge. The water is an iron grey and the sails of the *Jeanie Johnston* fill and strain with that stiff northerly. The sun glances across the glass front of the National Conference Centre. I love it at night, that building. The lights on. I told Finn that the front of it collapsed when they were building it. During a storm, I said. Gas, he is. He believes everything I say.

I make a bet with myself. Terminal one, I reckon. I do this on the airport runs. Keeps the boredom at bay. Receipt, definitely. He'll ask for a receipt. A euro tip.

I'm right about everything except the tip. No tip. English accent. Probably over for the day.

Blooms in Clontarf looks like the kind of flower shop women approve of. No cellophane and no diesel fumes. Silver buckets of flowers outside and a pink wreath in the shape of a loveheart on the front door that tinkles like Christmas bells when you open it. The smell inside is as strong as Janine's perfume. I breathe through my mouth.

The woman has a high, squeaky voice and speaks like a nurse. 'Good morning, sir. How are we today?'

I get to the point before I'm overpowered. 'Spring bouquet. Tulips and daisies.'

'Excellent choice, sir. And may I recommend some lilies also? We got them in this morning and they smell heavenly.' She pushes a bunch of them towards my face and the smell off them hits me like a fist.

She beams at me, with her head to one side, waiting for a reply.

I nod. 'How much?' I manage to say.

She's already wrapping them. White paper with pink roses. I have to admit it looks a lot better than cellophane. 'I can give them to you for thirty euros, sir,' she says, like she's doing me a favour. Still, I've saved twenty euros and hopefully the woman – Ellen Woods – won't be there and I can leave them with one of her neighbours and then on Friday, she'll say thanks for the flowers and I'll say you're welcome and after that, it'll be business as usual.

In the foyer of Ellen's apartment block, I press her bell. Number twenty-eight. The age I was when Kerry was born.

'Hello?' Her voice sounds wary, like she's not expecting anyone. Which is fair enough. It's not like she knew I was coming.

'Eh, this is Vinnie. Vinnie Boland. The taxi driver. You, ah . . .'

'Vinnie?'

'That's right. You gave me a dig out last Friday. In the cab. I had a . . . I wasn't well. You drove me to the hospital.'

'Yes?' She might as well have said, 'So what?' I can't blame her. She has the look of someone wearing a 'Do Not Disturb' sign around their neck.

'No, listen, I don't want to bother you or anything. It's just . . . I wanted to say thanks so there's a few flowers. Nothing major. I'll leave them here, on the table in the foyer, alright? I'm just letting you know. Just sayin' thanks, you know? For taking me to the hospital.'

The intercom static crackles down the line.

An elderly woman enters the foyer, takes one look at the flowers and says, 'What a beautiful scent.'

I'm gaggin' here. Still nothing down the line.

'So yeah, anyway, I'll let you go. And I'll pick you up on Friday. In the cab, I mean. If you're going to Portmarnock as usual. OK?'

'Yes. I'll be going.'

'Grand, so. I'll see you then. Usual time, yeah?'

'Yes. And . . . thanks for the flowers. There was no need.'

'It's just something small. You were . . . you were great, so you were. The way you knew what to do. I wouldn't have had a clue.'

'I used to be a doctor.'

'Always good to have a doctor in the house,' I say, in a jokey way.

She doesn't respond but she hasn't hung up. I hear the static.

'OK, then, I'd better get back to work. So . . . thanks again. See you on Friday. OK? OK. Grand. Bye now.'

I light up when I get outside. Look up at the building. Lovely brick finish. Gated. A bit of a palaver getting in and out. Behind the blinds of an apartment on the second floor, I see the silhouette of a woman. Standing there, looking down. It could be her, I suppose. She's usually outside, at the front gate, when I pull up on a Friday. I don't know which one number twenty-eight is.

Twenty-eight. Young for nowadays. To have a kid. Paula had to have a section in the end. An emergency C-section. I jogged alongside the trolley to keep up with it. She held my hand so tight, I couldn't feel it for ages afterwards. She was asleep when they lifted the baby out. Exhausted, the doctor said. We'd been in the hospital for a day and a night by then. I sat in a chair and they handed Kerry to me, swaddled in a blanket. Wide awake the baby was. Not a peep out of her. I was surprised by her hair. How much of it there was. Her eyes were blue back then. She looked at me. Straight at me, like she knew who I was.

'You're my little woman.' I didn't say it out loud. The doctors and nurses were still there, working at the gap in Paula's belly. I sat on a chair, looked at the baby.

'Do you think she's hungry?' I asked one of the nurses after a while. She smiled at me, the nurse. 'She'll let you know when she's hungry, Mr Boland.'

The pair of them slept all afternoon. I sat between them, one hand on the lip of the cradle, the other on the bed. I wasn't tired, even though I hadn't got a wink of sleep the previous night. I felt . . . weird. Nice weird. Like we were in this little cocoon, the three of us. Me and the pair of them. Like nothing could happen. Nothing bad. The world was going about its business and we were safe and sound.

Dear Neil,

I got flowers. I've had to arrange them in the coffee pot. I think the vases are in one of the boxes in the spare room. And before you ask, yes, they're still unpacked and no, I've no intention of unpacking them any time soon. I have everything I need.

Apart from a vase.

They look so out of place, the flowers. All cheery and fragrant.

The taxi driver gave them to me. The one I drove to the hospital, remember? Vinnie. A thank you, he said.

I remember the last time you bought me flowers. January last year. Four years married by then. I thought we were okay.

'My husband went to a symposium, fucked a junior doctor and all I got was this lousy bunch of flowers'.

You didn't know that I knew then, did you? What must you have thought? When I threw them in the bin? PMT? A bad day at the clinic? You said nothing. Retreated into your study. I swept up some petals that had landed on the floor when I grabbed the bouquet from you. Put everything in the brown bin. See? Even when I was angry, I was well-behaved.

You should see me now.

I'm sitting on the couch in my pyjamas at three o'clock in the afternoon watching repeats of Strictly Come Dancing *and eating digestive biscuits with slices of banana on top. Late lunch.*

I feel a sense of melancholy, watching the dancers. As if I used to dance and now that I can't, I miss it. But I never used to dance.

Isn't that funny?

Ellen

Ten

Fight club with balls. That's what Janine calls it. The five-a-side. At least one injury every Wednesday night. Nothing serious. Sprains, mostly. A few black eyes. Not surprising, the way some of the lads elbow their way onto a ball. One broken collarbone. Clavicle, it's called. A hairline fracture. Nothing major. Kenny got a concussion once but you can't really count that; he tripped over a pair of football boots in the changing room after the game.

I wasn't going to go this week after the thing in the car. Goin' to hospital and that. And Kerry acting up. But Kenny and Ma ganged up on me. Said it would do me good. Get out of the house. A bit of exercise.

One broken nose. I broke Andy Dolan's nose. Ah, a long time ago now. I still remember the crack of it. My hand in a fist, connecting with his face. The noise. The bright red spurt of blood. And the pain in my hand afterwards.

Bare-knuckle Boland, the lads called me after that. And I'm not a scrapper, as a rule. I'd say the last time I hit someone was in school. Primary school. Nine years old, I would have been. Some sixth classer claimed me after school. A big enough fella. Twelve, he was. 'You're claimed,' he said, pointing at me in the yard. An argument over territory. Some imaginary line he'd drawn that I'd stepped over. You had to go, though. If you were claimed. To the spot behind the football field. More than your life was worth not to show up. I managed to get one good punch in before he made mincemeat of me. Joey broke it up in the end. Barged through the crowd and yanked me away. Brought me home. 'Pick on someone your own size,' he said to yer man. Thomas Boyle. That was his name. He joined the French Foreign Legion, last I heard.

Really enjoy the Wednesday nights, though. Sixty minutes of running and tackling and shouting at the ref and no time to think about anything else. It's like a pause button, pressed in the middle of the week. You might get a few digs, a bit of abuse roared your way, but I'm fairly sure I'd never get a panic attack there. Maybe it's because I don't think about much when I'm on the pitch. Don't think about anything except the beautiful game.

'Cross it.'

'Clear it.'

'Pass it.'

'Throw it.'

'Head it.'

'Fuck it.'

Mostly good-humoured banter. On the pitch. In the changing room. And a pint afterwards. Post-match analysis, we call it.

Janine asks me about the lads. Any of them single? Separated? Divorced? Any of them having an affair? What kind of jobs do they have?

'We don't really talk about stuff like that.'

'What do you mean? You've been playing with them for years. You must know things.'

'I don't.'

'But . . . what do yiz talk about?'

I shrug. 'Football, mainly.'

'Give me strength,' Janine says, shaking her head.

Maybe that's the difference between men and women. We don't get involved. Not as involved as they do, at any rate. I know what teams the lads support. What position their teams are in the league. If they'll qualify for Europe. Who's on the transfer list. Chances of relegation. All that.

There's always a chance of relegation with Cardiff, let's face it. If it hadn't been for the local fella, Michael O'Sullivan, getting spotted by that scout back in the day, getting called up, I could have supported any team I wanted. A team that wins, once in a while. O'Sullivan only ended up playing for Cardiff for one season before he got injured. But still, once you start supporting a team, you don't stop.

An hour a week. Two, if you include the pint afterwards. You don't have to think about anything, or worry. It's only when you're on your way home and the thoughts come back, fill your head again. You only realise then; that they've been gone. While you were playing.

The beautiful game. It can be. It really can.

The Andy Dolan thing happened about two years ago. He was always sleazy.

'Handy Andy' he was called at school. He used to brag about how many times a day he could manage it. Always asking for a toilet pass.

And in the pub, after the game, twisting his neck this way and that, scanning the place for opportunities. 'Nice legs, shame about the tits.' Nudging and grinning. 'I'd give that a go.' Nodding at some youngone at the bar, in a short skirt and heels. 'Wouldn't throw her outta the bed for eatin' me battered sausage, wha'?'

Sniggering like a schoolboy. I didn't pay much attention. Why would you? He didn't have much to say.

It wasn't just him. It wasn't all his fault. I know that. Knew it at the time, bein' honest. Paula was on the antidepressants then. That's what they thought it was. Depression. The tablets made her manic. That's how they diagnosed the bipolar in the end.

You're not supposed to say manic any more. Elated. That's

what they're calling it now. I always thought elation had something to do with happiness.

That's not true.

She took the tablets and after a bit, she just . . . she turned into this heightened version of herself. Wired, she was. Up all night, pacing the floors, watching telly, loud enough to wake the kids, coming up with all sorts of ideas and plans. Joining a kibbutz. That was one. Me and her and the kids, tending crops and whatnot in Israel. She couldn't get over what a good idea it was.

And the money. Spending rings around her. I'd go to the bank machine and the overdraft would be used up and another two weeks to go before payday. The stuff she bought. All sorts. She was into crystals back then. White magic. That kind of stuff. She bought rocks on the internet. A fortune, some of them. Boxes of rocks in the hall and not a scrap of food in the fridge. I had to set up a different bank account. Put a few quid by.

Down the pub at night, getting up on tables to dance. She fell off once. I had to come and get her. She put one arm around my shoulder, reached down to my crotch, put her hand there. Squeezed. 'A fine specimen is my Vinnie,' she roared, eyeballing everyone in the place, daring any of them to contradict her.

The pity in people's eyes as I led her out.

He didn't sleep with her, Andy. It was more of a grope, I suppose, down the side of the pub. But he took advantage of her and that's a fact. She wasn't herself. I heard about it afterwards. Trish told me. 'I'm sorry to have to tell you, Vinnie,' she said, her hand gripping my arm. More pity.

I was up to here with it. I said it to Paula. She didn't deny it. 'Well, if you're not getting it at home . . .' She would have had sex morning, noon and night then and yes, there were times when I said no. Times when I was tired. When I'd had a long night. An early morning airport run. A five-hundred-mile round trip in the Stretch.

It was like, the more elated she got, the more tired I became. Like two ends of a see-saw we were. One up, one down.

He wasn't the only one, Andy. I know that. But he was there, right in front of me, dribbling the ball between his feet, setting it up for an equaliser, me in the goal trying to anticipate him, him kicking it, sending it into the back of the net.

'He shoots, he scores,' Andy shouted, pulling his jersey over his head, running around the pitch like a fucken fool.

I was the fool. I knew that. There was something impotent about knowing that. I didn't understand any of it. Couldn't do a thing to change it. That's how I felt as I walked over to Andy, tore the jersey off his head, laid into him.

Just one punch, really. That's all it took. I felt bad about it later, of course. But at the time, just for that moment, when my knuckles slammed into the bridge of his nose and I heard the wet squelch of it and knew I'd hit home, done some damage, just then, I felt something. Like I'd finally done something.

'He's been asking for that for years,' Kenny said afterwards. Two years ago. Water under the bridge.

'We'll sit here,' Kenny says to me in the pub, sitting on a stool and pulling an empty one towards him. I think it's for me until he lays his coat across it. Black and white squiggles all over it. 'Herringbone,' Kenny tells anyone who happens to glance at it. Either way, it hurts your eyes, lookin' at it. 'I'll take a pint, comrade, when you're ready.'

I stand at the bar. Andy slots himself beside me, waving a note at Mary behind the bar. His nose never looked the same after. It's bigger, like the swelling never went all the way down. And there's a bend on the bridge. But maybe that was always there.

He picks up his pint and his chaser, nods at me, heads down to the table where the rest of them are already shouting the odds.

I missed a load of Wednesday nights after that.

Paula was put on new medication after she got the diagnosis. Bipolar affective disorder.

The elation vanished pretty quick after they told her that. Depression set in and, honest to God, it was hard to know which one was worse. By the time I went back to the football, Paula was gone and nobody said a word about it.

Andy apologised. Said he was offside. Was going to say more but I stopped him. Said to forget about it. Neither of us mentioned his snout.

We carried on.

We carried on playing.

Eleven

The landline rings at seven o'clock the next morning. The screen says 'Withheld.'

'Hello?' It's freezing in the hall. Draughty as hell. I meant to ring that insulation fella back. Don't know what I did with his card. On top of the breadbin maybe.

'Is that you?' A woman's voice, low, hesitant.

'Who's this?'

'I wasn't sure if it was OK to ring. You said . . .'

'Who's calling?' My voice sounds tight. Strained.

'Oh, sorry, I thought . . .'

'Who are you looking for?'

'Is that John?'

'No, there's no—'

The line goes dead. I put the phone back on the base. I'm shivering now. The toes on my left foot are white. Bad circulation. Like Da. Bad genes. Bad start to the day; the phone, going off like that, this hour of the morning. Leaves me unsettled, when it rings like that. Or late at night. Bad news, when the phone rings then. Something's after happening.

I climb the stairs, use the banister to haul myself up. I'm breathless by the time I get to the top step. Have to sit on it, tuck my head in between my knees. Things are spinning. The landing. The walls. The bare bulb hanging off the ceiling. Meant to get a new light shade. Everything spinning and my breath stuck in my chest, no air getting in or getting out.

It feels like the one last week. In the motor. Except now there's no doctor in the back seat. All I can think about is the kids. Getting out of their beds, wandering into the landing, finding me like this. Or worse.

I think about Da then. The colour of his face when I reached him. A ghostly white. Like he'd been dead for hours.

I manage to crawl into my bedroom. Take a paper bag out of the bin. I kneel on the floor and blow into it, like Ellen showed me in the taxi. Suck the air out. Blow in. Concentrate on filling the bag. Emptying it. Filling it. The inside of my head is full with the roar of my body. My heart pounding and my blood racing through it and my pulse beating much too fast and my head fit to burst. I close my eyes and force myself to breathe. Slow as I can, like Ellen said. My legs shake with effort.

I think about Finn. Practising the other day for the Communion. Getting me to feed him little bits of wafer, pretending it was the body of Christ. His tongue hanging out and his eyes shut tight, trying not to laugh when I put it in his mouth. Laughing anyway. 'That tickles, Dad,' he said. Trying not to chew it. 'It's against the rules to chew it,' he told me. Using his tongue to try and prise it off the roof of his mouth. 'It's stuck,' he said. 'It's not supposed to stick. It's supposed to melt. That's what teacher said.' Me trying not to laugh. Pretending to cough instead. 'Are you OK, Dad?' he said, thumping my back.

This helps. The doctor said it would. Thinking about something. Something good. My breath comes easier now, the roar of the blood in my head quietens. I sit on the bed with my head between my legs. I didn't take any tablets yesterday and I was grand. Not a bother on me. I go into the bathroom, put one on my tongue and fill my cupped hands with water from the tap. Swallow it. The hand that reaches for the tap is shaking. I turn it off, grip the sides of the sink.

It was a wrong number. That's all. It's just, the landline rarely rings. And when it does, it's usually Paula. Or the odd time, her Dad, ringing to see how the kids are. Whenever the landline rings, I sort of brace myself. Don't think I realised that until now.

Just a wrong number. It happens from time to time. The odd time, it's some Chinaman trying to sell security for the computer. Short shrift. That's what those fellas get. Once, it was Ma, home late from the pub quiz – her team won and she got a spot prize: a six-pack of Smithwick's. 'You hate Smithwick's,' I said.

'There was something else I had to tell you,' she added. 'What was it? Oh, yeah, I'm locked out.' After midnight she rang. On the landline. Gave me a terrible start.

I ran up the road with the spare key. Her cheeks were pink from three sherries. Her coat was puckered at the front, buttoned up wrong. She wrapped her hands around my face. Frozen they were. 'There's my handsome boy,' she said, with a discreet burp at the end of the sentence. She giggled.

'Why didn't you ring me on the mobile?' I said.

'The mobile?' she said, like I was speaking Chinese.

I opened the door for her. 'Go on to bed, Ma. I'll poke my head in, in the morning.'

I put her to bed in the end. I was worried about the stairs. She sat on the bed and let me pull off her shoes. She sang through the whole procedure. 'When I Fall in Love'.

'Your father loved Nat King Cole,' she said, as I tucked the blankets around her chin. 'Did you know that, Vincent?'

'Yeah.'

It was just the phone. Ringing at this hour. Unsettles me. That's all.

By the time I've the coffee beans ground and the pot on the hob, I've warmed up and my hands have stopped shaking. A wrong number. Nothing to get wound up about.

Finn comes in, his hair like briars on top of his head. His shirt is inside out and his jumper is back to front. Without looking down, I know for a fact that his shoes are on the wrong feet. But I'm wrong about that. He hasn't put on his shoes and there's a hole in the heel of his left sock.

School socks. Add that to the list.

He sits at the table and I put a bowl with two Weetabix in front of him. Pour milk on top.

'Only one spoon of sugar,' I remind him.

'Can we get a dog?' he says.

'We have a dog.' Archibald shifts in his basket, farts, goes back to sleep.

'I mean, another one.'

'No.'

'We're growing tadpoles in school.'

'Really?' I pour myself a mug of coffee. Stick two slices of bread in the toaster.

'Yeah. We're going to be allowed have a go of them, when they turn into frogs.'

'What do you mean, have a go?'

'I don't know.'

The doorbell rings. It's Ma. 'Where's the most gorgeous fella that ever walked?' she shouts, striding down the hall.

'I'm here, Granny,' says Finn, in a voice that's soggy with Weetabix. I reach for the kitchen roll when I get back into the kitchen, wipe milk off his chin.

She puts her handbag on the table, turns to me. 'I'll take him to school this morning. Give you a chance to shave before you go to work. And you'd better give Kerry a lift to school. Make sure she's not late. I don't want her getting into trouble again, after her little stint in school.'

'How'd you know about that?' I run my hand down my face. The bristles scratch my fingers.

'Mrs Byrne told me. Last night at the bingo. I was helping the auldones. Marking their cards.'

Jaysus. Is there anything Kenny doesn't tell his mother?

'What did she do this time?'

'Nothing much. A bit of graffiti.'

'They were talking about that on the radio the other day. Self-expression, some of them were calling it. On Joe Duffy.' Ma loves Joe Duffy. She listens to his show every day. He's the one constant on her list of the five people she'd like to invite to her house for dinner. The other four change regularly enough. But Joe never shifts. Not for her. She has it all planned. Steak and kidney pie. That's what she'll make for Joe. 'I'd say he loves his bit of meat, that fella.'

'Well, they're calling it graffiti. Down at the school.'

She reaches for the kettle, fills it, turns it on. 'You'd think they'd go easy on Kerry, all she's been through.'

'Do you want a slice of toast? To go with your tea?'

She shakes her head. 'I've to drop a dress size before the Zumba weekend in May.'

'I thought it was samba classes you were doing.'

'No-one does samba any more, Vincent.'

Kerry walks into the kitchen. I told her to be up and in her school uniform by half seven. I look at the kitchen clock. It's coming up to a quarter to eight and she's in her pyjamas and dressing gown. But still. She's up. 'If you're ready to go by ten past, I'll give you a lift, OK?' I tell her. She nods.

Ma looks at her. 'The dead awoke and spoke to many,' she says. 'Cuppa tea?'

Kerry shakes her head and sits at the table. I give her the eye and she sighs and says, 'No, thank you, Granny,' in a pointed, sarcastic voice, which goes over Ma's head, thank God.

Ma puts two heaped spoons of sugar in her mug. Stirs it. Catches me looking at her. 'Well, since I'm not having the toast,

I can afford an extra spoon of sugar,' she tells me, testily. She squashes herself into a chair, between the pair of them. Kerry supports her face with both hands.

'How's Leonardo?' Ma says, nudging Kerry's arm with her elbow.

'Who?' Kerry says.

Ma sighs, bends her head to her mug. 'I don't know what they teach you down at that school,' she says.

'Erotic art, apparently,' I say. Nobody laughs.

Ma looks at me. 'Go on with you. Go and shave that mug of yours, do you hear me?' Kerry smirks and Finn giggles. They think it's gas the way Ma speaks to me like I'm a kid. Still, I go upstairs and shave. More than my life's worth to rile her.

Twelve

I'll check the shed when I get home from work today. See if there are a couple of tins of white paint for the school wall. I'll offer to give Kerry a hand. Maybe take her over to the school this evening. She'll say, Thanks, Dad. She might even apologise for the grief. And mean it. I'll say, No sweat, kid. No, I won't call her 'kid'. She hates that. No sweat, love. We could go to a café after maybe. Finn too. Stuff our faces with cream buns.

'Kerry. I have a plan,' I call out, walking down the hall. I open the door into the kitchen. There's a tall, gangly-looking yoke sitting on one of my chairs. Pale skin with angry red pimples across his forehead and chin. Earrings queuing along the edges of slightly protruding ears. A stud in his nose that looks like a cluster of whiteheads. Something on his lip too, although it's hard to tell if it's a morsel from his last meal or a piece of jewellery. Silver rings on most fingers. A tattoo – Chinese writing, of course – along his hand. The clothes are standard fare: hoodie worn over T-shirt with writing on it. Something smart-arsed, no doubt. I can't make it out. Black jeans. Converse.

'Howeya, Vinnie,' he says. He's slumped in one of my kitchen chairs, with his legs stretched across the floor, like an amateur obstacle course.

'Who are you?'

'Mark.'

'Mark who?'

'Whelan.'

'What are you doing in my kitchen?'

'I'm waiting for Kerry.'

Alarm bells. Loud ones. There's never been a boy in my kitchen before. Waiting for Kerry.

'Why?'

'What do you mean?'

'Why are you waiting for Kerry?'

The cockiness drains away. He bends his legs, tucks his feet under the chair. He manages, but only just. Long as barges, his feet. He scratches one of the spots on his face. It reddens, fit to burst.

'Cos she asked me to,' he finally manages.

I take the stairs two at a time, knock on Kerry's bedroom door. 'Kerry?'

'What?'

'I'm coming in.'

'I'm in me bra.' She knows how to push my buttons, that one.

'Who's your man?' I say, through the closed door.

'You know who he is.'

'I've never seen him before in my life.'

'I heard you. Interrogating him downstairs.'

'What's he doing here?'

'He told you. He's waiting for me.'

'Why?' I've my two hands on either side of the door frame now. Sort of leaning on it, waiting for her to answer. I know what she's going to say before she says it.

'We're going out.'

'Why?'

'He's my boyfriend.'

Fuck.

'You're too young to have a boyfriend.'

'I'm nearly fifteen.'

'You're fourteen years old.'

'You can't stop me having a boyfriend.'

'Yes, I can.' I haven't figured out how. But I will.

She yanks the door open. She's dressed, but only just. A low-cut top that would give Janine cause for pause. A tiny hankie of a skirt. Full-on Amy Winehouse make-up. A battered pair of Doc Marten boots. She got me to drive over them a few times, to achieve the look. ('I used to wear Docs when I was your age,' I told her. 'Yeah, right, Dad.')

'I'm going out.'

'You were suspended from school this week. You can't go out.'

'What, so I'm a prisoner now? I have rights, you know.'

I can't believe I didn't ground her. I forgot to, with everything going on.

'Well, you're certainly not going anywhere dressed like that.' I sound like Kenny's mother, when Kenny roots out his Speedos in the summer.

'Fine,' she says, closing the door again. When she reopens it, she has jeans on under the skirt and a cardigan over her top. 'Happy now?' she asks.

'Where are you going?' Did I say she could go? When did that happen?

'We're going to the cinema.'

We. It's 'we' now. I feel like I've arrived on another planet. Unfamiliar terrain.

'I don't know anything about this Mark fella.'

Heads for the stairs. 'He's in my science class.' She's in the hall now, putting on her jacket. 'Come on, Mark.'

'What about the wall? I was going to bring you over to the school after dinner. Give you a dig out.'

'You said we'd do it at the weekend.'

'I said *you'd* do it. I'm not the one who defaced school property.'

'Neither did I.'

I sit on the top step of the stairs. Exhausted, I am. She can do this for ever, Kerry. Arguing. She's brilliant at it.

'What time will you be home?'

'When the film's over.'

'What about the homework?'

'Done.' She reaches the hall, opens the door.

What about studying?'

'Done.'

'Seeya, Vinnie.' Mark smirks up at me. The victor. My thoughts are ugly. Violent. The things I'd like to do to that fella's spotty face. I glare at him instead, which has no effect on the smirk.

'OK, but don't be late.' I do my best to inject a bit of authority into the sentence.

The front door slams. I run to my bedroom, stand at the curtain, inch my face around it. There they are, walking up the path, laughing. It's been ages since I heard Kerry laugh. I'd nearly forgotten what it sounds like. She nudges him with her elbow, he pushes her with his hand in the small of her back, then pulls her back, now with his hand on the collar of her jacket, his fingers buried in the mesh of her hair. They're walking again, only now he's got his arm draped over her shoulder and she's got her hand tucked into the back pocket of his jeans.

Fuck.

I distract myself with coffee. The making of it. The smell of it. The house is quiet now. Ma took Finn to the zoo after school, along with the residents of the local nursing home. She has him in charge of pushing one of the wheelchairs. I told him not to go too fast with it. 'How fast is too fast?' he wanted to know.

Kerry and Mark. Mark and Kerry. In the cinema. In the back row. In the dark. I know about fifteen-year-old boys. I remember. Me and Paula. In my room. Studying. I studied every bit of her. I knew her off by heart. If she'd been an exam, I'd have got an A plus.

Kerry, though. It's different when it's your daughter. In some ways, she's cool as a cucumber. Like last autumn. October, I think it was. She strolled into the kitchen. 'I need a tenner.' A lot of conversations start like that.

'What for?'

'Tampons and sanitary towels.'

'Oh. Right. Well . . . have you . . .? Does that . . .? I mean, are you . . .?'

'Yes, Dad. I got my period.'

'Right.' I handed over the tenner. Then I told Ma. 'Leave it to me, son,' she said. And I did, more or less. My job was the handing over of tenners and the stockpiling of tampons and sanitary towels in a basket on a shelf in the bathroom. The basket was Ma's idea. And the hot-water bottle and the packets of Panadol. 'For the cramps,' she said, in a hushed voice.

It's not like I didn't know about periods and all that. It's just . . . well, it's tricky when it's your own daughter. And Kerry hates me saying anything about it. So I buy the things. And keep a note in my Calendar app so I know when she's likely to hate me more than usual.

She doesn't hate me. I know that. It's just . . . well, she doesn't talk to me. Not like she used to. 'She's a teenager,' everyone says. But it's not just that. I've let her down. Couldn't make things work with her mother. I do try talking to her.

'How was school?'

'Grand.'

'Do you have any homework?'

'Yeah.'

'Anything good on the box tonight?'

'No.'

That kind of thing.

She has four hundred and twenty friends on Facebook. I heard her saying that to her friend Sharon one day. Four hundred and twenty. I have sixteen. And who are these four hundred and twenty people anyway?

I used to know all her friends' names. Sometimes I see her now, in a massive throng of teenagers, moving around the shopping centre like a dark cloud. She pretends she doesn't see me. I can understand that, I suppose. I used to do the same with my ma when I was that age.

I had the sex education talk with her in the taxi. I was driving. Easier that way. I didn't have to look at her. I cleared my throat and began. 'The thing is, Kerry, you're growing up now and . . . well . . . there are certain things that you should probably . . . be aware of, so to speak . . .'

'What are you on about?'

'Well, I mean . . . what I'm saying is . . . like, for example . . . boys, for instance . . .'

'Are you talking about the facts of life?'

'Well, I suppose I . . .'

'We did that in school ages ago.' She sounded bored. Like we were talking about irregular Irish verbs or something.

'Okey-dokey, so.' I swear to God, I said that. Okey-dokey. I've never said that before.

She sniggered. Couldn't blame her. I struggled on. 'So, what I'm saying is . . . if you have any questions or . . .'

'I don't.'

'Right, so.'

That was that.

Dinner. I'll have to get a start on that. Finn'll be home any minute. I wrap my hands around the mug. Drink the coffee. Take a couple of deep breaths. Anytime yer man, whatshisface, Mark, appears in my head, I run him off. State of him. 'Vinnie.'

You'd never know what she's thinking, Kerry. Didn't say much when Paula left. Finn bawled, asked about her all the time. Still does, though not as much. But Kerry, a different story altogether. She nodded when I told her. About Paula leaving and about me not knowing if she was coming back or not. Nodded, like she already knew. She wasn't surprised. Then just got on with things. Went to school, came home, did her homework, texted her friends. All the normal things. The trouble in school didn't start til this year, really. The principal said it was 'understandable, in the circumstances'. Pious old witch. But who's to know if she would have been like that anyway? If Paula had stayed. Who's to say? It's just teenage stuff. Harmless enough, mostly.

I remember the first film me and Paula went to. *The Breakfast Club*, it was. I was sixteen. She was the same. Her hands around the box of popcorn, rings on each of her fingers, the nails painted black. She was a bit of a goth back then. Moody and melancholy. I loved it. The drama. I yawned, stretched my arms over my head, got ready to drop the left one across her shoulders.

'Get your feeler out of my face!' someone hissed from behind. I turned around. An auldfella. That's what I thought at the time. He was probably the same age as I am now. My arm ended up landing on her shoulders with more force than I'd intended. I was going to slip it down so soft she'd hardly notice. She laughed. 'Ssshhh!' The tosser behind us. Paula lifted one of her hands from the box of popcorn. Reached for my hand. Spread her fingers and slid them up through mine, like keys in locks.

She never took her eyes off the screen. I can't remember how the film ended.

Dear Neil,

There's nothing to report. Nothing has happened for weeks and weeks. Months, really. Nothing. Physio, counselling, dinners with my mother, watching the telly, the odd email from Colm, asking my advice on a patient or a medication. I know he doesn't really want my advice. He's just checking up on me, I think.

There's a strange kind of freedom in doing nothing. You stop moving and yet everything keeps on going. Pushing past you and around you. I'm like one of those little figures in a snow globe. Passive and still. Cocooned.

I turn the telly off and listen. The apartment is quiet. A strained kind of quiet. Like it's waiting for something to happen.

I look at my watch. The taxi driver – Vinnie – will be here in two hours to pick me up. He brought flowers the other day, did I tell you that already? Perhaps it's their scent that makes the apartment feel smaller than usual. Overpowering. I wouldn't say they'll last too long in here. Stagnant, Mum says. I pick up the vase and put it out on the balcony. Close the door, pick up the remote, turn on the telly. Jeremy Kyle. Perfect. I concentrate on a mother who is pregnant with her son-in-law's baby but I can still see them. The flowers. The blooms swaying like they're waving at me, trying to get my attention. I turn off the telly and pull the blinds across the patio door.

One hour and fifty minutes. I do my physio exercises (fifteen minutes), have a shower (ten minutes), get dressed (ten minutes). I heat a tin of tomato soup. Remember my home-made tomato soup? I made it for you when you had that bad flu. It's easy to make but I've no fresh tomatoes, no basil. There's nothing here. Nothing!

I bring the flowers back inside. Open a window, give them some air. It was a nice gesture, I suppose. The flowers. There was no need. Anyone would have done the same. I concentrated on the road, the traffic lights, the other cars. Tried not to think about driving. About me driving. Vinnie kept saying, 'Sorry.' He looked so uncomfortable. I should have pushed the seat back to give him more room. He had his face on his knees and his legs were bent and his hands spanning the dashboard as if he knew I hadn't driven in months.

It's strange. He's been picking me up every Friday for months and yet, it was only last week that I noticed him. He looks a bit like the man who used to come into the clinic and look after the plants once a week, remember? The tall, slim fellow, maybe late thirties, with dark hair and brown eyes. Pale skin. Muck under his fingernails and a quiet sense of purpose. He called you Neil instead of Dr Ryan and it drove you mad. You liked your title. Said you'd worked hard for it.

Vinnie doesn't have muck under his fingernails but there's something a little unkempt about him, all the same. Like he got dressed in a hurry.

I eat lunch, have a cigarette, watch Home and Away *and put a half load of washing in the machine before I allow myself to look at my watch.*

Twenty minutes to spare.

I used to get through two patients in twenty minutes, remember? Examine, diagnose, prescribe. Over and over again until the end of the day, then back the next day to do it all again. I don't think I ever liked it. I just did it and I'd be doing it still if things hadn't changed. I'd go back to being someone who never had twenty minutes to spare.

I imagine Vinnie thinks I'm odd. I never wondered what he thought of me before.

I'll be glad when this week ends. If it ever does.
I feel funny today. Like I've been jerked awake. And now I can't seem to go back to sleep.

Ellen

Thirteen

Ellen looks different today. I can't put my finger on it. And then I realise. She's got make-up on her face. Foundation. I don't get foundation. The smell of it. And the greasy feel. She's put it over the scar. Nasty-looking scratch. Fading, though. I've noticed that, these past months.

She gets in the back of the cab, as usual. 'Hello,' she says, reaching for the belt.

'Hello.' I glance in the rear-view mirror and I can't help noticing her mouth. She's wearing lipstick.

'How are you feeling?' she asks. The question seems strange. Only because she doesn't usually ask questions, I suppose. But it's the way she asks. A deliberateness to the words. Like she's been practising the line.

'Yeah, grand, fine, much better. Thanks.'

She nods and puts her bag on the seat beside her. 'The flowers are beautiful. Thanks again.'

'Don't mention it.' I clear my throat. 'Portmarnock, yeah?' I say, because that's what I always say and it's high time we were getting back to the way things were.

She nods and I pull away from the kerb and it's business as usual. I drive, she looks out the window, I park outside the clinic, she makes her way inside, I wait, she reappears. Twenty-one minutes today. Quickest time yet.

I open the door for her and she says thank you and smiles, and that's when I notice the eyeshadow. Brown. Suits her. Brings out the yellow. Amber, I suppose. Maybe she's going someplace after.

She looks at me and, for a moment, I get a terrible sense that she knows everything about me. Even what I was thinking just then. About her eyeshadow and that.

I get back in the motor and she says, 'I'm not going straight home today.' I was right, then. About the eyeshadow.

'Where to, so?'

'I'm not sure yet.'

'Oh. Right. Well, take your time. No hurry.' This never happens. Even the really strange punters know where they want to go.

She lets her head fall back against the seat. She hasn't put any foundation on her neck and the skin there seems very white. Delicate.

She shifts in her seat. 'Duncan – he's the physio – says I need to walk.'

'Walks aren't really my line of business, I'm afraid. But I can drive you to a place ... where you can walk. Where are you thinking? Dollymount Strand? St Anne's Park?' Wouldn't have had her down as a walker. Tricky enough, I'd say, with the crutches.

'A pier. I haven't walked down a pier in ages. Have an ice cream, maybe.' Nothing about the day suggests ice cream. One of those grey Dublin days where the clouds hang so low, you'd think you could touch them. Still. If this business has taught me anything, it's that people are peculiar.

'Howth?'

'Could we go somewhere farther away?'

'Sure. How about Dún Laoghaire? It's a fair stretch from here, mind. It'll be a hefty fare.'

'Will you wait for me? While I walk the pier? And then take me home?'

'That's going to cost you a fortune.'

She looks at me in the rear-view mirror. 'Will you?'

I nod, put my belt back on. 'Course,' I say, easing into the traffic.

For a while, it's business as usual. Her sitting in the back in her black coat looking out the window, me behind the wheel. It's always quiet in the cab with Ellen in the back. She doesn't say much and I'm not one of those drivers who shouts the odds about the behaviour of other road users. If I were, I'd be hoarse.

There's something about the quiet today that unsettles me. Perhaps because we're not going where we usually go. And now I'm thinking, maybe she always wore the bit of make-up – the eyeshadow and lipstick and what have you – and I just never noticed. Why would I? The punters can wear whatever they like, so long as they pay their fare. I suppose it's because of what happened. The incident. In the cab. It just feels a bit . . . different. That's what has me unsettled. I turn the radio on, catch her eye in the rear-view mirror. 'You don't mind, do you?' I say, because here's another departure from our usual routine. Me switching on the radio. She shakes her head. Returns her gaze to the window. She's looking. Really looking. Like it's interesting, the stuff passing by. We're going over the East Link. Nothing interesting about that. Or maybe I've just gone over it too many times.

Led Zeppelin on the radio. 'Could you turn it up?' she asks. Wouldn't have had her down as a Zeppelin fan. 'Stairway to Heaven', maybe. But not this one.

The pier in Dún Laoghaire is busy. Dogwalkers, people-watchers, joggers and ancient couples who hold each other now more for support than affection. I never really got pier-walking. You get to the end, turn around, head back. Pointless, really.

I stop the car. 'I'll wait here for you, alright?'

She takes off her seat belt but doesn't move. She fiddles with the strap on her bag. Shortens it. Lengthens it. Shortens it. She looks up. 'I haven't done this in ages,' she says.

'Done what?'

She shakes her head. 'Anything, really. I haven't done anything.'

Peculiar.

'You don't have to walk,' I say, jerking my head towards the pier. 'I can drive you back. If you like.' This seems to mobilise her and she sits up straight, one hand on the door handle.

'I'm here now, I might as well,' she says, and I see her grip on the handle tighten, as if there's a struggle going on and the outcome is undecided.

Maybe I'm a bit slow off the mark but it sort of dawns on me, around then, that this is kind of a big deal. For Ellen, I mean. Coming here, to Dún Laoghaire. Instead of going straight home after the clinic. Even the dullness of walking to the end of a pier, turning around. Walking back. Even that. There's something about it. I don't know what. But something. So when she says, 'I don't suppose you'd like to get some air?' I just nod and grab my jacket. Janine calls it 'fraternising with the clients'. We're not supposed to do that. Kenny does it all the time, of course. Well, he tries, at any rate. But Janine's never had to pull me up on it before. It's not something I've ever done.

But this isn't fraternising. It's just a walk. Least I can do, after her help last week. A walk on a pier. All the way to the end. And back again.

Fourteen

She's taller than I thought. Comes up to my shoulder. Handy enough with the crutches. She walks slowly but without any obvious limp and doesn't seem to favour one leg over the other. Car accident. That's the most obvious, with the scar and that. I could be wrong, of course. None of my business, either way.

It's colder out here. The sea wind, I suppose. It whips at the top of the waves, churning them like cream. The sea is a green-grey. Down below, the sleek oily head of a seal – a massive yoke – bobs on the water, then disappears with barely a splash. The sun is across the bay, pouring down the sides of the lighthouse at Howth, lifting it out of the gloom.

My mobile rings. It's Janine. I let it ring. She knows I'm here. It comes up on the system, where my car is. She loves that system. Knowing everything. But she'll want to know why I'm here and I've nothing to say about that. I haven't a clue.

Ellen doesn't say much. In fact, she doesn't say anything. And that suits me grand. Nice not to have to come up with something to talk about. We're just two people walking down a pier.

At the end, she stops, a little out of breath. It's a long enough pier and I'd say those crutches would take it out of you, after a while. Chip-fattened seagulls drift overhead and the ferry belches a long goodbye as it shifts to the east.

That's what Paula took in the end. The ferry. She packed light. One suitcase. A photo album. Pictures of the kids, mostly.

Her iPod. The letter that Maureen left for her. She kept it in the top drawer of her bedside locker. That was gone when I went looking. The note, on the kitchen table.

Don't look for me, Vinnie.

Ellen takes a packet of cigarettes out of her coat pocket, slides one out, offers it to me. There's another surprise. Wouldn't have put her down as a smoker. I take one even though it's a Silk Cut Ultra. Hardly worth your while. Still. Don't want to be rude.

We stand there, smoking and watching the ferry slip away. People on the deck, looking at the shore getting smaller. Some of them wave. I wave back. Ellen laughs. More of a giggle, really. Girlish. It sounds strange. Probably because I haven't heard it before.

We smoke. Then we walk back. 'Where to next?' I say, looking in the rear-view mirror. She tucks her hair behind her ears. There's a flush to her face, a brightness in her eyes. Ma always said the sea air was a tonic.

'Home, I suppose,' she says, and I can tell she doesn't want to go back. Not yet. I get that. I feel the same way myself some days.

'You still fancy an ice cream? Or a coffee?' I say. 'Warm you up?'

'I'd like a coffee but I'm not all that keen on going into a café,' she says.

'Takeaways?'

She nods and smiles, a small smile that gathers around the edges of her mouth. I'm pleased. Like I've answered a tricky question and got it right.

I get them in. Double espresso for me and a skinny cappuccino for her. I wasn't wrong about that. Back in the taxi, she takes the lid off hers, wraps her hands around the cup, inhales the steam. That's half the pleasure of coffee. The smell of it.

'You don't say much, Vinnie,' she says, after a while.

'Neither do you.'

She nods then. Agrees.

'You must think me strange,' she says.

I suppose I do a bit. When I stop to think about it.

She looks out the window at the line of traffic, limping up the road. 'Getting driven to the same place. Week after week.'

'I take people where they want to go. That's my job.' I don't tell her that she's the source of endless speculation at the depot between Janine and Kenny. Trying to work her out. Coming up with all kinds of theories.

'I was . . . in an accident.' There are hesitations between the words, as if she's speaking a language she's unfamiliar with.

I turn around. She smiles. 'I'm lucky, really. I fractured my pelvis. They thought at first I mightn't walk again. And look at me now, hobbling down a pier.'

'Hardly hobbling.'

'That's true,' she says, and she sounds surprised, as if she had been unaware of how much progress she'd made.

'When did it happen?' I ask.

'Eight months ago,' she says, swilling the dregs of her coffee around the bottom of the cup. 'That day, in the car, when you were . . . when you weren't feeling well. That's the first time I drove since the accident. I wasn't sure I'd remember.'

'It's like riding a bike,' I say. 'You never forget.'

'I should be getting back.' She lifts the cup to her mouth. Drains it.

I turn the key in the ignition. Indicate and edge into the traffic.

'Good to get back behind the wheel all the same,' I say.

Fifteen

'Vinnie! Over here, gorgeous.'

Janine's had a few already, by the sounds of her. She slips a hand down her top and into the cups of her bra, lifts one breast, then the other, looks down, inspecting them, smiles, pleased with the result. She wraps her hands around my face. Warm. 'D'ya like me top?' she says. Her hands rest on the side of each of her breasts, pushing them together, the line of her cleavage deep as a gorge. I nod. 'It's lovely,' I say, even though it could do with being a few sizes bigger. It's got to be bad for your circulation, a top that tight.

The pub is no great shakes but it's around the corner from the depot. Handy for a quick bevvie on a Friday night.

Janine's sister works the phone at the depot at night. She's younger than Janine and, if you talk to her for two minutes, she'll have told you about her husband – Rocko – their poodle – Beyoncé – and the apartment they bought in Lanzarote 'for a nursery rhyme', she says. Then she'll add, 'That means it was even cheaper than a song.' And then she'll laugh.

'Yeah, one huff and puff and you could blow that kip down, alright,' Janine said.

'So, how was your afternoon?' Janine says, dead casual, when I get back from the bar with the drinks. She's fishing.

'*Muchas gracias*, comrade,' Kenny says, lifting the fresh pint and wiping the bottom of the glass on the beer mat before guiding it towards his mouth. Careful not to get any drops on his purple jacket. 'Suede,' he says, even though no one asked. 'A beautiful material, yes, but very tricky to get stains out of.'

'Well? Janine ignores him. She's giving me the eyes. She's got the falsies on tonight, the lashes so long and curly, you'd wonder how she manages to blink.

'Same old, same old,' I say, guiding the pint towards my mouth. The pub might be no great shakes but the Guinness is a decent drop.

'Mine was grand too, thanks for asking,' says Kenny, winking at a youngone who passes us at a trot and ignores him.

'I thought you had a date with Carol?' I ask him.

'I thought you were coming back to the depot. After the Portmarnock run,' says Janine, lancing one of the cherries in her cocktail with a stick and putting it in her mouth. She sucks it like a sweet, her cheek bulging.

'I *did* have a date with Carol,' says Kenny.

'She dumped him, I'd say,' says Janine to me.

'She did *not* dump me.' Kenny sets his glass on the table. 'We met for coffee. Her treat. That was the arrangement.'

'*She* paid for coffee? For the two of you?' Janine widens her eyes, for effect.

'Yeah. She insisted. We went Dutch on the buns, alright. Carol's right, they're a rip-off in that place.'

Even Janine can't think of anything to say to that. 'Anyway, coffee's not a date,' she manages eventually, lancing the second cherry and flicking her tongue around the perimeter before depositing it in her mouth.

'What is it, then?' says Kenny, squaring up.

'Leave it out, would yiz?' They're as bad as Kerry and me when they get going.

Janine nods towards me. 'I mean, there's Romeo there, disappearing for the afternoon with Calamity Jane and you don't hear him calling it a date.'

Kenny stares at me, his mouth open wide enough to view the fillings at the back. 'Pure gold,' he told me when he got them put in. 'Well, gold plated, at any rate.'

I look at Janine. 'What are you talking about, disappearing?' I say, cagey as hell. She does this. She's good. That's how she kept tabs on her second husband, Jeremy, the serial adulterer. 'Maybe he was a sex addict?' suggested Kenny, trying to be fair.

'Maybe he was a bollix,' said Janine, who likes to call a spade a spade.

'You went on a date and you didn't even tell me?' says Kenny. He looks dejected. He can't hide it. He'd wear every single internal organ he has on his silken sleeve if he could. Not just his heart.

'You were in Dún Laoghaire,' Janine says. 'I saw it on the system. And the meter was still ticking away so she must have been there with you.'

'She wanted to go for a walk.'

'A walk?' Kenny says, disappointed.

'You were parked outside Insomnia for ages,' says Janine, poking my shoulder with one of her long nails.

'We stopped for a coffee. No big deal.'

'I knew it,' Janine says, with a smirk.

'Anyway, Carol didn't dump me,' says Kenny. 'In fact, it went very well. So well that we're meeting again. Next week.'

'For a touch of afternoon tea, is it?' Janine says. 'A right pair of Lotharios you two are. Kenny's bad enough with The Spinster Skinflint, but you should know better, Vinnie. Calamity Jane's a regular.'

There's no getting away from Janine once she's got her nails dug in.

'She wanted to go to Dún Laoghaire so I took her to Dún Laoghaire. That's what you're always telling us to do. Whatever the punters want.'

'You're not supposed to follow them out of the cab, Vinnie.'

She's about to use the word 'fraternising', so I cut in sharpish with, 'I needed a breath of air.'

'What about the coffee?' Kenny wants to know.

'Jaysus, I got us a couple of takeaways. We drank them in the cab and I drove her back to Clontarf. End of.'

Kenny and Janine exchange a glance.

'So what's she like?' Kenny asks.

I shrug. 'She's grand. Quiet, you know?'

'Did she tell you how she got the scar?' Kenny wants to know.

'And the limp?' Janine adds. She's never met Ellen but Kenny has filled her in.

I shake my head. I decide not to tell them about the accident. Like vultures, they'd be, picking at the bones of the story.

Janine sighs. 'I Googled her. She doesn't exist.'

Kenny looks worried. 'What do you mean, she doesn't exist?'

'She's not anywhere. I looked. Twitter, Tumblr, LinkedIn, Pinterest, the lot.'

'Just because someone's not on any social media network doesn't mean they don't exist,' I say.

'And she's not listed in the telephone directory,' says Janine, ignoring me.

'Lots of people aren't.'

'Maybe, but who doesn't have a Facebook page, tell me that!' Janine accompanies this piece of evidence with a dramatic raising of both hands, palms outstretched. After several seconds, she lowers them, reaches for her cocktail, finishes it and holds the empty glass in front of Kenny's face.

He nods, steps off his stool. 'Appletini?' he asks, and she smiles.

'Now there's a proper date drink.'

'Pity you're not on a date then,' says Kenny, brave after the few pints.

'Only because I am discerning.' Janine climbs down from the stool, pulls her skirt down and checks that her cleavage is still on show.

'We had an interesting conversation about waste,' says Kenny.

'Waste?' Janine says, with a face on her like she's just bitten into a lemon.

'Who?' I say, because I'm confused.

'Carol and I. She's a keen environmentalist, so she is.'

'Well, don't go telling her your engine size. She'd have a fit.' Janine laughs long and loud. Someone told her recently that she had a filthy laugh and she never wastes an opportunity to show it off. When she stops, she heads towards the ladies with her curious little walk, which is part-strut, part-balancing act. She manages, which is no mean feat when you consider the height of her heels. Long as knitting needles, they are.

'Pint, comrade?' Kenny asks. I nod. Finn's watching a film and having a pizza at Callam's house. His ma said she'd drop Finn home by nine. And Kerry's in the house. I rang a while ago. 'Stay out as long as you like, Dad,' she said.

'Why?'

'Chillax, Dad. Everything's under control.'

'Are you studying?'

'No.'

If she'd said yes, I'd be suspicious.

My phone rings and I pick it up, check the screen. It's Ma. 'Thought you were at your bowling tournament tonight,' I say.

'That eejit Alan Jackson dropped one of the balls on his foot and had to go to A&E. And he refused to go in the ambulance because he said they drive at a terrible rate of knots so I had to take him because I was the only one who wasn't drinking.'

'There's a bar at the bowling alley?'

'Don't be daft. They bring the drink in. In flasks. They just look like auldones, having their cup of tea.'

'Right.'

'Anyway, I called into your place on my way home but there was no one there. I wanted to borrow your blowtorch. Think there's a mouse in Joey's room.'

'What do you mean, no one there? Kerry's there. Isn't she?'

'Well, she's here now, alright. And the main thing is, no one's hurt.'

'Ah, Jaysus, what's after happening?'

'Don't be using that language in front of your mother.'

In the pause that follows, I feel it starting up again. My heart racing, a tightness in my chest, my breath sluggish in my throat.

'Is Kerry alright?' My voice sounds strange. Like someone's got their hand around my neck.

Kenny puts his pint down. Gives me the eyebrows.

'Is she alright?' I say again, louder now.

'She's fine, son. It's your car I'm worried about.'

'The car?'

'She took it for a little spin. Her and that fella of hers. The long, skinny one with the nappy rash on his face, God love him.'

The relief is like something solid. Kerry is fine. She has a boyfriend but she's fine. She took the car but she's OK. She's not hurt. I won't have to ring Paula. Tell her something terrible about her daughter. Not today, at any rate.

'Where's Kerry now?'

'In the kitchen. I made her tea. Three sugars. She's a bit shaken, so she is. Not so cocky now.'

'And the car?'

'Outside. Crashed into the back of my little runaround. You'll have to sort that out, Vincent. I can't be without my wheels. I promised I'd bring two of the auldones to Bray on Sunday. They're mad about the slots. They're counting on me, Vincent.'

'I'll sort it. I'm on my way.' When I look up, the pub is

rotating around me like a carousel and I have to bow my head and concentrate on breathing in and out and wait for it to stop.

'What happened?' Kenny puts his hand on my shoulder, pats me a couple of times. 'Vinnie?'

I reach into my pocket, take out the Valium and pop one in my mouth. The weight of it on my tongue is enough to quieten the roar of the panic. Magic little yokes. I'm able to straighten now, look at Kenny. 'I've to go,' I say. I fill him in.

'Joyriding?' He shakes his head. He's Kerry's godfather. Probably wondering where he went wrong. Him and me both.

I leave before Janine comes back. She'll have a tonne of questions that I don't know the answer to. I tell Kenny I'll ring him later. Let him know what the story is.

The usual thoughts on the way home. If onlys. If only I'd driven straight to the pub after I dropped Finn to Callam's. Not left the motor at home. I was only going for the one. No need to leave the car behind. Thought it'd be safer at the house than in the pub car park. Fool.

If only.

If only me and Kerry had one of those relationships you see on the telly. In the movies and that. I'd say something, she'd say something back. Conversations. We'd have a laugh, she might come for a walk with me and Archibald the odd time. No aggro. Or just a bit of aggro. The odd time. Finn still talks to me. Can't shut him up, to be honest. Kerry was like that once. You wouldn't have called her chatty as such. Not like Finn. But she'd talk to me. When she was younger. Before Paula left. We'd chat, me and her.

I scan the road for a taxi but of course there's none. Never a bloody cab when you need one. The pub's not far from the house. I walk quickly but I don't run. The Valium is working. I can feel it in the ends of my fingers. Down my legs. Around my head. A warm sensation, like someone giving you a rub. Still, I don't run in case it sets me off again. I walk. Light a cigarette. Nearly there.

If only.

If only Paula hadn't got sick. If I'd been a better husband. More attentive, maybe. Put the toilet seat down a bit more often. Not cut my toenails in the bedroom when she was there. 'That's disgusting, Vinnie,' she said. I don't know what was disgusting about it, to be honest. They're just nails. But I shouldn't have done it, all the same. It drove her mad. I kept forgetting.

The street is quiet. Blinds down at Benjamin's house. Lights off at Ailbhe and Grainne's. The flicker of the telly in Mrs Finnegan's front room. The *Late Late*, I'd say. Even though she's always complaining about Tubridy. 'Not a patch on Gaybo,' she says, any chance she gets.

The cars look parked for the most part. Ma's in front and mine behind. It's only when you get close enough you see the damage. The front of mine creased against the back of Ma's. Bits of glass on the ground from where my headlights smashed.

If only.

I take one more drag from the cigarette, toss it behind the lavender in the front garden. It's been growing there for years, with no attention from me or anyone else.

Resilient.

Sixteen

Ma's at the kitchen table, filling in a questionnaire for one of her competitions. She rarely wins anything – the odd box of teabags or packet of biscuits at one of her fundraisers – but that never stops her entering. I suppose you could call her resilient too.

'Where is she?' I say, reaching for the kettle.

'In her room. She's having a rest, she's fine,' says Ma, not looking up from the questionnaire. The tip of her tongue is trapped between her front teeth. She looks up then, her eyes closed. ' "I love Lyons tea because . . ." ' she says. 'In ten words or less.'

'Because it's cheaper than Barry's?'

Her eyes snap open. 'I don't scrimp on tea! I get the gold label. Nothing cheap about gold label.'

'Because it keeps you regular?'

She tilts her head, considering. 'Well, it does, but they hardly want to hear that kind of detail.'

'What's the prize?'

'Afternoon tea with Daniel O'Donnell. Imagine!'

'Is she on her own?'

'Who?'

'Kerry.'

'Of course. You'd hardly think I'd let that young pup up there with her, do you? I gave him short shrift, so I did.'

The kettle boils. 'Cuppa?' I say, getting the teabags out of the press.

'Go on, then,' she says. 'Just the one.' Her standard response. She's never refused a cup.

The doorbell rings and I answer it. It's Finn. I mouth a thank you at Callam's mother. Monica waves from her car, then drives away. 'Dad, you're home!' Finn launches himself at me. He does this every time. As if he can't believe I'm still here. He's getting heavy. Not as easy to lift as he once was. Getting too big for that carry-on anyway. But still. He's warm as a piece of toast. I set him down on the ground.

'Is murder a mortal sin?' he wants to know.

Jaysus.

I go back into the kitchen. Finish making the tea. 'Yeah, I suppose it is,' I say.

'No supposing about it,' says Ma. 'It's a mortaller, alright.'

'What about if you kill yourself?' Finn hauls Archibald out of his basket as he asks the question, tries to get him interested in a chewed-up tennis ball. The dog stands there with his eyes closed. Having none of it.

I press the teabag against the side of the cup with a spoon. Nice and strong. 'Where'd you hear about that?' I ask, casual as I can.

Finn holds the ball in front of Archibald's nose. Lets him have a good sniff before he flings it down the hall. The dog stands for a moment before he lumbers back to his basket, lies down again.

'Lucas Murray. He says it's a mortaller. Does that mean you go to hell, Dad?'

'There's no such thing as hell, son.'

Ma looks up. 'Of course there's a hell, Vincent Patrick Boland. There's a heaven, so there has to be a hell. It's common sense.' She shakes her head and tuts before returning to her page. She's filling in her email address now. mrsjosephboland@gmail.com.

'Lucas Murray says that if you even *try* to kill yourself, you'll go to hell because even trying is a mortaller. Is that right, Dad?'

I'm pouring the milk into the cups now. The teabag is still in Ma's cup. She doesn't like it taken out. Stewed. That's how she likes it. The milk spills over the rim of the cup. I try to think of something to say.

Kerry knew about Paula's attempt. Impossible to keep anything from that one. And she was that bit older, of course. Twelve. But Finn. He just nodded when I told him his mam was sick and had to go to hospital for a while. 'Will she be better for my birthday?' I think that's what he asked that day. And that night, a new line at the end of his prayers. Otherwise, business as usual.

'Lucas Murray doesn't know anything about anything.' Ma has put her pen down and is sitting stiff as a board in her chair.

'He's the best in our class at maths,' says Finn, taking the last chocolate digestive out of the biscuit tin.

Grocery shopping tomorrow. First thing.

'He's a cheeky pup, talking about things he knows nothing about.'

The doctor in the hospital didn't think it was a cry for help. A genuine attempt, he called it. Serious. She did it about four months before she left for good. I wasn't due home til dinnertime and the kids were with Ma, at a fundraiser for the hospice. A danceathon, Ma said it was. I'd forgotten my watch. My grandfather's watch. I used to think it was a bad omen if I couldn't feel the weight of it around my wrist. I slipped home. Slow day on the rank. Lunchtime, it was. The doctor said that if I'd come home any later, that would have been it, the amount of pills she swallowed.

'He said there was no such thing as Santa Claus too,' says Finn, pouring himself a pint glass of milk.

'Well, there you are, then,' says Ma, picking up her pen again. 'He knows nothing about nothing, that fella.'

'That's what I thought,' said Finn, taking his milk and biscuit to the table. Ma holds out her arms and he settles himself on her lap.

I put the mug on the table in front of Ma. Hold my cup with both hands, warming them. Finn looks at me, grins. 'Check out my moustache, Dad,' he says, pointing to the line of milk over his mouth.

'You'll have to start shaving soon.' I head for the door, my legs wobbly with relief. For a moment there, I thought Finn knew. About his mam. What she did. Or tried to do. I thought maybe some kid in his class had said something.

Some people might say that I'm not handling it. Not being honest. But what was I supposed to tell a five-year-old? And now, what can I say to a seven-year-old that makes any sense?

'I'm going to have a word with Kerry,' I say, opening the door.

'Good boy,' says Ma, the way she used to when I was a kid and did something for her, like clear out the grate and light the fire. 'Good boy,' she'd say. It was just me and her then, with Joey gone to Australia the day after his nineteenth birthday, after she gave him the few bob from Da's insurance policy.

Kerry's door is closed. I knock, give her a moment, walk in. She's sitting on the edge of her bed. She looks up and her eyes are red and swollen and her face – the bit that's not covered with her hair – is white and pinched. She looks so like Paula, sitting there. That's always a shock. A kick in your stomach. It winds you.

'I'm sorry, Dad,' she says, and her voice is small. A little girl's voice. My little girl. The one who begged me to come into school on parents' day and stand up in front of her class and talk about being a carpenter.

I steel myself. 'What the hell were you thinking?'

'I just . . .'

'You are grounded.'

117

'For how long?' She looks horrified.

'I don't know. Ages. And I'm docking your pocket money for the foreseeable.'

'I said I was sorry.'

'You shouldn't have done it in the first place. I left you here on your own. I trusted you.'

'It was an accident.'

'How is stealing my car an accident?'

'Crashing it, I mean. That bit was an accident.'

'You can't even drive.'

'I can. It's an automatic. A monkey could drive it.' The small little girl voice is gone. Maybe I imagined that bit. When she stands up, she comes up to my chest now. Getting taller. You don't notice it. Until they're squaring up to you.

'You could have been killed.'

'I wasn't, though. I'm grand. So is my boyfriend, thanks for asking.'

'You were supposed to be here. In the house. On your own. Not with that . . . boy.'

'His name is Mark.'

'That car is my livelihood. I can't work if it's off the road. I can't earn. You get that, don't you?'

'That's all you care about. Money.'

'That's not true. But I need to make a living. Those tenners you're always asking for don't—'

'Grow on trees. Yeah, I know, I heard.'

'Don't be cheeky.'

She picks up her earphones. Puts them in her ears. This is all wrong. I'm standing there and I've no idea what to say. How to fix things. Maybe that was always the problem. I never knew. Here I am, with the upper hand, for once – *she* took the car, *she* crashed the car – and yet, somehow, I'm the bad guy. How can that be?

I clear my throat. 'OK, so no pocket money and . . . and you're grounded for a week.'

She sits there, bobbing her head to a rhythm I can't hear. I can tell she's heard me, though. I can see it in the taut line of her shoulders.

'And no friends round either.'

She puts her finger on the volume button on her iPod. My iPod. Well, it used to be mine. Paula bought it for me. A birthday present or something. I still like the scratch of a needle on a vinyl, though. Even with the earphones in, I can hear the thump, thump, thump of Kerry's terrible music.

I leave the room before I do the thing I want to do, which is yank out the earphones, pull them until the iPod jerks out of her hands, throw it on the floor. Crush it with the heel of my shoe.

Instead, I take myself out of it, give her door a good slam and then I have to sit on the top step of the stairs because anger like that – or maybe it's frustration – takes it out of you. Leaves you drained.

There's only myself to blame, of course. I've let her get away with things. On account of everything. Tried to make it up to her, I suppose.

Finn and Ma are on the couch in the front room, Finn asleep with his head on Ma's lap and his knees tucked into his chest. His hands are clasped, as if he was in the middle of a prayer. Not all that unlikely, given his current fervour. I carry him upstairs and put him into bed, take his shoes off but leave his clothes on. I should really wake him. Make him go to the jacks. The bedwetting is no worse nor better than when he started. He murmurs something in his sleep, turns towards the wall, curled in a circle. I put my hand on the side of his head, feel the tickle of his pulse against my palm. In the end, I don't wake him. I tuck the duvet around him. Hem him in.

'I've got it,' says Ma when I get back downstairs.

'What?' The day feels like it should have ended hours ago. It's half nine on a Friday night. My body feels heavy. That'll be the Valium, pulling at me.

'I love Lyons tea because . . .' She looks at me, makes sure she has my full attention before she says, in the same voice she uses to call out the bingo numbers, '. . . because it's tasty and hot, just like Daniel O'Donnell!'

She lowers the page. 'There!' she says, her cheeks flushed with the excitement. 'What do you think?'

'It's the winner, alright.'

'You're just saying that.' She grabs the arm of the couch. Uses it as leverage to haul herself up. You think someone's invincible and then you see them doing something like that, a small grunt of effort escaping. The hands she uses to tie her scarf around her head are bloated, her wedding ring a glint now, buried under the creases and folds. I go and get her coat, help her into it. She turns and pats me on the shoulder. 'Thanks, son, you're a gentleman. That's always been your problem.'

No one can insult you with a compliment the way Ma does.

Dear Neil,

The physiotherapist says that soon, I won't need the crutches. I said I will need them. He smiled, like he expected me to say that.

Medical professionals can be so smug, can't they?

Still, I'm feeling better this evening. Not so maudlin. I walked down the pier at Dún Laoghaire today. Haven't done that in ages. We used to do it, the odd Sunday afternoon, remember? You'd have an ice cream, I'd have a coffee and a cigarette and you'd nag at me to quit and then we'd go for a drink and some dinner. Even then, on those odd afternoons off, we'd end up talking about the clinic. I wonder what we would have talked about if we'd never set up the business?

Vinnie drove me to Dún Laoghaire after my physio appointment. Walked the pier with me. And no, it's not what you think. Not everyone is like you.

But yes, I asked him to walk with me, which I agree is out of character. It's a long pier and, I don't know, it's been a long week, for some reason.

He's taller than the guy from Plants n' Pots, *actually. Maybe six three or four. I never really noticed before. He opened the car door but didn't offer me his hand and he looked at the sea as I struggled out. We didn't talk much and he matched my pace as if it were his own. The wind slipped the scarf off my face and I left it there, around my neck. I think I even forgot about it, for a while.*

It's still hard to say 'No' when people ask if you have any children. Vinnie's got two kids. We never said never, you and me. We just agreed that now wasn't the right time. Now was never the right time. For either of us.

Your face that day, when I told you I was late.

How many tests did I do in the end? You kept going out to buy more. 'This brand is supposed to be very accurate,' you said, handing me another pregnancy kit. When we'd exhausted the supply, you cooked. You always cooked when you had something on your mind. It helped you work things out, you said. Monkfish and spinach. That's what you cooked that night. Noodles in a sticky sauce. I had seconds, unusual for me. I remember thinking it was the baby, this sudden increase in appetite. Eating for two. We told our patients that that was a myth, eating for two. And there I was, doing just that.

You used the word 'options'. I nodded. I'd already thought about it. So many reasons why not. The conference in Bali at the end of the year, our tickets already booked and a locum organised. The plans for the clinic. Refurbishment. Extension. Recruitment. The hours we worked. The demands of our patients. Our staff. How could a baby fit into lives so tightly wound?

The Bali conference happened last month. I gave Colm my ticket. I didn't ask him how it went and he didn't volunteer any details. It's funny, the things that happen in the end.

I wish we'd reacted differently that afternoon. Hugged each other or something. We ate monkfish and discussed our options.

I had seconds.

That's how I knew what option I was going for.

Ellen

Seventeen

The good thing about the recession is that people are doing nixers again. Kenny knows a mechanic who agrees to come over the following morning. Ray. 'He doesn't have any sense of style but he knows what's what under the bonnet.'

Ray is a small, narrow man with a massive gut straining against the zip of his anorak. His legs are bandy, as if they're buckling under the weight of his belly. He looks at the cars, shakes his head, strokes his chin.

I'm on to him.

'I know the damage is only superficial but I need to get the taxi back on the road pronto,' I tell him, like I'm familiar with such things. I keep meaning to do a course on car mechanics but I haven't got around to it yet.

He lifts the bonnet of the taxi and peers inside. A sharp intake of breath. More head-shaking, accompanied now by a concerned expression. Probably totting up his bill. I'll have to cough up for the damage. Even if the insurance covers it, I don't want the boss to get wind of it.

Ma arrives then and tells Ray about the old people and Bray and the slots. 'I need my car back by eleven o'clock tomorrow morning,' she says, standing as straight as her arthritis will allow and folding her arms across her chest.

'No problem,' he tells her.

'Don't let me down,' she says, tucking her handbag into the crook of her elbow and heading up the road. He watches her go and you can see by his face that he won't let her down. He wouldn't dare.

'What about my motor?' I say.

He shakes his head. 'You're going to need a new bumper, I'd say. A bit of panel beating, definitely. And the lights fixed.'

When I think of what could have happened to Kerry in the car last night, my breath seems to get trapped in my chest.

'You alright?' Ray asks.

'Bit of indigestion,' I say. 'So, when will the car be ready?'

'It'll take a few days.'

I should have said the taxi belonged to Ma. Too late now.

Saturday crawls by. Kerry stays in her room, coming down only to make toast every few hours. She leaves the buttery knife on the counter. Crumbs all over the place. Paula used to go mad about stuff like that. Buttery knives and crumbs and empty milk cartons in the fridge.

Being grounded is worse for me than it is for Kerry, to be honest.

Finn has football practice on Saturday afternoons. Usually I drop him and Callam there and then go to work. Monica brings them home again. It's a grand system. Apart from that time last year when she came round to drop Finn off afterwards and there was no one in the house. I was a bit late getting back. They were standing at the front door when I arrived.

'Sorry about that, Monica. The traffic . . .'

'Don't worry about it, Vinnie. It never eases up, that traffic.'

'He should have gone to his granny's. She's only around the corner. He knows well.'

'Ah, no, I couldn't leave him, the poor motherless little pet.'

I open the front door, tell Finn to go upstairs and get changed. Then I turn to Monica. She's looking into the house, down the hall. The kitchen door is open, last night's dinner dishes still on the table.

'He's not motherless,' I say.

She snaps her head around. Looks at me, alarmed. 'No, I just meant . . . he's such a brave little soldier, you know what I mean.'

'He's not motherless,' I say again. 'He's a great kid. He's doing grand.'

'Of course, of course, I didn't mean anything by it.' She grabs Callam's hand, yanks him down the garden path, can't wait to get away.

It was a bit awkward for a few weeks after that. But the kids are great friends. Blood brothers, Finn calls himself and Callam. I was a bit concerned the first time he mentioned it. 'Yiz didn't cut yourselves or anything? Mix up your blood?'

'Is that what blood brothers are supposed to do?' Finn asked, his eyes like a pair of saucers in his head.

'Eh, no.'

Today, I walk the boys to the football pitch. No choice. Then I decide to stay. Better than going back for more silent treatment from Kerry. I text Monica to let her know that I'll drop Callam home after the game.

My breath erupts from my mouth in clouds. I blow into my hands, shove them deep inside my pockets. It's mostly fathers, standing on the sidelines. They all seem to know each other, a fair bit of back-slapping going on when one of their youngfellas scores a goal or manages a tricky little tackle. One of them has a flask and paper cups. Pours out coffee. Hands the cups around. It's instant. I can smell it from here.

'That's it, Johno, put it in the back of the net.'

'Good man, Philip, well played.'

'Mark him, Anthony, don't let him away with that.'

'Move yourself, Peter. You wouldn't catch up with your granny at that pace.'

'FOUL! Ref, is there something in your eye? That was a foul.'

You'd think it was the Premiership.

Finn surprises me. He's handy. He's on the wing, fast as a bullet, a skinny little yoke, not a pick on him. When he runs with the ball, his legs are a blur. He kicks the ball to Callam. 'Great cross, Finn,' I roar. I don't usually roar. Maybe I did once or twice. Like when Thierry Henry did his Hand of God with the ball, threw it into the net and that was it for Ireland. Endgame. We were so close that time. I might have shouted then, but show me a man who didn't. Roaring crying, some of the fellas in the pub that time. Weeping into their pints.

Callam, who won't be spotted by a scout any time soon, smiles and waves at me before Finn's cross bounces off his head and somehow manages to dribble into the goal. He doesn't even notice until his teammates rush at him, jumping and shouting, like little mini-Man-Uers. Gas, they are. Infectious too. I'm on the sidelines, smiling my head off.

I call into the depot on the way home. The boys love the depot, especially when the Stretch is in. They turn on the stereo and sit in the back and press all the buttons they can get their sticky fingers on. Janine lets them. She has a soft spot for kids, and Finn in particular.

'How's Messi?' she says, when she sees him. She rummages about her pockets, finds two Club Milks, hands them to the boys. 'There's a couple of cans of Coke in the fridge, lads. Help yourselves.'

When they're in the kitchen, she looks at me, shakes her head. 'I heard about Kerry's little joyride. Is she alright?'

Kenny, of course. He'd tell you his PIN, if you asked him nice enough.

'She's grand. The motor's not looking so good.' I nod towards the Stretch. 'Any bookings for tonight?'

Janine looks at the computer. 'There's a pick-up from the airport later. Drop off at the K Club. But Kenny's doing it.'

'I'll talk to him. He won't mind swapping with me.' He owes me. I told his ma it was me who left the birdcage door open. Tweetie Pie, she called the canary. Had him for years. God knows where he ended up.

Janine looks sceptical and I can't blame her. Kenny loves wearing the Stretch clobber.

'When are you getting your motor back?' Janine says.

I shrug. 'Not sure. Monday, hopefully. We can keep it between ourselves, can't we? No need for the boss to know.'

She fixes me with a look. Nods slowly. 'But you're in my debt, Vinnie.'

'I know.'

'Big time.'

'Yeah.'

'Well?'

'What?'

'What are you going to do for me?' She's giving it her best Marilyn. The hand on her hip, the fluttering eyelashes, the smile around the corner of her mouth.

Jaysus.

'Wine,' I say. She looks unimpressed, even though she's fond of her jar.

'Fizzy wine.' I amend it. She's mad about bubbles.

'Prosecco, Vinnie,' she tells me, raising her eyes to the ceiling.

'Prosecco, then,' I say. 'And flowers.'

She opens her mouth, so that's when I jump in with a quick, 'Not from the garage.'

She smiles. 'You're comin' on, Vinnie.'

'I've been schooled by the best,' I say, and her smile widens. Then she wraps her arms around my neck and hugs me. I surrender myself to it because there's no point doing otherwise. She's mad about hugging. Trees an' all.

'Are you my dad's girlfriend?'

Janine releases me so quick, I stagger a little. Finn and Callam are beside the Stretch, with their cans of Coke, nudging each other and stifling their giggles with their hands cupped over their mouths.

'I am not,' says Janine, indignant. 'My boyfriends are tall, dark, handsome and loaded.' She winks at the lads and turns to me, looks me up and down. 'Three out of four is good, but not good enough. Isn't that right, Vincenzo?'

'Whatever you say, Janine.'

'Now, go on, the lot of yiz. Some of us have work to do.' She opens the door, leans against it. 'Are you too old for a hug now, Finn?'

'Yeah.' He scoots through the door, quick as a flash.

'What about you, Callam?'

The smile slides off Callam's face as he wonders how to say no to a grown-up without being cheeky.

'Go on, son,' I say, putting my hand on the poor lad's shoulder. 'I won't let her near you.'

'I'll get yiz the next time,' she roars down the street at us. I wave and she nods.

'I hope you're studying up there,' I roar up the stairs when I get home.

No answer.

'Kerry?'

Nothing.

'KERRY!'

'WHAT?'

'Don't roar at me like that.'

'You were roaring at me.'

Fuck sake. I'm only in the door.

'I'll ground you for longer if you don't watch your lip.' Christ, the very thought of it.

I belt into the kitchen before she says something else and I'll have no choice but to make good on my threat.

I put the kettle on, open the cupboard, reach for the box of teabags. Nil stock.

I make a list. We're out of everything. Finn walks to the shops with me.

'Do you think you'll ever get a girlfriend, Dad?'

Christ, why can't seven-year-olds ever talk about the weather?

'No, I don't think so. Sure, I'm too old.'

'Dano's dad has a girlfriend, and he's even older than you, I'd say.'

'Look, is that a finch? It is. Look at the colours on it, Finn.' There's no finch but it works because he darts up the road for a look. A bit of peace in my head. Then he comes back and says, 'What age do you have to be to get a girlfriend?'

The Stretch is great when the punters seal the glass partition between them and you, and leave it there for the duration. The ones who want it down are usually younger, maybe made a few quid in the boom and managed to hold on to a bit of it. They're inclined to want to tell you all about it. The ones who want it up are generally older and probably sick to death of the sounds of their own voices. They're the ones I like. They're not as free with the tips as the others, who like to splash the cash about when everyone's watching, but still, I prefer them. Nice and easy.

Kenny gives me the K Club run, only after I threaten to ring Carol and tell her that he doesn't run a fleet of Stretches all over the country. And that he likes Kenny Rogers.

'I don't like Kenny Rogers.'

'You went to see him at the O2.'

'I thought it was Kenny Everett. I just saw the Kenny bit and assumed.'

'Kenny Everett's been dead for nearly twenty years.'

'I didn't get the memo,' he says, handing over the outfit in the dry-cleaner's bag. A hat and gloves, the lot. The boss calls it 'vintage'.

The weekend drags. I was going to paint the wall with Kerry on Sunday but Miss Pratchett left a message on the phone on Friday to say there was a hockey final on, and that the weekend was no longer convenient. 'Some evening during the week would probably suffice,' she said in her message.

I get the motor back on Tuesday, after two more Stretch runs, both with the partition down and the punters going hell for leather at the minibar and tellin' me allsorts.

I find myself thinking about Ellen. Wondering about her, more like. Just bein' nosy, I suppose. I'm sort of waiting for Friday to arrive to see what she'll do. If she'll go back to the 'partition up' scenario that was always the way before . . . well, before the hospital palaver.

Or partition down, like last Friday.

It's when I'm out the back having a smoke, I get around to thinking about her. Wondering about her, more like. And then I flick the butt down the side of the shed – needs to be revarnished and it's sagging a bit, if I'm honest – and go back inside the house. I do the usual – homework with Finn, the few roars at Kerry, watch a bit of telly, make the dinner, pour Cif down the loo – and I forget about her.

Just getting on with things. Nothing else to be done.

Eighteen

I don't get a chance to get to the school til Thursday evening.

'I've a tin of paint that'll do you,' Kenny says. 'Left over from painting my bedroom last year.'

'I need outdoor paint.'

'It'll be grand.'

'You painted your room purple, though.'

'It's more violet. Nice and bright for a school wall.'

I go to Edges. Pick up a tin of white outdoor paint. Last one in the shop. 'First Holy Communions,' the man says, by way of explanation. 'People dickying up their properties.'

I nod, hand him a note. The doors and skirting boards at home could do with a coat. The worse for wear, with the traffic through the house. No time to think about that now. I leave the shop.

I arrange to meet Kerry after school, at the wall. Down by the bicycle shed. I've got the rollers, the brushes, the trays, the paint and an old sheet to lay along the ground and drape over the few stray bicycles still chained up. All she has to do is show up, and she's late. I can't even have a smoke, waiting for her. There's a 'No Smoking' sign. A fair few butts behind the wall, mind.

I'm about to ring her when she arrives. Strolling along, no hurry on her. No apology either. For being late. Barely a greeting. A mumble. That's what I get.

I button my lip.

'Right, then,' I say, handing her a brush and prising the tin open with a screwdriver. 'Let's get started, shall we?'

'Do you like it?' she says.

I look at her, confused. 'Do I like what?'

She sighs. Another black mark against me. Haven't a clue what I've done this time. No surprises there.

'My painting,' she says then, nodding towards the wall.

'Oh.' I look at the wall. I hadn't thought of it as a painting. Not like something you'd see hanging up in a gallery. The Mona Lisa or what have you. I glanced at it when I arrived, alright. Before I started fuming about her no-show. And wondering if I'd enough paint in the one can to cover it. And if it needed more than one coat. Stuff like that. That's what I was thinking about.

Practicalities. Someone has to think about the practicalities. Not that you'd get any thanks for it.

Blobs, really. Blobs of paint. That's what I saw when I glanced at it. It's only when you look properly, you can see it's a woman. No, two women. Sort of tucked around each other to make a circle against a backdrop of bright colours so you really have to study it to notice that it's two women. And yeah, they've no clothes on but you'd have to be staring pretty hard to notice that. Their bodies are made up of these swirls of colour and they've both got long hair, over their vitals. Their faces look a bit funny. It's the eyes, I think. All different sizes. And the noses and mouths aren't where they should be, strictly speaking.

'The faces. They're a bit . . . out of proportion, aren't they?' I say.

Kerry raises her eyes. Shakes her head. 'They're supposed to be like that.'

'Oh. Right.'

I notice her name then. Her signature. At the bottom right-hand corner of the wall. 'A bit of a giveaway,' I say, nodding at it.

'It's my first public exhibit. I didn't want anyone else taking the credit.' The chin's up and the eyes are narrowed, like she's expecting trouble. An argument. Between me and her. Wouldn't be the first one today.

Maybe I'm tired. Drove a fare to Bray this morning. He did a runner. Jumped out at a red light. Not the first time it's happened, of course. Still, wears you out. Punters. People. Do your head in. Whatever it is, I don't have the stomach for an argument. Not another one.

'Let's get started,' I say, handing her a pair of overalls.

'I'm not wearing those things,' she says, holding the overalls between the tip of her thumb and finger, like they're contaminated.

'You are.'

'I'm not.'

'You are.'

'I'm not.'

Jaysus.

'Here,' I say, 'before you put them on, I'll take a photograph of you. You and your painting.'

'Why?' Immediately suspicious.

'Your first exhibit,' I say. 'We should take a picture of it, all the same. A keepsake.'

She doesn't say anything but moves to the edge of the wall, stands there while I get my phone ready. 'Say Vincent Van Gogh,' I tell her. She doesn't, but she stands there all the same, lets me take the picture. When I look at it later, there's a hint of a smile about her face. She looks lovely when she smiles.

She puts the overalls on in the end. We get to work. She's not a bad little worker, Kerry, when she puts her mind to it. It's only as I paint over it, I notice all the little details. Misshapen trees and brightly coloured birds perched on their branches and the moon, shaped like a cube, but the moon all the same, with its silvery light. The jet stream left behind by a plane and, right in the corner, a tiny little car. A taxi, it is.

'What are you smiling at?' she says.

I nod at the taxi. 'You've put me in the picture,' I say.

She rolls her eyes. 'You're not the only taxi driver in the world, you know.'

'Your ma was fond of arts and crafts herself, you know. Remember she did that pottery class? Made the vase? We called it the Leaning Tower of Pisa. Remember?'

No answer to that. She's working away. Most of her painting is covered now. I dip my brush in the tin. Whistle a bit. Take the weight out of the silence.

'I'm never going to have kids.' She goes on painting, not looking at me. Like it's nothing, what she's saying. There's a bit of paint in her hair.

I shrug. 'You might change your mind. When you're older, like.'

'I won't.'

'I think I'd make a great grandad.' I smile, keeping it light. She doesn't smile back.

'I don't want to end up like her.'

I stop painting. Look at her. The overalls make her seem small, standing there with her rigid jaw and her angry eyes.

'Your mother had a difficult time,' I say. 'She . . .'

Kerry laughs. A short bark of a laugh. Brittle and dry. 'She doesn't give a toss about us. You included.'

'That's not true. She loves you. You and Finn. She just . . . she wasn't . . .'

'Anyway, I'm not having kids. I'm just saying.'

She's painting again, slashing at the wall with her brush. We're nearly finished. I have that dull, heavy feeling inside my stomach. It's my fault, really. I tried to explain it to her as best I could. Told her it was nothing to do with her. It wasn't her fault. *Sometimes, people get sick.* That's what I said. Something like that.

Will she come back when she's better?

She didn't say much, Kerry, but I remember that one. That question. Made a dog's dinner of it, of course. Went round the houses with that one. *Yeah, I'd say she . . . when she's feeling better . . . right as rain in no time . . . needs a bit of rest . . . home soon, I'd say. Home before you know it. Home in two shakes of a lamb's tail.*

I suppose I was trying to protect her. Protect them both.

You do your best. It's only looking back, you realise you're short. You've fallen short.

'That's the lot,' I say, putting the roller in the tray and looking at the wall. 'Clean as a whistle.'

She reefs herself out of the overalls, tosses them in the bag. She looks tired. A lot on her plate at the moment, with the Junior Cert coming up.

'How about a bag of chips on the way home?'

'I'm on a diet, remember?'

'We'll get low-fat ones.'

That earns me a small smile.

'I wouldn't have called it graffiti, all the same,' I say, gathering up the bits and pieces.

'Pity you're not Miss Pratchett, then, isn't it?' she says, crossing her arms.

'Prachett the Hatchet, wha'?'

'Dad!' She glances around to see if anyone heard me. There's no one here. It's just us.

'Come on,' I say, picking up the bag, slinging it over my shoulders.

'Can I have a cheeseburger too?'

'Yeah.' The promise of chips has lightened the tension. I think about putting my hand on her shoulder. Saying, 'Good job.' I don't in the end. Don't want to ruin it.

'Can I have a tenner for tomorrow?'

'What for?'

'Geometry set.'

'A tenner for a geometry set?'

'Yeah.'

'OK.'

Dear Neil,

Dr Deery says I should think about what I miss about you. She says it's important to (a) acknowledge that there are things I miss, (b) list them, and (c) accept that you're gone and move on. This, she says, is closure!

Because she called it 'homework', I did it. It's the ex-prefect in me, I suppose. Here's my list:

1. *The smell in the kitchen when you cooked dinner.*
2. *Your habit of taking off your glasses and cleaning them with the tail of your shirt when you were trying to work something out. You looked vulnerable without your glasses on. Not as sure of yourself.*
3. *Your laugh. Everyone at the clinic could hear it, even with your door closed. The patients loved your laugh. Loved you. They always asked for you. I was the better doctor, you said. But you could make them laugh.*
4. *Ordinary things. Like the creak of the stairs, the twist of the radio dial, the low hum of your shaver in the bathroom, the filled-in crossword in the paper. Just, I suppose . . . the fact of you . . . in the house. You only realise the comfort of somebody else's noise when it's not there any more.*

I told Dr Deery that the list of the things I don't miss is much longer. She didn't laugh. Even you'd be hard-pressed to make her laugh. An occasional smile, small and benign.

'Oh, I forgot to mention his organisational skills,' I said then. 'He would have unpacked the boxes in the spare room. Found a place for everything.'

A place for everything, and everything in its place. Isn't that what you used to say?

'What boxes?' Dr Deery says, looking up from her notebook.

'Oh, just stuff, really. When I moved into the apartment. I unpacked some of them but . . . it's just odds and ends from the house. I haven't needed any of it.'

'You moved into the apartment six months ago?' she asks, her pen poised. I nod, and she writes something. A black mark, I'd say.

She nods at my list. I'd like to know what she thinks. I'd love a 'Good', or a 'Fair', even. Some sort of grade. She nods and asks me how I feel about what I've written.

How do you feel, Ellen?

How do you bloody well feel, Ellen?

It's exhausting.

She tells me I should think about unpacking the boxes.

In the taxi last Friday, Vinnie asked me what my plans were for the weekend. Just being polite, I suppose. Making conversation. I haven't had plans in ages. I don't think watching Charlie Chaplin films with your mother counts, does it? It hasn't bothered me before. It's just when you say it out loud, it sounds a bit . . . I don't know . . . sorry. 'Nothing,' I said. Then I changed it to 'Nothing much.' Sounds a bit better. Takes the edge off.

Dr Deery says it's important to get out there, interact with people, engage with the world. But it's when you do that, you realise how small your life has become. A tight little circle of me and the apartment and the treatments and watching telly with my mother.

And that was fine. It's fine until you show it to somebody else.

I am embarrassed by the smallness of my own life. Dr Deery says this is a good step.

Coming to, she called it.

Ellen

Nineteen

Friday happens to be a gorgeous day. One of those spring days in Dublin that hints at a vague promise of summer. I notice buds swelling on the pear tree and Mrs Finnegan across the way is at her front windows with a J-cloth, whistling while she works, like one of the seven dwarves.

I hoover out the motor; hang one of those air-freshener trees on the back of the rear-view mirror. It's a bit strong, the smell. I take it down and put it in the pocket of the door instead. Lavender. 'That'll have you all Zen,' said Morris at the garage where I bought it. 'It's a yoga term,' he explained.

Bloody yoga. They're all at it.

Still, the car looks well and doesn't smell too bad.

'Where are you going all dressed up like that?' says Kerry.

'Like what?'

'Like a dog's dinner.'

'It's the shirt your granny got me for Christmas. Thought I should get some wear out of it.'

'Christmas was three months ago.'

'About time I put it on.'

'You smell weird.'

'What kind of weird?'

'Are you wearing Granny's perfume?'

'No! It's just a bit of the aftershave Finn got me for my birthday last year.'

'He got that in a jumble sale. It cost fifty cents.'

'He was robbed,' I say then, and it works because I see her, trying not to smile. She's in better form today, since it's the last day of her internment, as she calls it. Thank Christ.

I splash my neck with cold water. Maybe it *is* a bit strong, that stuff. Especially when you consider the lavender in the car.

'What did you do to your hair, Dad?' Finn asks on the way to school.

'I brushed it.'

'Oh.'

The jeans aren't as comfortable as my old ones. A bit stiff. At every traffic light, I'm pulling at them, like Janine with the ends of her skirt.

The day wears on. Tips are down. It could be the lavender. Even after I wrapped it in a bag and put it in the boot, you can still smell it.

Kenny looks me up and down at the airport rank, wolf-whistles. 'Nice threads.'

'Maybe you're rubbing off on me.' Although he's fairly casual today. A white cotton shirt with long pointed lapels and brightly coloured vintage cameras printed all over it, tucked into mustard jeans with a discreet little bell-bottom. Hard to tell if he's wearing shoes or boots underneath the bell-bottoms. Boots, I'd say. He's mad about boots. Authoritative, he says.

'Job interview?' says Kenny.

'No.'

'Funeral?'

'Give over.'

'What, then?'

'Nothing.' I rub my hands together. It's cold enough once you're standing around, but I'm not getting my jacket out of the car. If Kenny sees that, he'll have a field day. It's not that it's all that nice or anything. Just . . . I don't wear it very often. Hardly ever. The only reason I have it today is . . . well, it happens to go grand with the jeans. Same dark blue. That's all.

'You picking up Calamity Jane this afternoon, comrade?'

'Dunno.'

'Be a shame for her to miss your little makeover.'

'Fuck off.'

'That's it, isn't it? Kenny's hit the nail on the head, hasn't he?'

'No. I've a meeting later. At Finn's school.' This is not, strictly speaking, true. But it could be. They're forever having meetings at that place.

Kenny winks at me and starts humming 'Love Is in the Air', wiggling his hips while he's at it.

Later, Janine rings. 'Kenny says you're all dolled up today.' I can hear the smirk in her voice. 'Are you coming to the pub later?' she asks.

'No.'

'It's Friday. But you already know that, don't you?'

'I'm aware of the days of the week, yeah.'

'Send me a photo of your little outfit.'

'Fuck sake, Janine.'

'Do it or I'll take you off the system.'

She'd do it too. She's done it before. That time I said she was like yer woman from *The Weakest Link*. Mental, she went. I didn't mean she *looked* like her.

I get out of the car. Take the shot. Text it to her.

Wick Woo, she texts back, with one of those smiley faces, winking. *Tonite cud b yr lucky nite, Vincenzo . . . j xxx*

I look at the photograph. Tosser. My hair plastered down like that. I pull my fingers through it, get it back to the way it was. Kerry's right. A dog's dinner. When was the last time I wore that jacket? Finn's christening, was it? No, it was after that. The day I picked Paula up from the hospital. Brought her home. Finn made strange with her. Kerry barely spoke to her. Even Ma was shy around her for those first few weeks, phoning before she arrived at the house. 'Just seeing if it suits,' she'd say, breezy as you like. As if this wasn't out of the ordinary, her giving prior notice of a visit with a phone call. She had a conniption when her phone bill arrived.

The call comes through at four o'clock. 'Anyone around the Clontarf area?'

Usually she asks for me. 'I'm close,' I say, cool as you like.

'Thought you might be, Vincenzo,' Janine says, and hangs up before I can think of something smart to say.

Twenty

Ellen's not where she normally is. Outside the gates, waiting. I pull up at the kerb, give her a few minutes.

Still no sign.

My phone rings. I take it out and look at the screen. I don't recognise the number. I answer it anyway, which I don't normally do, but I have a feeling it might be Ellen.

It is.

'Vinnie?'

'Yeah. Howeya, Ellen.'

'I hope you don't mind me ringing you directly like this. I rang the depot and got your number off Janine.'

'No, it's . . . it's fine. Is everything OK?'

'I'm just . . . I have a bit of a problem, to be honest.'

I wasn't expecting this. 'What kind of a problem?' I ask, cautious.

'It's so stupid. I've never done this before.'

'What?' I've my hand on the door handle, imagining allsorts.

'It's just . . . well, I've locked myself out. The fire alarm went off in the building and I walked up the corridor to see what was going on. I was sure I'd put the door on the latch.'

'There's no fire, is there?'

'No, it goes off sometimes. I keep meaning to complain to the management company about it.'

'Would they have a spare key, the management company?'

'No.'

'How about any of your neighbours?'

'No.'

'Anyone else?'

'My mum, but she's gone away for the weekend.'

'You're on the second floor, aren't you? Number twenty-eight.'

'Yes.'

'Any chance the patio door out to the balcony is open?'

'It might be . . . I had a cigarette out there this morning. I don't remember locking it when I came back in.'

'OK, I'll see if I can locate a ladder. Is there a caretaker?'

'I don't think so. I've never seen one.'

'I'll ring you back in five minutes, OK?'

'Sorry about this.'

'Don't worry. We'll get it sorted.'

There's a maintenance shed around the back but no sign of a caretaker or a ladder. I walk back around the front of the building and work out which apartment is Ellen's. There doesn't seem to be anyone in the apartment on the ground floor directly below hers. I can't see anyone anyway. I look around. All quiet, not a sinner about. I drag their table against the wall surrounding their patio and, without giving myself too much time to think about it, hoist myself onto the top of the wall. Ellen's balcony is directly overhead. It's out of reach but not by too much. I could reach it if I jumped. I'm fairly sure I could.

I jump. My fingers reach for the wrought-iron railings, find them, wrap themselves around them. Now I'm dangling in the air, my arms stretched above me, aching with my weight. I tell myself not to look down, and then I do and the ground is far away. It didn't seem such a distance when I had both feet on the ground. Still, there's nowhere to go but up. I swing my body like a pendulum, then lift a leg and slot my foot into the space between two rails, gain a bit of purchase before I hook the other leg over the top of the railings and haul the rest of myself over. In the end, I sort of fall onto the balcony. I lie there for a moment, gasping for breath, part exertion and part, I don't know, adrenalin, maybe. Or stupidity. When I manage to stand up, I lean my hands on my knees, struggling to get my breath back. Automatically, I reach for the bottle of pills in my pocket. But I'm not having a panic attack. I'm just out of breath. Out of shape, let's face it. But not panicking. That's something.

Still, I'll have to sort myself out, fitness wise. Press-ups or something.

The patio door is unlocked, which is just as well because there's no way I'd risk climbing down. A fire brigade job, it would have been.

I step inside.

The immediate impression is that nobody lives here. The apartment is more than quiet. It's still. No radio. No stereo.

There's not a sound in the place. Not a breath.

I'm in the living room. Bare essentials. A stiff-looking chair. A leather couch. The telly on, the sound muted. One of those monotonous chat shows, it looks like, all teeth and tans.

Along one wall, a sturdy wooden sideboard, with nothing on it but a few envelopes, sealed but with no address on them. A layer of dust over everything. An empty bookshelf.

An archway leads into a kitchen. It's warmer in here. More lived-in, somehow. Maybe because of the coffee machine and a cardigan hanging off the back of one of two kitchen chairs, parked under a small wooden table. Her keys are on the table. I pick them up and step into the hall, past a shelf where a spider plant has come to a withered end. Ma always says it's impossible to kill them, spider plants. Looks like she was wrong.

I open the front door and Ellen is there, leaning on her crutches. It strikes me then that I've never seen her without her coat. Her clothes are more informal than I would have imagined.

Dark, skinny jeans, bright yellow T-shirt. Her feet are bare and her toes are long and thin. Her hair is wet and sticks up in spiky tufts around her head, making her seem younger. No scarf. The scar looks out of place on her face, the red jagged line like a roar against the smooth, pale skin. Perhaps because her face is . . . well, it's nice. Pretty, I suppose.

'How did you do that? Did someone lend you a ladder?' she asks.

'Not exactly,' I admit.

'You didn't climb up! Did you? You could have fallen. I should have phoned a locksmith.'

'Cost you a fortune, those boyos,' I say, stepping back and holding the door open for her. She walks inside, past me and the air stirs between us, catching her scent, touching me with it; sweet. Coconut, maybe. Shower gel, I'd say.

'Thanks a million, Vinnie.'

'No problem. So, are you ready to hit the road?' It feels funny, being in her apartment. Wrong, somehow.

'Could you give me five minutes to dry my hair and put my shoes on? Sorry, but I'm a bit behind now.'

'Sure, yeah.'

'There's coffee in the jug in the kitchen. It's fresh, if you want a cup.' I nod, and she disappears through a door off the hall, closes it behind her.

It seems like a reckless thing to do, all the same. A stranger in your home. A taxi driver. Dodgy as hell, some of them.

In the kitchen, the coffee smells good; earthy and strong. I open a press, take out a mug, find a spoon, pour the coffee.

I sit at the table. A few bits on it. A mobile phone, a flyer for a new dry-cleaner's up the road, a stack of takeaway menus, a plastic bottle of pills, a tube of prescription cream.

The only thing on the wall is a calendar. A page for every month. A freebie from a bank, it looks like. A black diagonal line scored through the square of each day up to today. I get up, walk over to it, lift the page. The same last month. And the month before that, all the way back to January. Black lines, through every day.

Maybe she's moving out. That could be why the place is so sparse.

I sit down. It's awkward as hell, really. Being here. I feel like I'm prying in some way that I can't explain. And I'm not. I'm just sitting here, drinking coffee, waitin' for a fare, that's all. But you can't help noticing stuff, all the same. Human nature, I suppose. Like, no pictures or photographs anywhere. Not a single one.

I concentrate on the coffee. Don't want Ellen to catch me gawking, making assumptions. Not that there's anything to assume. An apartment like this doesn't tell you much about a person. Doesn't tell you anything.

When she comes into the kitchen, her hair is dry and she has a pair of runners on. She pours herself a coffee, inhales the steam just like before and sits on the other side of the table. Then she looks at me and sort of smiles, shakes her head.

'What?' I say.

She blows on the top of the coffee, takes a sip. 'It's just a bit weird,' she says, after a while.

'What is?'

'You're the first person I've had in the apartment since I moved in. Apart from my mother. And the guy who came to connect the electricity and the gas.'

'When did you move in?' I ask.

'About six months ago. After I got out of hospital and the rehab place. After the accident.'

I nod again. I'm like one of those toy dogs you see on the back windows of little old ladies' cars. Nodding their heads off.

I drink my coffee. Compared to Ellen's apartment, my house is like Heuston Station on a bank holiday. I can hear the coffee going down my throat every time I take a mouthful. That kind of quiet could do your head in, I'd say. After a while.

I finish my coffee and reach into my pocket for the keys of the motor. Don't want her to think I'm getting too comfortable.

Instead of standing up, putting her cardigan on, she says, 'What're your kids' names?'

'Kerry and Finn. She's fourteen and he's seven.'

'They're lovely names.'

'Yeah, they're grand. Paula picked them.'

'Your wife?'

'Yeah, I suppose so. Technically, at any rate.'

'You're separated?'

I shift in my chair. 'Well . . .'

'Sorry, it's none of my business.'

'No, it's grand, it's just . . . she left. Over a year ago. Fifteen months.'

I suppose I knew. The minute I woke up that morning. Paula's side of the bed was cold, the duvet undisturbed there. I couldn't remember her getting into bed that night, pushing her cold feet into the bend of my knees. I looked at the dressing table. Stuff missing. Her perfume, hairbrush, various lotions and potions. Gone. I got out of bed but didn't check her wardrobe. Not then. Instead, I went downstairs. Down to the kitchen. Where she sat sometimes, at the table, drinking tea and smoking cigarettes. She said she liked the house at night-time. The quiet. She said she could think.

The kitchen, neat as a pin that morning. She must have scrubbed it during the night, the antiseptic smell of Dettol hanging like clouds in the air. The note, a white rectangle in the middle of the table, her rings on top of it.

I didn't read the note for ages. I stuffed it into my pocket, along with the rings. Got the kids up for school, made the lunches, gave them lifts, walked the dog, went to work, came home, made the dinner, watched a bit of telly, went to bed. I didn't tell them for nearly a week, the kids. They were used to Paula's comings and goings by then.

Finn cried.

Kerry didn't.

For a while, I was like a ship with no rudder. Just drifting. Going from day to day. Getting on with things. What else can you do?

'Did she ever come back?' Ellen says. Her voice sounds far away, like she's in another room, but I realise it's not her who's far away, it's me who's not quite here. I sit up straighter in the chair, clear my throat, fold my arms.

'No,' I say. 'She's in touch sometimes. Postcards, mainly. The odd phone call.' I'm about to stand up, suggest we leave, and then I don't. Instead, I say, 'It's a bit of a relief, bein' honest.'

It's out of my mouth before I can drag the words back. It's not something I've said before. To anyone. It's a horrible thing to say.

True, though.

When Paula was there, you wouldn't know what to expect coming in the door after a day's work. There could be some stranger sitting at the kitchen table with her, having tea. Some random door-to-door fella that she might have dragged in. Jehovah's Witnesses. Mormons. Salesmen. Beggars. 'I get lonely, in the house on my own all day,' she'd say.

Sometimes, she'd prepare elaborate four-course dinners. Have a tantrum if Finn didn't eat it. 'It's not your cooking, love, it's just Finn. He doesn't like plum sauce.' I tried to placate her.

'All the effort I went to,' she shouted, grabbing the plate in front of Finn and shoving it in the bin. Finn crying. Paula crying. Kerry finishing everything on her plate, then leaving the kitchen, silent as a shadow, up to her room.

Sometimes, toast for dinner. 'I didn't have time. I can't do everything. You expect me to do everything. I'm like a slave in this house. A skivvy.'

Me with the takeaway menus. 'How about a Chinese? I got some nice tips today.'

She could be drinking. The house could be cold and dark. Or steaming hot with the heat on full blast, the music blaring, the windows thrown open for the whole neighbourhood to hear. The breakfast dishes might be on the table. Or the place could be like a new pin, with black bags lining up in the hall, ready for the charity shop.

You'd just never know what was going to greet you every day when you turned the key in the lock. So, yeah, it's true.

There was relief.

Part of me was relieved.

I look at Ellen. 'You probably think that's an awful thing to say.'

She shakes her head.

'She was grand until she had the kids.'

'Post-natal?'

'They thought it was. Then there was a bit of an incident and she had to go in someplace. It took a while before they realised it was bipolar.'

'That's hard on a family,' says Ellen.

'It was hard on her, alright. Took her a long time to accept it. I'm not sure she ever did.'

I don't know why I'm saying all this. Spouting off.

'Where did she go? When she left, I mean.'

'She went to this place in England first. It's like a retreat type of a facility. In Manchester.'

'I know it.' Ellen nods. Hard to remember she's a doctor.

'I only found out where she was when I got the bill in the post.' I pick up my mug, drink some coffee. That was some day.

The bill arriving. Two weeks after she'd left. I'd been frantic. She'd never been gone this long before. And this was the first time since her attempt. She'd been in hospital for six weeks after the attempt, and when she came out, things were better. Not brilliant or anything. But quieter. Calmer. I thought things were getting better. We got through Christmas and I thought we were home sailing. By the time I got around to taking the decorations down, she was gone.

The guards were sympathetic but there wasn't a lot they could do. Paula hadn't broken the law. She was a grown-up. She'd done this before. She'd come back before. 'We'll put out a few feelers, alright?' they said.

Don't look for me, Vinnie.

That's what the note said. But I had to look for her. She was my wife. I was her family. And she was mine.

'Is Mammy back yet?' Finn's question, every day after school. Like she was at the shops. Like she'd be back any minute.

'She's not coming back, you big baby,' Kerry said, one day. Finn cried again. Kerry looked at me and she looked so young and so confused, like she couldn't believe she'd said it. She wanted me to contradict her. To say, *Of course she's coming back, don't be silly.*

I should have said something to her. To both of them. I didn't. I couldn't think of a single thing. I got in the car every day. Drove to every place we'd ever been. I stuck posters to every lamppost in the city, train stations, DART stations, bus stations. I persuaded the consultant at the hospital to speak to the guards, try and get them to take it seriously. I got Janine to help me set up a Facebook page.

The bill put a stop to all that. The size of it, for starters. Had to borrow the money. There was no other way.

'That's a great facility, that place in Manchester,' Ellen says.

I nod. 'I could do with a week in there myself, sometimes. A bit of peace and quiet.' I smile and she smiles back and the oppressive silence of the apartment lifts a little.

She looks at me again, with expectancy, as if she's waiting for me to ask her a question. Maybe ask if there's a husband. A partner. Someone. A significant other, Janine calls them. I might ask if we were in the motor. If she was in the back seat. But here, in the close silence of her apartment, it feels a bit . . . I don't know, inappropriate, maybe. She could get the wrong idea.

But I'm curious now. And she's asked me stuff. Maybe it would be rude not to ask her anything.

'Shall we go?' The question takes me by surprise, the abruptness of it. It's like those sliding panels in the confessional that the priest shuts when you're done admitting all your wrongdoings. When the panel slides shut, you're plunged into a darkness that's as thick as treacle. You can't see your own hand in front of your face. You have to feel for the door.

'Yeah. Sure. Let's go.'

We don't say much after that. Ellen gets in the back seat and looks out the window. I drive to Portmarnock. Business as usual. She looks a bit tired now.

I keep driving, say nothing. I've said enough already. Not every day of the week I'm sat in someone's kitchen spilling my guts.

I drive her to the physio place. Wait outside. Thirty-two minutes today. Back to normal.

I don't say, 'Home?' like I usually do when she gets back in the car. That sounds a bit too familiar, now that I've been inside the place. 'Clontarf?' I say instead. She nods.

It's back to the way it was before but it doesn't feel right any more. It feels awkward as hell. I say nothing. Just drive.

When I stop outside her place, she hands me the cash, opens the door, steps out, arranges her crutches on either side of her.

But then she bends, looks in at me. 'I like your jacket, by the way. It's nice with those jeans.'

'Oh . . . thanks . . . it's ancient, I don't usually wear it but . . . I've a meeting later at the school . . . have to be presentable.' The lie comes out nice and easy, since I've already given it a dry run with Kenny.

She nods and smiles and opens her mouth, like she's about to say something, then closes it again and shakes her head like she's having an argument with herself. Then she says, 'You know, I came across my cookery books the other night.'

'Are you into cooking?'

'I haven't cooked in ages.'

'I make dinner every night. But I don't think you'd call it cooking, exactly. More like defrosting.'

'I used to do this tomato stew thing. With chorizo and chickpeas.'

'Sounds tasty.'

'I found the recipe. Thought I'd try it again. You could . . . you could come over and eat it with me. If you like. I'd like to say thanks.' She nods towards the balcony, which seems, now that I'm looking at it again, a hell of a lot higher up than it was earlier. 'For today. Helping me out.'

'Ah, there's no need for that.' I shift in my seat.

'OK.' She puts the strap of her handbag across her shoulder and arranges her hands on the crutches. 'I'll see you next Friday, then.'

'What day were you thinking?' I say then. It comes out as one word, I say it that fast.

'Oh, well, I hadn't thought that far ahead, really. It was just . . . an idea.'

'How about Wednesday night?'

Kenny can get someone to fill my spot on the five-a-side.

'Wednesday. Yes.'

'Great.'

'Don't expect too much. I'm a bit . . . rusty.'

'Anything that's not fish fingers and oven chips will be a step up.'

'Seven o'clock OK?'

'Seven. Yeah. Grand. Lovely.'

She smiles. It's startling, her smile. Unexpected. She looks different when she smiles. Younger. She turns and walks towards the gate. I drive away quickly. I don't want her to think I'm sitting here staring at her or anything.

Dear Neil,

I told Dr Deery that I'd invited a stranger to the apartment for dinner. Perhaps I wanted to see if she could make any sense of it.

She says it's a positive step. Besides, she says, Vinnie's hardly a stranger.

'You have to give yourself permission to be happy.' I hate when she talks like that. It reminds me that I'm in therapy.

Were we unhappy? I didn't have time to stop and think about it back then. You must have been. That's why you had the affair, I suppose. Or affairs. You had more than one, didn't you? You must have been unhappy. Or bored. You always said you had a low boredom threshold.

Perhaps I'm bored. Maybe that's why I invited Vinnie. But no, I don't think it's that. I opened one of the boxes the other night. I couldn't sleep so I took a knife from the kitchen drawer and went into the spare room. Opened the one nearest the door.

Stacks of our recipe books. Mine, really. You never really followed recipes. A pinch of this, a splash of that. A natural, you were.

And CDs. Joni Mitchell and John Lennon. The Doors, Bob Dylan. You said I had a bit of a hippie vibe when you met me. Maybe I had, back then. My hair halfway down my back and bangles clinking around my wrists and my silver toe rings. I cut my hair when I qualified. It was too impractical for work, always getting in the way. I've kept it short ever since. Don't know why, really, since there's no need now. Habit, I suppose. Maybe I'll grow it back someday.

I saw my apartment today. Really saw it. Maybe because Vinnie was here. I locked myself out and he arrived to collect me in the cab. He climbed onto the balcony and let me in. I shouldn't have let him. He might have broken his neck. But I didn't think he would. There's a suggestion of strength about him. Maybe because of his height. He opened the door and let me in and it was like seeing the place for the first time, in a way. Like I was a visitor in my own apartment.

You look in the front room and you see that the person who lives here watches a lot of television. There are box sets, TV guides and remotes within easy reach of the armchair that faces the telly.

You look in the fridge. The person who lives here eats ready-made dinners. Cans of soup. Pre-sliced cheese. Tins of tuna.

You look in the bedroom. The person who lives here sleeps alone.

You look in the bathroom. At the brown paper that's taped over the mirror. The person who lives here doesn't look at herself.

Vinnie doesn't mention any of that. He drinks a coffee and takes me to the physio clinic.

We have nothing in common, me and Vinnie. I used to think that was important. But look at you and me. We had so much in common. Our professions, where we came from. We both liked classical music. Cooking. Watching Wimbledon every summer. We were workaholics. Both of us.

Maybe I'm lonely. Dr Deery doesn't think so. She says I'm very self-sufficient. I've always been content with my own company, I suppose. I just didn't have time to realise it before. And I don't feel lonely.

So why did you ask him to dinner? That's what you're wondering, isn't it?

Me too.

But the idea of the smells of home-made food wafting through this apartment appeals to me. Perhaps it's as simple as that.

And I have to admit, it was nice today, the sound of voices in the kitchen. The sound of conversation. The apartment seemed so quiet afterwards.

You were larger than life. Noisy. Always working on a plan. When you were gone, everything was so quiet. Quieter still when I moved in here.

Perhaps I just need to make a little noise.

Ellen

Twenty One

'Dinner at her place? You know what that means, don't you, comrade?' Kenny turns Janine around, places his hands on her haunches and simulates pelvic thrusts, despite the tightness of his trousers. Janine obliges him by bending at the waist, backing her rump into Ken's crotch and panting. The other drivers at the depot don't even look up from their newspapers. Used to that pair's antics by now.

I feel a bit funny about Wednesday night. It's not a date, exactly. I know that. But still. It feels strange.

'I've a bit of a rendezvous myself, this very evening, so I have,' says Kenny, letting Janine go. She pats the huge halo of red curls – *they're Titian, Vinnie* – around her head with both hands and glares at him.

'What grand plans have you made this time?' she asks. 'Going to bring her to your house to observe a shoe fetish in action?'

It's true that I helped Kenny turn the spare room into a walk-in wardrobe, most of which is taken up with shelves for shoes and boots. Janine finds it difficult to accept that Kenny has more footwear than she does.

Kenny hooks his thumbs into the pockets of the black silk waistcoat he got in the charity shop in Killiney. A better class of second-hand threads in Killiney, he says.

'I'm picking her up from work and taking her to the Leprechaun Museum. She's interested in leprechauns. Another thing we have in common.'

'Since when have you been interested in leprechauns?' Janine asks, with great scorn.

Kenny shrugs. 'Ages.'

'You never mentioned it.'

'I don't have to tell you everything, you know. Besides, we'll only be able to go if she gets out of the clinic on time. Colm – that's her boss – only took over the practice in the last few months and he depends on her completely. She's worked there since it was set up. There's nothing she doesn't know about the place.'

'Hmmm,' says Janine, unimpressed with Carol's in-depth knowledge of her workplace. She always gets a bit antsy when Kenny's going on one of his dates.

Me and Paula didn't go on dates. Not really. We started walking home from school together – she lived down the road, so it made sense. Then we started sitting together in the canteen at lunchtime. We both sat at the back of the lab in Biology class. I heard that we were an item from Kenny. Who else?

'You're going with Paula.'

'Am I?'

'How far have you gone with her?'

'What are you talking about?'

'Have you felt her tits?'

'None of your fuckin' business.'

Everyone assumed we were a couple, and after a while, so did we. There was no conversation, as far as I remember. No proposition.

After Da died, things changed between us. Ma was in bits. Joey went to Australia a few months later. I stayed at the airport and watched his plane take off. Ma bawled. Everyone gawked at us. Paula hugged her. She was good at dealing with sadness. Other people's sadness. She knew what to say. What to do.

We rang each other every night. Hours we'd spend, on the phone. 'You saw her all day at school, for the love of God,' Ma would roar at me. I'd make myself scarce when the phone bill arrived. I don't remember what we talked about now. There was never a lull in the conversation.

We'd go to the pictures the odd time. Long walks around the cobbled lanes of the quays. Out to Howth Head. Red Rock. We went to the zoo once. I bought her a panda bear in the shop. A rip-off. But it was worth it. She kissed me when I gave it to her, her tongue darting inside my mouth, hesitant and unsure. The warm surprise of it.

I spent most of 1987 kissing her. But dates? We never really did dates. Yeah, I'd bring her for the odd meal, when I was flush. We'd walk to the place. Or get the bus. Maybe that's why it didn't feel like a date. It was just me and Paula, walking up the road, holding hands, like we always did. Even after we got married. I'd say, 'Do you fancy slipping over the road for a pint?' the odd Saturday night. She didn't drink pints. Shorts. Vodkas, mainly. Vodka and diet Coke, not that she needed the diet bit but you know what girls are like.

So the idea of Wednesday feels a bit funny. Weird, like. Even though it's not a date. Not at all. It's getting your dinner handed to you by someone who wants to say thanks.

A bit of dinner.

That's all.

I spend ages deciding what to wear. State of me. Jeans and a shirt. Different jeans to the ones I wore last Friday. Paula brought these ones back from London, that time she went with Trish for the weekend. They were always a bit roomy around the waist. I find a belt.

I don't say anything to the kids. Not that there's anything to say, exactly. They assume I'm going to play football with Kenny and the lads. The usual Wednesday night. No point in complicating things.

It's just dinner. Meat and two veg, maybe a glass of vino, a cup of coffee. That machine of hers is snazzy. Makes lovely coffee, so it does. A bit of dessert. Or crackers and cheese? That might be more her style. Then it's thank you very much and goodbye. End of.

Ma and Finn are in the kitchen, making spaghetti and cheese. Finn is in charge of grating the cheese. There's shreds of it everywhere. Archibald lumbers around the kitchen, bending his head and pushing his tongue along the floor like a mop. He loves a bit of Kilmeaden.

Ma stands at the hob, her face pink and moist from the steam. She picks out a strand of spaghetti from the pot, throws it at the tiles on the wall. It sticks. 'What does that mean again?' she asks him.

'It's ready,' says Finn with authority, standing on a chair to get the bowls.

'Right, so. I'm off,' I say.

Ma looks me up and down. 'You're not playing football in that get-up, are you?'

'Just have a quick run to do in the Stretch before the game. I've me gear in the bag. I'll get changed at the club.'

She'd never let up if I told her where I was going. She's like an episode of *Questions and Answers*, except with her, it's just questions.

'You know I've to leave by half eight, don't you? The Swingin' Sixties are meeting tonight. I said I'd do them a few sandwiches. I've the eggs hardboiling there.' She nods towards another bubbling pot where several eggs are jostling for position.

'I thought it was the Nifty Fifties you were in?' It's hard to keep up with her.

'I am, but the Swingers have just set up and I said I'd give them the benefit of my experience.'

'Grand. Kerry's at the library with Sandra. She'll be back by eight. And Ma, don't go calling them Swingers.'

'Why not?'

'Because . . . just don't, OK?'

Finn puts the bowls on the counter and looks at me. 'I lost a tooth today, Dad.'

'Another one?'

'Yeah. I'm like Mrs Finnegan across the road now.'

If I'd said that as a youngster, Ma would have flicked the back of my leg with the corner of a tea towel and told me not to disrespect my elders. Now, she smiles and ruffles Finn's hair. 'Don't forget to put it under your pillow,' she tells him. Finn leaps from the chair and wraps his arms and legs around me. I nearly topple over.

'Will you French kiss me, Dad?'

Jaysus.

'What do you mean?'

'We did it in school today. Loads of stuff about France. I'll show you.' Before I can prise him off me, he puts his hands on either side of my face and kisses me twice, once on each cheek.

I'm supposed to be there at seven o'clock. I arrive at ten to. I wait in the car. I bought flowers but in the end I just bring the bottle of wine. Leave the flowers in the boot.

If it were a date, I suppose I'd bring flowers. That'd be the thing to do, I'd say.

But it's not.

It's not a date.

I ring her bell.

Twenty Two

She buzzes me in and I walk up the stairs instead of taking the lift. A bit of exercise, since I'm missing the football game. I stand in front of her door and knock. There's one of those little peepholes in the door and I wonder if she's there, on the other side, looking at me. I smile in case she is. Then I stop because why would I be smiling, standing in a corridor by myself?

Cretin.

I pat the pocket of my jeans. I can feel the shape of the bottle of Valium through the denim. I don't think I'll need one but it's comforting to know they're there, all the same.

Ellen opens the door and I remember to smile then. Hold out the wine. She takes it, looks at the label. 'That's a really nice one. Thanks, Vinnie.'

'I don't know a lot about wines so I get the ones with the medals on them. They can't be too bad if they've won medals. That's what Finn says.'

She laughs. A quiet laugh. Like a hum. Now she's turning and walking down the hall, towards the kitchen. 'Come on through,' she says, turning when she gets to the kitchen door. She's wearing a dress. First time I've seen her in a dress. Blue with white flowers. Daisies, I think. It's pretty. It falls just below her knee. Navy leggings down to a pair of flip-flops, the glint of sliver around her toe. Her toenails are painted green. Lime green. The leggings accentuate the slim length of her legs. I hardly notice the crutches now. They make no sound against the carpet in the hall.

The apartment is the same as before but feels different. Warmer, maybe. The telly's still on and muted. Music in the background this time. Classical, I think. Not as bad as you'd think.

'Smells good,' I say, shrugging my jacket off. Otherwise, I'll freeze when I get back outside.

'I made that stew I mentioned. I used to make it all the time and it was nice. People said it was nice.'

I wonder then who she means by 'people'. I imagine her and her husband at either end of a long table – oak, I'm thinking – with guests seated along both sides, everyone passing bowls of this and plates of that, drinking deeply from goblets of wine, talking about . . . I don't know, politics. Or the theatre, maybe. Highbrow.

I can't think of a thing to say.

Ellen hands me a large wooden bowl, with leaves in it. 'Would you mind tossing the salad?' she says, putting two oversized wooden spoons on the counter beside me.

'Sure.' I pick up the spoons and look at the contents of the bowl. No tomatoes, no hardboiled egg, no scallions, no red peppers. Ma would not grant this the title of 'salad'.

'What are you smiling at?' Ellen says, splitting a baguette down the middle with a knife.

'Just thinking about my ma, actually.'

'Do you often think about your mother when you're tossing a salad?'

'I don't toss salads all that often, to be honest. The kids aren't keen on them.'

She nods and returns her attention to the bread. Now she's spreading butter on it. Scattering herbs. She pushes a fork through a clove of garlic until it's mashed to a pulp, lays it along the blade of a knife and slides it along the baguette. Her movements are fluid. You can tell she's done this before. She has long, slender hands. Delicate fingers. You could imagine her feeling for glands on a child's neck. Pressing gently, her face serious and intent.

I stop tossing. I'd say it's tossed enough by now. Hard to know, really. She wraps the baguette in tinfoil, puts it in the oven. She looks at me. 'Wine?' she says.

'Ah, no, I'm grand, I've got the motor.'

She nods and sits on one of the two chairs at the table. The silence stretches, makes me nervous. It doesn't seem to bother Ellen. Maybe she's used to it.

'Will I open the bottle?' I say. 'Pour you a glass?' I will her to say yes. Give me something to do, now that I've sorted the salad. Make a bit of noise. She smiles, nods. I get busy, rattling around the cutlery drawer, finding the corkscrew, opening a cupboard, getting a glass out. The wine opens with a pop that sounds much louder than it should.

I don't know what I was thinking. Saying yes to dinner. Awkward as hell. I look at my watch before I remember that I've forgotten to pick it up. Again. I'd say it's half-time at the five-a-side. Kenny's probably limping by now.

She swills the wine around the glass, lifts it to her face, inhales it, just like she does with the coffee.

I could do with a coffee now. The machine on the counter looks expensive. I wonder if she has a grinder.

I sit on the other high stool, opposite her. Cast around for something to say. Eventually, I come up with, 'Do you miss being a doctor?'

Surprises her, the question. She wasn't expecting that. You can see it in the way she sets her glass down, carefully. Picks up the bottle and pours another measure in. Slowly. Buying a bit of time. Eventually she says, 'No.'

Now, I am surprised. I was expecting her to say yes. She seems like someone who would be a good doctor. Careful.

She shakes her head, slow and deliberate as though for emphasis. 'No,' she says again, 'I really don't.'

'The hours can be brutal, can't they?'

She shakes her head again. 'It's only now I'm realising that I never really wanted to be a doctor. It's just . . . it was assumed. My parents were doctors, my brother's a vet, my great-grand-father and grandfather, a couple of uncles, aunts, cousins – all doctors. It's like a pandemic, running through the family.'

'Better than swine flu, all the same,' I say, and she smiles.

'I did medicine in Trinity. I was good at that bit. Studying and assignments and projects and all that. It was after I qualified and started working that I realised it wasn't really for me. But I kept on with it. It never occurred to me to do anything else. Besides, I was busy. You don't get much time to think when you're busy.' She looks at me with a small shrug of her shoulders. 'How about you?'

'Me?'

'Have you been in the taxi business for long?'

I shake my head. 'About eight years now. Feels longer.'

'You don't like it?'

'What's to like? But it pays the bills, I suppose, if you put the hours in. And it's flexible too, so I can manage with the kids.'

There's a pause then and she looks away, towards the oven.

I jump into the space where the conversation has faltered and say, 'I'm a carpenter by trade. I liked that.' I miss being a carpenter. I don't say that. Sounds a bit poncy. 'I had my own business. In demand I was, back in the day.' I laugh to take the brag out of it. Sounds like I'm trying to impress her. But it's true. We *were* in demand. Me and my employees. Only two of them and one just an apprentice. But still. Used to get such a kick out of it. Answering the phone, saying, 'Good morning, Boland's Joinery, how can I help you?' Even Janine couldn't have faulted my phone manner back then.

She looks at me, nods. 'I thought there was something creative about you, alright.'

'Hardly creative. Although we did a bit of the bespoke stuff for a while. At the height of it. 2004. That was a mad year. Out the door with work, we were.'

Sometimes I think about the pieces I made back then. Things that people were only dying to throw money at in the boom. Huge, wall-mounted wine racks, blanket boxes, built-in units for fifty-inch plasma screens, vast bookshelves, rocking chairs, garden furniture. Perhaps still in place, in abandoned houses, repossessed by the banks. The idea that Ellen thinks there's something creative about me feels . . . yeah, it feels nice. Good. Like there's more to me than just driving people around. Taking them wherever they want to go.

'What about you? Did you work in a hospital or a private practice or what?'

She picks up her glass, takes a sip, sets it down. 'We set up a clinic, Neil and I. A practice. In Rathfarnham. That's where we lived.'

'Neil? He's your husband?'

'Was.'

'He's not in the picture any more?'

A brief pause. Then, 'No.'

She leans across the counter to pick a tortilla chip out of the bowl between us. I smell something lemony. Her hair, maybe. And something else. Something burning. I stand up. 'The bread,' I say, pointing at the oven. 'Oh!' she says, reaching for the oven gloves.

It ends up being a lovely evening. Any initial awkwardness I might have felt disappears. I wonder why I felt awkward in the first place. Or even if I did.

I set the table, she rescues the bread, stirs something around a pot, pours me a glass of pink lemonade, which turns out to be

166

lovely. 'Refreshing,' I say, and try not to think about what Kenny would say if he could see me now, drinking home-made lemonade out of a wine glass with my pinkie sticking out.

We eat. It's delicious. Nothing from a tin or the freezer. I try not to wolf it.

'The salad's lovely,' I say. 'Very nicely tossed.'

She smiles at that. We say 'cheers', clink our glasses like we're a couple in a restaurant. I have the one glass of wine. Rude not to. I'm not a big wine fan but it's not bad. 'Robust,' I say, and Ellen smiles.

Bowls of ice cream and tinned peaches for dessert. Ellen apologises. 'I'm not good at desserts.' Afterwards, I offer to make the coffee. I'm dying to have a go on the machine. No grinder. But a fresh bag of good coffee, all the same. Fair trade.

When I think back, it's hard to remember everything we talked about. But it was good, the conversation. It flowed between us. I'm pretty sure about that.

She seemed interested in the kids. What class they were in, what hobbies they had, the usual. I wondered about her then. If she'd ever wanted kids. Her and Neil.

I told her a few taxi stories. The little American with the goatee who wanted to know why we have traffic lights on the roundabouts. 'Just . . . you know . . . to be sure, to be sure,' I told him. He laughed all the way to his hotel. He rang his ma to tell her. Mom, he called her. It was four o'clock in the morning in New York. He said his mom didn't mind.

Ellen told me a doctor joke:

Patient: I feel invisible.

Doctor: NEXT!

I'd say she was a good doctor, no matter what she says. Something about her voice; discreet and low. Something about the way she doesn't fidget. The way she listens. The stillness of her.

I look at my phone. Ten o'clock. 'I'd better make tracks, I told

Kerry I'd be home by half ten,' I say. We're on the couch now, at either end. She sits with her legs stretched on a stool in front of her, her flip-flops dangling over the edge of it. I wonder about the accident then. What happened.

I realise that I haven't really noticed her scar this evening. I mean, it's there, of course it is. But I just . . . I don't know . . . I haven't seen it, I suppose.

'Thanks for coming over,' she says.

'Don't mention it.' I swear to God, that's what I say. *Don't mention it.* Tool.

There's a pause then and I wonder, for a horrible moment, if she expects me to invite her to my house. For dinner. Spaghetti Bolognese and Kerry shouting the odds from her bedroom? No way.

She picks up her crutches, propped against the arm of the couch, and stands up. 'As I said, you're my first guest since . . . well, since forever, really. I'm glad I remembered how to . . . you know, how to do things.' She waves an arm towards the kitchen so I'm assuming she's talking about dinner and the fact that it's not from a tin and that.

I stand up. I have to get my jacket, my car keys. They're in the kitchen. I make a move. She follows me. I'm aware of her, walking behind me. If I stop walking, she'll bump into the back of me. I slow down in the kitchen, just enough to lift the jacket from the back of the chair, slide the keys off the table. I keep moving. I'm in the hall now. Here's the hall door. This is the bit I'm anxious about. The bit at the door.

What about a handshake? A bit formal? I have to do something and she might get the wrong impression if I lean in for a peck on the cheek.

In the end, I stop at the door, turn and smile and say, 'Thanks for a lovely evening,' like a right plonker. I turn back towards the door and now I'm fumbling at the latch, trying to get the bloody thing to open.

She says, 'Here. I'll do it.' Steps forward. The hall is so narrow, it feels like she's right up against me even though she's not, and then she opens the door and turns back to me, reaches up and kisses the side of my face.

No awkwardness. No fumbling around like an eejit. Just her, reaching for my face with her mouth. A brush more than a kiss. Soft.

'Goodnight, Vinnie. Thanks for everything.'

'Yeah, goodnight now, take care.'

I'm wondering how to negotiate the confines of the doorframe with her standing there and that's when she moves back, graceful as a dancer even with the crutches, standing in the shadows. She tucks a stray piece of hair behind her ear and smiles at me, and that's when I realise just how pretty she is.

I open the door wide and wedge the toes of my left foot between the door and the floor. Women always say that men have low pain thresholds and in my case, it's true. It's all I can do not to howl with the pain.

I manage to say goodnight and walk away. I try not to hobble but I'm pretty sure that's what I do, all the same.

Dear Neil,

I found the baby books in one of the boxes. What To Expect When You're Expecting. *All those ones.*

She would have been five months today. I wonder what we would have done. Would we have marked the day in some small way?

I'd like to think we would have noticed it at least. Mentioned it to each other, perhaps in a congratulatory way, stopped for a moment to take a little pride in our achievement.

I still get those emails. The ones from that website I registered with when I found out.

The last email talked about 'little games'. Dropping things just to watch us pick them up. It says, 'Don't tell her "no".'

Once you got used to the idea of the baby, you were great. So excited. We both were. We would have played the little games. We wouldn't have told her 'no'.

Or perhaps we wouldn't have noticed the five month anniversary. We would have dropped her at the crèche on our way to the clinic, perhaps kissed her fat little cheek. I always imagined her as chubby, a great feeder, smiley. She might have waved at us. A jerky, uncoordinated wave. The email said, 'Waving is a possibility at five months but not to worry if your child hasn't mastered this particular skill!!'

Lots of exclamation marks in each update!!!! Perhaps because everything is new and exciting.

I wish we hadn't fought so bitterly that last day. It should have been water under the bridge by then, your indiscretion, as you called it. Even now, writing this, my fingers thump against the keyboard. Regret. Such a hopeless noise. I said I forgave you but it turns out, forgiveness isn't as easy as all that.

I managed to make a very acceptable dinner for Vinnie the other night. I can see you raise your eyebrows in that wry, amused way you have and yes, you were much better than me. But I can cook. It's just . . . you used to do most of it, especially during those last months.

Beef Wellington; your swan song.

I found your pasta-making machine today. In one of the boxes. I might make ravioli for Mum. About time I did something nice for her.

Dr Deery isn't all that interested in ravioli. She is, however, interested in Vinnie. I tell her I'm taking her advice. Interacting with people, like she's always encouraging me to do. I want her to be pleased with me. I know she's often disappointed with my contribution. I'm used to being top of the class, as you know. She offered a cautious 'That's good' when I told her I'd walked to the shops to get the ingredients for dinner, instead of ordering online.

Then she asked me why.

She always asks why.

'Why did you walk to the shops instead of ordering online?'

I said I didn't know. I hate saying I don't know. Although I think it's something to do with spring. It's pushing in on all sides. Making me notice things. Bright green shoots rising out of the muck and the way the light lingers in the evening and the surprising warmth of the morning sun on my back when I walked home from the deli last Wednesday with a bulging shopping bag, just like an ordinary person on an ordinary day walking home to an ordinary flat to make an ordinary dinner.

I felt ordinary. It was nice.

Dr Deery nods as if I haven't said, 'I don't know.' As if I've answered her question and she agrees with whatever I've said. Christ, I'd hate her job.

She wants to know what Vinnie said. About the scar. And the crutches.

I said he didn't say anything.

She nods, and writes something in that annoying notebook of hers. Maybe 'Vinnie'. And a smiley face.

Ellen

Twenty Three

It's been fifteen months. Longer. Since I've kissed anyone.

I'm on the escalator in Arnotts on Thursday evening when I work it out. Finn tugs my hand. 'Can we get a milkshake after we get my First Holy Communion outfit, Dad?'

'OK.'

I should be thinking about something else. There's loads of stuff I could be worrying about. Tonnes.

I kissed three girls before Paula. Marjorie Brennan, Anna Fitzpatrick and Siobhan Burdock. Marjorie Brennan always had bits of food in between her teeth. Anna Fitzpatrick was the only girl in the class who had braces and I worried I might somehow get snagged on them. Number three was Siobhan Burdock. A wet kisser. I remember the skin around my mouth, soaked afterwards. She took my hand and clamped it against her breast, moved it around. It should have been more exciting.

Then I kissed Paula, one dull day in March. We were sharing a smoke in Fairview Park. In the middle of a copse of trees, so we wouldn't be spotted in our school uniforms. I thought about it for ages before I did it. I put my hand on her shoulder. The relief when she didn't shrug it off. The softness of her lips. The sudden ferocity of my erection. Her shiver when I put my fingers on her neck. 'Are you cold?' I said, zipping up my coat so she couldn't see the telltale strain against the crotch of my trousers.

She shook her head. 'Do that again,' she said.

Four girls. That was it. I would have been fine with that. I would have kissed Paula until I was too old to stoop to reach her. A quivering, forgetful old man, bending on arthritic knees. That was my plan. Not that I formulated a plan in any strict sense.

At the bottom of the escalator, Finn slips his hand into mine. 'If I get lost, I'll go to the security guard in the shop and tell him my name, OK?'

'You won't get lost.'

'I know, but if I do, I'll give the security guard your mobile number. I know it off by heart.'

My phone rings. It's Ma. 'Why aren't you at home?'

'I'm out with Finn. Is everything OK?'

'I'm just back from my yoga class. Saw the lights off. I was worried.'

'Yoga? You haven't been able to touch your toes since 1956.'

'Yoga's not about touching your toes, Vincent. It's about centring yourself.'

'Right.'

'Where are you?'

'Arnotts.'

'Don't tell me you're buying the poor lad's get-up for his Communion.'

'OK, then, I won't.'

'I told you that Margie and me would bring him. Margie does the window display at the Vincent de Paul charity shop. She has a great eye.'

'I have to go, Ma.'

'What about Kerry?'

'I left her in Topshop. She promised to buy something suitable for Finn's big day.'

'Don't impulse buy, whatever you do.'

The sales assistant has the brisk manner of someone who loves telling people that she doesn't suffer fools gladly.

'What size is he?'

'Size? I'm . . . not sure. He's seven. Seven years old.'

She sighs and snaps a measuring tape off a clip on her belt. Wraps it around Finn's waist, then down his leg. 'Wait for me in the changing room,' she says, straightening.

She's back in two minutes. Maybe sooner. Hands me three suits. Navy pinstripe. Beige linen. A dark brown double-breasted one with a waistcoat. Each fits perfectly.

'I'd recommend the brown one. It'll hide all manner of stains.'

'I like this one,' says Finn, pointing at the beige linen.

'A devil to iron,' she says, regarding me with pale, suspicious eyes. 'And it's dry-clean only. Even then, you'd never get chocolate out of it.'

I look at Finn. His little face with his big brown eyes and his mop of dark hair. Everyone says he's the image of me but I don't see it. A handsome devil, Janine says. He has his hands clasped together in front of him, imploring me. Or sending a quick prayer upstairs.

'We'll take this one,' I say, picking up the beige linen suit.

'Suit yourself,' she says, looking me up and down. 'What about you?'

'What about me?'

'You're going to need something snazzy for the occasion.'

'Ah, no, I'm . . .'

Finn tugs at my sleeve. 'You will, Dad. Callam's mam bought his dad a new suit. It's yellow.'

The woman looks appalled. 'Yellow?'

Finn nods. 'And she won't let him wear his runners with it even though he says the shoes she got are hurting his bunions. She says it's the shoes or the spare room and there's no bed in the spare room, only a stool and you couldn't sleep on a stool, could you?'

In the end, the sales assistant persuades me into a grey jacket. Charcoal, she calls it – and a pair of black jeans, a white shirt and a tie that I'm never going to wear. I draw the line at the man bag.

Apart from anything else, it's two hundred and fifty euros. I can understand why men end up buying them, though, with yer woman on the job. She insists that I try everything on. Steps back. Looks me up and down. Nods. Says, 'You'll do.'

Finn is more effusive. 'You look deadly, Dad. Even better than Adam's dad and he was in an ad.'

'What ad?'

'For dog food. Pedigree Chum, I think.'

Kerry texts me.

Bought a 'suitable' outfit ;) Thanks for the money. I'm getting the bus home now, OK?

I text back.

OK.

She was supposed to meet us afterwards. Still, I text 'okay.' I think it's because of the winky face. She doesn't usually do winky faces.

Three hundred and twenty-eight euros, the lot. I hand her my credit card. I'm pretty sure there's enough room on it for the clobber. Still, I'm relieved when it goes through. I'll have to make inroads into that. Pick up a few more shifts.

Finn makes a terrible racket with his milkshake, his cheeks dented with the effort of sucking the stuff up through the straw. I get a double espresso. You'd need something after shopping.

'Are we poor, Dad?'

'No. Why d'ya ask?'

'We never get the Kellogg's cornflakes like Callam. We get the Centra ones.'

'They're just as good.'

'Yeah.' He drains the cup, takes the lid off, licks inside.

'Is this bad manners?' he says.

'Yeah.'

'Why didn't you tell me to stop?'

'I was just about to.'

'Do you think I'll get loads of money for my Communion?'

'You're not supposed to be thinking about the money. It's about the . . . whatdoyacallit . . . receiving the body and blood and that.'

'It's weird, isn't it? Drinking someone's blood.'

'It's wine, really.'

'Does wine taste like blood?'

I remember the wine at Ellen's house the other night. Robust, I'd said. Eejit. Made her laugh, all the same. 'No, wine is made from grapes.'

'Does it taste like grapes?'

'Not really.'

'Do you want to hear my sins?'

'What sins?'

'For the confession. We've to say our sins.'

I'd love another coffee. 'Go on, then.'

'I told Granny a lie, I said a bad word, I stayed up past my bedtime when you were in the pub, I didn't brush my teeth on Monday and I stole an apple from Mrs Finnegan's tree.'

'There are no apples on Mrs Finnegan's tree. It's April.'

'I didn't really steal one but teacher says you have to have five sins and I couldn't think of another one.'

'It might be better if you don't mention me being in the pub.'

'Why not?'

'Just . . . because.'

'Are you not supposed to be in the pub?'

'No, I am, it's just . . . you probably don't need to go into that much detail.'

'But if I say that you weren't in the pub, would that not be a lie?'

'No . . . just . . . Do you want another milkshake?'

'Yes, please.'

*   *   *

Kerry and Mark are sitting at either end of the couch when me and Finn get home. Red faces on the pair of them.

I look at the clock on the mantelpiece. Do a quick calculation. They've been here for twenty minutes at the most. But teenage boys can manage a fair bit in twenty minutes.

'Shouldn't you be doing your homework?'

'I did it at school.'

'How about some studying?'

'Went to the library at lunchtime.'

'Right.' It could be true. She did really well in her mocks. She must be doing something.

'I'm sure your mother will be wondering where you are, Mark.' You always mention the mothers. They're the ones who'll be wondering. You never say fathers.

'She knows I'm here.'

'It's time for you to go.' It comes out abruptly. Like a command. Too late to take it back now. It does the trick, all the same. Mark stands up.

'See ya tomorrow,' he tells Kerry. There's something a little unflappable about him. I can't seem to insult him enough.

The kitchen is in rag order. Press doors open. Weetabix stuck like cement to the sides of cereal bowls on the table. Kerry's schoolbag on a chair. Finn's football boots spilling from a bag on the floor. The sink full of brown, greasy water. I pull the plug. Pick up the dishcloth. Sniff it. Bin it.

Kerry and Mark are still at the front door. I'm in the kitchen but the draught down the hallway has slammed the kitchen door shut and the only way I can see what's going on is to look through the keyhole and briefly, I consider it. I really do.

She crashes through the kitchen door, the handle banging off the wall, crumbling another piece of plaster.

'Take it easy, will you?'

'What did you have to do that for?' She stands there, hands on her hips. She's giving the impression that she's mad as hell but her eyes are bright and I'm afraid she might cry and I haven't got a clue what I'd do then. Not a notion.

'I'm protecting you. Trying to.'

'You don't trust me,' she says then.

'It's him I don't trust.'

'Why not?'

'He's fifteen, love. I know what fifteen-year-old boys are like.'

'You were going out with Mam when you were fifteen.'

'Yeah, and maybe we were too young.'

'That's easy to say now. When you've wrecked it all.'

'I didn't wreck it. Things happened.' I make a huge effort to lower my voice. 'It's . . . it's not easy to understand when you're a kid. It's . . . complicated.'

'I'm not a kid. And that's a cop-out. Saying it's complicated. That's what adults say when they can't think of anything else.' She turns her back to me and I know that she's crying now. Doesn't want me to see. 'Listen, Kerry, love, I . . .'

She rushes to the door, opens it, slams it behind her. I hear her feet thumping up the stairs. I hear my breath charging through my body. I put my hands on the back of a kitchen chair. Lean on it.

It's easy to do the wrong thing with your kids. I'm always amazed how easy it is. I should go up to her. Talk to her. Tell her she's right. It *is* a cop-out. Saying it's complicated. Tell her I don't have the answers. Tell her I'm doing my best and that I know it's not always good enough.

Tell her I try. I fall short.

Talk to her. That's what I should do.

I put the kettle on, go out the back garden, smoke a cigarette. There are times when I'm pretty sure I'm not a good father. I try not to think about it, mostly. Just get on with it. But there are times – like now – when I'm positive.

179

Twenty Four

The limo rolls into the depot. Kenny hops out, gets the clothes brush from the shelf and sweeps it along the legs and sleeves of his tuxedo. 'Very hairy man in the Stretch this afternoon. I think he was moulting.'

When he's finished, he walks towards me and Janine and puts his hand on my shoulder. He got real touchy-feely after those mindfulness classes he took during the boom and he hasn't been able to break the habit. 'So, how did it go the other night, Vinnie?'

They're both eyeballing me.

'Grand.'

'Late night, was it?' he says, nudging Janine and winking.

'No.'

'And did you manage a spot of . . .?' Kenny reaches for Janine's waist with both hands.

'Getoffme,' she says, flicking his ear with a lethal fingernail.

'That hurt, so it did,' he says, wounded.

'Well, keep your hands to yourself, then or I'll knock you sideways with a sexual harassment claim.'

'But you love a bit of sexual harassment, you're always complainin' that no one does it any more, how PC the world's gone.'

'That's neither here nor there,' she says, picking up the phone. 'Good afternoon, Any Road Taxis and Limousines, Janine speaking, how may I help you today?' she says in a voice that is unrecognisable as her own.

I'm kept busy for most of the morning and that's just the way I like it. Less time for thinking about things. There's an unemployed solicitor on his way to another interview in the back seat when Ellen texts me. I'm stopped at lights, which is good, because it gives me a bit of a start, the text. Like she knew I was thinking about her.

Hi, Vinnie. I found a key down the back of the couch. Maybe it fell out of your pocket the other night? I'm having a check-up at the hospital later. I could meet you in town and give it to you if that's convenient? Ellen

A key? I'm not missing one. It could be Kenny's spare front door key. He gave it to me after that time he was away with his mother – auditioning for *The Voice*; a duet, apparently. Months ago now. Must have been in that pocket all this time. I'd say he's forgotten I have it. I certainly don't need it back in a hurry.

I text back.

Great. Was wondering where that was. Can meet in an hour if that suits? Vinnie

I drop the solicitor at Citywest, then head back into town, park the motor and ring Janine. Tell her I'm taking an hour off.

'You're what?'

'I'm due a break, amn't I?'

'You never take breaks.'

'I'm taking one today.'

'Are the kids OK?'

'They're grand.'

'What's goin' on?'

'Nothing.'

'You know I'll get it out of you, Vinnie. Might as well tell me now. Make it easier on yourself.'

'I'll tell you later.' It's the only way I'll get her off the blower.

Ellen is already at the corner of Merrion Square when I arrive, a solitary figure standing alone, the crowds moving around her, careful not to jostle her. She's back in her long black coat, her hair hidden under a black beret, tilted so it covers a lot of the scar, the crutches on either side. A small, brief smile moves across her face when she sees me.

'Hi, Vinnie,' she says. There's a smudge of lipstick on the corner of her mouth, as if she applied it without a mirror. In the back of a cab on the way in, maybe.

She hands me the key and that's when it starts raining. Lashing, the drops ricocheting off the pavement. All of a sudden, everyone's running.

'Here.' I take off my jacket and hold it over our heads, against the worst of the deluge. 'We should shelter til this stops.'

She nods towards the National Gallery behind us. 'The coffee is good in there.'

'That'll do.'

We walk towards the entrance, the rubber tips of her crutches making a squelching sound against the wet ground.

It's a beautiful building. I hadn't noticed that before. Elegant, I suppose. I've never darkened the door until now. I took the kids to the Natural History Museum once, a few doors up. A fair while ago now. Eerie, it was, the glassy, dark eyes of the stuffed animals following you from one end of the displays to the other. It wasn't long after Paula left. I took them loads of places then. Better than sitting in the house waiting for the next batch of questions I couldn't answer.

'This is boring,' Kerry said, more than once. Finn ran from one end of the place to the other, like one of the animals come back to life. The woman in charge told him to pipe down and that set him off again, crying and asking where his mammy was gone. I took them to McDonald's then. A bit of peace in my head while they got stuck in to their Happy Meals. You often see fathers in there with their kids. Weary but grateful. A sort of a refuge.

It isn't one particular thing that prompts us upstairs, into the gallery itself. It's a combination of circumstances. For starters, everyone has the same idea and by the time we get inside, the queue for the café is out the door. We stand in the foyer and that's when the man at the reception desk tells us that admission is free today because of some anniversary they're marking. Then there's the lift doors, sliding open as we walk past. Ellen looks at me and I shrug in an 'I don't mind' type of a way, although an art gallery is as alien to me as a beauty parlour, let's face it. Then a busload of Americans surrounds us and we're sort of swept, like driftwood, towards the lift in a sea of Aran jumpers and Kilkenny Design bags. Somehow, I've become a man who walks piers and drinks wine and strolls through art galleries.

I feel very unlike myself.

'I used to come here often,' Ellen says, stepping through a set of double doors. She knows her way around but her steps are cautious, like a climber negotiating a foothold.

I recognise some of the painters' names. Monet and Renoir. Makes me feel a bit less conspicuous. There are allsorts in here. All ages. Tracksuits and business suits. The Americans are decked out in truly shocking shades of green. Nobody pays a bit of notice to me.

In one of the rooms, Ellen sits on a bench in front of a painting. I can see only the right side of her face, the side that's not hurt. Her skin is quite flawless there, pale and still. It strikes me then how difficult it is, to have your injury, your story, I suppose, on display all the time. Like a finger pointing, drawing the attention of strangers.

Her feet look tiny in her runners. You'd never think she had such long, slender toes. The light of the day moves around her and is reflected in those curious amber eyes, transforming them from their pale yellowy-brown to a harvest orange.

She clocks me looking at her, turns her head towards me and

it's too late to look away so I just smile because what else can I do? I look at the painting then, wrap my hand around my chin. Concerned, I told her earlier. That's the way you look at a painting. Like you're *concerned*. She adopts my pose and looks at the painting too. Concerned. Maybe she's forgotten I was staring at her before. Not staring, exactly. Looking. I was looking.

'*The Meeting on the Turret Stairs*,' I say, reading the title of the painting.

'It's a farewell,' Ellen says. 'They were ill-fated lovers. Her brothers have been ordered by their father to kill him. They'll never be together again, so the story goes.'

'Uplifting,' I say.

'At least they get to say goodbye,' Ellen says, collecting her crutches and standing up.

It's in the café afterwards I think about what it would be like to kiss her. I think it's the way she puts her mouth around the rim of the cup. Sort of folds her bottom lip against it and tips the coffee inside. There's a lull in the conversation and she takes a sip of her coffee and that's what does it. I'm not usually like this. Even Janine says it. *There's nothing sleazy about you, Vinnie*, she says, shaking her head like it's an area I've neglected.

'Have you . . . seen anyone since your wife left?'

A head-butt. That's what the question feels like. I don't say anything.

Ellen colours. 'I'm sorry, that's none of my business, I don't know why I—'

'No, no, it's grand, it's just—'

'No, really. I've been on my own too much lately. I'm . . . inappropriate.'

I shake my head. 'I don't have the time, to be honest. The kids and the job, I'm pretty busy, y'know?'

She nods and pokes at the froth at the top of her coffee with the edge of a spoon.

'What about you?' I ask.

She shakes her head. A slow but fairly certain shake. 'No,' she says.

I'm thinking that's an end to that particular strand of conversation, when she looks up. 'I don't think I'm cut out for relationships.'

'I'm sure that's not true.'

She shakes her head again. 'I think it's a skill, being in a relationship. It doesn't suit some people.'

I'm shaking my head, disagreeing. But maybe there *is* some truth in it. In some ways, my life is easier since Paula left. The thought rises to the surface of my mind, like a piece of wreckage.

'I was married to my job,' Ellen says. 'We both were. We were good at that bit of the relationship. The business side of things. We were hardly ever in the same room together. We were like flatmates except we lived in a house instead of a flat and we didn't put our names on the butter and the milk in the fridge.' She smiles then, a small smile, an effort to take the sting out of it. Regret, perhaps. That one stings like a nettle, God knows.

I look at the clock on the wall. 'I better get going. Finn's got a football match at six and I've to get a few hours clocked before I take him.'

'I didn't think it was so late,' she says, looking at her watch, a little Timex on a narrow black leather strap.

'I've to pop in to Eason's. Kerry left her English play on the bus the other day. *Romeo and Juliet*. I've to get her a new one. But I can drop you home after that. The motor's parked around the corner.'

'Not at all, I'll get a cab.'

She stands without using her crutches, although her hands are on the table. I pick her coat off the back of her chair and hold it behind her so she can slide her arms inside, one at a time. Then I pick up her crutches, hand them to her. I worry then that I shouldn't have done that. She never mentions them, the crutches. But she smiles and says, 'Thanks, Vinnie,' in a way that makes me think she doesn't mind.

At the rank, she stops. 'This is me,' she says, tucking herself into the queue. I know some of the drivers on this rank. I could get her bumped up the line but something tells me she wouldn't appreciate that. Wouldn't like to draw attention to herself.

Here's me, being awkward again. Glancing about, shuffling my feet. I feel like I did the other night, like a boy on a first date. I'm a bit long in the tooth for that carry-on.

'I hope you didn't mind me dragging you around an art gallery,' she says, looking up.

'Wasn't as bad as I thought.' I grin, and she smiles.

'You won't be late for Finn, will you?' She looks worried.

'No, but I'd better head. You'll be alright here.' It's not a question. I make sure of that. She nods, and I head off at a clip.

It's like the season has infected me. There's a bit of a spring in my step.

Dear Neil,

I went back to the National Gallery the other day. I used to go there when I needed to think, remember? Or if I was stressed about something. Work, usually. I'd forgotten what a lovely space it is. It was like getting a call from an old friend.

I told Dr Deery about it after she'd commented on my unusually cheerful disposition. She didn't say 'unusually' but I could tell that's what she thought, all the same. I said I was there with Vinnie and she seemed unsurprised, even though we hadn't planned to go. It just ended up being one of those things. I think he liked it in the end. I think it took him by surprise.

Later, she asked me what I wanted to be when I was a child. I must have looked confused because she repeated the question.

My parents didn't wonder whether David and I were going to be doctors. They talked about the kind of doctor we would become. Orthopaedic surgeons or neurologists or GPs or vets.

Dr Deery nods and writes something in her notebook. One word, I think. 'Doctor', perhaps.

I remember when Faye's eldest was five and insisted on wearing a tutu and a sheriff's badge everywhere. To the shopping centre, even. He told me he was going to be a ballet dancer and a sheriff when he grew up. I don't remember David ever talking about being an astronaut. Or me dreaming about becoming, I don't know, a rock star or something outlandish like that.

Yes, I loved painting as a child. My mother funded art classes and workshops and materials and I understood it was a hobby.

I wonder about the baby then. Our daughter. Would we have presumed she would become a doctor, like the two of us? I want to say no. The person I am now – after everything – says no. But

187

if we were still together, still running the clinic, then . . . I don't know. Everything was so busy, so hectic back then. There was barely time to think.

Lots of time now. Too much time.

Dr Deery asks about the last time I painted a picture. I couldn't remember. I didn't even do Art for the Leaving Cert. She gives me an assignment. I am to paint something. Anything. I tell her I have no materials. She says that's part of the assignment. I have to buy things. Paper, paint, brushes.

OK, I say.

You can't buy them online, she says. You have to go to a shop. I open my mouth to protest. Maybe to say that I don't know where an art supply shop might be. She shakes her head with that smile of hers that manages to be both small and authoritative, and the arguments I had prepared are left unsaid and already I am thinking about the type of paint I might use and whether or not I will paint on paper or a piece of stretched canvas.

I know you'll be surprised. I am too. I ended up doing a charcoal sketch of the living room in the apartment. It was only when I finished I realised how empty it is. How devoid of stuff. It looked like a waiting room in some colourless institution. I tore it up.

I got Mum to sit for me in the end. I always liked people's faces. The stories they tell. Mum was embarrassed at first. 'I don't have any make-up with me.' I told her I'd paint on lipstick and eyeshadow and blusher. 'Russet,' she says, settling at last into the armchair. 'That's the colour of my lipstick.'

'Oh, mine too,' I say, surprised. I paint and we talk about brands of lipstick. She favours Max Factor. Has done for years. I switch between brands and can voice opinions on many of them. She likes this. I can tell. Her head nods, even though I told her not to move. She's making notes in her head. We've never done

*this before, she and I. Had an in-depth discussion about lipstick.
Not really a discussion. More like a chat. As we chat, I paint,
and she relaxes into the chair, forgets I am painting her.*

*'That's really good,' she says, when I'm finished. I am ridicu-
lously flattered. I say, 'It needs a lot of work,' and that's when
she puts her hands on my shoulders and looks at me. 'You've
always been hard on yourself.' That's what she says. For a
moment I think she's going to pull me against her long, thin
frame, hug me. We've never been tactile. Instead, she squeezes
my shoulders, nods at me. Then she walks into the kitchen and
takes two Marks & Spencer's dinners out of the bag she's
brought. She heats my meal first. 'You must be hungry after all
that painting,' she says, like I'm a kid and she's one of those
mothers who are in the kitchen when you get in from school,
with flour on their fingers and an apron on. I nod, and I'm not
just being polite this time.*

I'm hungry. I really am.

Ellen

Twenty Five

First Holy Confession. Finn practises his sins on the way to the church. We walk, Ma striding along, the pair of us struggling to keep up with her. 'We don't want to be late,' she says, when I suggest she slows down.

'Is it a sin to be late for your First Holy Confession?' Finn wants to know, getting ready to add it to his list.

Ma considers the question, then shakes her head. 'We're not going to be late, so it doesn't matter if it's a sin or not.'

'Yes, but *is* it a sin?'

'No, it's not' I say, looking down at him, his face shiny and pink from the vicious scrub Ma gave it with the facecloth before we left.

'I'll check with Father Murphy when I see him at the church spring clean,' Ma says, winking at him.

Finn nods and goes back to reciting his list. The morning is brisk and bright and there are the beginnings of tulips poking their heads above the earth along Mrs Finnegan's flower bed.

'Spring has sprung,' Ma says, when she sees them. I feel like that too.

I even did a bit of a spring clean in the house last night. After I dropped Ellen home from the clinic. Put a bit of John Lennon on the stereo. 'Working Class Hero'. 'He says the f-word in that song,' Kerry says, walking through the front room where I'm taking down the curtains. Grubby, they are. 'That's art,' I tell her.

'So I can use bad language so long as I sing it, is that it?' she says, smirking. I bundle the curtains, aim them at her and she shrieks and legs it.

By rights, I should be in bad form. Kenny rang when I was driving Ellen back to Clontarf. 'I'm really sorry, Vinnie. I can't go to the match on Saturday.'

'But it's Bohs and Rovers. You can't miss it.'

'Sorry, bud. No can do. I'd forgotten about the auditions for A *Streetcar Named Desire*. I'm goin' up for the part of Stanley Kowalski. It could be my big break, comrade.'

'It's the local amateur dramatics society, Kenny.'

'Everyone has to start somewhere.'

'So what am I supposed to do with your ticket?'

'Sell it on eBay.'

'I haven't a clue about eBay.'

'You'll get the hang of it, comrade. Listen, I've to go. Practise me lines.'

'OK.'

'Really sorry, Vinnie. I was all set for the match. Got the sheepskin coat back from that specialist dry-cleaner's on time an' all. They did a great job on it, mind. Looks as good as new.'

'Goodbye, Kenny.'

'Bad news?' says Ellen from the back.

I shrug. 'It's not life or death, I suppose. I have tickets for the Bohs match at Dalymount tomorrow night and Kenny's after pulling out on me.'

'Would you not go on your own?'

'Ah, yeah, I'll go, alright. Wouldn't miss it.' I glance in the rear-view mirror. 'Don't suppose you're a football fan, by any chance?'

She shakes her head. 'I've never been to a football match.'

'They're good craic. Great atmosphere.'

'Are you asking me to go?'

'No. I was just sayin'. They're enjoyable.'

191

Silence then. I look in the rear-view mirror and she's looking back at me. 'Why?' I say. 'Would you come if I asked you?'

'I might.'

'Well, then.'

'Well what?'

'Do you want to go?'

'You guarantee craic, atmosphere and enjoyment?'

'I can. And I'll throw in a hot dog at half-time.'

'I've never eaten a hot dog.'

'Well, here's your chance.'

So there I am, piling the curtains in the machine and thinking about Saturday night. It's not a date. It's football. Football is straightforward. Bohs at Dalyer playing Shamrock Rovers. Great atmosphere. A few songs. Hot dogs wrapped in paper napkins. Choice of mustard or ketchup. Cans of Coke. Easy as pie. No room for awkwardness. No need, when it's football.

The kids couldn't get over me with the rubber gloves on yesterday. It's not like I'm a stranger to the hoover or the Mr Sheen. But I went at it yesterday. Threw the windows open, aired the place out, filled two black bin liners with stuff I should have thrown out years ago. Bits of Finn's old toys, two broken clocks, a radio that hasn't worked in years, remote controls for tellies long retired, a box of tapes from the eighties, misshapen stumps of candles lining the tub in the bathroom. Paula loved candlelight when she was in the bath. She'd lie in there until the water got cold. I told her she'd set the place on fire some day.

The church is pretty packed. Not just Finn's class getting ready to confess. A few other schools in the area are here too. Most of them with their parents. The mothers powdered and perfumed and the dads balding and fidgety, wondering how long it's going to take.

Finn spots Callam and pulls at my hand til we're at their pew. I nod at Monica and her husband. Can't remember his name.

Dermot or Declan, maybe. Monica smiles at me. Her smiles are sometimes nervous, since the 'motherless' incident. They shuffle along the bench and we squeeze in. Finn and Callam begin a conversation in stage whispers.

'Ssshhh,' hisses Ma, leaning across me. 'It's a sin to talk in God's house.'

'But if you're talking to God, is it a sin?' Finn wants to know. I catch Dermot or Declan's eye and we share one of those parental expressions: a combination of knowing smile and pained grimace.

'Kneel down there and say a few prayers, like a good boy,' says Ma. 'You too, Callam, love.' If Monica is unimpressed with the religious instruction being doled out by my mother, she doesn't say.

Ma leans towards me, hisses in my ear, 'Where's Kerry? I thought you said she'd meet us at the church.'

'I did. She will.'

Ma consults her watch. 'She'll be late if she's not careful.'

'She'll be here,' I say, twisting my neck around to see if she's skulking at the back.

'Well, I hope she'll be dressed appropriately,' says Ma, pulling her rosary beads from her handbag. The cross glints in a line of sunlight that cuts through one of the small windows set high in the wall of the church.

'I told her to put something decent on.'

'Hmm,' is my mother's response. She doesn't sound convinced.

The kids don't go in the boxes any more. The confession boxes, with the wooden panel that slides back and reveals the side profile of the very priest you didn't want to get. They go to the altar now. No closed doors, no dark spaces, no whispered sins. So when it's Finn's turn, I can see him up there, troubling the priest – the youngest one, Fr McIntyre, I think – with the sins that he has learned by heart.

He used to be the smallest in the class. He's really stretched. He's still one of the skinniest, though. I should have brought him to the barber's yesterday. The fringe is halfway down his face. At least I remembered to put his uniform in the wash. Draped it on the radiator last night. Stiff this morning, but dry as kindling. I ironed the collar of his shirt. It's the only bit that you can see, so long as you don't take off the jumper. 'But what if it's really warm in the church?' Finn wants to know.

'It won't be. It's always like an icebox in that place.'

'But I'll be on the altar. The candles might be lit. They'd warm the place up, wouldn't they?'

'You'll be grand.'

'But what about—'

'OK, fine, hand us the bloody shirt.'

He opens his mouth and I say, 'I know, I know, that's a bad word, I shouldn't have said it.' He hands me the shirt and I get the iron out of the press again, plug it in, set up the ironing board and iron the rest of it. Takes me five minutes. Less. Should have done the whole thing in the first place. Another lesson learned.

Kerry arrives. I hear the clip-clop of high heels against the floorboards and I turn around and there she is, wearing Paula's shoes, a dangerously short skirt, a faceful of make-up and yer man, whatshisface, on her arm. Mark. Smirking at me like he knows I want to burst every spot on his face but I can't, on account of the First Holy Confession and the church and the priests and the kids and that.

They clatter into the pew beside us. Beam at me. The pair of them. Like they've been drinking. They wouldn't have been drinking, would they? It's not even noon. Teenagers don't drink before noon. Even awful ones. I struggle to remember me and Paula at that age. We drank, yeah. But at reasonable hours. And only on Saturday nights, surely? In Fairview Park. Paula went into The Plough on Abbey Street the odd time, if her auld lad had had a good day on the horses and slipped her a few quid. She'd put her hair up, a load of make-up on her face and her ma's high heels on her feet and she'd sail past the bouncer. Not like me. Even after I was eighteen, I had to bring my ID. Years I spent, getting slagged about my passport photograph.

The congregation stands, and when it looks like they're not going to bother their arses, I turn and frown at Kerry and Spot-For-Brains beside her, and eventually, with a great show of bad grace, they haul themselves up, sniggering and slouching. Something glints on the side of Mark's nose. A stud or a spot.

Finn's class lines up on the altar to sing a hymn. Kerry leans across me to say something to her granny. I don't smell drink off her. You'd smell it, wouldn't you? The alternative is that they're on a natural high. The pair of them. Happy. That's almost worse.

Ma nudges me in the ribs, making me grunt. 'Are you not taking any photos of the little fella?' she hisses, nodding towards Finn, who's walking in a line down the central aisle now, his hands clasped and his face a massive grin. 'I can't wait til it's over, Dad,' he said this morning.

'Why?'

'Because then I'll be absolved of all my sins.'

'Oh, right.'

'Except my original sin, of course. That's a stain on my soul forever.'

'Really?'

'Yeah, on account of Eve eating the apple in the garden of Eden, remember? She wasn't supposed to do that. It was the only thing she wasn't supposed to do so that's why they couldn't stay in the garden, see?'

I nodded. Kenny is right. I should have sent him to the Educate Together.

I take three photos, one of the side of Finn's head, one of the back of his head and one with his eyes closed. I'll take more outside. Have to make a fuss of him. His First Confession. He'd been worried about the penance but he only got one Our Father in the end, which, compared to Callam's two Our Fathers, three Hail Marys and one Glory Be, was pretty good going, Finn reckoned.

It's only when we get outside that I realise Mark is wearing make-up and it's just possible that Kerry put it on him because it's pretty much the same as hers: white face and eyes ringed with thick black pencil.

Kerry gives me a Champions League final smile.

'What do you want?' I say.

'Just a tenner.'

'What for?'

'Credit for my phone.'

'I gave you money for credit on Wednesday. That can't be gone already.'

She blows a bubble with her chewing gum, bigger and bigger until it bursts all over her face. Mark laughs. He's like a hyena, I swear to God. Except worse. Worse than a hyena. I'd paste him up against the wall of the church if I thought I could get away with it. And the funny thing is, I'm not usually violent.

I take my wallet out of my back pocket. Look inside, take a twenty out. 'I want change,' I tell her. I always forget. She knows that. No wonder I'm always broke. I'll be driving taxis until I'm ready for the grave.

'Are yiz not coming to the reception?' Ma says grandly, as Kerry and that yoke move away.

Kerry grabs Mark's hand. Smirks. 'Would you like to go to the parish hall and drink tea with little old ladies and kiddies? It'll be great fun!'

'Don't be smart,' I say.

'There's buns and fizzy drinks too,' Finn says.

'Who are you calling a little old lady?' Ma says, drawing herself up to her full height.

'I didn't mean you, Granny,' Kerry says, smiling, giving Ma one of her sudden, quick hugs. She gets Finn in a headlock, teases his fringe with her hand til it stands on end, crackling with static. 'Later, kiddo.' She walks away at a trot, Mark in her wake.

'What time will you be home?' I call after her.

'I won't be late,' she calls back, without turning around.

We make our way to the reception in the parish hall where we are offered thin sandwiches, thick slices of Madeira cake and cups of grey-looking tea.

'This is deadly, Dad, isn't it?' says Finn, pausing as he races by me with Callam. He has a can of Coke in his hand and two jelly snakes hanging out of either side of his mouth.

I take a sip of cold, weak tea. 'Yeah, it's great.'

'So,' says Monica, brushing dandruff off her husband's jacket. 'You all set for the big day? Finn says you're getting a bouncy castle. That's lovely.'

Fuck. The bouncy castle. He mentioned it ages ago and I said I'd look into it.

'You're on the ball,' Monica goes on. 'I had to ring loads of places before I managed to get one and that was months ago.' She turns to her husband. 'Will you stop shuffling, you're making me nervous.'

'It's these shoes. They're killing me, so they are.' I look at the shoes, shiny and stiff, just out of their box. I would have gone for the spare room with the stool.

Bouncy castles. I'll have to sort something out. Kenny might know someone.

'Ma, are you doing anything tonight? Only I'm going to Dalyer and I'm not sure if Kerry will be home before I've to leave.'

'Well, it's the semi-final of the Stars in Their Eyes competition at the Nifty Fifties tonight,' she says, removing the crust from a quarter of a ham-and-egg sandwich, pushing it into her mouth and swallowing it down with a mouthful of the terrible tea.

'I suppose I could be at your house at seven, if that's any good to you? I've the film appreciation at five, but I won't stay for the talky bit. Desperate wafflers, some of them.'

'What about Stars in Their Eyes?'

'That shower!' she says, slamming her cup on the table so the remaining tea clears the rim and forms a puddle on the paper tablecloth.

Why did I open my mouth?

'They knocked me out in the quarter-finals. It's not who you do, it's who you know in that place.'

'I thought you knew everyone. And who did you, eh, do?'

She allows herself a small smile. 'Yer woman. That French one. *Je ne regrette rien*.' Here's where she starts singing. When she sings, she seems old. Properly old. Her voice is wheezy and breathless. It's also fairly tuneless, and that's me being nice.

> *Non, je ne regrette rien*
> *Ni le bien qu'on m'a fait*
> *Ni le mal; tout ça m'est bien égal.*

She has her eyes closed now; her left hand is circling, like she's washing a window. I put my hand on her shoulder. A gentle hint. She shrugs it off.

Non, je ne regrette rien . . .

It's Finn who manages to stop her in the end. He and Callam are attempting a trick Callam saw on the telly. Where you yank the edge of a tablecloth and pull it clean off the table without disturbing any of the bits on it.

They manage to yank the tablecloth off the table, but not without disturbing the bits. There's an almighty clatter as teacups and pots and saucers and plates meet a fairly sticky end on the floor of the parish hall.

'It worked when I saw it on the telly,' Callam says, as his mother pulls him away from the debris.

I find some kitchen paper, tear a wad off the roll and bend to mop up the worst of the spillage before someone slips on it.

'What's going on?' says Ma, opening her eyes and lowering her hand.

'Sorry, Dad,' says Finn.

'It's alright son. Grab the bin over there. I'll put the broken bits into it.'

'I really wanted to get through today without sinning.'

'That was an accident, not a sin.'

'Are you sure?'

'Positive.'

'Phew.' He runs to get the bin and I watch the skinny little streak of him. A rasher. That's what I used to call him when he was brand new. 'How's my rasher?' I'd say when I picked him out of his little basket. I don't know why. There's nothing all that great about rashers. He was a great baby, though. They both were, really. 'It's nothing to do with the babies being good,' the doctor told me. 'It's the hormones. The hormones can act up sometimes.' That's not how he put it exactly but that's the general gist. The hormones. They can run amok. I knew about the hormones but I thought they kicked in *during* the pregnancy, not afterwards.

We had some of our best times when Paula was pregnant. Me rubbing the bio-oil into her bump. Like a football it was, perfectly round. A zip-off bump, Maureen called it. Some women look like they're carrying the baby all over their bodies but Paula never had a pick on her, apart from the enormous bump out front. She looked like she might topple over, it was that big.

And the sex. Well, it was pretty amazing when she was pregnant, being honest. I was a bit funny about it, what with the baby an' all, but she insisted. I'd meet fellas in the pub the odd night and they'd slag me, sympathise and offer me the lend of their blow-up dollies to tide me over. They hadn't a clue. She rang me at work when she was expecting Finn. Right in the middle of a shift. In the middle of a fare.

'You've to come home.'

'Jaysus, is it the baby?' Doing a U-turn so fast, my fare bangs his head off the back of the passenger seat.

'I need a ride.'

'To the hospital?' Skid marks along the road, as the engine roars.

'No, you big eejit. I've another three months to go.'

'So the baby's not coming?'

'No, but I might not be either if you don't get your skinny little arse back here, pronto.' She hangs up.

I spot a rank ahead, indicate, pull in to the kerb. Turn to my fare in the back, who's rubbing his forehead and wincing.

'Sorry about that,' I say.

He shakes his head. 'Your first time?'

I stare at him, wondering if I'd hit the speaker button on the phone in my panic.

'Eh, well, it's just . . .'

'I remember my wife ringing me to tell me that she was in labour with our first baby.' He's smiling now, marinating in the memory.

'The thing is . . .'

'Don't worry, I won't delay you. You've an important job to get to. I understand.'

'Yeah.'

He reaches into his pocket, hands me the fare and a nice tip. 'For the day that's in it,' he says, with a wide smile.

I spend the tip on flowers. She flings them on the floor when I hand them to her, pulls me through the hall door. Slams it shut with her foot. We make it as far as the stairs this time. I have a red mark on my back for hours afterwards, where the edge of the step digs into my skin.

'I can't believe you stopped at the garage to pick up flowers,' she says afterwards.

'I didn't get them in a garage,' I say.

'It was an emergency. You should have come straight home.'

Sometimes, I didn't know if she was being serious or not. I grinned at her. Drew the hair off her neck, kissed her there.

'You'll know next time, right?'

'I'm only in the company a wet week. I can't be ducking off home for no reason.'

'No reason?' She sits up. Slides her hand up my leg. 'God, I love your cock.'

She said stuff like that. Deadpan.

Christ, the sex. Glorious, it was. I suppose a part of that is youth. Maybe everyone's memories of youthful sex are glorious. But I don't think I believe that. And that's not me blowing my own trumpet or anything. I'm nothing special. But with Paula, I felt pretty special. She could make me feel like that.

Any time she wanted.

Pity I couldn't do the same for her.

Twenty Six

I love everything about Dalymount Park. Dad supported Bohemians – Bohs – all his life and me and Joey followed suit. He'd bring us to the matches, often as he could. Sit us on his shoulders on the walk home. Stride home, he would, like it was nothing, having me and Joey up there. He'd get us a bag of chips to share and I'd lean down and feed one into his mouth every so often. He'd shout 'CHIP' and I'd slot one in and he'd pretend to bite my fingers and I'd whip my hand away, real quick, laughing, lick the salt and vinegar off the tops of my fingers and sit up there, watching the city settle into night and the people below, tiny from up there, scurrying along with their shopping in plastic bags.

The smell of the newly mown grass on the pitch, the heave of the crowd, the roar when a goal is scored, the strained silence before a penalty is taken. My fifth birthday was the first time. It never fades, the feeling. When I walk into the place.

I meet Ellen outside the stadium. I offered to pick her up but she said no, she'd meet me there. 'I've been studying,' she tells me when we meet. She fishes a book out of her bag. Holds it up. *Football for Dummies*. 'I ordered it last Friday,' she says. 'I wanted to get to grips with the basics before the match.' She looks at me and colour creeps across her face then, as if she is embarrassed by the purchase.

I smile, oddly touched. The trouble she took.

She's wearing jeans, boots and one of those padded, puffy jackets that Kenny calls the devil's work. She's got a black and red scarf tonight. The Bohs colours. I wonder if it's a coincidence. The scarf, wrapped around her head and neck like a cowl, covers the scar, which I presume is the purpose of it. I worry about the crutches in the crowd. I don't think she's all that used to crowds. She doesn't mention it but perhaps walks a little slower than usual.

I get coffees from one of the vans parked outside. 'Wrap your hands around that,' I say. 'It'll warm you up.' The sun is sliding towards the horizon, like an egg yolk, runny on a plate. Whatever heat there was in the day has lifted into the clear sky, darkening now. Azure. I didn't know it was a colour until last week, when Kenny was buying that Fred Perry shirt on eBay.

She takes the cup and smiles. 'Thanks, Vinnie.' She pulls the scarf away from her face, lifts the lid and inhales the steam.

'What's wrong with that lady's face, Dad?' A kid, about Finn's age, walks past us. His dad grabs his hand, yanks him along, grimaces an apology at me, doesn't even look at Ellen. 'You're hurting my hand, Dad.' The kid starts to cry but the man continues to pull him along until we can't hear him any more.

I feel my face flush with embarrassment. This is my place, after all. My suggestion. Ellen seems unconcerned. We finish our coffees. 'Should we take our seats now?' she asks.

I have good seats. It takes a while to get there but there are no more comments as we make our way through the crowd.

Once we're settled, she takes a naggin of brandy out of her bag along with two paper cups. Pours a healthy measure into both of them. 'Keep us warm,' she says.

'Nice touch.' She lifts her cup towards me and we say 'cheers', and we turn our faces towards the pitch and drink.

The game begins. Bohs against their nemesis, Shamrock Rovers. I stop worrying about Ellen and whether or not she'll be bored. That's the great thing about football. The beautiful game. It takes you away. I'm aware of her arm, all the same. Against mine. Not pressing or anything. Just . . . there. I feel the heat of her through her sleeve, in spite of the chill gaining on the evening.

'That's a corner,' she says, with admirable authority.

'You're a fast learner,' I tell her, and she nods without taking her eyes off the pitch. I don't blame her. It's a cracking start, with Bohs scoring five minutes into the first half. The pair of us are on our feet, roaring approval at Molloy, who heads the ball into the net from the edge of the box.

It's game on now, with Bohs on the offensive and Rovers on the back foot.

Ellen strains forward in her seat, taking slugs of brandy from her paper cup every so often. She doesn't look like a woman who's never been to a match before. Her football lingo is already better than Kenny's. And she knows the offside rule.

Nearly half-time and still one–nil. Bohs are getting a bit sloppy though and Rovers find a gap in the defence with a minute to go to the break. Here's Bryan Rooney, not someone you'd normally worry about but he's got momentum and his face looks like it's set in cement as he flies up the field, with no sign of Hall, who's supposed to be marking him. Rooney shoots, and McCarthy hurls himself towards the ball but it's too high. He can't reach it. He's never been what you might call lofty. The ball flies over his head and bounces against the back of the net.

The whistle goes.

We wrestle through the crowd and make it to the hot dog stand. Get in the queue.

'I'd say we can still beat them,' she says. 'A game of two halves and all that.'

'It's 'we' now?' I say, amused. 'Looks like Bohs have got themselves a new fan.'

She nods. 'Makes it more exciting when you're up for a team.'

'Yeah, for sure. And I agree, it's still all to play for.'

She wants ketchup and mustard. Fried onions. The lot. I order two, the same. We queue for fresh coffees. It's too cold for Cokes. We bring them back to our seats. Silence for a while, the pair of us munching away.

'I didn't expect that to taste so good,' she tells me, wiping the corners of her mouth with a napkin when she's finished.

'They taste better at a match, I always think. I make them at home sometimes. For the kids. But they're never the same.'

'Are you a good cook?'

'Eh, no. I wouldn't say good, as such.'

'What would you say?'

I search for a word. 'Passable,' I come up with, after a while.

'Are you warm enough?' I ask her.

She nods. 'I put a thermal vest on. It's done the trick.'

'I tried to buy thermal long johns in Dunnes the other day,' I tell her, 'but Kerry said she'd burn them if I brought them home.'

'I can see why she'd say that.'

'She would, too. She's as good as her word, that one. She'd have a pyre in the back garden.'

'Must be tricky. Bringing up a fourteen-year-old girl.'

'She's grand, once I'm doing what she wants. Dispensing tenners and making her favourite dinners and driving her places.'

'What's her favourite dinner?'

'Lasagne. Except I don't know how to make it. I can go as far as spaghetti Bolognese. That's where my Italian cookery prowess ends, I'm afraid.'

'Lasagne's easy,' she says. 'I could show you how to make it, if you like?'

'I'm pretty much a lost cause in the kitchen department, I'm afraid.'

'Everyone can learn. If they want to.'

'You make it sound like it's just a question of choosing.'

'It is.'

'OK, then.' I smile and I'm pretty sure if Janine saw me, she'd say it was a flirty smile. She's big on categorising facial expressions.

There I am, at Dalymount Park, smiling and maybe even flirting. I don't know what it means, being honest. Any of it. All I know is . . . I like it. And I want to see her again. Even if it means learning how to cook lasagne.

The second half begins and we turn our attention to the pitch. Both teams are anxious for another goal and this anxiety translates into some pushing and shoving and a fair few fouls, most of them made by Bohs' centre forward, Cathal Brady, who gets a yellow card for his troubles. Brady-the-Butcher, we call him. He argues with the ref until the manager can be heard roaring from the sidelines. 'Zip it, Cathal.' He's a dirty player, alright. Mouthy too. Kenny's not fond of him. 'He looks like someone dragged him through a bush backwards. And that's even before the match starts.'

'Looks like it's heading for a draw,' Ellen says, looking at me with those amber eyes, bright with cold. Her cheeks are pink now, from the wind. And her mouth. I try not to look at her mouth but I do anyway and it's a beautiful mouth, the lips full and red. Not lipstick red. Just red. Natural, like.

The crowd starts shouting and I turn my head towards the pitch, glad of the diversion. There's Brady-the-Butcher, chasing McGinn, who's gaining on the Bohs goal. McGinn makes it to just inside the penalty area when Brady slips his boot around McGinn's ankle and he stumbles like a drunk in stilettos before succumbing to gravity and falling into the mud. He lies on the pitch, clutching his ankle and making an awful racket. The ref shakes his head. I see him mouthing at the player, *Get up, Fernando Torres*. For a moment, I think we're going to get away with it. Brady's putting on a good show, proclaiming his innocence, but the ref's having none of it. He points at the spot, takes the red card out. Brady fumes off the pitch.

Penalty for Rovers.

I cover my eyes. 'Are you not going to watch?' Ellen asks. I shake my head. 'Hearing it is bad enough,' I say, and right on cue, I hear the torturous groans of the Bohs fans, the triumphant roars of the Rovers supporters.

Two–one to Rovers and the ninety minutes are up.

'Is that the end of the match?' Ellen asks, looking disappointed.

'Should be about three minutes injury time to play.'

The fourth official at the halfway line holds up the board. I'm right. It's three minutes.

'That's pretty impressive,' Ellen says, bemused.

I'm not hopeful. No Brady, and Larkin's getting substituted for MacLochlainn, who lumbers onto the pitch with no sense of urgency. He should have been put out to pasture long ago. Don't know why the manager keeps him on. He couldn't hit the side of a barn with a banjo.

'A lovely head of hair on him, all the same,' said Kenny at the last match, after an opponent kicked a ball that bounced off the back of MacLochlainn's head before dribbling into the Bohs net. Can't understand why he's being let loose again.

Rovers are playing short passes, holding possession, not taking any chances. Barely worth staying to watch the rest of the match.

I glance at my watch. Less than a minute left. I hate this bit. Once you accept it's over, it's not so bad. It's those few minutes beforehand. When you know you're going to lose but still, a flicker of hope persists. That's the killer.

Rovers' centre half, Bissett, passes the ball to Hardy and he passes it back and they do that over and over again in a way that is almost hypnotic. That's when Costello appears, as if out of nowhere. Kenny calls him the strong, silent type. A defender. Doesn't make a lot of fuss. I've told Kenny you can't go around calling footballers strong, silent types. That's just . . . not on. But I agree that Costello's the workhorse of the team. Reliable, focused, grounded. A safe pair of hands.

All of a sudden Costello's there, right beside Bissett and, with the lightest of tackles, he eases the ball from between his feet, politely, as if he asked permission first. Hardy stands there, looking confused, like he doesn't know what just happened.

Costello's not known for his speed but now he's streaking up the pitch like he's on fire. He looks up. There's a gap between the last two Rovers defenders and the goal. There could be a chance.

Costello catches MacLochlainn's eye and nods. The Bohs fans groan. A chant about a three-legged donkey reverberates around the stadium. It's not for the sensitive, this game.

MacLochlainn's running now. I suppose I should be grateful he's running in the right direction, towards the Rovers goal. He races past the last two defenders just as Costello kicks the ball. The defenders' arms shoot up. They're already shouting, 'OFFSIDE.'

We're on our feet now, all the Bohs fans chanting in unison:

> Carefree wherever you may be,
> We are the famous Bohs FC,
> We don't give a fuck if we never win the league,
> Cos we are the famous Bohs FC!

Ellen chants along.

MacLochlainn keeps running. The ball arches across the field, lands just in front of him. His first touch is renowned for being abysmal and, true to form, he makes a swipe for the ball with his left foot and misses. Now we're booing, along with the Rovers fans.

He finally gets the ball under control, turns towards the goal. The Rovers goalkeeper – a massive slab of a man – advances. It's just the two of them now. MacLochlainn and the keeper. We haven't got a prayer. MacLochlainn glances behind, sees a flock of Rovers players bearing down on him like a plague. He looks ahead again, never stopping and, somehow, a glimmer of hope is persuaded into my head. Twenty yards out with just the keeper in his way.

Football is all about statistics. Fans are mad about statistics. A few of these come to mind. Like the fact that MacLochlainn hasn't scored a goal all season. Like the fact that he missed the last three penalties he took. Like the fact that he's the oldest player on the team. Like the fact that his hamstring isn't what it was. Or his Achilles heel. Or his right knee. It's been years since he was declared Man of the Match.

But now he's all we've got and somehow, despite the odds, the glimmer of hope persists.

MacLochlainn takes a swing at the ball with his right foot and it launches into the air. Time stands still as it soars in an arc, graceful as a swallow. The keeper stretches his gigantic hands towards it and the ball grazes the tips of his fingers and for a moment it looks like he'll stop it but, somehow, the ball keeps going until it slams into the back of the net. MacLochlainn rubs his eyes as if he can't quite believe it. Who could blame him?

The crowd erupts. Ellen leans towards me. 'Could that be offside?' she says, worried.

I nod, because that's what I'm thinking too. I keep my eyes on the ref, who approaches the linesman. They huddle. It's impossible to tell what's going on. The Rovers fans are shouting, 'OFFSIDE, OFFSIDE, OFFSIDE,' while the Bohs supporters chant, 'GOAL, GOAL, GOAL.' I concentrate on the ref and the linesman. So does Ellen.

Finally, the ref nods at the linesman, then walks with purpose onto the pitch. He looks up and for a moment seems to catch my eye, then looks away and points at the centre circle and the crowd erupts again, into a mass of boos and cheers.

You'd think it was the World Cup final and we'd won instead of drawn. But somehow, it feels like a win.

MacLochlainn. I didn't think he still had it in him. He begins a lap of honour around the pitch as he's pronounced Man of the Match, but it's cut short when he trips over his bootlaces.

'What does that mean? When he points to the circle? I didn't get to that bit in the book.'

That's when I kiss her.

I turn towards her and I'm pretty sure I'm about to say what it means.

And then I kiss her.

Maybe it's the match. The sweetness of a draw that feels like victory. The beautiful game. The way it infects you, makes you think anything is possible.

Or maybe it's her face. The way the cold flushes against her pale skin. Or her amber eyes and the way they've settled on me. Or just her smile. The way she's smiled at me, like she's thinking good things.

I don't know.

I kiss her.

Right there, on her full, beautiful mouth in the middle of Dalyer where anyone could see.

I don't think about anything. No words float to the surface of my mind. I am a series of sensations.

The strangeness of her mouth. Her lips. How different it feels. To kiss someone who's not Paula.

The cold softness of the skin on her face. I'm touching her face.

The surprise. Of her kissing me back. The shock. A few weeks ago, she was a fare who never said a word.

When I lift my face away from hers, she says, 'I suppose that means we drew.'

I nod.

She puts her hand on my sleeve, just above my elbow. 'You know, I just wanted to say . . . thanks for bringing me. I'm . . . it's nice, you know. Being out. Doing things again. It's, good, so just . . . just thanks.'

'Do you want to go someplace? When we get out of here?' I'm not ready to go home. Not yet.

'Yes,' she says. 'We could . . . go back to my apartment.' Her voice is low. Almost a whisper. An invitation.

Different answers crowd into my head, like supporters spilling across a pitch at full-time. The one I end up saying is, 'Yes.'

Twenty Seven

In the back seat of the taxi, the space between us seems wide. The feeling I had, back at the stadium, it's not gone exactly, but it's subsided enough to realise that I'm nervous. I never do things like this.

The city passes in a blur of lights. Ellen is chatting to the driver about the match. 'I'm a Shels man meself,' he says, looking at her in the rear-view mirror. 'Still,' he concedes, 'I saw the comments on Twitter, it sounded like a hell of a match.' Ellen nods and tells him about the penalty just before full-time. And then MacLochlainn, the unlikely hero, picking us up and carrying us across the line with twenty seconds to spare. She sounds animated and informed. Like she's a regular football fan. Like I never kissed her.

I shouldn't have kissed her.

For better or worse. That's what I promised. Richer or poorer. In sickness and in health. I said them dead slow, the vows. Meant every word.

And now, here I am.

'We could . . . go back to my apartment.' She didn't mention a drink. Or a coffee. Nothing like that. Just . . . her apartment. Us, going back there.

Sex. I can't remember the last time I had sex. I've only ever slept with Paula. Joey asked me once: how many women. I told him to mind his own business. He would have laughed.

The taxi jerks to a stop and I look out the window. We're

here. I hand the driver a note. 'Keep the change.' It's only a few coins but it keeps the morale up. Keeps you going.

For a moment, I don't move. The engine idles. Ellen looks at me then.

'You OK?' she says.

'Yeah, grand, it's just . . .' I look at the place on my wrist where my watch should be. 'I'm wondering if it's a bit late?'

'Oh. Right. Sorry. I didn't think . . . do you need to go?'

'Let me just . . .' I take my phone out of my pocket. Scan the screen. A text from Ma at eight o'clock to say Finn's fast asleep. Another text, twenty minutes later, to say Kerry is home and fed and in good form. A smiley face at the end of that one.

'Everything alright at home?' Ellen asks, her voice low with concern.

I put my phone in my pocket. 'Yeah, yeah, it's grand.'

She looks at me, and there is a question on her face but I don't know the answer.

The taxi driver's face appears between the front seats, his eyebrows pitched high. 'Well?' he says, directing the question at me. 'Are yiz comin' or goin'?'

'It's fine if you need to—' Ellen begins.

'No, no, I don't,' I say, louder than necessary. 'I mean, I can stay, for a little while.'

The taxi driver nods, turns back into his seat, eyeballs me in the rear-view mirror, unimpressed. I get out of the car.

It's a bright night, the half-moon glancing yellow light across the bay, etching the crooked line of the Dublin mountains against the sky. The taxi roars away.

I take my cigarette packet out of my pocket. It's only now I notice the photograph on the back of the pack. A drooping cigarette with the caption, *Smoking may reduce the blood flow and cause impotence*. I take two cigarettes out and shove the pack in my pocket before she clocks it.

'Want a smoke?'

She nods. I hand her a cigarette, she puts the tip in her mouth and I light it for her. My eyes settle on her mouth and I twitch my head away.

There are steps leading to the gates of her apartment block and, without discussing it, we sit there. You can see the lights of Howth Head, flickering along the headland. I used to tell Finn that it was a treasure chest. It looks like one in the dark. 'That's where the pirates hide their treasure,' I told him.

'It's not a very good hiding place,' Finn said, unimpressed.

It's so quiet, I hear the cigarette paper burn as I inhale. I try and think of something to say. Things were great at Dalyer. Should have left it at that.

Shouldn't have kissed her.

It's Ellen who says something in the end. 'Look . . . Vinnie . . .' she says, throwing her half-smoked cigarette on the ground and crushing it with her crutch. 'The thing is . . . I mean, we're both adults and . . .' She tapers off. I nod. Don't know why.

'I don't want you to think that this is what I do,' she says, pointing towards the gates.

I don't know what she's talking about.

'I mean, I don't bring men back to the apartment. That's what I mean.'

'Oh, I didn't—'

'You're the first one.' She laughs. A small, nervous laugh. 'Although, technically, I haven't managed to get you inside the door, so I'm not sure that counts.'

I want to say lots of things. It's just . . . it's difficult, I suppose. I feel like I'm out of practice. Rusty as the hinges on the shed door.

'To be honest,' Ellen is saying, 'I haven't been with anyone since Neil. And even before. We worked every hour. We were always tired. It seems stupid now. Such a waste of time. All that work. I don't know what it was all for now.'

I'm stuck on the word *been*. *Been with*. That's sex. I'm pretty sure that's what it means. Ellen looks at me. An expectant look. My turn, I suppose. To say something. I take a chance that I'm right. 'I haven't been with anyone either. Not since . . .' I don't want to say her name. Drag her into another of our conversations. 'Not for a long time,' I say instead.

She nods her head. There is a trace of relief in her face. I feel it too. Like we're standing on the same spot. We've got some common ground. Makes you feel a bit less . . . I don't know . . . alone, I suppose.

She laughs then. A sudden sound.

'What?' I say.

She hesitates for a moment. Then, 'I was going to seduce you, you know. That was my plan.'

'I get that a lot.' I keep my tone light and it works, because she laughs again.

I love when she laughs. Things seem so easy when she laughs.

I shouldn't have kissed her. Complicated things.

Out of the blue, Ellen says, 'Do you think your wife will ever come back?'

'I don't know.' That's the truth. I don't know. I haven't got a clue.

Ellen is looking at me, like she's waiting for me to say something else. I shake my head. 'I don't think so. She . . . I don't think she liked being married. We were young. Maybe we were too young. We'd been going out for years. People just assumed that we'd get married, have kids, live in North Strand. I wanted all that. But, looking back, I don't think that was what she wanted. She just . . . went along with it until it was too late to back out.'

It sounds so obvious, when I say it out loud. Have I thought that before now? If I have, I've stamped it out, like a fire.

'We wanted different things. I'm only realising that now. She said she wanted to travel. I thought a couple of weeks in Spain every year. A few city breaks.'

I look at Ellen. She's listening to me, nodding like I'm making sense. 'The doctor said it had nothing to do with what she wanted in the end, with her having a different idea of what our life was going to be like. He said it was an illness, simple as that. Could happen to anyone. But I wonder . . .' I stop there, cup my chin with my hand, feel the scratch of the stubble against the backs of my fingers.

'What?' Ellen says.

'Just . . . even if she hadn't got sick, maybe things still wouldn't have worked out.'

'You don't know that.'

I shrug. 'I suppose I don't. It's just . . . maybe we could have saved ourselves a lot of . . . trouble, I suppose, if we'd stopped to think about things. Think about life and what we wanted out of it. You don't when you're young. You think you're invincible then, don't you? Like you have all the time in the world.'

She nods and reaches into her handbag for the hip flask. Takes a swig, offers it to me. The heat of the brandy going down lifts me, the way it spreads through my chest like warm fingers.

Ellen lights another cigarette. 'I can't blame youth on me and Neil. I was thirty-six when we got married. Neil was fifty-one. I did my residency under his supervision at the hospital. We were colleagues for years. We got on great, worked really well together. Maybe we mistook that for something else. Something more than it was.'

'Did you love him?' Somehow, it's easier to ask a question like that when it's dark and you're nowhere in particular, sitting on steps that are lit by the orange glow of streetlights.

Ellen takes the flask from me. Drinks from it. Hands it back. 'It's hard to know now, after everything. He was charming, ambitious, driven. Everybody loved him, you know one of those types of people?' She looks at me and I nod.

'He loved Spanish food. Tapas and paella. Our last holiday was in Spain. It was supposed to be a reconciliation. Things hadn't been great between us. Seville and Cordoba. All over the place. I drove – I loved driving back then – and we ate tapas and paella, and at night, we'd pull into these little guesthouses and ask for a room. We stayed for a week. It was hot during the day. Cooler at night, especially up in the mountain villages. I think that's where our baby was conceived. In Ronda, maybe. Sorry, I don't mean to be . . .' She puts her face in her hands and for a moment I think she might cry. There's something fragile about her in the shadows of night, like one of those shells you find on the shoreline, breakable as an egg.

I put my hand on her shoulder. 'I didn't know you . . . had a kid.'

She shakes her head. 'I don't. Or I did. It's hard to know how to put it.' She lifts her head, looks at me. I am surprised all over again by the colour of her eyes. The strange beauty of them.

'You don't have to explain,' I say.

She tells me anyway. There is something like relief leaking through the words. Perhaps she hasn't said them before. Not out loud.

'I was six months pregnant. Nearly six and a half, really. Twenty-six weeks. Then the accident happened and I went into labour.'

'I'm sorry, Ellen.' I put my hand on her arm.

She shakes her head. 'It was my fault. I got distracted. At the wheel. Neil and I were fighting. She was so small, the baby. I could hold her in one hand. They let me hold her.'

I shuffle over on the step until I am beside her, put my arm around her and she lets her head fall against me. We sit there for a while, quiet and unmoving.

'I'm tired, Vinnie.' She whispers it. I nod. I can feel it. Her tiredness. The ache of it, deep inside her.

When I stand up, pins and needles rush up and down my legs. I reach for her hands, pull her gently up, onto her feet, reach for the crutches. She slots her arms through the hoops at the top, leans on the handles.

'You should get some rest,' I say.

She nods. 'I'm sorry,' she says, and her voice is tired too. Maybe from all the talking. She doesn't usually do much of it.

'For what?'

'All this . . . stuff I'm telling you. I've managed not to think about any of it and now, all of a sudden, it's in my head. I can't stop thinking about it. It's . . . exhausting, to be honest.'

I nod. I know.

I don't kiss her when I leave. She says, 'Goodnight,' and I say, 'Goodnight,' and she turns away and so do I.

I start walking.

I was going to seduce you, you know.

I walk and I try not to think about that. A drizzle starts up and I pull the collar of my jacket up around my neck and walk faster. By the time I reach Fairview, it's a deluge. Still, I don't hail a cab. Sometimes it's nice to walk in the rain. Clears your head.

I think about Paula. Sometimes, it feels like she lives in my memory. Like she's taken up residence there.

I know what Ellen means. It's exhausting. All the thinking. All the remembering.

Twenty Eight

Sex.

I haven't thought about it in ages. Now, it's in my head, pacing the floors. I can't stop thinking about it.

I've never slept with anyone else.

The first time was my sixteenth birthday. Paula said it was her birthday present to me. We did it in her mother's bedroom. Even though her da slept there as well, she always called it her mother's room.

It took me ages to get my breath back after. I don't know what I said. 'Thanks,' maybe. State of me.

Paula said, 'You'd better perk up again, Vincent Boland. I'm just getting started.'

We did it two more times that afternoon, the third while her mother was downstairs. I could hear her putting the kettle on. 'Get off me,' I hissed at Paula, who had me straddled on the bed. She smiled her slow, secret smile and covered my mouth with hers. I forgot about her mother in the kitchen making tea. I forgot about everything. She had that effect on me, Paula.

There was no stopping us after that. I learned how to unhook a bra with one hand while the other was buried in her hair, or between her legs. She'd shout when she came. Words like 'Jesus' or 'Fuck' or 'Vinnie'. I'd kiss her mouth, swallow her noise.

'How come you never make a sound, Vinnie?'

'You're making enough of a racket for both of us.'

We did it in sand dunes. Donabate, Portmarnock, Dollymount. The sand got everywhere. We'd share a cigarette after, lying on our backs, watching the ferries inch along the horizon.

'I'd love to go to France,' Paula said. I propped myself up on an elbow. Looked at her. The bright green eyes and tanned face and her long blonde hair and her generous curves. Traced the freckles that straddled her nose with my finger.

'I'll take you to France,' I said, with all the conviction of a sixteen-year-old boy. Everything seems possible at sixteen. It's a question of *when* rather than *if*.

When she first went on the medication, the doctor talked about the side-effects. Mentioned her libido and the effect the meds might have. Paula wasn't worried. There had never been any problem in that department.

And then there was.

She'd insist on sex anyway. It took me so long to make her come, I'd be sore afterwards. And the humour was gone out of it. It was a serious business now, like a war declared. An enemy to be defeated.

I haven't thought about it in so long. And now, I can't stop. I'm thinking about sex. I'm thinking about Ellen.

I was going to seduce you.

I'm still thinking about her saying that the next morning. I need to distract myself. I poke my head in the front room where Finn's watching the telly. 'Do you want to go for a swim?'

'YES!'

It's been a while since I've exercised. Apart from the five-a-side, and that's more like an exercise in avoiding injury. I used to swim. Before the kids came along. Fifty lengths in thirty minutes, a couple of times a week.

'That's my kind of six pack,' Paula'd say, running her hands across my chest, down my stomach, grabbing the hem of her dress and lifting it over her head.

'Ah, Jaysus, I'll be late for work.'

'Lie back, Vinnie. This won't take long.'

The doctor at the hospital said exercise would help with the panic attacks. Dr McDaid too. Swimming is a good form of exercise. Better than yoga anyway.

Finn can swim but wears one armband in the water. 'Just in case,' he says.

'We'll stay in the shallow end,' I say, easing it down his arm. His skin is bluey-white, the cage of his ribs visible beneath. You'd never think he eats me out of house and home.

He's able to stand just shy of the five-foot marker now. 'You're getting tall,' I tell him. I lift him over my head. 'Stand on my shoulders and jump.'

'I can't. The water's too far down.'

I bend my knees. 'There. You can do it.'

He does it. He jumps, his arms flapping like he's trying to fly. He explodes into the water, resurfaces, reaches for me. 'Did you see that, Dad? Did you see me jumping?'

'I told you you could do it.'

'Can I do it again?'

'Go on, then.'

He's still doing the doggy-paddle. I show him the breast-stroke. The front crawl. He swims a width. Then another. He jumps in from the side when the lifeguard isn't looking. He swims underwater, through my legs and back again, grazing my shin with his toenails. Have to clip them when we get home.

I leave him splashing in the shallow end and manage ten lengths. Out of puff. Big red face on me. Still, it's a start, I suppose.

Finn picks up the abandoned armband on the way to the changing room.

'I don't think you need that any more,' I say.

He puts it in his bag.

'We could come again next week. I'll show you the stroke I used when I won the Olympic gold medal.'

'You weren't in the Olympics, Dad.'

'I was. Calgary in Canada. 1988.'

'Really?'

We're home and it's only eleven o'clock in the morning. Kerry's still in bed. I'm about to roar up the stairs at her and then I don't. She's been fairly busy this week, with school and homework. And no phone calls from the school lately. I leave her. She could do with a bit of a break.

I iron the uniforms, take a packet of ham and a pan of bread out of the freezer for the school lunches, push the sweeping brush across the floors downstairs. Every time I stop, it's the same thoughts. About Ellen. About sex.

I was going to seduce you.

Proper Sunday dinner. How about that? I could roast a chicken. I could invite Ma. About time I did something to say thanks. Maybe Janine and Kenny too. Why not? I've the whole day ahead of me.

I'm setting the table and trying not to think about Ellen and sex when she texts.

Had a great time last night. Thanks for bringing me to the match. Do you still want me to show you how to make lasagne? Thursday at 7pm suit? Ellen

She doesn't say anything about sex. Or seducing me. But that's what I'm thinking about, all the same. I can't help it.

Yes, that would be lovely. C u then.

Janine is suspicious. 'What's going on, Vinnie?' she says, when she arrives at six.

'A bit of dinner is all.'

'What's the occasion?' She walks into the hall, looking around like someone's about to jump on her.

'No occasion. Just thought I'd feed you, for a change. You've fed us often enough.' This is true, especially in the beginning when I had to Google poached eggs. Fried eggs I could manage but poaching was a different animal altogether. Finn loves a poached egg. He spears the top with a piece of toast and lets the yolk dribble onto his plate. They're actually not that hard to make. It's all about timing.

'Something smells tasty,' Kenny says, thrusting a brown paper bag at me and taking off his jacket. A fitted, tartan affair. Mustard and black. 'I didn't know tartan was back in,' Janine tells him.

'It was never out, my little flower. It's a classic design. Bit like yourself.'

I empty the bag. Cans of Guinness, and slabs of chocolate for the kids.

'Vodka and tonic?' I ask Janine.

'Slimline?'

'Of course.'

'Why'd you get slimline? Do you think I'm overweight?'

'I got it because you like it.'

'Fair enough,' she says, handing Kenny her coat. He feels it before he hangs it up.

'I love the feel of a good mohair,' he says.

'Give over,' Janine says.

Kenny pours Guinness into a glass, leaving space at the top for his customary dash of blackcurrant. He looks up when Kerry walks in. 'How's my favourite god-daughter?'

'Grand.' It's not just me she's monosyllabic with, but at least Kenny gets a smile.

'I thought you'd like this colour,' says Janine, handing Kerry a bottle of black sparkly nail varnish. 'It's from Kate Moss's new collection.'

'Thanks, Janine, it's gorgeous,' says Kerry, pocketing it.

The doorbell rings and Kerry runs to answer it.

The hob hisses as water in the pot of peas overflows and runs down the side. I lift the lid, add some cold water, lower the heat. When I turn around, Kerry is in front of me. 'Mark's at the door. We're going out for a pizza. Can I have a tenner?'

'I've made dinner.'

'Howeya, Vinnie.' Mark's in my kitchen again, that smug grin all over his spotty face.

I nod. 'Mark.'

Kerry stands beside him. His hand encircles her waist. She smiles at him.

The cheek.

'Well, can Mark stay for dinner, then?'

'Set another place at the table.' Keep your friends close and your enemies closer. Isn't that what they say?

'Sorry I'm late.' Ma appears, hands me a box of After Eights. 'I couldn't get rid of that fella selling his paintings.'

'I hope you didn't let him in, like the last one.'

'Of course I did. It's perishing out there.'

'He could be a mugger, for all you know.'

'I'd be well able for him if he was. A skinny little whippet of a thing, God love him.'

'Did you buy anything, Mrs Boland?' Janine asks.

'Ah, the pension won't stretch to art any more, what with the butchering those eejits above in Leinster House are after givin' it.' She struggles out of her coat, takes the spoon out of my hand and starts stirring the gravy. 'I'll get those lumps out for you, son.'

There's barely room for everyone around the table. Benjamin's place across the road is a lot bigger, according to Kenny's mother, who got her nose in on the pretext of collecting for the local hospice and coughing like a mad yoke at his door, so he had to let her in for a glass of water. According to Mrs. Byrne, Benjamin has knocked down nearly every wall inside his house.

She told Benjamin she couldn't take water but she'd be able for a drop of brandy, if he had any. She stayed for over an hour.

'What's for starters?' Kenny says, picking up his knife and fork. He and Janine are at the head of the table, squashed against each other. Kenny doesn't look like he minds.

'It's far from starters you were reared,' Janine tells him.

'We're doing starters in Home Economics at the moment,' says Kerry. Her tone is conversational. Agreeable.

'Pity you didn't let me know earlier,' I say. 'You could have given me a hand.' The wrong thing to say, I know it at once. She tosses me a look that is neither conversational nor agreeable.

'We did Caprese salad the other day,' Mark says.

'I love a bit of French food, all the same,' says Ma, pouring the gravy into the boat and setting it on the table.

Mark looks at her but doesn't correct her and – briefly – my thoughts towards him become less malevolent.

'Can I have some wine?' Kerry says.

'NO!' That's me, Kenny, Janine, and Ma, in unison, like the roar of a picket line.

'Who's for what?' I say, carrying the chicken over to the table.

'I'm a leg man myself,' says Kenny, smiling at Janine.

'Chance'd be a fine thing,' says Janine, pouring wine for her and Ma.

The chicken could do with bein' bigger. Should have got two. The oven's too small. Could do with a new oven. One side of the grill doesn't turn on any more. That's another day's work. Still, I get a bit of meat on everyone's plate and there's more than enough spuds and peas and gravy and stuffing to go round.

It's warm in the kitchen. A bit stuffy, maybe. But cosy, like. There's loads of noise. Good noise. And Kerry's saying things. I'm finding out allsorts.

'I got a B1 in Maths in the mocks,' she's telling Janine now. 'The teacher says I'll get into the honours class for the Leaving. And Applied Maths if I want to.'

'You didn't tell me that,' I say. It's only when it's said that I realise how I've said it. You wouldn't call it conversational. Or agreeable. It sounds more like an accusation, the way I've said it.

She shrugs, not looking at me.

'But that's great news, love. Well done.' That's what I should have said in the first place. Why couldn't I have said that in the first place?

'We're going out now, OK?' Kerry says, looking at Mark and nodding towards the door.

'There's ice cream,' I say.

'I'll be back later.'

'What time?'

'I'll text you.'

'Where are you going?'

Janine nudges my arm with hers, gives me the 'go easy' look.

I make coffee. Dole out the ice cream. Open the tin of fruit salad. No one wants any except for Ma. She demolishes the lot. 'That's two of my five-a-day done.'

'You should give those things up,' says Janine when I head out the back garden to have a smoke. 'They'll kill you.'

'He doesn't smoke enough to kill him,' says Finn. 'Do you, Dad?' His little face puckers with worry.

'No, son, a couple a day is all.'

The one after dinner is usually my favourite one of the day. I throw it away, half-smoked. Should think about giving them up. Never should have started. Kenny nicked a couple out of his dad's pack years ago. We were fourteen, I'd say. Kenny ended up puking his ring up afterwards. I wasn't mad about the taste of them but I kept going til I couldn't stop. Twenty-eight years at it now. I could wear one of those patches, I suppose. Stop Finn worrying.

When they leave, I clear up, put Finn to bed. It's only when I'm downstairs, on the couch, I realise that nobody mentioned Paula tonight. Not even Finn.

The bag where Finn keeps her postcards is under his bed. He's out for the count when I go back into his room. I check the sheet. Still dry. He smells of chlorine and shampoo. His nails are clipped. I forgot about it but Ma noticed. 'Givvus those claws,' she said.

The postcards are in date order. One a month for fifteen months. Fifteen postcards. The first one in January last year, from England. She said she was lucky to get into that place. Not a hospital, exactly. More like a refuge, she said. Therapy. Counselling. Medication. A balanced diet. All calm on the home front. Except it wasn't home.

I told her that, any time she rang.

The last phone call was Finn's birthday in February. She sang 'Happy Birthday' to him. He held the receiver away from his ear. She always had a bit of a shrill voice when she sang.

The last postcard was sent in early March. Now it's April. Something tightens inside my chest and I sit for a moment on the floor beside Finn's bed. Breathe deeply. Slowly. Like the doctor said I should. Finn stirs and I wait for him to settle again before I put the cards back into the bag and slide it under the bed.

I go downstairs. Pour myself a finger of brandy. It burns going down but then spreads out, releasing the tightness inside. Worry is what it is. A regular squatter. The doctor says I should try not to worry. Hard not to, when it comes to Paula.

Twenty Nine

It's Thursday. Finally. Only seven o'clock in the morning, but still. Thursday. Any time I think about Ellen – her face and her mouth and how she tasted when I kissed her – I work out the square roots of various numbers. That does the trick, some of the time.

'Four more weeks til the Communion. That's twenty-eight sleeps,' Finn tells me, when I pick him up from school. Half two. Four and a half hours left.

'Yeah.'

'It's going to be deadly, isn't it? The Communion party.'

'Yeah.'

'Especially with the bouncy castle.'

'Yeah.' Fuck. The bouncy castle. Kenny said he'd have a think and get back to me. I'll have to get that sorted.

'Do you think my teeth will have grown back by then?' He sticks his finger into his mouth, runs it along the smooth pink of his gums.

'Maybe.'

'Cos I've to say a reading and it's tricky reading out loud with no teeth.'

'A reading?'

'Yeah. Everyone put their hand up but Miss Crean picked me. She says she doesn't mind about my teeth.'

Something surges inside me and I think it might be pride. 'One of the seven deadly sins, son,' I can hear Ma say. 'Pride.'

'You'll be great, son, with or without your choppers.'

'Will you be back by five?' Ma wants to know, when I drop Finn to her house afterwards. 'Only I promised Mrs Nolan I'd do her hair this evening. She's burying her husband tomorrow. Wants to look her best.'

'Mr Nolan died? I didn't hear.'

'Finally. He held on for far too long, that fella. He was always the same. Never knew when to quit.'

A slow enough afternoon on the rank. On a whim, around four o'clock – three more hours – I decide to pick up my watch. 'Knew you'd be back some day,' says the jeweller, standing behind the counter in the same ancient double-breasted suit that looks like it was made for a bigger man. He bends slowly, opens a drawer and takes out the watch. 'Good as new,' he says, stroking the face with long, narrow fingers.

'You've shined it an' all.'

'A bit of cola, would you believe. Brings them up lovely, so it does.'

'Go way.'

'May I be struck be lightning if I'm telling a word of a lie.' He stands still, his arms outstretched, looking upwards.

Nothing happens. He smiles.

'How much do I owe you?'

The amount is paltry. I wonder how he manages to make any sort of a living. He tells me business is looking up. People are getting their watches fixed again.

He nods towards my left hand. 'That ring a yours is looking slippy on that finger. Could be it needs a bit of a resize.'

'Ah, no, it's—'

'I'll measure you up. Only take a minute.'

My finger feels strange without the band. The skin underneath is a pasty white. I rub it with my thumb. Encourage some life back into it.

'I could do it straight away for you. Won't take long.'

'I've the cab parked on a yellow outside.'

'Come back for it, so. I'm open every day except the Sabbath. I'll have it ready for you. It'll be as good as the day your missus put it on your finger.'

I pull out into the traffic, my eyes drawn again to the space on my finger. I don't know why I didn't take it off before. The kids, maybe. Although they probably wouldn't notice. But if they did. The exposed skin feels like a statement.

It's just a resize.

That's what I'll say if the kids say anything.

Thirty

Half six, Thursday.

'Where are you off to looking like that?' Kerry wants to know. I got Ben & Jerry's for a treat. Worth the expense. She's nearly smiling.

'Like what?' I'd love to ask her if I look alright. I haven't got a clue any more. Black jeans and a grey-and-black top that Kenny gave me for my birthday. 'Blokes don't buy clothes for their mates,' I told him, not for the first time either.

'Who's going to buy you new threads if I don't?' he said. 'Besides, the horizontal lines will bulk you up a bit.'

'Do you not think it's a bit . . . snug?'

He shakes his head. Emphatic. 'With those wide shoulders and your skinny little waist, you can carry off that fitted look, no problemo.'

'Right.'

I cover the new top with my old leather jacket.

I arrive at seven, then wait in the motor for a few minutes. Bit OCD arriving on the dot.

I make myself wait for five minutes. The minute hand tracks its way around the face of the watch. Hard to believe it's been doing that for nearly a hundred years, especially when you consider how long five minutes takes.

I have a fancy bag for the wine. I've bought flowers again and bring them in this time.

'Hi, Vinnie.' She smiles like she's glad to see me. I thrust the bottle and flowers towards her. 'Thanks,' she says, pushing her nose against one of the roses and inhaling. 'They're beautiful.' She straightens and looks at me and there's nothing for it but to look at her. Her feet are bare. There's something a little shocking about bare feet. Intimate.

Her dress is red. It looks like it's made from tissue paper, a little slip of a thing. Her toenails are silver, and around her left ankle a fine silver chain with tiny red stars hanging from it at intervals.

She's matching.

She's beautiful.

She steps back from the door so I can pass by and I make it to the kitchen without touching her.

She opens the fridge, takes out two bottles of beer, hands one to me.

'So, what's the plan?' I say, taking a drink and putting my bottle on the counter.

'Just like I said. I'm going to give you a cookery lesson,' she says. A smile spreads across her mouth.

'I'm not exactly Gordon Ramsay material, bein' honest.' She laughs with her mouth closed until it's too much and then – real slow – her lips part and lengthen, revealing the white line of her teeth and I swear, it's the sexiest thing, her laugh. It really is.

'Lasagne's easy, I promise,' she says. 'And it's Kerry's favourite. Plus, I was thinking that you could make it for Finn's Holy Communion. You were talking about getting something from the deli but this would be much nicer and a lot more economical too. You could do a big green salad and some garlic bread to go with it.'

'It sounds easy, when you say it.' I take a drink from the bottle and the beer goes down the wrong way and makes me cough and there she is now, beside me, banging my back and I catch her scent then, something warm and spicy, like cinnamon. She stops banging my back but leaves her hand there. I feel the heat of it through my jacket. I think about her wrist, the narrowness of it, how pale the skin is there, almost transparent.

'You OK?'

I nod, clear my throat. 'Grand, yeah. Thanks.' Her hand falls away.

'Don't look so nervous.'

'I usually go by the instructions on the back of a tin.'

'Here.' She holds out an apron with an L-plate on the front of it. 'I bought this for you.'

'I'm not a complete novice. I do a fairly acceptable scrambled egg, you know.'

'Doesn't matter. You're to wear it.' She tosses the apron at me and I catch it. I feel self-conscious taking my jacket off. It's the top. It looks so new. The style's probably too young for someone like me. Ellen will think—

'I like your top,' she says.

'Oh. Thanks.' I drape my jacket across the back of a chair. Make a note to buy Kenny a pint.

'Alright, so. What do I have to do?'

She grins. 'Nothing illegal, I promise.' There's a ton of stuff on the counter. Parsley and mincemeat and onions and mushrooms. Allsorts. Already, I feel nostalgic for the sound of the plastic sleeve getting ripped off the lid of a ready-made lasagne. The ding of the microwave. The warmth of the plastic tray on your knee.

'You've your work cut out for you,' I tell her, putting the apron over my head. I roll up my sleeves.

We start with garlic. 'You need to crush it,' she tells me, after I manage to peel a few cloves. She leans across, drops a clove into something that looks a bit like a tin opener. 'Here,' she says, taking my hand, guiding it to a handle. 'Pull this down. Like this.' I feel her breath on my arm, warm and ticklish. She moves away, watches me. I crush the garlic. She nods and I feel pleased, like I've done something spectacular.

What am I like?

I chop an onion into minute little pieces. Diced. That's what that is. My eyes smart and water. Ellen tells me to whistle. I whistle the theme tune to *Match of the Day*. It works.

I lace a sauce with red wine and then bring it to the boil to get rid of the alcohol – so the kids can eat it – but keep the flavour. A doddle, really.

The white sauce is tricky. Ellen makes it with cornflour. A cheat, she calls it. Easier than a roux, she says. Whatever that is. I stir the sauce and grate cheese and nutmeg. Nutmeg is the secret ingredient, she says. I tell her about Finn and the tomato ketchup. She laughs. She makes me a coffee with her complicated machine. To keep me going, she says. But, weirdly, I'm enjoying it. This cookery class. Making something from scratch. A bit like carpentry that way.

'You're a natural,' she tells me, when I manage to arrange the layers of meat sauce, the white sauce and the rectangles of lasagne one on top of the other until they reach the top of the dish. I sprinkle cheese over the top, lift the dish, slide it into the oven. 'That wasn't as bad as I thought it was going to be.'

'It can be a bit nerve-wracking, alright,' she says. 'Doing something you haven't done before.'

She looks at me. The kitchen is quiet now, without all the chopping and grinding and crushing and mixing and scraping and stirring. There's not a sound. It's like the world has stopped. Like it's straining to hear something.

The silence between us crackles with static. The air is loud with it.

My throat is dry. I have oven gloves on my hands. Huge pink oven gloves. I take them off. Put them on the worktop. She's still looking at me. Right at me.

Along the line of her neck, a pulse rises and falls. My breath sounds too loud. I walk towards her. She lifts her hand, holds it like a stop sign, then puts it on my chest. I cup the back of her neck with my hand, rub my thumb along her mouth. Her breath catches in her throat and when I bend to kiss her, it's like something has given inside me, like a dam has burst, and I'm all over the place, all at once, and there's something ferocious about it. Something furious. I'm not thinking about anything. Or maybe I'm thinking about Ellen's mouth. Her mouth on mine. Her tongue in my mouth. The suck of her lips.

I bite her neck. She pulls my hair. I slide my hands over the rise of her breasts, my fingers grazing the hard length of her nipples, trail them down the front of her dress. I reach the ends, slip them under the material and up the length of her glorious legs, her thighs, the curve of her bottom. She wraps her arms around my neck and her legs around my waist and I carry her like this into her bedroom. Lie her on her bed.

From someplace, a guttural noise. I wonder what it is before I realise that it's me.

Thirty One

I come. And come. And come. I keep on coming. There's no end to it. It's magnificent. But a bit out of control at the same time. There's a swell at the back of my throat. A stinging sensation behind my eyes. Like I'm going to cry.

Jaysus.

I squeeze my eyes shut, bury my face in the hollow of her neck, lick her there. She's salty. She tastes like the sea in June. Dollymount Strand. I concentrate on thinking of the view from the beach. The ships easing out to sea, making the waves that Finn loves to jump over. The pigeon houses on duty. The Twin Towers, Kenny calls them. The pushing at the back of my throat eases. The tight hotness behind my eyes subsides. It'll be alright. Now I feel Ellen tightening around me, the steady pulse of her, the moan that issues from her mouth. I come some more.

Afterwards, we share a cigarette. She closes her eyes when she pulls on the filter. Releases the smoke in a long, gentle sigh.

We don't talk. I accept the cigarette, pull on it and hand it back to her. I feel empty and full, at the same time. Full with the feeling you get after sex. Empty too. Like I've crossed some kind of line. Left Paula behind. Like we're at either end of a pitch. Facing each other but getting smaller, with the distance between us.

'Are you thinking about Paula?'

'A bit, yeah.'

Silence then, the cigarette going back and forth between us.

'Are you thinking about Neil?'

She nods.

'What're we like?' I say.

She smiles. I turn on my side, prop myself up with an elbow. Look at her. She's beautiful. The failing light of evening softens the whiteness of her skin and accentuates the gentle curve of her body. The sheet drapes across the jut of her hips and my eyes travel the line of her legs, to her toes, sticking out at the bottom. She stretches her arms over her head and, with this movement, her breasts rise, fuller than I'd imagined, the nipples still hard and flushed. She doesn't seem at all self-conscious about her body. Why would she be? Not like me, with the boxers already back on. Might be because she's a doctor. She's seen allsorts, I suppose.

I don't really think I was going to start snivelling. Why would I? Having sex? It was probably just . . . I don't know, it's been that long since I've . . . I'm not a crier – and I'm not being all macho, saying that. It's just . . . it's not something I do, as a rule. The times in my life when I've cried I can remember vividly because they don't happen all that often. Getting stitches in my head after Darren O'Neill threw a stone at a crow and missed. The stone and the cut didn't hurt as much as the look of the needle in the doctor's fingers, with the bit of thread attached to it, the doctor coming at me like I was a hem that needed taking up.

Joey going to Australia. I'd say it was because it was so soon after Da. I didn't cry at the airport, like Ma. She went to bed when we got home and I went into Joey's room, except it didn't feel like Joey's room any more with the mess gone and the wardrobe door hanging open with the glint of the empty hangers swaying on the rails.

Of course, I must have cried when I was a kid and fell down and cut my knee or whatever but those two times are the ones I remember with the sharpness of yesterday.

And that afternoon. When I came home from work early. I think I knew. The minute I opened the front door. Something about the air in the house. The stillness. Paula's coat on the hook, the handbag on the table with her keys beside it, laid out. I put my hand on the side of the kettle. It was cold. I called her name. 'Paula?' My voice loud and shrill in the dense quiet of the house.

I took my time walking upstairs, the steps moaning beneath my weight. The bedroom door was closed. I moved towards it and it felt like a dream, when you move but make no headway. I stopped at the door.

'Paula?'

I can't see anything at first when I open the door. The room is in darkness, the blinds down, the curtains drawn. I blink and the room comes into focus, the rectangle of wardrobe, the oval of mirror above the dressing table, the corner of rug, curling towards the ceiling. The figure on the bed looks much too slight to be her. Prescription bottles with no lids on the bedside locker. Empty. A vodka bottle on its side, dripping its remains onto the floor below.

It takes me a moment to see it. To take it in. I stand at the door, just stand there, blinking through the dark. I know. I know what this is. Still, I stand there, straining for something. A sound, perhaps. The sound of her breath, the rise and fall of it.

But other than the drip from the bottle, there is no sound at all.

The ambulance men said that the speed of my actions probably saved her life. But there was nothing quick about me in those first moments.

I walk to her side of the bed, sit on it, the springs jangling and sharp beneath us. It's the heat of her that finally jerks me awake. It's shocking, the heat. I wasn't expecting that. I push two fingers into the soft skin of her neck and her pulse glances against them, vague, like the feathery flutter of butterfly wings.

I pick her up. I remember thinking how light she'd become. She lies like a coat in my arms. Threadbare. I run with her, out the door, down the hall, into the bathroom. I don't know why I go there. I remember the urge to get out of the room. Leave its dark airlessness behind me.

Her head, hanging down the side of my arm, bangs against the edge of the sink. The sharp crack of it. Later she will have a bruised mound on her forehead. She moves in my arms. I set her on the tiles. Roll her onto her stomach. Squat beside her and prop her chest over my knee. Open her mouth and force my hand in. I feel her throat contract against my fingers. 'Come on, come on, throw it up!' I'm shouting now. Roaring. My fingers rub against the fleshy mounds at the base of her throat. I ram them down further, nearly gagging myself. Her stomach heaves. I feel the movement against my leg. My knee is numb, trembling against the tiles. She makes a sound. A choking sound that comes from somewhere deep inside her. I reef my hand out of her mouth and the stuff roars out of her. A violent arc. Projectile. It hurls against the pedestal of the sink, the side of the bath, the grooves between the tiles. The smell is sour. I breathe through my mouth but I can taste it, the smell.

I phone the ambulance. I sit on the bathroom floor, leaning against the door, Paula's head in my lap. I hang up. Look at her. Little white pills cling to the ends of her hair. The bile makes them glisten. I feel spent. My body aches and my heart is like an animal, throwing itself against the bars of a cage. I don't know what I feel but I do know what I don't feel and that is shock. Surprise. There's nothing like that. In fact, there's almost relief. That she's done it now. Got it over with. Out of her system. We can move on.

'You'll be alright, love,' I say, pushing her hair off her face. 'The ambulance is on the way, you'll be right as rain.'

She doesn't answer and I think perhaps she's asleep but when I bend my face towards hers, her eyes are open and staring.

'Paula?' It comes out like a whisper.

'You weren't supposed to come home,' she says. Her voice is dull. Disinterested, almost. She moves her head away, curls herself into a small circle on the bathroom floor, so all I can see is the tight curve of her back.

When I cry, I don't make a sound. I don't want her to hear me.

I look at Ellen. Wonder what she's thinking about Neil. Maybe she's remembering sex with Neil. Comparing us. The thought is pathetic, I know, but it persists, all the same.

I feel the easy space between us shift and lift, like dust motes. I want to prolong it, whatever it is. This lull. 'Do you just have one brother?' I say, keeping my tone light. Conversational. Keeping Neil and Paula at bay.

'Yes,' she says. 'David. He's married, lives in Kilkenny with his wife and their three kids. They have an equestrian centre.'

'That sounds like a nice way to earn a crust.'

She nods. 'He's a vet. He loves it.'

'Do you see him much?'

'Not really. After Neil and I set up the practice, we didn't have much time to see anyone. Apart from the usual: Christmas and Easter, and Communions and Confirmations, things like that. Then the accident happened and I . . . I don't know . . . I suppose it was hard to know what to say. To anyone. Things were so different afterwards. I wasn't pregnant any more and Neil was gone and . . . I was busy with physio and stuff like that and . . .'

Ellen turns her head and looks at me. She opens her mouth like she's going to say something but in the end, she shuffles towards me til her face is buried in the crook of my shoulder and when she cries, her body heaves and shudders and I fold my arms around her and let her go.

Dear Neil,

I dreamed about you. We were in Barcelona and I was wearing the dress you bought me for my birthday there. Remember the green silk one? You dragged me around half the shops in the city before you settled on that one. And yes, it's true, you had a good eye for fabric and cut. Marching through a boutique, pointing at the wares and saying – at the top of your voice, of course – 'No, no, no, no,' then stopping at something that caught your eye and saying, 'Now this is more like it,' and you'd yank it off the hanger and hold it against me and yes, you'd usually be right, it was more like it.

I kept a couple of the dresses you bought me but the rest went into black sacks. I think Mum gave them to one of the charity shops.

But the green dress. I loved that one. I looked for it when I woke up but I couldn't find it. And it's not easy to lose things in this little apartment of mine. I like its diminutive size. Something cosy and safe here. Needs a bit of personalising. It's on my list of things to do.

About time, you might say. Things to do. You always were the organised one. You had the head for business. And the appetite. Voracious is a word that might have been coined just for you.

Nothing really happened in the dream. We walked down Las Ramblas, moving through the crowd like ghosts. A street performer played Puccini's 'O Mio Babbino Caro' on an ancient violin and you slipped your hand around my waist and we danced for the first time. The last time.

People walked around us and through us, like we weren't there. We kept on dancing.

When the music ended, you were gone.

Ellen

Thirty Two

Things are on the up.

The weather, for starters. It's May now and there's real heat in the sun, most days. I don't think it's lashed since the night of the Bohs match and that was over a week ago now.

I know for sure that things are on the up when I get a fifty-euro tip. 'I'm spreading the love,' the fare says, a woman in her sixties, I'd say. Hard to tell, with the way Ma plays fast and loose with her age. Her number, Finn used to say. *What's your number, Granny?* She refused to say.

Fifty euros. A single note, pressed into my hand, as well as the fare.

'Prize bonds,' the lady said, by way of explanation. 'Forgot I even had them til I got the call. There's one catch.'

'What's that?' There's always a catch.

'You must spend it unwisely,' she says, and she winks as she gets out of the cab.

I ring Ma and ask her if she'll mind Finn after school. 'So long as he doesn't mind a bit of muck,' she says. 'We're planting a few hanging baskets at the daycare centre this afternoon.'

'He loves muck,' I tell her.

I park at the gates of Kerry's school and wait. I see her before she sees me. She's in the middle of a gang of kids. She throws her head back when she laughs and her dark hair parts and I see her face, her eyes closed and her mouth spreading a smile across it.

It's nice, seeing her like this. Out in the world, independent, animated. She looks like any other kid – teenager, I suppose. She looks beautiful and somehow carefree, like nothing bad will ever happen to her. Like she knows the world is full of possibilities and it's just a question of choosing.

She spots me and I roll down my window.

'Aren't you supposed to be at work?' she says.

'I was. Got the afternoon off. Thought we'd do something.'

'Like what?' She looks wary. Suspicious. Like I'm a stranger offering her sweets or something. I struggle to resist the bait. I want this to turn out good.

'Hop in. I'll tell you on the way.'

She sighs and straightens, turns her head towards her friends.

'I have to go,' she tells them. There's no need for her to say anything else. They get it. They're like fans at an away match that's not looking good. Stoic and loyal, despite the odds. They smile sympathetically. I nearly expect one of them to start singing 'You'll Never Walk Alone'.

She gets in, tosses her bag on the back seat, puts on her belt and sits there with her arms folded tight. 'Well?' she finally says.

Lately, I've been trying to remind myself of fourteen. Nearly fifteen. What was that like? How did that feel? It's trickier than you'd think, remembering. I don't know if Da ever picked me up from school. Maybe a few times from primary. Not from secondary school. I don't think so. And yeah, I probably would have been mortified if he had. He drove an ancient Fiat back then. Bright yellow, it was. The Banana Peel, Kenny called it. Yeah, I would have been morto, alright.

'We're going to Edges,' I tell her.

'The hardware shop?'

'Yeah. We're going to pick up some paint.'

'Why?'

'Graffiti,' I say, smiling away like a fool.

'What about it?'

'I just thought you might like to do some, you know, graffiti, in your bedroom. Art, like. On the wall. In your bedroom.'

'Graffiti?'

'Yeah.'

'On my bedroom wall?'

'Why not? It's your bedroom, isn't it?'

'You're going to buy me paint and let me splash it over the walls in my bedroom?'

'Yeah, that's right.' I'm enjoying this, to be honest. Her look of confusion. Disbelief. I'm getting a kick out of it.

'OK,' she says, putting her earphones in and settling back against the seat. I hear the familiar thump, thump, thump of that dance-y music she's keen on. She closes her eyes and I drive the dirty streets and that's fine by me because she's not kicking up and we're in a car going somewhere and if anyone looks into the motor, they'll see a father and his daughter, not fighting, not talking, just sitting together and moving forward and that's something, so it is. In any man's language.

It was Ellen's idea actually. She came up with it that night. At her apartment. We got up afterwards and ate huge portions of lasagne as if we hadn't eaten in days. It was delicious. We washed it down with glasses of milk, like a pair of kids. I thought it might have been a bit awkward. After the sex, I mean. But it wasn't.

Sometimes, when I've been in the motor all day, I feel like I'm on automatic pilot, going through the motions. But then, the odd time, I might round a corner and suddenly become aware of something. A landmark, maybe, like the statue of Big Jim on O'Connell Street, his powerful arms straining for the sky. Or something quiet, maybe, like a pair of swans floating down the Grand Canal in the early morning, oblivious to their grace. And it's like, all of a sudden, I'm there. Really there. Like I've come to.

That's how it felt, in Ellen's kitchen, drinking milk. I noticed everything. The way she closes her eyes when she laughs and how she tilts her head to the side when she listens, like what I was saying made sense. So I told her about Kerry and the trouble at the school. Ellen didn't agree that it was graffiti. She called it an art form.

In Ellen's quiet, serious voice, it seemed like a reasonable idea, letting a kid paint whatever they want on their bedroom walls. I kissed her when she said it and she said, 'What was that for?' and I said, 'Nothing,' but still, I kissed her because, yeah, why not? What was the big deal?

Kerry takes ages at the hardware shop, choosing colours. I give her the note. The fifty-euro note. 'That's the budget, alright?' She nods. That's grand with her. Fifty euros. That'll do the job.

At home, it takes a while to get the room organised. She spends time gathering her books and jewellery and the mountains of clothes that live on the floor. She places everything in a tall pile on the landing. I haul the furniture out. The dust comes off the stuff in clouds. I put a dust sheet over the bed, which is the only stick of furniture left in the room when we're done. 'Should we give it a bit of a hoover and polish?' I say. 'Before you start, I mean?' She withers me with a look and I say, 'No, you're right, why change the habit of a lifetime?' and for a second I think I've wrecked it and then she smiles and it's a real slow smile, one that looks like it'll never make it and then it does and I think we're safe enough.

'This wall, then?' I say, nodding towards the widest one, untroubled by the bed.

'It's got the light switch on it,' she says. 'It'll get in the way.'

'You could paint over it. Or maybe make it a part of the scene.'

'Do you think so?'

She looks at me then and it's such a genuine question, and she's asking me like she thinks I might have some kind of an answer so I say, 'Yeah, absolutely, why not?' and she nods and says, 'It might work, alright,' and I swear to God it feels like Cardiff just stuffed Manchester United to claim the Premiership title.

I leave without being asked to. I just say, 'I'll leave you to it, alright, love?' She nods and I close the door behind me and walk downstairs to the kitchen to make dinner. Hungarian goulash, God help me. Still, Ellen reckons I have potential. I don't even think she was joking. She gave me the recipe for the goulash after we'd finished the milk and the lasagne, and that was when I noticed the time. I stood up real quick and said, 'I have to go.'

She stood up too. 'Yes, of course. I'll get your jacket.' She handed me the recipe and walked me to the door of the apartment.

I should have said that I'd told Kerry I'd be home at midnight at the latest and now it was ten to, and if Finn woke up and I wasn't there, he'd be upset and he might cry and I'd feel awful for not being there when I said I'd be there.

But I didn't say any of that because, well, it's too much and it's too messy and it's too involved. So instead, I said, 'I had a lovely time,' like a right fucken dope, and she smiles and says, 'Me too,' and I tell her that I can't bring her to the physio clinic tomorrow because the motor's due her NCT and she says, 'That's fine,' and I say, 'See you soon,' and she nods, and I leave without telling her that I don't want to leave. Not yet. Not so soon.

The recipe is a Delia one, which means – according to Ellen – it can't fail. It's a good day for it. Rain lashing against the windows now, making them look cleaner than they deserve and the smell of garlic and onion softening in the pan and my daughter upstairs splashing paint on a wall in her bedroom.

Here are the things that no one tells you about home-made food. It makes your house smell lovely. Like a place where you'd want to arrive after a day's work. And it's quick. Quicker than fast food. By the time you drive to the Chinese, order, wait and drive home. Or even ring your order in and wait for delivery. Quicker than that. It's in the oven before you can say chicken balls and curry chips, I swear to God.

'She's looking for a canvas, that's all.' That's what Ellen said when I told her about Kerry and the graffiti that night.

'What do you mean?'

'She wants to express herself, I suppose. A way of speaking to the world. Trying to get someone to look at her and get her.'

'*I* get her.'

'It's not the same; you're her father.'

'I do my best, you know.'

'Of course you do. You're her father. You love her.'

'I do.' I tried to remember the last time I said it to Kerry. I love you. Did I ever say it? I must have. It's hard to know.

After we ate, Ellen made me a coffee. An espresso, good and strong. She handed it to me, picked up the remote and pointed it at the telly like she was turning it off. Except it was already off. It was never on. She looked surprised.

'Sorry,' she said. 'I'm the last person you want to take advice from. And I'm not, I'm not giving you advice, I just . . .'

'You're right, all the same. I don't get her. You're definitely right on that score.'

'What I meant was, you don't need to get her, that's the thing. You just need to give her a canvas. That's all.'

I wonder how she's getting on, Kerry. I'm not going up. Going to leave her to it. The smell of the beef and tomatoes and paprika and wine coming from the oven is making me remember that I had no lunch. I take a banana from the bowl and text Ma.

When will you be back? There's dinner for the pair of u.

A moment later:

What are you making? (remember I'm on that Zumba diet!) There in half hour.

This was followed by her usual winky, smiley face with the semi-colon and the bit of a bracket.

Kerry doesn't come down for dinner. Says she's in the middle of the thing. I can't argue with that, since it was me who started it.

Kenny rings after dinner.

'Beverage?'

'No.'

'No, just at the moment?'

'No.'

'No for the rest of the night?'

'Yeah. Maybe. I dunno.'

'Kerry out with her fella?'

'No.'

'What, then?'

'She's painting.'

'What?'

'Kerry. She's painting.'

'Yeah, I heard you. What is she painting?'

'The wall in her bedroom. She's doing . . . a mural, I suppose.'

'And you're just letting her?'

'Yeah.'

'Good man.' He hangs up and I realise then the reason why I like Kenny. Just . . . I don't know, he accepts things. Doesn't ask too many questions. Doesn't judge. I love that about him. I really do.

'Can we see your wall, Kerry?' Finn asks when Kerry finally appears, paint-splattered and hungry. I'm glad it's Finn who's asking. I hand her a bowl of goulash, which she inspects with distrust, then delivers a forkful to her mouth. I can tell she likes it. Her cheeks flush with the heat of it. 'Can we, Kerry?'

She sighs, shrugs, nods. We follow her up the stairs.

It's not graffiti. Or art, like the one she did on the school wall.

'It's a cartoon,' I say.

Kerry rolls her eyes. 'It's the Gorillaz,' she tells me.

'What do you mean, gorillas?'

'They're a band, old man,' Kerry says, punching my arm. 'That's Noodle, and 2D and Russel and Murdoc. On Plastic Beach.'

'Is that an actual place? Plastic Beach?'

'You're such a dinosaur.'

'In my day, bands were made up of actual people. Human beings.'

'In your day, people drew on the walls of caves and wore animal pelts.'

'A regular stand-up, you.'

'So, what do you think?' She stands still, looks at me. She wants to know what I think.

'I think it's fantastic, love. You're a great painter.'

She looks at me and smiles a small, brief smile like I'm not her da.

Like I'm someone she knows.

Someone she likes.

Thirty Three

I text Ellen a photograph of Kerry's wall the next morning before my shift starts at eleven. This is my first contact with her since the other night and I've spent a long time wondering what to text. Or if I should text at all. Phoning might be best. More grown-up, maybe. But I don't want to be pushy. Or seem needy. A phone call so soon might come across as a bit grasping.

A jaunty text. Something that says I'm thinking about you but not in a pushy or needy or grasping way.

I am thinking about her. Nothing pushy or needy but still, a fair bit, all the same. And there's loads of things I should be thinking about instead. Or at least, as well as. For instance, is Kerry at the library, studying for her exams the way she says she is? Or is she somewhere with yer man, whatshisface, with the silver ball bearings across his mush. A powerful magnet might put paid to his shenanigans, if I could get my hands on one.

Kenny gave me a few numbers to ring about the bouncy castle. I rang them all.

'For next year, yeah?' one of them said.

'Eh, no, it's this year. Three weeks' time.'

He laughed, like I'd said something funny.

'I've one left I could give you,' another fella tells me. 'But it's usually for hen parties. It's got a massive—'

'Ah, no, you're alright' I said, before I hung up.

One woman cried when I told her that Finn presumed I had it booked already. 'I'm a Cancer,' she explained. 'We're terrible emotional.'

The last fella quoted Benjamin Franklin. 'Fail to prepare, prepare to fail,' he said, his voice knowing and full of regret.

Then, this morning, the dishwasher finally gave up the ghost after a particularly shuddering cycle that ended with a roar, then ominous silence. When I opened the door, water gushed across the floor like a spring tide.

Instead of mopping it up and calling a plumber and putting out the brown bin and collecting a load for the washing machine and refilling the dog's water bowl and paying the gas bill, I made a cup of coffee and sat at the kitchen table and composed my jaunty text as the water lapped around my feet.

You were right about the wall. And about Kerry. Here she is beside the finished product, smiling!!

I press 'Send' before I can deliberate about smiley faces and X's and O's and what have you. I'm more a talker than a texter and even then, my phone conversations are bare minimum.

My phone pings and the kitchen's so quiet now that the dish-washer has given up, I jump at the sound.

Glad to hear it. Kerry's a talented painter. E

The promptness of her response emboldens me. The water has soaked through to my socks. I pick up my phone.

Would you like to do something?

I press Send. Put the phone on the table, facing down, so I can't see the minutes ticking by. This is needy, pushy, grasping. The phone pings, shifts a little through the crumbs on the table.

One word.

Yes

Wednesday night at 7pm? I'll pick you up.

Another word.

Yes

They can do without me at the five-a-side for another week. Loads of lads on the reserve bench, angling for a game.

I take off my shoes and socks, roll up my jeans and wade through the water, grab the mop and bucket and get stuck in. I think I even whistle a little as I dry the floor. The water, still a little warm and sudsy from the rigours of the machine, laps between my toes in a not unpleasant way.

I put the things I need to do on a list in my head. Janine recommends lists. She also recommends decluttering and something called feng shui but I haven't done either of those. She's on the money about the lists, all the same. Makes things seem a bit more manageable.

I mop and I make a list and I think about Wednesday night.

Janine's not right about everything, though. She says men can't multitask, and look at me now.

Dear Neil,

Dr Deery asked me to describe myself today. Of all the questions she's asked, this was one of the most difficult. I've never thought of myself in terms of adjectives. Attributes. I have been things to other people. A daughter, a student, an intern, a doctor, a wife. I've been all these things without giving any of them much thought. Now I have time to think, it seems like I'm somebody else. Somebody who has a good relationship with her mother. Somebody who doesn't want to be a doctor. Somebody who loves to paint.

Somebody who can make a friend.

I've made a friend.

I told Dr Deery that I was writing to you and she didn't tell me not to. But she said I have to be honest with you.

I made a friend and his name is Vinnie. We talk. We didn't talk for a long time and then, one day, we did. I surprised myself. I was never really the talkative type. Looking back now, I think it was because I was busy. There was never enough time.

I slept with him. It's harder to write than I thought it would be. I didn't plan to. It just happened. This is not me getting back at you. Yes, it's true, I was angry with you. Before. But that's not why. It really isn't.

It's nice, not being angry. I feel calmer and sort of . . . more hopeful. About the future. Even though I have no job and I live in an empty flat and I have no plans. But that doesn't mean I'll never have any plans. I realise that now.

I don't know what's going to happen. Or if anything will happen.

But yes, I want to see him again.

In the end, I come up with some kind of answer for Dr Deery.
  'I think I might be somebody who is open to possibilities.'
That's what I tell her in the end. She nods, as if she already
knew this.

Ellen

Thirty Four

At exactly a quarter to six on Wednesday evening, Finn gets a stomach bug. First, he eats his dinner. I manage to get him to eat fish even though he hates fish unless it's Donegal Catch or fish fingers. I hide the bits of cod and coley in a cheesy sort of sauce, cover the dish with mashed potatoes and bake it. According to the recipe, the preparation time is twenty minutes and I manage it in about forty-five minutes, which I reckon is pretty good for a beginner. He mills it, asks if it's OK to lick the plate. Kerry eyes her plate suspiciously and says, 'This is new.' I tell her fish is good for your brain and low in calories and she says, 'I know,' in a bored voice, then asks for seconds.

It's been a good week. Janine came over last night with her toolbox and sorted out the dishwasher. 'Something about a woman with a spanner in her hand, wha'?' said Kenny, who drove her over since her car was in for a service. 'I've known a few spanners in me time, alright,' said Janine, before a fair bit of her disappeared inside the machine. Kenny managed not to stare too long at the tops of her stockings, visible beneath the hem of her skirt and held in place by black suspenders. It was a huge effort on his part and he left shortly afterwards, declaring himself 'out of sorts'. I'd had a grand day at work – no fifty-euro tips or anything like it but only one complaining customer (because I stopped and let a car out when I knew the customer was in a hurry) and one drunk-ish woman who insisted I was the spit of John Cusack and asked if I could stop so she could get into the front seat and keep me company. I told her the seat belt in the front was broken. She didn't say another word after that, which is pretty unusual when it comes to drunk-ish women, in my experience. I paid the gas bill, remembered to put the right-coloured bin out and picked Kerry up from the library, saying I happened to be in the area, which was not, strictly speaking, true.

Now, it's a quarter to six on Wednesday and I'm standing in my bedroom with a towel around my waist, getting ready to shower the day off myself before I head over to pick Ellen up. Kerry bangs on the wall separating her bedroom from mine and tells me to stop singing, she can't get any studying done, and that's when Finn arrives in my bedroom, with the dog's bowl in his hands, up to the brim in vomit. 'Sorry, Dad, I didn't make it to the toilet on time.' I put my hand on his clammy forehead and he throws up on my bare feet. 'Sorry, Dad, I was trying to aim for the floor.'

I ring Ellen after Finn throws up again, this time on the floor tiles in the bathroom. 'Nearly made it that time, Dad,' and I know we're over the worst because a wan smile struggles across his white face. I wipe him down, put clean pyjamas on him and carry him to bed. 'Will you read me a story?' I nod, but the little fella's asleep before I have the book picked, the long, thick eyelashes dark against the paleness of his skin. I sit with him awhile.

'Finn is sick,' I say.

'Oh. Sorry. Is it . . .?'

'Ah, it's nothing serious, I don't think. A stomach bug. It's doing the rounds in the school, by all accounts.'

'I hope he's better soon.' Her voice sounds far away, like the line is bad.

'Yeah. Think it's just a twenty-four-hour thing.'

'So . . . I'll see you on Friday then?'

'Friday?'

'My physio appointment. In Portmarnock.'

'Oh, yeah, Friday, yeah.' I don't know why I'd forgotten. Probably because I was concentrating on Wednesday. Looking forward to it. Really looking forward to it.

I'll see her on Friday. Only in the car but still, we can talk then. I'll see her.

I want to see her. I realise it when she says, 'Goodbye,' and hangs up. Maybe I should have suggested doing something after the physio. I'm useless on the phone. Coming up with great things to say when the line's already dead.

Thirty Five

My phone rings. It's Janine. 'Calamity Jane never rang to book you.'

'I'm on my way over there now.'

'She rang you direct?'

'I was talking to her, yeah.'

'You holdin' out on me, Vinnie?'

'Course not. I just haven't had time to enter it into the system yet.'

'I'm not talkin' about the system.'

'I've to go. I'll be late.'

'Kenny says you got the hair cut.'

'I had to get Finn's mop sorted for the Communion. Yer man scalped the pair of us.'

'You'll be buyin' balloons next. Walkin' along beaches with the balloons in one hand and yer arm around Calamity Whatsherface.'

'I've no plans to buy balloons.'

'Not yet, maybe.' She sighs, as if it's just a matter of time. 'I suppose there'll be no sign of you in the pub tonight?'

'There's a practice mass for Finn's class at seven.'

'Is it serious, then? You and her?'

'I've to go, Janine.'

'You used to tell me everything.'

'No, I didn't.'

'Well, I used to be able to drag everything out of you.'

That's closer to the truth.

Ellen is outside the apartment block, standing beside a large cardboard box and a bulging black plastic bag.

'You running away from home?' I say.

'I did that already,' she says, but there is a small smile lurking around the corners of her mouth.

It's been a week and a day since I've seen her. She looks different. Could be her hair. It's getting longer, a dark frame against the paleness of her face. She looks at me with those curious amber eyes and I try not to stare at her mouth and think about reaching for her and cupping her small face with my hands and breathing her in and kissing her for a long, long time.

I try not to think about any of that.

'You OK?' she asks.

'Yeah, grand, not a bother.' It's too late now, to kiss her. If I was going to do it, I'd have done it by now. Wouldn't I? Should have stepped out of the car and just grabbed her. Not grabbed her, exactly, but . . . just . . . I should have kissed her. That's what I wanted to do. Minute I saw her.

'So,' I say, nodding towards the box. 'What's the story?'

'It's a bouncy castle. And a generator. I borrowed them from my brother. For you. Well, for Finn, I mean. For the Communion.'

'Oh.'

'You mentioned it last week. That you were looking for one.'

'Right.'

'You *do* still need it, don't you?'

I nod. 'I do. I really do.'

'I'd say it'll fit in the boot, won't it?'

I open the boot, lift the box in. When I turn around, she's there beside me, handing me the bag. I take it. 'Thanks,' I manage, finally.

'Don't mention it. David was delighted to offload it. His kids are a bit old for bouncing now.'

'No, really. Thank you. You have no idea how much I appreciate this. It's . . . it's very thoughtful of you.' I think about Finn's face when he sees the box, the way he'll smile with his entire body and jump up and down with excitement. I feel like doing a little jump myself. The kindness of the gesture. The thoughtfulness. Then I catch sight of her collarbone. The straight line of it, visible above the neck of her top. I stop thinking about bouncy castles.

'To be honest,' she says, 'it was a good opportunity for me to get in touch with him. I invited them for dinner on Sunday, David and his family. It was high time. So you did me a favour, really.'

I close the boot and turn around but she's not there. She's arranging her crutches into the well of the front passenger seat, then folding herself inside.

I get into the car and she looks at me. 'Is this OK?' she asks.

'Course.' Although it feels strange, all the same. I'm used to seeing her face in the rear-view mirror.

'You can see so much more from here,' she says, and there is a faint shake in her voice and I think about telling her she can sit in the back, like she always does. But I don't tell her that. Instead, I indicate and ease out onto the road. 'You alright?' I ask after a while, habit causing me to glance in the rear-view mirror.

'Yes,' she says.

I drive and she looks out the window and it's pretty much business as usual except she's up the front and there's a bouncy castle in the back. We talk. I tell her about the moderate success of the goulash. I say moderate because Ma was slow to endorse it, poking at the meat with the prongs of her fork. 'It's very orange,' she said, suspiciously.

'That'll be the paprika,' I told her.

'Hmm,' she said.

Ellen tells me about her own mother, sitting for a portrait. 'She made me give her long hair. Like Cher's, she said.'

'And did you?'

She nods. 'And I made it darker too. And glossy. Least I could do. She's been very good to me.'

I pull up outside the clinic and look at my watch. 'Bang on time,' I say. 'How's that for service?'

Ellen nods, picks her bag off the floor. I get out, walk around to her side and open the door, like I always do, but she doesn't move. I bend down. 'You OK in there?' She nods without looking at me and picks up her crutches. I stand back so she can make her way out of the car. She walks a few paces away, then stops and turns. Her face is flushed. 'What's the story?' I say.

She shakes her head. 'This is embarrassing.'

'It's just physio. You've been doing it for a fair while now. Nothing to be embarrassed about.'

She glances towards the clinic, then back at me. She really does look embarrassed. I can't work it out.

'Remember last Thursday? When you were leaving the apartment?' she says then, in a rush of words.

'Yeah,' I say.

'And you said you couldn't take me to physio the next day because you had to take your car in for the NCT.'

'Yeah, sorry about that, I tried to change the time but I—'

'I actually didn't have a physio appointment.'

'So that worked out alright then.'

'And I don't have an appointment today either.'

'Then what are we—?'

'I was going to go inside. Sit in reception. Come out after twenty minutes, like I usually do.'

'Why?'

'He doesn't want to see me any more. The physiotherapist.

Duncan. He says I'm fine. So long as I continue to do the exercises and do some more walking. Every day, he says. I have to walk. And do the exercises. But I . . . I don't need to come to the clinic any more. That's what he said. A couple of weeks ago.'

I shake my head. Janine's right. I'm no Sherlock when it comes to the mysteries of women. I haven't got a clue what's going on.

'So,' I say, because she's looking at me like I'm supposed to say something now. 'You don't agree. You want Duncan to give you a couple more sessions. Just . . . to be on the safe side. Before you stop with the physio. Is that it?'

She leans heavily on her crutches. Concentrates on a spot on the ground. 'No, that's not it.' She looks at me, then back at the ground. 'I just . . . I got used to seeing you. Every Friday. And then I started looking forward to them. To the Fridays. You were . . . you are . . . easy to talk to and you just seemed to take me at face value and that was nice. I . . . I liked that.'

The penny floats in front of my face like a heat shimmer before it drops.

'So there's no physio session?'

She shakes her head. 'No.'

'Oh.'

She looks up then. 'I'm sorry, Vinnie. Wasting your time. But I wasn't sure what the situation was. Between us. You left so abruptly last week and then you cancelled on Wednesday and I know Finn was sick but still, I started thinking . . .'

'Started thinking what?'

'I wasn't sure. If you wanted to . . . see me again or . . . I don't know . . . maybe you regretted the other night. I know you've lots going on in your life and I don't—'

'I should have kissed you.'

Now it's her turn to look confused.

I blunder on. 'When I picked you up today. I thought about it and I didn't do it and I don't know why but I should have. It's just . . . I'm not used to this and I don't know what to be saying or doing half the time.'

'You could kiss me now,' she says then. 'I mean, if you like.'

I walk towards her and I swear, it feels like the longest walk, and when I reach her I bend my head towards her face and she closes her eyes and when I kiss her, she kisses me back and it feels like we know each other. Like we've known each other for a long time.

There's a café across the road and I get some takeout coffees. We sit on the wall outside the clinic and drink them. 'I would have liked to stay. The other night, I mean,' I tell her.

'Would you?'

'Yeah. But I was late enough as it was. That was why I had to go so abruptly.'

'You don't have to explain.'

'And I'm sorry about Wednesday.'

'There's nothing to apologise for. I was just feeling . . . a bit exposed, I suppose. It's been a long time since I've ventured out of my shell.'

'Finn vomited in the dog's bowl and on my bare feet. That actually happened.'

'Why are you smiling?' she asks after a while.

'I was thinking about Duncan,' I say.

'Why?'

'I just wondered what he'd make of us, sitting here drinking coffee.'

'He'd be jealous because you're so handsome.'

'Oh.'

She laughs. 'You really don't know, do you?' She puts her hand on my shoulder. I bend to kiss her again but I'm too eager and I end up smacking my nose against hers, like a right apprentice. My eyes water. 'Sorry about that, I'm . . . I'm out of practice.'

She smiles, rubbing her nose. 'We both are.'

Neither of us say anything, so after a while I say the first thing that comes into my head, which happens to be, 'Look . . .' with no idea of what I'll say after that.

'I know,' Ellen says, which is confusing, since I don't know.

'I know what you were going to say.' She looks serious now. She looks like someone who knows what I am going to say.

'You were going to say it's complicated,' she says.

I don't think I was going to say that but I nod because, when you think about it, it's not straightforward. Me struggling with the kids, worrying about Paula, and Ellen trying to come to terms with the break-up of her marriage and her grief. It's not your average boy meets girl. Then again, I've done your average boy meets girl and look where that got me. Oddly, I smile. She smiles too, like it's contagious.

This time, when I bend to kiss her, there is no collision. No damage done. Just her mouth. The sweet flesh of it, soft against mine. She runs her hands up my arms, curls them under the collar of my shirt in a way that is unfamiliar and exciting. I pull away. 'Complicated isn't necessarily a bad thing, mind,' I say.

She nods slowly.

'And, let's face it, I could do with a lot more practice,' I continue, encouraged by the smile sweeping across her face.

'Maybe we could practise on each other and see how it goes,' she says, easing herself off the wall and reaching for her crutches.

I nod, not trusting myself to speak. My response might have been more suited to a football match, with Cardiff ahead by more than they deserved.

Dear Neil,

I rang Faye.

If she was surprised, she didn't say. She sounded pleased, in fact. Said it was lovely to hear from me. She was always the easy-going one. She was in the canteen at the hospital. Her lunch break. The background noise was so loud, I could barely hear her. I'd forgotten that, how noisy that place is. And the smell of mushroom soup everywhere. Even when it wasn't on the menu, it still smelled like mushroom soup. Remember?

I said I was sorry. For not being in touch. She asked about my leg. The physio. All that. I told her I'd had plastic surgery on my face. We had a laugh about that. When we were young, we said we'd get plastic surgery on our chests. A reduction for her, an enlargement for me. I ask about Barry and the kids. She said Barry's driving her crazy but she always said that, right from the start. She told him he wasn't her type and he said he didn't care and she said, 'On your head, be it.'

I'm not sure I have a 'type'. It was your work I admired at first. I respected you as a doctor. It was only years later we became lovers. At that conference in Donegal. You tapped my shoulder during the talk on hospital hygiene. Bent towards me and whispered in my ear. 'I think we should get the sex thing out of the way.'

You made me laugh.

There's a position at Beaumont. Faye told me about it. Part-time, short-term contract so I wouldn't have to commit.

The idea of being a doctor again provokes a dull, heavy feeling, like a headache getting started.

I suppose I can't sit in this apartment forever. The money will run out sooner or later.

Faye wants to meet up. I said I'll call her. She said, 'Don't leave it too late.'

I know she's right.

It's time to show my face.

Ellen

Thirty Six

The only way to fit the bouncy castle into the back garden is to dismantle the shed. It's on its last legs anyway.

Kenny helps. He's wearing what he calls his DIY outfit: bright orange overalls and a matching bandana around his head. The overalls don't look like they've seen much in the way of DIY. Immaculate, they are.

Most of the stuff in the shed is for the bin. Mismatching wellies. A fishing net with a hole at the bottom. An ancient kettle. A cushion with the stuffing oozing out of it. Paint cans, their hard dregs stuck to their bottoms. A raincoat with a broken zip. A flask with no lid.

'A veritable treasure trove,' says Kenny, peering in and shaking his head.

'Just give us a hand, will you?'

It doesn't take us long to clear it out in the end. Most of the stuff ends up in black bags.

Finn brings us glasses of Ribena. We sit on upturned buckets and peer into the empty shed.

'I'd say one good swing of an axe should do it,' says Kenny, nodding at the slope of the roof. It takes a few swings in the end. We take turns. There's something about demolition that brings out the boy in a man.

'She's about to surrender,' says Kenny, mopping his brow with the bandana. 'Stand down, Vinnie. Give us a go.'

I swing the axe one more time. What's left of the shed

staggers under the blow, sways and moans before toppling to the ground.

'Ah, Vinnie, it was my turn.'

'Sorry, couldn't help it.'

He nods, understanding.

We bag the wood and the rubbish.

'There's a skip outside Mrs Hall's place. We could dump it in there,' says Kenny. 'She's away for the night, visiting her sister in Bray.' He's on the Neighbourhood Watch committee so he always knows who's where, doing what.

'We can't do that, Kenny.'

'We can. I've already taken stuff out of the skip so we'll be square.'

'What the hell did you take out of a skip?'

'She threw the kennel in. Nearly new, it was. She bought it only six months before Charlo went under the Ikea truck. All those flat-packs. He never stood a chance.'

'You don't even have a dog.'

'I'm thinking about getting one.'

I blame *Marley and Me*. Since he saw that film, he's got this idea that getting a Labrador like Marley might help him get a woman like Jennifer Aniston. Not that he'll admit it. But that's the case, all the same.

'There's no way your mother would have a dog in the house.'

'What do you think I nicked the kennel for? I've put it in the back garden. Letting her get used to the idea first.'

'She'll never go for it.'

'She's halfway through the *Lassie* box set I got for her. Loving it, she is. It's only a matter of time.'

I look at the black bags. 'I'll bring this lot to the dump.'

'Suit yourself,' says Kenny.

The bouncy castle is still in its box in the cupboard under the stairs. I haven't told Finn it's there; only that it'll arrive the night before the Communion. Otherwise, he'd plague me to pump it up. He's got this idea that he can churn milk into butter if he drinks a pint of it, then bounces for long enough in the castle. 'Does he really think that?' Ellen wanted to know the other afternoon.

'He seems fairly convinced,' I said.

'He's such a funny kid.'

'Funny weird, maybe.'

It was one of those days where the light of afternoon reaches for you in lazy slants through the blinds in the apartment, makes you think that time is nothing but a myth.

I stay for an hour or so usually, a couple of afternoons a week. When Finn has his football practice or tae kwon do. It doesn't feel like time, the time I spend there. Maybe it's because I never took time off before. Not to do nothing. Well, not nothing, exactly. Just nothing that's on the list of the things in my head that I'm supposed to be doing.

Or maybe it's because her apartment is not a place I associate with anything other than her. There's time to think. I think about the kids. About the very fact of them. I mightn't always know what to be doing with them, what to say, but I wouldn't be without them. I know that much.

The thoughts I think in Ellen's apartment aren't the ones that race along. They're ones that arrive and sit for a while and stare you in the face, like footballers on the bench, determined to get a game.

Ellen says, 'You look very serious.'

I say, 'Come here.'

She leans over and kisses me and I gather her up and carry her to her bedroom and I put her on the bed and she reaches for me and time stops again, for a while.

'Are you thinking about sex?' Kenny asks.

'What kind of a question is that?'

'You are, aren't you?'

'No.'

'Why not?'

'Because I'm not.'

'I would be, if I were you.'

'Would you give over.'

'Did you invite her to the Communion?'

'No.'

'Why not?'

'Are you going to help me with this lot or not?' I point at the black bags strewn across the grass.

'Keep your hair on, Casanova. I'm only sayin'. You should ask her. She sorted you out with the castle an' all. And you've been seein' her a fair bit. And you know what the women are like. Even if they say no, they still like to be asked.'

'You should be one of those whatchamacallems . . . agony aunts.'

'I suppose I should,' he says, as if I'm not taking the piss. 'Give something back. Share the benefit of my experience with the rest of the world.'

'Jaysus.'

Janine's just as bad. Interrogating me. 'Have you had the conversation?' she asked the other day.

'What conversation?'

'The "where is this thing going?" conversation.'

'It's only been a few weeks.'

'Never too soon to set out your stall.'

'What stall?'

She rolls her eyes. 'Don't come crying to me, lover boy.'

I'm keeping things simple. Trying to, at any rate. Enough complications going on. Janine likes complications. Adds to the excitement, she says. But there's something grown-up about me and Ellen. We talk. There's no shouting and roaring. Just two people in a room. Talking. We've things in common, after all. Irish history, for example. We visit the exhibition at Collins' Barracks. And music. I burn *The Luke Kelly Collection* for her. She says 'Raglan Road' is her favourite song on the album.

We're both reading again. Ellen hasn't read in a long time, she tells me. And she's still not, not really. Nothing new, at any rate. Instead, she's rereading. She likes knowing what's going to happen in the end. Comforting, she says. She lends me *The Catcher in the Rye*. Holden Caulfield reminds me of Kerry a bit.

There are no demands. No givers, no takers, no hassle. Just two people, enjoying a quiet life, a few hours a week. It's not what I was expecting. I wasn't expecting anything. I'm fairly sure I had resigned myself to the same old, same old. Thought that was it, nothing else was going to happen to me.

And now this.

The newness of it. The strangeness.

Maybe this is what a relationship is like when you meet as adults and not half-baked teenagers like me and Paula. Always squabbling, we were. Like kids. Paula said the make-up sex made it worth it. Or during the fight, sometimes. Angry sex, she called that. 'Harder! Fuck me harder.' Me worrying that she'd wake the kids, and knowing afterwards that somehow, it was never hard enough.

The garden looks much bigger, with the shed gone and the grass cut. I take down the clothesline. I can see one of Finn's friends thinking it's a tightrope.

Five days to the Communion. Ma brings down armfuls of tulips. Arranges them on windowsills around the house. Nicked from Phoenix Park, no doubt. The park ranger is wise to her at this stage. I think he turns a blind eye, to be honest. It's been years since he's chased her.

Finn persuades me to allow five of his pals from school into the garden tomorrow after school. 'They want to see the shed, now that it's demolished,' he says.

'Why would they want to do that?'

He shrugs. 'Dunno.'

'No more than five, mind,' I say.

'We might be hungry,' Finn says, not quite looking at me.

'Pity about yiz.'

'We could have pizza. They're easy to make. No mess. We could eat them in the back garden.'

'Go on, then. I'll get some pizzas in.'

'Pepperoni?'

'Yeah.'

'And Coke?'

'No way, yiz'll be as mad as hatters.'

'But we're having Coke on the Communion day, aren't we?'

'Yeah. Just one glass each, mind.'

'Two for me, seeing as I'm the main attraction.'

'Go on.'

'I know I'm not supposed to talk about how much money I'm going to make on Saturday, but if I make enough, I'll buy you something, OK?'

He runs out of the room before I get a chance to respond.

Kerry walks in. 'What are you smiling for?' she says.

'Nothing.'

'Do I have to go to the Communion?'

'Yeah.'

'Can Mark come?'

'Does he eat lasagne?'

'You're buying lasagne?'

'I'm making it.' I'm enjoying this. Kerry's look. Her disbelief. Trying to work me out. It feels deadly.

'You don't know how to make lasagne.'

'I do now.'

'How?'

'I took a cookery class.'

'You?'

'Yeah. A friend of mine gave me a cookery lesson.'

'Is she the friend you went to the "gig" with the other night?' She sniggers. I didn't call it a gig. I said a concert. It's been years since I've been to one. I'd forgotten how live music gets inside you, the beat and thump of it. I was hoarse the next day, all the roarin' I did. And I wouldn't be a massive Van Morrison fan, like Ellen is, but I knew most of the stuff anyway and it was . . . yeah, it was pretty exhilarating, bein' honest.

'Yeah . . . Ellen.' It feels weird, explaining yourself to your kid.

'Is she your girlfriend?'

'No.' Girlfriend sounds frivolous. We're both married, for fuck sake. Or were, at any rate.

'What, then?'

'I told you, she's a friend. And a fare. She drove me to the hospital that time.'

'What time?'

'I wasn't well. In the car. A good while ago now.' The panic attack feels like it happened a long time ago. To somebody else.

'You never told me.'

'No, well, it was nothing, really. I didn't want you to be worrying.'

'Is she coming to the Communion?'

'I . . . I don't think so. I'm not sure. Maybe.' Maybe Kenny's right. And Ellen can say no. I'll tell her that. No big deal. Except that it is a big deal.

It is.

Like this conversation. I never expected me and Kerry to be having this conversation. About Ellen. Didn't expect it to come up so soon. Was putting it on the long finger, like I do.

'So can Mark come? If he promises to eat your lasagne?'

'OK.'

Kerry moves to the fridge, opens it, scans the shelves.

'So what do you think?' I say, as she picks up a yoghurt. Diet ones. She insists.

'About what?'

'About me seeing if Ellen wants to come to the Communion.'

She shrugs, closes the fridge door, gets a spoon out of the drawer. She's heading for the door now.

'Kerry?'

She turns, looks at me. Shrugs again. 'Whatevs.' She turns and leaves the kitchen. No slamming doors. No stamp of feet on stairs. No shouts or roars.

That went well.

I'm pretty sure it did.

Dear Neil,

The world is made up of people who don't mention my scar and people who do.

The woman in the corner shop where I get my cigarettes knows my name. She says, 'Ah, howeya, Ellen,' like she's known me for years, or hasn't seen me for years. She asked straight out, the first day I went into the shop. 'What happened, love?'

The woman in number twenty-one knows everything about everyone and is only dying to ask me about it but doesn't know how to weave it into the conversation. I see her trying, every time she meets me. A muscle throbs in her jaw with the effort of not mentioning it.

The physio talks about it but in a breezy, professional way so you'd barely notice. Or maybe I'm just getting used to it. I think I might be.

Vinnie has never mentioned it. It's like he hasn't even noticed it. I forget about it when he's around. It becomes unimportant. There's something appealing about that kind of acceptance. How quiet it is. How kind.

You would have been interested. In an objective, medical way. You would have been interested in the length of it. The rise of it. The colour. The width. The pull of the skin around it. The surgeon did a good job.

I think it's fading. All scars fade in the end. Someday, it will be a fine, white, jagged line, connecting the corner of my eye to my jawline.

I was lucky.
I know that now.

Ellen

Thirty Seven

I ring Ellen. She sounds worried. 'Everything OK, Vinnie?' I don't usually ring. I text.

'Look, I know it's late notice but I was wondering if . . .' I stop there. It's too much. I shouldn't ask her. It's too soon, or something. My family . . . you can't just shove someone in the middle of all that.

'If what?' she says.

I take a breath. 'If you'd like to come over to the house on Saturday. You know we're having a bit of a do for Finn and I just thought . . . since you showed me how to make the lasagne and everything, I'd . . . you might . . .' I fade out. I don't know what the hell I was thinking.

'I don't know, Vinnie.'

I don't blame her. I haven't asked her to the house before. Bedlam at the best of times. Didn't want to send her running.

'Look, you don't have to. But I'd like you to. I just . . . I wanted you to know that.'

Silence then, on the other end of the phone. She's thinking. I want to know what she's thinking. And then again, maybe I don't.

I know what I'm thinking, though. I know that I want to spend time with her. I'm sure about that. Rub my thumb along her mouth, kiss her, over and over. Go to bed with her in the afternoon. A hundred times. More. I want to be the one who makes her laugh. Makes her smile. Takes her out.

I want things to be less complicated.

'It's Finn's big day,' she says then. 'I don't want to . . . get in the way of that, Vinnie.' Her tone sounds flat.

'Are you OK?' I ask.

'Yes, it's just . . . I got a letter from Neil's solicitor. The house . . . it's sold. That family who made the offer signed the contracts. They're moving in at the end of the month. I've to clear out the last of my stuff.'

'I could come with you, if you like.'

A pause. Then, 'Thanks, Vinnie.'

'No sweat,' I tell her.

Another pause. Then, 'I'd like to come. On Saturday.'

'Really?'

'Just for an hour or so. I could help you dish up.'

'No, there'll be no helping. You'll be our guest.'

'OK. If you're sure.'

'Say around two?'

'Fine.'

'See you then.'

'Yes.' I hear her uncertainty. It's not something she wants to do. She's making herself do it. She's made herself do a lot of things recently. It wouldn't take much to dissuade her so I just hang up before she changes her mind.

I think about her getting the twenty questions treatment from Ma. Maybe a touch of cold shoulder from Kerry. Flirted with by Kenny. The up and down inspection by Janine. And Trish said she'd call in. I didn't even invite her. She just said she'd 'pop in' with her kids. Like she was doing me a favour.

I take a breath. Release it slowly, like the doctor advised. I haven't had a Valium in a couple of weeks now. Haven't needed one. I'm wondering how I'll introduce Ellen to people. Around here, we don't call women 'friends'. Women are your ma. Your wife. Your girlfriend. Your sister. Your neighbour. They're not your friends and if you call them that, you're only asking for trouble.

'Friend-of-mine' sounds better.

'This is Ellen. She's a friend-of-mine.'

I think it's good. About the house. Being sold. Her and her husband – Neil – can, I don't know, move on a bit, I suppose.

Saying where people are from when you're introducing them. That can be a good distraction.

'This is Ellen, from Clontarf.'

'Oh! What part?' People always ask that. That'll distract them.

'This is Ellen. She showed me how to make the lasagne.' That sounds good. People might think she's with a catering company maybe. Even though catering companies are a bit Celtic Tiger, but still.

No, Ma will have the full story in five minutes flat. Probably haul it out of her at the doorstep.

A while ago, there wasn't all that much to tell.

It's a bit different now.

It feels a bit different.

I put the kettle on. Use two teabags. A heaped spoon of sugar. Drink it in the back garden, with a fag. Think about Ellen. About explaining her.

Nothing occurs.

Should have thought this through before I opened my beak.

Now I'm just thinking about her. Thinking about Ellen. I'm sitting on the step at the back door, thinking about Ellen and smiling. I only realise I'm smiling when I get up to poke the butt through the grid of the drain. I catch my face in the kitchen window. The reflection of it. Smiling away like a fool.

State of me.

It's weird, being happy.

It catches you unawares. You think everything is going along, just like normal, then you catch your reflection in a window, and there you are, smiling away at nothing.

Dear Neil,

I'm running out of things to paint in the apartment. Mum says we should go to St Anne's Park, I could paint something in there. A tree, perhaps. She says she'll come with me. Bring a picnic, since the weather's been so mild. I laugh and she says, 'What?' defensively and I say I can't imagine her sitting on a rug in a park drinking tea out of a flask. 'Do you even have a flask?' I ask and she says, 'Not yet,' and there's that steely glint in her eye that suggests she'll have a flask and a picnic basket by sundown.

She hugged me today. When she was leaving. I told her that I'd been thinking about my dream job. I'd love to work with kids. Teach them how to paint. Be an art teacher. In a secondary school, maybe. I have no idea how to go about it. But I think I'd love it. How about that for a surprise?

She hugged me and then she kissed me. On my scar. I don't know if this was deliberate, the geography of her kiss. She complains of being short-sighted but refuses to wear her glasses. I thought she would feel bony but it was soft, her hug. Vinnie invited me to Finn's First Holy Communion. I didn't tell Mum. Maybe because I'll end up not going. That's what's awful about having too much time on your hands. You don't just have second thoughts, but third and fourth ones. Besides, it's a family thing. I probably shouldn't go. I don't know why I said yes.

I told Mum I wasn't quite ready to paint in public. Could you imagine me, in the park, with an easel? Still, her idea must have resonated with me somehow because later, I went out and bought the most colourful, extravagant bunch of flowers I could find. The florist stared when I walked in but collected herself quick enough. A professional. I used every colour on my palette to paint them. It's more frantic life than still life. There was paint in my hair when I finished. My phone rang and I answered it and it was Vinnie and he wanted to know if I'd come in from a run or something and I realised I was out of breath, like I'd just unfolded myself from a vigorous yoga stretch.

I think it was exhilaration.

I haven't done yoga in years. Haven't even thought about it. I used to love it, remember? Those Thursday-night classes. And then we decided to extend the clinic's opening hours and I missed a few, then a few more before I stopped going altogether. It's only now, thinking about it, I realise how much I miss it.

What do people bring to a Communion party? You'd tell me to Google it, probably. Or reach for two bottles of wine from your rack. Not the ones at the top. Second row, maybe. I don't know why you bothered buying those ones at the top. 'They'll be worth a fortune someday,' you said.

I went to the house the other day, to clear out the last of the stuff. Vinnie drove me there. 'I'll wait outside,' he said. He knew. That I needed to go in on my own. Some goodbyes are like that.

The bottles were still there, on the top shelf of the rack. I left them behind. Maybe the family who are moving in will drink them. Or sell them. Or keep them until they're worth a fortune. Someday.

Ellen

Thirty Eight

' "Jesus loves the sick and the sad." '

That's the first line of Finn's reading. Kenny beams, distinct-ive in a suit – pale green tartan – and a pink shirt. 'It's cerise,' he announces. His tie – also green – has a picture of the crucifixion on it. 'Had to order it specially from the Vatican gift shop,' he says. 'Pure silk. Feel it.'

Kenny leans towards me. 'Great delivery,' he whispers, and I have to agree.

Jesus loves the sick and the sad.

Something inside me swells. Pride, maybe. I can't help it. He's so pale and skinny and he's lost that many teeth. And more besides. But still. There he is. Standing on a box behind the lectern on the altar. Speaking into the microphone that is bent low so he can reach it.

He was ready in five minutes this morning. Had the outfit laid out at the bottom of his bed. The socks, underpants, even his hairbrush, and God knows it isn't often a brush gets pulled through that mop. He had the sheet and the pyjamas in the linen basket already by the time I went in to him.

'Sorry, Dad.'

'Don't worry about it, son.'

'I think I forgot because I've loads to think about today. And I've to do the reading, remember?'

'We'll have a great day.'

'Yeah.'

The smell of urine is sour but faint. Usually, I'd take the mattress off the bed. Spray Febreze on it. Put it in the back garden to air out. Can't do that today. No room in the garden, for starters, with the bouncy castle and the patio furniture Ailbhe and Grainne lent me. I open the window. Let a bit of air at it that way.

The only thing Finn needs help with is the top button of his shirt. 'I'd say Mam didn't send a postcard because she's sent a First Holy Communion card instead. It'll probably be in the post. And I know I'm not supposed to talk about the money, but I'd say there'll be something inside. But I won't mind if there isn't. But I'd say there will be. Would you, Dad? Would you say so?'

'You've a cornflake in your hair,' I say, removing the soggy article. 'How'd you manage that?'

He thinks about it, then shakes his head. 'I don't know.'

'Did you brush your teeth? What's left of them?'

He nods, opening his mouth and breathing all over my face so I can smell the toothpaste. He knows me well.

There's a fair crowd in the church. It's nice, all the same. Make a bit of a fuss of the lad on his big day.

Ellen said she'd be at the house later. Around two. It feels strange. The idea of Ellen being in the house. As my guest. And what else? I'm not sure, but the uncertainty isn't the stressful kind of not knowing. It's more like . . . I don't know . . . 'exciting' sounds a bit daft. It's been a while since I felt excited. And I don't just mean sex. I mean seeing someone. Having them around.

After I invited her and she said yes, I put the voucher in the pocket of my jacket. The one for the night in the fancy hotel in Derry that the boss slipped into my Christmas pay packet.

'A little something for all your hard work, Vinnie,' he'd said, with a discreet wink. I'm fairly sure he was referring to him asking me to drive him home when he'd had a few too many at the Christmas party. Instead of going to his house in Blackrock, he directed me to a little redbrick terrace on Great Western Square in Phibsboro. 'Our little secret, Vinnie,' he said, tapping his nose with his finger and stumbling out of the motor.

I'd forgotten all about the voucher until recently. I could suggest it for June, when Ma takes the kids on her annual pilgrimage to Knock.

All Ellen can say is no but, well, she said yes to the Communion. It's just the one night. I think about the two of us in those fluffy white dressing gowns, drinking coffee and making plans. Nothing major. A visit to the Giant's Causeway maybe. She could bring her paints. And we could go to the Brandywell. See a match. She said she'd like to go to another one. Or we could stroll along the walls and look out on the city. The peace of it now, after the Troubles.

I'll ask her. When everyone's gone. I'll persuade her to stay and have a drink with me when it's all quietened down. Then I'll ask her. No pressure, I'll say. Just some time out.

I think about waking up with her. Opening my eyes on a gorgeous June morning and seeing her there beside me. A feeling hatches inside me and I think it might be excitement. Maybe even optimism. Or both. Whatever it is, I find myself ringing the hotel. Enquiring about availability.

'You'd be better off making a provisional booking, sir,' the girl says. 'We fill up pretty quick that weekend.'

'OK,' I say, 'I will.' There's caution in my hands and I'm flinging it into the wind.

Ma is sitting at the end of the pew beside Callam's granny. Rita, I think her name is. Mrs O'Dwyer. Lives two roads over. They're acquaintances more than friends, her and Ma. But at this stage, with their numbers dwindling, they make do, I suppose. She's gone all out, Ma. She had the hair in rollers most of yesterday. And she got the colour in too. She says it's called 'Cobalt Shimmer', but it's a blue rinse, all the same. Her and Margie went shopping for her outfit. Days, it took them, to settle on one. It's a pink dress. Bright, Ma says. Loud might be another word. She couldn't wear the shoes in the end. Even after she'd asked the cobbler to cut the toes out of them. Had to settle for the black lace-ups she's worn for years. And thick tights to hide the purple knots of her varicose veins. A lilac jacket – *It's a blazer, Vincent* – with silver buttons and a carnation in the lapel, to match Finn's. She looks great, bein' honest. She loves a bit of an occasion. Something to dress up for. She glances at me, frowns, signals with her hand. It's only then I realise I'm meant to be kneeling, not sitting.

I kneel. What would it be like if Paula were here? It's hard to imagine her today, when everyone is in such great form. She was so sad, especially those few months before she went into the hospital. It was vast, her sadness. I'd bring her out in the motor on Sunday afternoons. We'd sit in the car at Howth Head and look at the sea. Ireland's Eye. Ireland's Tear. Lambay. I'd tell her stuff about me and Joey, when we were kids, getting into all sorts of trouble. Harmless stuff, really. We stole a boat once. Borrowed it just. A small wooden yoke. We rowed out to Ireland's Eye. Around it, and back again. 'The size of the seals out there, Paula,' I'd say. 'Big as houses, some of them.'

'Why is Mammy crying?' Finn wanted to know, on one of those Sunday-afternoon drives. We were parked at St Anne's. Finn was in the back seat beside Kerry, who didn't say much. Finn wanted to go to the playground. Get an ice cream. The usual. Paula shook her head any time I suggested we get out of the car.

'What's the matter?' I asked her. She said, 'Sorry,' over and over again. She wasn't really crying. There was no sound. It looked like she was leaking, with the tears running down her face. Like some part of her was dissolving. And there was nothing I could do about it. I drove her home. Gave her the tablets. Put her to bed. Took Finn out to Fairview Park. Kerry didn't want to come. I pushed him on the swings. Bought him an ice cream on the way home. What else could I do? He was five. He didn't understand. None of us did.

' "Jesus loves the sick and the sad." '

Proud as punch, I am. He gets through the whole lot without a glitch, unless you count him saying 'lice' instead of 'life' so it comes out as 'Jesus gave the gift of lice to the world,' but no one notices. Except Janine. I see her smiling to herself. She won't say a word. Nearly as proud of him as I am.

The day is glorious, like Jesus himself has banished the low, dirty clouds from the city for the day that's in it. Outside the church, families gather in semicircles for photographs. Finn poses with Kerry and Ma, Kenny and Janine. The dress Kerry bought in Topshop is gorgeous. A bit on the shortish side but a dress all the same and it's not black. It's green. 'That's a bottle green, Vinnie,' Kenny says.

She's gone easy on the make-up too. She wraps her arms around Finn, hugs him, kisses him. 'Smile,' says Kenny, shaking under the weight of an enormous contraption of a camera he got last Christmas when he was going through his artistic phase. He talked about composition. Depth. Tone. Perspective.

Kerry smiles. She looks younger when she does that. Like a kid again. 'Keep smiling, Kerry,' I say, taking my iPhone out of my pocket to snap them.

Monica grabs my elbow. 'Call in to us, Vinnie,' she says. 'On the way back from the church, if you like. Have a drink. The boys can have a bounce. Our bouncy castle has a slide an' all.'

'Ah, no, you're grand. I need to get home. Get the food organ-ised. But thanks.'

'What are you doing food-wise?' she asks.

'Lasagne.'

'Lasagne? From the local place? I heard they had rats. Big as dogs some of them, Mrs Finnegan was saying. Droppings all over the floor the other day, apparently.'

'Eh, no, no . . . I . . . I made it myself, matter of fact. It's a doddle, really. Nothing to it.'

She looks at her husband then, her nose wrinkled. Like he's just farted. 'Did you hear that? Lasagne.'

He shrugs, winces, shifting from one foot to the other.

'Those shoes still giving you jip?' I ask him. It's hard to look directly at him, with the glare. Finn was right. It's yellow, his get-up.

'Bunions, you know yourself.' His smile is grateful. I wouldn't say he gets a lot of TLC at home. I nod, even though I don't know anything about bunions, thank God.

Monica gets back to me. 'Yer man would put an egg on the frying pan without cracking it first, I swear to God. Hasn't a clue.'

'Well, I suppose cooking's not . . . everyone's cup of tea,' I say, fairly feebly.

'Hmmm,' says Monica, scalding the poor fella with another glare. 'Well, we'll pop in to you then. Later on, of course. If you'd like.'

'Well, we—'

'Just for an hour or so. Let the lads compare their hauls, eh?'

Jaysus.

Finn runs up, out of breath. 'Dad, I know I'm not supposed to talk about the money but I'm only talking to you about it so that's OK, isn't it?'

'Well . . .'

'I went behind the bush there to count it so no one would see me and so far, I've made eighty-five euros and that's not including the fiver Kenny gave me for ice cream. He said the real cash is in the card but you can't make your First Holy Communion without a ninety-nine. That's why he gave me the fiver. But don't worry, Dad, I won't say anything about the money to anyone else, OK? Just to you, and that doesn't count, does it? I'll let you know when I get to a hundred, OK?'

He's gone before I can get a word in.

The house is full of people already and the doorbell keeps ringing. Neighbours, mostly. They want to get a look at Finn. Take a picture of him. Press a note or a card into his hand. Ailbhe and Grainne arrive. Kenny answers the door. I know it's him because I hear him say, 'Ah, the lovely ladies.' Janine raises her eyes to the ceiling.

'Can I do anything to help, Vinnie?' Trish appears beside me, one of the shoulders of her top halfway down her arm, her bra strap digging into her skin. That'll leave a mark, I'd say. I'm washing lettuce leaves and scallions at the kitchen sink. The smell of her perfume gets right up my nose, stings my eyes.

'You wouldn't throw an eye on the kids on the bouncy yoke for me, would you? I'm worried there'll be a bit of horseplay out there.'

She nods but doesn't move. Looks at me washing the lettuce and scallions instead. 'Quite the little homemaker, aren't you?' she says, nodding towards the dishes of lasagne waiting for the oven to heat up. She puts her hand on my shoulder, runs it down my arm. 'Paula doesn't know what she's missing.'

I turn the tap off. 'Excuse me, sorry,' I say, reaching for the handle of a press. Trish steps back, her hand coming away from my arm. She stands at a curve, so her breasts – her finest assets, she announces to whoever happens to be listening – strain against the thin material of her top. There's an inch of grey at the roots of her hair. Her feet will kill her later, in those shoes. I ask her if she'd like a cup of tea. It can't be easy, raising those boys on her own. Fairly wild, those lads. You'd have your hands full.

'I'd prefer a gin and tonic,' she says. 'It's a celebration, after all. Isn't that right?' She winks at me and I give Janine the eye, but she's busy explaining to Kenny why she's only given him six out of ten for presentation and ignores me.

'You go on out to the garden,' I tell Trish. 'And I'll get someone to bring a drink out to you, alright?'

'I'm grand here, Vinnie.'

'Kenny,' I shout, over her shoulder. 'Kenny, you wouldn't make Trish a gin and tonic, would you? The gin is in the sideboard.'

Kenny walks over. 'Hello, Trish, my angel, you're a vision in pink, so you are.' He turns to me. 'What would you give me out of ten for this outfit, comrade?'

Fuck sake.

The doorbell goes again. I look at my watch. It's after two now. It could be Ellen.

Finn leaps off the castle, makes a run for it. I intercept him at the back door. 'It's alright, son, I'll get it. You go and play.'

'But it might be someone with a card,' he says, worried.

'I'll send them straight out to you if it is, alright?'

It's a woman, tall and angular with the kind of short, wiry hair that doesn't move, wearing a stern, no-nonsense black trouser suit although there is a small frill at the neck of her white blouse that looks like it landed there by accident. 'Hello,' she says, smiling to reveal long, red gums and small, childlike teeth. She extends her hand towards me. 'You must be Vinnie.' She enunciates every letter in every word so it takes her longer to say it than it should. She shakes my hand – only once, but once is enough, the grip she has. She undoes the clasp of a small leather handbag and takes out an envelope. 'For your boy. I put a book voucher in it. I don't believe in giving children money. They could buy alcohol or . . . drugs, perhaps.'

'Oh, that's very—'

'Carol! You're here!' Kenny runs halfway down the hall, then slides the rest of the way on his socks, which are the same pink – cerise – as his shirt. Because he's been bouncing in the castle, he has divested himself of his hand-stitched Portuguese ankle boots, which look light brown but are, in fact, taupe, according to Kenny.

'Delighted you made it, pet. I was worried you wouldn't get away from the clinic on time.'

'Colm insisted I leave at lunchtime, even though I told him I could stay as long as he needed me. He's so thoughtful, bless him.' She offers Kenny her hand and he bows his head to kiss it. Carol smiles at me over Kenny's bent head. 'I'm Kenny's plus-one. He *did* tell you I was coming, didn't he?' She frowns now, twitches her pale blue eyes towards Kenny, looks him up and down. 'You're looking very . . . flamboyant,' she tells him.

'Thanks. You're looking very well yourself,' he says.

'Come in,' I say. 'I hope you're hungry.'

'Kenny told you I'm a vegetarian, I'm sure.'

'Yeah, course he did.' I'll fecking well kill him. His plus-ones are rarely straightforward. Kenny glances at me, mouths *Muchas gracias, comrade*. I give him the fingers behind Carol's back, try and remember if there's a tin of chickpeas in the press I could do something with. Maybe Ellen will have a suggestion. If she turns up.

The doorbell rings again before I make it back to the kitchen and I tell Kenny to get Carol a drink – *Goodness, is it not a bit early in the day?* – and excuse myself.

It's only Mark. I have to let him in. I promised Kerry. I scan the street outside for Ellen. No sign.

In the front room, Ma is giving Ailbhe and Grainne the third degree. 'So, girls, are you going out with any nice young boys at all? Or 'meeting'? Isn't that what they're calling it these days?'

'We're gay, Mrs Boland,' Ailbhe tells her.

'Would you go on out of that, the pair of you,' says Ma, laughing her first-glass-of-sherry laugh. 'Lovely young girls like you.'

She's seen them kissing. In Phoenix Park one Saturday morning. They were walking home with their newspapers and their coffees and they stopped, like couples sometimes do, on the footpath. Kissed each other. An ordinary kiss. Nothing X-rated or anything. But a kiss, all the same. Ma was with me and Finn. We were on our way to the playground. 'They get on great, that pair,' said Ma after a while.

Mark makes for the stairs.

'Eh, excuse me? Where are you going?' He stops and turns. Smiles at me, like I'm some eejit who came down in the last shower.

'Kerry's room.'

'No, you're not.' The temptation to open the front door and drag him through it and close it on his spotty face isn't as fierce as usual. Probably because of the day that's in it. I don't have the time.

'OK,' he says. Down he comes, cool as you like.

'She's in the kitchen. Go on.' I toss my head towards the kitchen door and he moves down the hall, like a stick insect, all angles and bones. You'd have to admire him in some ways. I've barely been civil and still, he comes back for more, smiling while he's at it.

Kerry pours him a Coke and gets him a slice of the chocolate cake Mrs Finnegan made for afters. I don't say a word. What's the point? He's already stuffed half of it into his gob. She leans towards him. Kisses his mouth that's stuffed with chocolate cake. In plain view of everyone. My mother. The neighbours. Everyone.

I look around but no one's paying any attention. Janine catches my eye, throws hers skyward and tosses her head towards Carol, who is telling Kenny about the new filing system she devised, a numerical one rather than the traditional alphabetical. 'There was just too much confusion with the Mcs and the Macs and the O'Byrnes and the O'Beirnes and the O'Briens and the ones that insist on the middle initial and then there are the "women's libbers"' – she puts inverted commas around the words with her fingers – 'insisting on their maiden name while their children take the father's name. No, the numbers are proving very efficient. Colm said so.'

I check my watch. Twenty past. She said she'd be here around two. Twenty past now. She might have changed her mind. Wouldn't blame her. Not really. Might do the same, in her shoes. Still, I'm going to have to dish up soon. Otherwise, the adults will be pissed, drinking on empty stomachs. Finn went around with bowls of Doritos and nuts but no one's eating them. They're too busy talking and drinking. I'll have to dish up. Don't want people getting locked on Finn's big day.

I Google chickpea recipes. There's something I can do with a tin of tomatoes and some garlic and herbs that sounds easy enough. I mention it to Kenny who tells me that Carol is afraid of pulses since she found a tooth in a tin of beans once. She asks him to take her to Clontarf Castle because she got a voucher from her sister for lunch for one. Kenny only has to pay for his own, she tells him.

'I could sift through the peas,' Kenny offers. 'Make sure there's no foreign matter.'

'No, you go on, the pair of you,' I tell him.

'We'll be back as soon as we can,' Kenny says, apologising. I tell him to take his time.

A while later, the doorbell rings again. Finn rushes in from the garden and mouths *One hundred and fifteen euros* at me before darting for the loo. Too much Coke, that fella. He's wired.

She's wearing the blue dress with the daisies. The same one she wore when she cooked me dinner that first time. It makes me feel fantastic. Ellen, wearing that dress. I've a feeling it might be her good dress. Like she wore her good dress for me that first time. Her long, slender toes poke out of a pair of silver sandals and her nails are painted the same colour blue as the dress. No make-up, only some mascara and a trace of lipstick that makes me want to kiss her mouth. No hat pulled down over her face today. No scarf.

'I like the get-up, Vinnie.' She smiles at me with those curious amber eyes, and I realise I'm wearing the L-plate apron. Put it on when I was making the garlic bread so I wouldn't get any butter on my shirt, then forgot all about it.

Learner.

That's me.

Thirty Nine

Ellen surprises me by being well able for everyone. Even my mother. Once Ma finds out she was a doctor, she forgets about her being a 'friend-of-mine'. She glances at Ellen's scar but doesn't mention it, although she nods at Ellen's crutch and asks if she's saving up for the other one, which is her version of a joke. Ellen laughs and tells her she only needs the one now, and instead of interrogating her, Ma nods and pulls up the hem of her dress and points at her knee. 'Gives me terrible jip when I'm doing the bit of Zumba sometimes,' she tells Ellen.

'I love Zumba,' says Ellen, surprising me again.

'A lot more sensuous than that line dancing,' says Ma, sitting on the arm of the couch and lifting her knee as high as she can, towards Ellen's face.

Jaysus.

Mark and Kerry are sitting in the bouncy castle while Trish's pair and the little lads two doors up impress each other with somersaults and backflips. Finn and Callam have retreated upstairs, to Finn's room. Counting their swag, I'd say. Janine has been cornered by Callam's dad, who, free from the constraints of his wife's disapproval, is talking at a rate of knots. Something to do with fishing – his hobby, although he hasn't indulged in years – and what types of bait you use to entice different varieties of fish. The poor fucker. How's he supposed to know that Janine hates fish, has a low boredom threshold and a great capacity for bluntness? Honesty, she calls it. It's only a matter of time before she holds up her hands and says, 'Sorry, I'm going to have to stop you there,' and walks away, leaving him wondering where she's gone, if she's coming back and, eventually, when he realises that she's not, trying to work out where it all went wrong.

There's a sense of summer about the place. Bees busy in the purple-tipped stems of the lavender out the front. Proper, honest-to-goodness sunshine, bright and warm. Enough to make you think about putting a bit of cream on Finn's face. Maybe even digging out the sandals.

I spend a lot of time at the kitchen sink. Washing up, drying up, putting away. Getting drinks and divvying out second helpings of lasagne and chocolate cake. Ellen helps. I keep telling her not to. 'It's no problem,' she says. I think she's enjoying herself. 'Will you stay for a drink?' I ask her. 'When everyone's gone, I mean. I . . . wanted to run something by you.'

'What kind of something?'

'A little plan I have. For you and me. Nothing major. And not til June, if that's OK?'

She smiles. Nods.

There they are again. Optimism and excitement. Like supporters, cheering from the stands.

I light candles on the cake before I cut it. Birthday candles, but why not? Finn blows them out. Wants to know if he could make a wish. 'Of course you can,' Janine says. 'You blew them all out, first time. That entitles you to one wish.' She says it with such conviction, it sounds true. We clap and cheer and sing 'For he's a jolly good fellow' and I swear, the look on Finn's face, the smile across it, it's worth all the work. The worrying. I've made loads of mistakes but I got today right. I'm pretty sure I did.

The doorbell rings.

I'm not expecting anyone else. Everyone who's supposed to be here is here. Out the back, most of them, the day's so good.

Apart from Ma and her cronies, who are dug in, in the front room. '. . . friend of Vincent's,' I hear Ma say. 'She's a doctor, as a matter of fact.'

The bell goes again. Could be Kenny and Carol back already. I hope not. I peel off the rubber gloves, look out the kitchen window. Ellen is sitting on the edge of the bouncy castle with Finn. He's talking and she's listening intently, nodding every now and then.

I turn off the tap, walk out of the kitchen, down the hall. Upstairs, I hear Kerry and Mark laughing their heads off. I told her not to bring that fella up those stairs. I'll talk to her later about it. When everyone's gone. Or maybe tomorrow. The day is going that well. Be a shame to spoil it now.

The doorbell rings a third time, the noise shrill and insistent. 'I'm coming, I'm coming, keep your hair on,' I say, wiping my hands on my trousers before remembering that I've the good ones on.

Looking back, I see myself now. Walking down the narrow hallway, towards the door. Wiping my hands on the trouser legs. Shouting, 'I'm coming, I'm coming, keep your hair on.' Through the mottled glass of the front door, a silhouette. I pause the memory. Examine the outline of the person on the other side of the door. The hands moving through the long blonde hair.

I should have known then, had I stopped to think about it.

But I don't stop to think about it. I move towards the front door. Glib as you like. Unsuspecting. Careless. I don't pause in real life because people don't, do they? It's only when you're looking back.

You can see it all then.

I open the door. Wide. Like I haven't a care in the world.

For a moment, nothing registers. I see her. Of course I do. But it's like my eyes haven't sent the message to my brain yet. I stand there, seeing her but not really believing her.

In my memory, the moment stretches like elastic.

'Howeya, Vinnie.' When she speaks, the elastic snaps.

'Howeya, Paula.' That's what I say. Normal as anything. Like she's just arrived back from work. Or the shops. Or from a night out with Trish.

Something like that. Ordinary.

'Howeya, Paula.'

Forty

The door into the kitchen slams in the draught, making me jump. Paula shivers. The air here, in the hall, is cooler, the light dimmer, the sun having cleared the house and settled at the back now. My heart is racing, thumping inside my chest. I grip the edge of the door, feel the warm wood beneath my hand, try to think of something to say.

I've thought about her so often. About her coming back. Standing on the doorstep. Coming home. I've thought about what I would say. And now I can't think of a thing. Not a word.

'Are you going to invite me in?' she says.

'Yes. Of course. Sorry. Come in.'

She's wearing a dress. A jacket. High heels. An outfit. Like mothers do, at their kid's First Holy Communion. When she bends, I notice the suitcase. Suitcases. Two suitcases. Huge ones. She picks one up, drags it towards the door.

'Here, let me . . .'

She puts it down and I pick it up. Heavy, it is.

Two heavy suitcases.

'Don't worry, I'm staying with Trish but there's no answer at hers so I came straight here.'

'She never mentioned it.'

'She doesn't know yet.' When she laughs, she sounds like herself. Her old self. Before the trouble.

'Trish's here.'

'I should have known. Probably drinking you out of house and home.'

It's funny, the things people say. In one way, it's like she was never gone. It's like a conversation we've had a thousand times before. Like a continuation of a conversation we were having before she left.

I carry the suitcases in. Slide them underneath the hall table. When I turn around, there she is. Standing there. Looking at me. Smiling.

'So,' she says. 'How've you been?'

She looks well. Healthy, her skin no longer stretched across her bones. Sturdier, with the weight back on. She's tanned, her eyes bright, her blonde hair blonder now. Longer too. Halfway down her back now. She looks different. She looks happy.

I think about Ellen. *This is Ellen. She's a friend-of-mine.* That's what I told everyone. She shook Finn's hand. He was delighted with that. He loves when people take him seriously. Kerry didn't say much. A brief nod, maybe. But Ellen said that she'd heard Kerry was into painting and that she had a friend, Orna, who was a painter and, while she hadn't seen her in a while, she was sure that, if Kerry wanted, Orna would let Kerry spend a few days in her studio in transition year, if she was interested in a bit of work experience.

It was nice, Ellen mentioning a friend. It made her seem more . . . well, more ordinary, I suppose. She had a life. Has one.

Kerry nodded and said, 'Yeah, maybe,' but her face was pink, which is what happens when she's excited. She smiled too. She couldn't help herself.

'You're looking well,' Paula says. 'Love the apron.'

'Yeah, didn't want to ruin the shirt, y'know?'

She nods. 'You brush up nice, Vince. You always did.' Vince. Mostly she called me Vinnie. But sometimes, Vince. When I'd done something she liked. Brought home a copy of *Hello!* and a

Terry's Chocolate Orange. Something like that. 'Thanks, Vince,' she'd say.

'Who is it, Vincent?' Ma roars from the front room. A lull in the conversation, probably. She hates that. Before I can say a thing, she appears in the hall, two high circles of pink staining her cheeks and a bit of chocolate icing smeared at the side of her mouth. She sees Paula and stops. 'Jesus, Mary and Holy Saint Joseph, would you look who it is.'

'Hello, Mrs Boland,' says Paula, in a small voice. She knows my mother. This could go either way.

'You took your time,' says Ma, stepping into the hall and closing the front-room door behind her. She likes knowing everyone's business but isn't as fond of sharing her own. She knows the likes of Mrs Finnegan will have their hearing aids at full tilt for this.

'I know,' says Paula. 'I wanted to be better before I came home.'

Home. It sounds strange, her saying that.

'And are you better?' Ma wants to know.

'Ma, she's only just arrived, will you let her—'

'I am,' says Paula. 'Much better, thanks.'

I open the door into the front room. 'Ma, will you go in and ask your guests if they'd like a cup of tea or something?'

Ma looks at me and there is something in her expression that unsettles me. Like the way I look at Kerry sometimes, when I'm telling her something she doesn't want to hear.

'Don't do anything rash, Vincent,' she says, before I manage to close the door behind her.

'She hasn't changed,' Paula says, smiling.

I shake my head. 'I wouldn't say she's going to now.'

Ma never really understood. That Paula was sick. 'We all get a bit down from time to time, don't we? You won't get any better lying in a hospital bed, moping and taking tablets,' she said.

'You have to get out and about. Fresh air. Keep busy. Get a few early nights. That'll sort you out.'

Six weeks, Paula spent, in St Pat's. Six weeks almost to the day of the attempt. The genuine attempt, the doctor called it. Visiting was hard. There were days when I didn't want to. I couldn't get over all the stuff you could do there, if you wanted to. Art and pottery and music and yoga. Allsorts. Paula slept a lot. 'Worn out,' the nurse said.

'Mam?' It's Finn, at the kitchen door. For a moment he stands there, not moving. Paula's hands fly to her face. Cover her nose and mouth. She's looking right at him but it's like she doesn't quite believe it. When she crouches, stretches her arms towards him, he runs, a blur, down the hall and launches himself at her, so hard she nearly falls.

'Mam! I knew you'd come back! I wished you would. When I blew out the candles. I got them all. All the candles. On my first try.'

It's difficult to make out what Paula is saying. Her face is buried in his neck, like she's trying to inhale him. She might be crying. Or not. It's a series of words, I think. Or just one word, over and over and over again.

'Sorry.'

I think that's the word.

I think that's what she's saying.

Forty One

Finn makes it alright in the end. He takes her hand and drags her down the hall, through the kitchen, into the garden. Shows her the bouncy castle. How he can do a somersault. A forward one and a backward one. How he can run at the wall of the castle so that it catapults him back into the middle. Paula claps, the bangles around her wrist jangling.

Finn stops bouncing, stands beside her and pulls at her arm so she bends towards him. Whispers in her ear. The money, I'd say. He's telling her about the money. I see her nodding. Hugging him again.

'PAULA!' It's Trish. She's just heard. She races into the garden, flushed with surprise and gin. They wrap their arms around each other, both of them talking at the same time. Ailbhe and Grainne move towards her, standing in front of her so I can't see her any more. I'm watching from the kitchen window. It's like watching something on the telly. It doesn't feel real. Finn bouncing up and down, his eyes on Paula as if he's afraid that if he looks away, she might not be there when he looks back. The neighbours gathering around her, shaking her hand, hugging her, laughing at something she's said.

She was funny, Paula. She could give you a laugh.

Ellen's not funny. Not like that. She'd make you smile rather than laugh. She's careful. Thinks about what she's going to say before she says things.

Ellen.

I scan the garden but there's no sign of her. She could be in with the old dears. They have her tormented with questions. Lining up, they are. Worse than pension day at the post office.

This is Ellen, she's a friend-of-mine.

Ellen, Paula. Paula, Ellen.

Ellen, this is my wife, Paula.

Paula, this is Ellen. From Clontarf. Yeah, she's . . . she happens to be a friend-of-mine.

In the end, there's no need for any of that. The kitchen door opens and Carol and Kenny walk in, back from their lunch. Carol asks if there are any nuts in the chocolate cake when I offer her a slice along with a cup of coffee. 'Are you afraid of nuts too?' Finn asks, running in from the garden for a glass of Coke. She looks down at him. Forces a smile. 'No, dear. Allergic.'

That's when Ellen manages to escape from the front room and she walks into the kitchen. When Carol sees her, it's like someone has turned the volume down in the room. It's quiet, all of a sudden.

'Ellen?' Carol looks at Ellen, says her name like it's a question. Like she doesn't quite believe it. 'What are you doing here?'

For a moment, it looks like Ellen might not say anything at all. She leans heavily on her crutch, looking like she wishes she'd brought the other one after all. Then she says, 'Carol,' and it's as if she's flicked a switch because Carol rushes towards her and wraps her arms around her.

'I am so, so sorry I didn't make it to the funeral. I just . . . I couldn't face it. You know how much I thought of Neil. And you, of course. I'd heard about your injuries. I couldn't bear to see you like that. I hope you understand. Ellen?'

When she releases Ellen, Carol is crying. She looks at Kenny, who hands her the cerise handkerchief sticking out of the breast pocket of his jacket. Carol blows her nose loudly. 'Sorry,' she says. 'Sorry, it's just . . . I wasn't expecting . . .' She tries, and fails, to finish a sentence.

Kenny extends his hand towards Ellen. 'You must be Dr Ryan's wife? You ran the clinic in Rathfarnham?'

Ellen nods. 'Dr Ryan is – was – my husband. Neil. I'm Ellen Woods.'

'I'm sorry about your husband's death. Carol says he was a lovely man. A great doctor.'

Ellen nods again, glances at me, like she's waiting for me to say something, except that I can't think of a thing. Nothing occurs.

In the end, it's Paula who does the talking. She walks into the kitchen from the back garden and spots Kenny. 'Kenny Byrne!' she shouts. 'Come here to me.'

Kenny's mouth drops open but whatever he was about to say is smothered against Paula's hair as she pulls him towards her and hugs him.

'You're back,' he manages to say when she releases him. She nods and smiles, and it's only then I remember the gap between her two front teeth and it's so fundamentally her, that gap, I feel winded. Like it's just sunk in. She's back. Paula's back.

'This is Carol,' Kenny says, putting his hand around Carol's elbow and tugging her gently towards Paula. 'She's my—'

'Carol Cousier,' Carol declares, handing Kenny his sodden handkerchief and seizing Paula's hand. 'Sorry, I'm a bit . . . emotional.' She nods towards Ellen, by way of explanation.

Now Paula looks at Ellen, turns her head towards me, then back to Ellen. Studies her, like she's a knot she's trying to untie. Here's where I should say something. Where I come in. I clear my throat but Paula gets in before me.

'I'm Paula,' she says, extending her hand towards Ellen. 'Vinnie's wife.'

Ellen smiles, shakes Paula's hand. When Paula releases her, Ellen looks at her watch. 'I'd better go,' she says, lifting her handbag that's dangling from the handle of her crutch, putting the strap on her shoulder.

'We should meet for a coffee,' Carol says, trying not to stare at Ellen's scar. 'Catch up.'

Ellen nods, and I lift her jacket from one of the hooks on the back of the kitchen door. Hand it to her. She takes it without looking at me. Puts it on.

'You a friend of Kenny's?' There is a studied casualness in Paula's tone that stops Ellen at the door.

Finn nearly topples Paula when he wraps his arms around her legs. 'Mam, come on, I want to show you my triple-decker backwards flip on the bouncy castle!'

Everybody laughs, and there's a sense of relief in the laugh, like we've been holding our breaths. Paula allows Finn to lead her back into the garden.

I move to the kitchen door, hold it open as Ellen walks into the hall, towards the front door. She stops when she gets there, her hand on the latch, her head down.

'I should have told you about Neil.'

'Why didn't you?'

She shakes her head. 'You just . . . assumed he'd left, and it was nice, not having to explain.'

'Fuck sake, Ellen.'

'I was driving when the accident happened. It was my fault. I didn't want you to think bad things about me. I didn't want you to feel sorry for me.'

'You should have told me.'

'You should have told me Paula was coming back.'

'I didn't know. I swear to God. I had no idea.'

She shakes her head, slow and resigned. 'I'm sorry, Vinnie. I wish things weren't so complicated.'

I pull my hand down my face, stubble scratching against my skin. 'Me too.'

She opens the door, steps out, walks through the garden, out the gate, down the road. I watch until she disappears around the bend. Until I can't see her any more.

When I close the door, turn around, Paula is there, in the hallway, her face in shadow. Unreadable.

'I was just saying goodbye,' I say.

Forty Two

The day ends pretty soon after that. Suddenly, everyone has somewhere they need to be. Someone they need to meet. An errand they need to run.

'But we haven't had the bit of a sing-song yet,' says Ma, annoyed. She looks at Paula. Something else to blame her for.

I help Ma into her coat. Press a piece of chocolate cake, wrapped in tin foil, into her hand. 'For later,' I tell her.

'I'll stay,' she says. 'Give you a dig out. State of the place.'

'I thought you had the book club tonight.'

'Fifty Shades of Rubbish,' she says. 'Mrs Hall picked it. She's always been a sex maniac, that one. Making eyes at the security guard in the Jervis Centre and poor Mr Hall barely settled in the grave.'

'Thanks for the present, Granny,' says Finn, like I instructed him. He wasn't to say money. Thanks for the money. And under no circumstances was he to specify the amount. Thanks for the ten euros. That was out of the question.

'Come here to your auld granny,' says Ma, holding out her arms. When she bends, you can hear the bones in her back creak, like a tree in a gale. 'Who's the bestest fella in all of Ireland?'

'I am,' says Finn, obligingly.

Kenny and Janine leave together, Carol having left earlier, citing a migraine. 'It's brought it all back to me,' she told me at the door, dabbing her eyes with another of Kenny's handkerchiefs. 'Poor Neil. I'll never get over it.'

Kenny and Janine gather around me at the door, oddly united. 'You going to be alright, Vinnie?' says Janine, putting her hand on my arm and squeezing gently.

I nod. 'Yeah, grand.'

'Ring me if . . . you know . . . you need anything,' says Kenny, his voice devoid of his usual grin.

'I will, yeah.'

He shakes my hand then, which is odd. We're not hand-shakers, as a rule.

Ailbhe and Grainne are behind them. 'We'll get the patio furniture during the week, Vinnie. There's no rush.'

'Thanks for coming.'

'We wouldn't have missed the little man's big day.'

Ma's cronies file out one by one, smelling of mothballs and lavender, wrapped in their winter coats, despite the lingering heat of the day.

'See you soon, Vinnie, the good Lord willing.'

'Please God, we'll still be here to celebrate the lad's Confirmation.'

'A credit to you, Vinnie, that lad of yours.'

'You were worth rearing, Vinnie, no matter what your mother says.' Mrs Finnegan cackles like a hen when she says this.

Finn cries when he realises Paula isn't staying in the house. Awful hearing him cry, after his big day.

'I'll only be over the road,' Paula says, kneeling in front of him, holding his small, round face between her hands. 'And I'll be back later on. To talk to you and your dad. And see Kerry too.' She looks at me, and I nod. What else can I do?

She stands up, drags the suitcases from underneath the hall table. 'Did Kerry say when she'd be back?'

I shake my head. I don't know where she is. When she left. Only noticed her text a while ago.

Gone out with Mark for a bit. See you later. K xxx

'Come on, missus. We have some celebrating to do.' Trish appears beside Paula, grabs one of the suitcases. Her face is red now. She sits on the top of the suitcase. Looks like she's done a fair bit of celebrating already.

Paula looks at me. The look is cautious. Unsure. It could be Kerry, looking at me like that. 'I'll come over later, yeah? When things have quietened down. So we can talk.'

I nod. 'Do you need a hand with those cases?'

Trish waves me away. 'We're grand. They're on wheels.' They walk away, the sound of the wheels against the path not loud enough to drown out Trish's laugh, loud and grating. It's only when I hear it, I realise I have a headache.

I go at the kitchen like a lunatic, cleaning, sweeping, mopping, sorting, wiping. I put the last slice of chocolate cake on a plate, fill a glass with milk, bring it in to Finn, who's in the front room, his new football on his lap. Ellen was the only one who gave him an actual present. If he was disappointed when he opened the card and nothing fluttered out, he didn't show it. The football was wrapped in blue paper and green ribbons. A round parcel. You could tell what it was before he opened it.

'Supper,' I tell him, taking the ball and setting the plate on his lap.

'I'm not supposed to eat in the front room,' he says.

'I'm making an exception,' I tell him. 'Since it's your special day.'

'I usually have cereal for supper. Or toast.'

'So you don't want the cake, then?'

'No, it's OK, I'll eat it.' Like he's doing me a favour, the cheeky sod.

For a while, there's no sound other than the devouring of cake and the gulping of milk.

'Was that nice?'

'Yeah.'

'Did you have a good day?'

'Yeah.'

'Good.'

'When is Mam coming back?'

'I'm not sure.'

'Is she coming for a sleepover?'

'I don't think so.'

'But if she wanted to have a sleepover . . . that'd be alright, wouldn't it?'

'You're a messy git, d'you know that?' I nod at the crumbs on his lap and the couch.

He smiles, and it's pretty much a chocolate-cake smile.

'You'll have to give those teeth an almighty scrub tonight, all the junk you've had.'

'Is it bedtime?' He doesn't seem too put out by the idea. He's only dying for me to send him to bed. Seven-year-olds never say, 'I'm tired.' You have to be the one to let them know.

He barely makes it to the end of the story, his eyelids struggling to stay open.

'Dad?' he says, when I bend to kiss his cheek. He smells of toothpaste and soap. His hair is sticky. I'll throw him in the bath tomorrow.

'Go to sleep,' I say, switching off the lamp on his bedside locker.

'Will Mam be here tomorrow when I wake up?'

'You'll see her tomorrow, yeah.'

'Is she going to live with us again?' With the light off, I can't make him out. I can just hear his voice. He sounds so small.

I put a hand on his head. 'Don't worry about a thing, Finn. We'll sort it out, alright?' In the dark, I hear him turning onto his side, settling there, perhaps asleep already.

You say stuff to kids and the thing is, they believe you.

They think you've got it all worked out.

Forty Three

She doesn't ring the bell, she knocks on the window instead. A quiet knock. 'Didn't want to wake Finn,' she whispers when I open the door. She's taken off the dress. The high heels. The jacket. She's back in her leggings. A long T-shirt. Flip-flops. She looks like she used to. The old Paula.

She looks great.

I bring her into the front room, like she's a visitor. Which she is, I suppose. Hard to know what's what.

'What will you have?' I ask her.

She nods towards the mug in my hand. 'I'd kill for a cup of rosy,' she says.

I nod. 'I'll just . . .' I point towards the kitchen, like an eejit.

'Here, I'll make it. I'd say I can still find my way around the place.' She walks past me and I catch her scent and it takes me back. Right back. I swear she smells the same as the first day she walked into the Biology lab and sat on the stool beside me, only because it was the only free stool in the place.

I sit at the kitchen table and watch her.

'You've put the mugs up here?' she says, closing the cupboard where they used to be and opening one of the top ones.

'Yeah, Finn can reach that one now and it saves me bending.'

'He's got so big,' she says then.

'Costing me a fortune in trainers.'

'What about Kerry? Is she not home yet?' She glances out the window at the day draining away. 'It's nearly dark.'

'She'll be home in a little while.' I struggle to keep my tone neutral.

'Did you tell her I was back?'

Back? What does that mean exactly, back? For good? For a holiday? What?

I shake my head. 'No.'

'Do you want another cup?'

'Yeah. Thanks.'

'One sugar and a splash of milk?'

'Yeah.'

'Nice to see some things haven't changed.' There's something brittle in her tone.

We sit at the table and drink tea. If someone looked in the kitchen window, they wouldn't think there was anything strange about it. A man and a woman – husband and wife – sitting at a kitchen table, drinking tea. Perfectly ordinary. It's so quiet, I can hear the clock in the hall ticking away. Her Auntie Joan got it for us, as far as I remember. A wedding present. I've never heard it tick so loud.

'So,' I say, at the same time as Paula says, 'Well,' and that makes us laugh. Not laugh, really. Smile, or something. Turns the volume down on the silence. Loosens it a bit.

'You go,' she says, nodding at me.

'Don't even know what I was going to say, bein' honest.' That's true. I've no idea.

She circles the rim of her mug with her finger. I'd forgotten that. The way she does that.

'I'm better now,' she says, pushing the cup away and rearranging herself in the chair so she's straighter. She folds her arms and looks right at me. 'I'm doing well. I'm working, taking my meds, meditating, doing a bit of yoga. I feel good.'

'That's good. Great. That's great news.'

She nods. Worries at the corner of her mouth with her teeth, so I know there's more. 'The thing is, Vinnie . . .' She stops, gathers her hair in her hands, twists it, lets it fall.

I wait. Pick up my mug.

'I had to go. When I left that time. I . . . had to, there was nothing else I could do. Not then.'

I nod. 'I know. But it was hard on the kids,' I say, and she winces, like my words are something physical, making a run for her.

'I'm sorry, Paula, but it's true. The pair of them. Kerry didn't say much but—'

'She never said much, that one.' Again, the sharp tone.

'Everyone has their own way about them.' A wave of protectiveness rises out of nowhere, reaches for me, surprises me, the force of it. I mean, yeah, most times I could swing for Kerry. But she's a good kid. And a great big sister. Always been mad about Finn. Hasn't been easy for her, all this. Especially at her age.

'She should be home by now.' Paula looks at her watch, wrapped tight around her wrist. Dangling off her, it was, the last time I saw her.

I stand up. Pick up the cups. Carry them over to the sink. 'So, what are your plans?' I say, turning on the tap. The noise of the water against the enamel fills the kitchen, slackens the tension. I rinse the cups, rubbing the lipstick off with my fingers, set them on the draining board. When I turn, she's there. Beside me. Like she's been a hundred times before. A thousand, maybe. For a moment, it's like nothing's changed. Like the past never happened. The pair of us. In the kitchen like this. The mugs on the drainer, the clock ticking in the hall. I could say, 'Anything on the box?' and she'd say, 'Nah,' and I'd say, 'Early night so?' and she'd grin and put her arms around me and press herself against me and I'd lift her hair, kiss her neck, and she'd go upstairs and I'd check the doors and put water in Archibald's bowl and turn off the lights and follow her up.

This close, I can see the downy blonde hairs above her mouth, the slight cleft in her chin, the sprinkling of freckles across her cheeks and the bridge of her nose, darker now from the sun.

I turn off the tap.

'I've missed you, Vince. I've missed your hands on me,' Paula says, and her voice is a whisper.

It would be so easy right now. To go back. Rewind. Play it again. Play it different. Make it better, this time round.

The key turns in the lock and the front door opens. Paula springs away from me, like she used to when Ma would come home early, trying to catch us out.

'Kerry?' I call out.

The sound of keys being thrown on the hall table. The thump of a bag being set on the floor. The toss of her jacket on the banister.

'Kerry?'

Paula stands behind a chair, her hands on the back, gripping it.

'Keep your hair on, I'm coming, and before you ask, yes, I was in Mark's house and yes, his parents were there and no, I didn't walk home on my own, Mrs Whelan gave me a lift, alright?'

The kitchen door opens and there she is, framed in the architrave, her face full of the strained patience she reserves for conversations with me. She stops. Stands there, looking. For a moment, I don't think she recognises Paula. The hair would throw you, I suppose. The length of it. And the colour. Nearly white, the blonde.

I see a reel of emotions playing across Kerry's face. Shock, maybe. Disbelief too. Confusion, definitely. I wish I'd phoned her. Let her know. She looks so lost, standing there. I could kick myself. The things I should have done. I could fill a book with that list.

Kerry recovers herself. Turns to me, her face a mask of teenage boredom. 'What's she doing here?' she says.

Paula steps out from behind the chair, like she's surrendering. 'I came to see you. And Finn.'

'Why?' Kerry's tone is neutral. You couldn't take exception to it.

Paula shakes her head, spreads her hands, like she's going to say, 'I don't know.' She doesn't say that. Instead she says, 'I missed you.'

For a while, nobody says anything. Then Kerry shrugs, which is pretty much her staple response to a lot of things I say, but Paula's not to know that.

'I'm tired,' Kerry says. 'I'm going to bed.' We stand in the kitchen, me and Paula, listening to the sound of our daughter walking up the stairs, her bedroom door closing, the springs on her bed creaking as she sits on it.

Then silence.

'Fuck.' Paula says it under her breath, almost to herself.

'She'll come round.'

'How do you know?'

I don't know. I don't know anything. 'Look,' I say. 'Why don't you go back to Trish's. Get some rest. Things will seem better in the morning.'

'You sound like your ma, saying that.'

'Well, maybe she's right.'

'I've screwed everything up.'

'She just needs a bit of time. Get used to having you here.'

'What about you?'

'What about me?'

'Are you going to get used to having me here?'

'Look Paula, it's late and—'

'Didn't take you long.'

'What?'

'That fancy piece in the house today. I'm not thick, Vinnie.'

'Will you keep your voice down.'

315

'Ellen? Is that her name?'

'She's a friend. A friend of mine. That's all.'

'Yeah, right.'

'She showed me how to make the lasagne for today.'

Paula laughs at this. The kind of laugh with no humour in it. 'Lasagne?'

'It's really just Bolognese sauce with a few extras,' I say. Later, I will rewind this conversation. No matter how many times I hear it, it will come out wrong. One of those conversations that ploughs on, regardless.

'Fish finger sandwiches. They were your speciality, as far as I remember.'

'That was a good while ago now. I've made my way around the kitchen a few times since then.' It comes out sharper than I intended. I don't realise I'm angry until I say that.

'Don't bother seeing me out.' She picks her handbag off the floor, tucks it under her arm and marches towards the door. 'I know my way.'

Forty Four

Sleep won't come. I lie in bed, waiting for it, and lie there still, long after I realise it's a no-show.

Finally, I get up. Check on Finn. The Cardiff City duvet in a heap at the bottom of the bed, one leg dangling over the edge, his foot nearly touching the floor. I lift his leg onto the bed, check the sheet. Dry. I shake the duvet out, spread it over him. He insisted on following Cardiff, even though I told him they were no strangers to relegation. He insisted, all the same. Said you never know what might happen.

I stand at Kerry's closed door. I don't go in. She'd go mad if she woke up and saw me. Invasion of privacy. That's what she'd call it. Through the door, the low rumble of a snore. She gets clogged up this time of the year. A touch of hay fever, the doctor said. I'll go to the chemist on Monday. Get her some Zirtek. At least she's asleep. That'll do her good. I'll talk to her tomorrow. About her mam. Paula. I don't know what I'll say but I'll come up with something.

The kettle sounds noisier at night. And tea is the last thing I need. I know that. But the lure of its comfort is too strong. I drop in a teabag, fill the mug to the brim. A spoon of sugar. A drop of milk. A Snack bar. It's only when I demolish the chocolate I realise I'm hungry. Didn't eat much today. Too busy. Still, Finn enjoyed it. That's the main thing.

The little face on him. When he saw her. In one way, I'm delighted for him. That she came back on his big day. But there's the worry too. Digging a hole in my gut. You can't help it, I suppose. Worrying. You're never done worrying about kids. Ma still says that.

I feel the familiar tightening in my chest, my heart thumping like a fist, much too fast. I've no pills left. Didn't need to get more. Things were going well. Great, really. Should have known. Things never stay the same. Especially when they're good. Things always change.

Meditation, the doctor said. A bit of yoga. I pick up the mobile and Google it. Yoga. Reams of stuff comes up.

I never wanted to give it a name. Her condition. For ages, I said 'baby blues' whenever anyone asked. 'A spot of the baby blues,' I'd say, like it was a cold. The flu, even. Something common. Nothing some hot drinks wouldn't sort, a few early nights. Fresh fruit. Fibre. A weekend away. A new pair of shoes.

Something that she would recover from.

Even when the doctor said, *Post-natal depression*. Even when he said, *Severe post-natal depression*. And *Bipolar Affective Disorder*. Even then.

'You don't believe me. You think I'm feeling sorry for myself. Wallowing. That's what you think. Isn't it?'

I was afraid, bein' honest. Words like *depression* and *bipolar*. I'm not proud of it. But there it is, all the same.

Fear.

And me, goin' around the place like a fool. *Yeah, a touch of the baby blues is all.*

Nothing to worry about.

The woman on the YouTube clip calls it the Downward-Facing Dog. It looks peculiar. Awkward as hell. Hands and feet flat on the ground and your backside cocked in the air.

She's like a piece of elastic, the woman. Gets herself into the position, no sweat. Talking away while she's doing it. Smiling an' all, like she's enjoying it.

I start by kneeling on the floor, then putting my hands down, arms straight. After this, you have to straighten your legs and push your arse towards the ceiling. It's tricky, doing everything at the same time. Keeping your arms and legs straight and tucking your head between your arms. When I manage it, she tells me to stay like that for a bit. She doesn't say how long. It looks painless when she does it. She tells me to breathe. What the hell else would I be doing?

Downward-Facing Dog. I don't know where they're going with the dog reference. You'd never catch Archibald doing anything like this.

From down here, I notice how the floor needs a sweep. And a mop, while I'm at it.

She says to clear your mind. Not think about anything. Breathe.

The muscles in my arms twitch with effort. I close my eyes. Breathe.

It's hard not to think about things. Clear your mind. I think about an empty pitch. Nothing in it but a pair of goalposts and lines, straight and white against the bright green of grass. The thoughts crowd the stands, straining to get a look-in.

Me and Paula, driving to Galway. A weekend away. Ma insisted. 'It'll do yiz the world of good,' she said. She was like me back then, with the remedies. A hot-water bottle. A meaty stew, full of iron. The right combination of those kinds of things, and Paula would be as right as rain. That's what she said, waving us off. 'You'll be as right as rain when you get back, you'll see.'

I bought her a necklace on Shop Street. Three lovehearts dangling off the chain. 'One for Kerry, Finn and me,' I told her, touching each of the silver hearts, already warm against her skin.

'You big sap,' she said, but she smiled and she kissed me and we ate minestrone soup and pizza in an Italian restaurant and slow-danced at the Spanish Arch where a busker played. He put his fiddle in the case when the song was done, took a picture of us with my camera. I gave him a fiver and we walked to Eyre Square with our arms around each other and it wasn't til I got to the hotel, I realised she was crying and she didn't know why and I didn't know why and she wanted to go home and I said I couldn't drive because I'd had two pints of Guinness and she said she'd take a bus or a train and I said it was too late, there were no more buses or trains. People looking at us, standing in the foyer of the hotel. She kept saying the same things over and over. How she had to go home. Right now. How she couldn't stay, not for the night, not for another minute. How she had this feeling. That something terrible was going to happen. She kept saying it, louder and louder. *Something terrible is going to happen.* Her face was distorted. I could hardly make her out. She looked like someone else. A stranger, nearly.

I drove her home. Drank two espressos and drove her home.

I rang Ma from the toilet of a garage on the N4 in the early hours. Told her we were coming home. Said Paula wasn't well. Told her to say nothing.

She said nothing. Just looked at Paula's face, gathered up her stuff and said it was just as well, because now she could give Margie a hand on the panel at the Strictly Come Waltzing night at St Mary's the following day. 'Margie wouldn't know a tango if it came up and stuffed the stem of a rose in her gob and marched her across the room, and I'm not tellin' tales out of school. The world and her mother-in-law knows that.'

'Whatcha doing, Dad?'

I open my eyes. Between the gap in my legs, I see him at the door. From this position, he's upside down. His hair is like an overgrown hedge this time of night, in spite of his recent hair-cut, sticking up all over the place. His pyjama bottoms stop above his ankles. I swear to God they fit when I put him to bed.

'There it is,' I say, lowering my knees and my head to the floor and sticking my arm under the couch. I push my hand across the floor, feel something soft and pulpy, pull it out. 'The very thing,' I say. It's an instruction manual for the DVD player and, from the looks of it, Archibald's been at it.

I stuff my phone into my pocket, pick myself off the floor, my knees making a terrible racket.

'Are you going to watch a DVD, Dad?'

'Eh, no, not right now. But, you know, it's handy to have the manual to hand. In case the player breaks or something. Know what I mean?'

'Were you doing yoga?'

'Eh . . . I was, yeah.'

'Callam's mam does yoga sometimes. Says it stops her from giving out to Callam's dad. She still gives out to him, though. Is that why you're doing it?'

'Eh, no. Just . . . you know . . . a bit of exercise and that.'

I'm upright now. A bit dizzy. I focus on Finn. 'What has you out of the scratcher at this hour?'

He shrugs with bony shoulders. 'Dunno.'

'What about a jam sandwich and a hot chocolate?'

'Yeah.'

I make him a hot chocolate and he drinks it at the kitchen table. I get the bread, the butter, the jam. 'Strawberry do you?'

'Yeah.'

The sugary smell of the jam, the very act of spreading it across a slice of buttered bread, calms me, slows the thoughts galloping around my head like a carousel. I put the sandwich on a plate, hand it to him. 'So, what are you going to buy with your Communion money?'

Finn's hand, halfway to his mouth with its cargo of jam sandwich, stops. 'I thought I wasn't supposed to talk about the money.'

'It's a lot of rent you got there. Good to have a bit of a plan.'

'Well, I was going to buy everyone a present.'

'Everyone?'

'Yeah. You and Mam and Kerry and Granny.'

'Right.'

'I already know what I'm getting you and Kerry and Granny but it's a surprise so I'm not allowed to tell you.'

'I see.'

'I'm not sure what Mam likes but I'll find out tomorrow and then I'll know.'

When Finn finishes, I stand up. 'Bedtime,' I say. 'Again.'

I sit on the edge of his bed until he's asleep. Between the gap in the curtains, I can make out Trish's house, on the bend in the road. The house is in darkness. Why wouldn't it be at this hour? I think about Paula over there, in the dark. I wonder if she's asleep.

I'm better now.

That's what she said.

Any time a thought about Ellen strays into my head, I cover it. In my mind, the cover is a dustsheet. One of those you throw over pieces of furniture in a house you're moving out of.

Dear Neil,

Dr Deery thinks it's a good idea. To talk about it. Or write it down at least. I'm going for option two. She wasn't surprised.

    So trivial, really, the details. An ordinary day. Summertime. Hot and dry. Tar, melting on the road.

    We fought again that morning. Shouted at each other across the bedroom.

    You went to the clinic. I didn't.

    It could just as easily have been you. Driving that day. Instead of me. You put your car in for a service. Rang me that evening from the garage. Asked if I would pick you up. Said you didn't want to fight. You wanted to go home and make us some dinner.

    I thought about not picking you up. Then I said OK.

    I picked you up.

    One small shift and everything changes. I remember little things about the day. Insignificant things.

    18.45. The time I pulled up outside the clinic.

    22°. The temperature outside, according to the car.

    Our conversation. So normal.

    'Can we swing by the dry-cleaner's?' you said.

    'It'll be closed by now.'

    'You hungry?'

    'Yes.' I was always hungry by then.

    'What would you like to eat?'

    'I'd love pasta.'

    'Carbonara?'

    'The version with the peas, and the cheddar instead of parmesan?'

'Yes.' You nodded. Asked me to stop at the deli round the corner from the house. You wanted to pick up some of their fresh pasta. Cracked black pepper tagliatelle, you said. You didn't feel like making your own. Too tired, you said.

An ordinary conversation. We'd had conversations like that hundreds of times before. My hand was resting on the gearstick and you covered it with your hand and I let you. Perhaps because I was tired and I didn't want to disturb the fragile nature of this peace between us. Perhaps because I knew it wouldn't last. The peace.

I could feel the swell of my bump straining against the zip of my trousers and thought about maternity clothes and where I might buy some, or whether perhaps Faye could lend me hers since she had 'shut up shop', as she put it herself. Six and a half months pregnant and still in some of my own clothes. Faye couldn't get over it. Said that she was like a heifer at that stage.

These are the thoughts. The observations. The details. The things I remember when I think about it, which I never do. I'm doing it today because Dr Deery said I should and I've always been a good girl and done what I'm told.

The accident itself. I don't know. The tar. I've mentioned that. The bend in the road. The tree on your side. Sycamore, I think. The black jeep roaring towards us. An accident black spot, the garda said. I remembered then, when he said it, the posy of flowers on the side of the road. I noticed it as I took the bend.

Someone else has lost something here.

Ellen

Forty Five

Ma rings the following morning.

'I'm not myself.'

'Who are you, then?'

'Don't be smart, son.'

'What's wrong with you?'

'A bit of a cold is all.'

'Must be serious, if you're ringing instead of calling round.'

'I'm a bit tired with it. I'm getting on, you know. Not going to be sixty-five forever.'

'Well, you've been sixty-five for years now so you never know.'

'Don't be cheeky.'

I don't call in to Ma's all that much. She's in my gaff that often, there's no need. I let myself in. There's a musty smell in her house, like the windows haven't been opened in ages. There are crumbs on the table in the kitchen and the cat – Doris Day – is on the counter, licking the bottom of an empty tin of tuna, her nose shiny with brine.

'Getouttathat,' I roar at the thing. She ignores me so I pick up a tea towel, wave it towards her. Doris takes her nose out of the tin and barely registers me before she strolls down the counter, hops onto the lid of the bin, jumps to the floor and squeezes herself through the catflap in the back door.

'Ma?'

The house is dark, with the curtains drawn across every window. There's a chill too, as if it's been a long time since the sun gained access. I open all the curtains and a few windows as well. I look in the fridge. There's not a lot in there. A couple of eggs. A chunk of cheese, uncovered. A jar of salad cream, with yellowing bits hardening around the lid. A few carrots rolling around the bottom of the vegetable drawer. The shelves could do with a scrub. A basin of hot, soapy water and a scouring pad. That's what's required. Ma would be the first to say it.

I climb the stairs. The banister shifts and creaks under my hand and the walls along the stairs could do with a lick of paint. I'll have to sort it this summer. Kenny might give me a dig out.

I knock on her bedroom door, stand outside until she tells me to come in.

'Is that you, Vincent?' Her voice is missing its usual volume and conviction. She blinks as the light from the door cuts through the gloom of the bedroom. I move to the curtains. Pull them apart.

'Who else would it be?'

She struggles into a sitting position and I take the cushion from the chair at the dressing table and slide it behind her back. She leans against it, sighing. 'I thought, when you first appeared at the door . . .'

'What?'

'You were the image of your father, standing there.'

'You thought it was Da, coming to get you? Bring you to heaven?'

'Don't be blasphemous. You're not too old for a clip around the ear.' When she coughs, her chest rises and falls with the force of it and her breath seems laboured.

'Sorry, Ma, I was only messing.' I shouldn't have said that. It's alright to mess with her when she's in the full of her health. But there's something frail about her today. In the bed, with her wisps of blue hair hanging in thin lines around her face instead of set in their usual robust curls.

'Would you get me a glass of water so's I can take my vitamins?' She nods at the table beside her bed where bottles of pills stand in lines.

'I've got an hour before I've to go to work. I could get a few messages for you, if you like. The presses are fairly bare.'

'Have you been nosing around my kitchen?'

'No.'

'I don't have time for housework and grocery shopping, you know. There are people depending on me, Vincent. I can't let them down. Those bingo numbers don't get called out by themselves, you know.'

'I was only asking.'

'Well, don't.'

'Grand.'

'What about yer woman?'

It was only a matter of time before Paula came up. Ma was fond of her from the beginning. Said it was nice to have another woman about the house. Brightened the place up, she said.

It was a different story when she left. Did a runner, Ma called it. She never really got it. How a woman could do that. 'Whatever about leaving a fella,' she often said, 'but leaving your own children behind. To fend for themselves? Well, that's just . . . I can't even . . . I'd call that . . .' She never finished those sentences. She couldn't find the words.

'They're not fending for themselves,' I reminded her, over and over. 'They have me. And you, don't forget. They're doing alright. Aren't they?'

'It's not the same, Vincent,' she said, shaking her head.

On this point, there was no changing her mind.

'She wants to bring Finn to the park.'

'What did you tell her?'

'I said she could.'

That wasn't my first response. 'Finn's a bit tired today.' That's what I said when she arrived on the doorstep first thing this morning, with her plans. 'He's still in bed. Knackered after all the excitement yesterday. I'm not sure he's—'

'You don't trust me with the kids.' Her tone is flat. Matter-of-fact.

'It's not that.' Except it is.

Paula looks at me like she knows what I'm thinking. She always said my face was like a book with really big writing that anyone could read. 'I've taken my medication today, Vinnie.'

I go downstairs, make Ma a cup of tea. She doesn't want anything to eat. 'I already had my breakfast,' she says, but I see no evidence of that in the kitchen.

'Should I give Dr McDaid a ring? Ask him to call in?'

She shakes her head. She looks a bit better, now that she's had the tea. Taken her tablets. They don't look like vitamin supplements.

'That doctor friend of yours seems like a nice girl,' she says.

'Ellen? Yeah, she's . . . nice.'

She usually texts around this time of the morning. Just something small. *How are you?* Or she might send me a photograph of a painting she's working on. Or a suggestion for Wednesday night. The pictures or something. I wouldn't call it a routine or anything like that. Just, she'd have texted by now.

'Do you feel like getting up? Getting dressed? It's lovely out, so it is. You could sit in the back garden, if you wrap up.' She looks old, lying there. Like a proper old woman. I think if she gets up and puts her clothes on and does something with her hair, she'll feel better.

I'll feel better.

She shakes her head. 'You go on, son. I'm going to take it easy today. But could you ring Tom from the Swinging Sixties and tell him I won't be able to help out at the aqua aerobics this afternoon? I said I'd make up a batch of sandwiches for afterwards. Egg and onion. They love my egg-and-onion sandwiches, bless them. Starving, they are, after the swim, the auldones. We work them pretty hard, mind.'

'You might be feeling better by this afternoon.' I can't believe she's not going. She always goes. Everywhere. Even when they don't ask her. She barges her way in. Her and her smelly sandwiches wrapped in greaseproof paper.

She shakes her head. 'Go on with you, Vincent, you've things to be doing.'

'I'll get Kerry to look in on you later. She's got a half-day.'

'Tell her to bring the little fella down with her. I'm dying to hear how much he made.'

'I'm surprised he didn't tell you yesterday. Like Scrooge he was, keeping count.'

'He said he'd take me to Rome to visit the Pope if he got enough.' She laughs, then but the laugh turns into a cough that sounds sore and chesty.

'You might need an antibiotic for that,' I say, handing her a glass of water. She waves it away. Draws the blanket to her chin.

'I'm going to have a rest,' she says. 'I was in the middle of a lovely dream when you arrived. Me and your da were on the DART to Bray. We had our free travel passes, the pair of us. I'd the sandwiches in the bag. And a flask of tea. We were going to have a go on the bumpers. Play a few slots. Climb Bray Head afterwards, maybe.' Her eyes are closed now, and the corners of her mouth are curled in a smile. She never talks about Da. Not really. Not like this.

I bend and kiss her cheek, the skin there worn and soft.

'Do you miss him?' I say, surprising myself with the question. She's not someone you ask questions like that. She's a strong person. Busy and matter-of-fact. At least, that's the way she always seems to me.

'Every day,' she says.

Forty Six

'Can Mam stay for dinner?' Finn wants to know. Paula is standing in the kitchen when he says this, her arm draped over his shoulder. There's a blob of ice cream down the front of his T-shirt. Chocolate ice cream. He grins his grin. The one that makes people say yes when they want to say no.

'Yes,' I say. I look at Paula then. 'If you'd like to, I mean.'

She smiles and nods. 'I'd love to stay,' she says, and her tone is deliberate and careful, like she's not just talking about dinner, but Finn doesn't notice and I have the meal to think about so I keep myself busy with that and Finn takes Paula's hand and brings her upstairs so he can show her the football kit that Kenny got him last year.

His room is tidy enough, as far as I remember. And there was no messing with the mattress this morning. His sheets were dry.

I give Ma a quick buzz. 'How are you feeling?'

'Much better.'

'Did you have anything to eat?'

'Kerry came in at lunchtime. Made me some toast.'

'Is that all you had?'

'That's all she can make. Still, she does it just the way I like it, the pet. And a good strong cup of tea.'

Maybe I could give Kerry a few cooking lessons. We'd probably end up killing each other. Still, I could suggest it.

'Did she say anything? About Paula being back.'

'Not a word, bless her.'

I don't know if I'm relieved or worried by this. One thing I do know: I'm not surprised.

I text Kerry.

Dinnertime. Your mam's here. She'd like to see you.

My finger hovers over the 'Send' button. If I tell her Paula's here, she mightn't bother coming home. But if I don't tell her, she'll feel ambushed, like last night.

I decide it's best to be honest with her. I send the text.

'Something smells lovely.'

When I turn around, Paula's at the doorway.

She nods towards the hob. 'A regular Gordon Ramsay you've turned out to be. Finn says you're making carbonara.'

'It's just pasta, really. Nothing special.'

'Salad and all.' She picks a bit of celery out of the bowl. Examines it before she puts it in her mouth.

'Trying to get the kids to have their five-a-day, you know.'

She smiles. 'You're a good dad, Vince. You always were.'

I open a cupboard. 'Do you want a glass of wine with your dinner? There's a few bottles left over from yesterday.'

She shakes her head. 'Better not,' she says. 'I try not to any more. My doctor says I shouldn't, with the medication an' all.'

'Grand,' I say, closing the cupboard door. This is new too.

I want to ask her what she's doing here. What she's doing back. In my kitchen. Our kitchen. What her plans are. Her intentions.

'I'm starving!' says Finn, running into the kitchen. I pour milk into three glasses. Finn's telling us about a complicated game he was playing with Trish's boys in the playground when I hear the key turn in the front door.

I put pasta bowls on the table.

'Very swish,' Paula says, picking one up.

'Got them in a sale. Half nothing, they were.'

I open the cutlery drawer. Get out spoons and forks. Put them in a metal heap in the middle of the table.

Finn picks up a fork and spoon. 'You have to twirl the spaghetti on the spoon with the fork,' he tells Paula, demonstrating,

The kitchen door opens.

Kerry's home.

'Ah, there you are, love,' I say, like I've been looking all over the place for her.

She stands there.

'Your dad invited me for dinner,' says Paula, her tone bright as day.

'Wash your hands before you sit down, love.'

'I'm not hungry.'

'It's spaghetti carbonara,' Finn says, anxious that Kerry should know what she's missing.

'I ate at Mark's.' She has her hand on the door handle, itching to be gone.

'Would you not stay for a bit?' says Paula, pulling out a chair. 'I'd love to talk to you.'

'You haven't talked to me for the last year and a half so I can't see what's so pressing now.' The monotone is back and I can see now what it's for. How it cloaks her anger. Her confusion.

'Come on, Kerry, sit and have a bite with us. Something small, even. I made salad.'

'There's garlic bread,' says Finn. I can see by his face that he reckons this just might clinch the deal.

Kerry shakes her head but smiles at Finn, tousles his hair. 'I've homework,' she says. She doesn't slam the door or even close it. She leaves the room. Walking. Her normal pace. Up the stairs. The usual creaks, no stamping. Her bedroom door opens. Closes. Music, almost immediately. But not loud. Nothing you could argue with.

'She's moody because she's a teenager,' Finn tells Paula. 'I'll probably be moody too. When I'm that old.'

Paula ignores him. I think perhaps she hasn't heard him.

We sit at the table. I dish up. Still three settings. Different people. I know there's no point wishing things were different, but sometimes you can't help yourself.

'Will I say grace?' Finn wants to know.

'Go on,' I say, 'but not a big long one. It'll be stone cold.'

'Dear God, thanks for dinner. And thanks for sending Mam home. Amen.' He grins at Paula. She looks at me and I get up and fiddle with the dials on the oven, like I'm checking I've switched it off.

Finn does most of the talking. When he stops, I get him to start again. 'Tell your mam about the spelling test.'

'The one where I got twenty out of twenty?'

'Yeah, that one.'

When he runs out of stories, he turns to me. 'Can I show her the money?' he wants to know, his face flushed with his windfall.

I nod. The relief when he brings her upstairs. I know we have to talk. Me and Paula. The future, I suppose. What's going to happen. I sit at the kitchen table. Rub my face with my hands. Try to get myself together.

Paula makes me a coffee after dinner. Insists. A cup of tea for herself. Mops up the milk Finn spills. Tells him he's a sloppy Joe. Asks me about my day. 'Anyone good in the taxi today?' She always used to ask that. *Anyone good?*

I tell her about the fella proposing to his girlfriend of seventeen years. He asked her in the back seat. She waited until he lifted the lid. Examined the ring. Then she said no. There didn't seem to be much in the way of hard feelings. She pecked him on the cheek and got out at Ringsend. He asked me to drop him at the jeweller's. See if he could get his money back.

'Is it OK if I put Finn to bed?' Paula asks.

'I don't need anyone to put me to bed,' Finn tells her, put out.

'I mean, read you a story. You're not too old for a bedtime story, are you?'

'No.'

'Here, I got you one.' From her bag, she pulls a book. Offers it to him. He looks at it but doesn't take it. 'I don't read picture books any more.'

'Finn! Don't be rude.'

Finn's bottom lip wobbles, the way it does before he cries. 'I wasn't being rude, Dad. I was just sayin'.' Daggers, he's giving me. I realise then that he won't cry. Won't let himself. Not in front of Paula. It's like a hard lump in my throat, the realisation.

'He's well able to read, that fella, but he still likes us to read him a story at bedtime, the lazy lump.' I stretch my face into a smile. 'You could read him a chapter of *Matilda*? If you like?' I reach for the empty dinner plates, stack them on top of each other.

'Or two chapters,' Finn says, smiling.

'Get up those stairs, you chancer,' I tell him, swiping at his legs with the tea towel.

He jumps back. 'Missed.' He hares out the door, up the stairs, Paula running after him. I hear them laughing, the pair of them. It feels strange and familiar, at the same time.

Forty Seven

In some ways, it's like she never left.

She stays at Trish's but she's in our house a lot. The doorbell goes and there she is, on the step. I'd like her to text first. Give us a bit of notice. I don't ask her. I don't know how to.

She takes Finn to the pictures, to the bowling alley, to the Leprechaun Museum. Kenny told her about it.

She asks Kerry to go to the pictures, to the bowling alley, to the Leprechaun Museum. Kerry gives her different variations of the same answer. I tell Paula to give it time.

I go with them when I can. Those afternoons I spent in Ellen's apartment. Lying in her bed. Drinking coffee on her couch. Now, I spend them with my son and my wife.

I am a tourist in my own city. With my own family.

It should feel more ordinary.

I check my phone. I find myself doing this at intervals. As if I'm expecting a text. A missed call, maybe. I'm not. I don't think I am.

'What are you doing?'

'What?' We're in TGI Friday's. Finn's face is hidden behind a massive cup of Coke.

'You keep taking your phone out. You expectin' a call?' There's a sharp edge to her voice. Paranoia. That was one of the signs. Before. But it's not paranoia. It's a question. I put my phone in my pocket.

I'm not expecting a call. I already rang her. Ellen. A few days ago. Told her I was sorry. She said she understood. I rang the

335

hotel in Derry. Told them I had to cancel the June weekend. A family thing, I said. They were nice about it. Said these things happen.

Paula puts Finn to bed every night, tries to wrestle a conversation out of Kerry, comes downstairs and makes tea in a pot, just like she used to. I haven't bothered with the pot in months. A teabag in a cup does me. We sit on the couch and she tells me things. Like about Spain. How it's too hot. How the Spaniards deliberately misunderstand her when she speaks Spanish. How her dad drives her spare, insisting on drinking in the Irish pub and flying the tricolour off his balcony. About her job at the salon in one of the beachfront hotels. Her boss is a tosser and the head stylist isn't properly qualified. 'They're holding the job open for me,' she says. 'In case I come back.'

In case.

She finishes her tea and then she leaves and there she is, the next morning, on the doorstep, asking if Finn is ready to go to school, saying she'll walk him, suggesting the zoo in the afternoon.

He hasn't wet the bed since his First Holy Communion. Nearly a week ago now. Seems a lot longer than that.

I think about Ellen more than I should. Wonder why she couldn't tell me. About her husband. Neil. God love him. He was only fifty-six when he died. Only a few years younger than Da. And Ellen behind the wheel, pregnant. A hard thing to live with.

I miss her. I miss doing nothing with her. In her apartment, in the lull of the afternoon. I miss the sound of her voice, the low weight of it. The quietness of her, the way she listens. It's a rare skill. You don't realise how rare until you come across someone who can listen. The world is full of people talking over each other most of the time.

I feel different when I'm with Ellen. I feel like someone else. Someone calm. A million miles away from a panic attack.

'What are you thinking about?'

Paula always asked that question. I usually said, 'Football.' Drove her spare.

'Do you want another coffee?' I nod at her empty cup.

'I asked you a question.' She keeps the tone light. Pushes Finn's fringe out of his eyes like she's not waiting for an answer. But she is.

'Eh, just, a match. Good few weeks ago now. Bohs stuffed Rovers, two–all.'

'How did they stuff Rovers if it was a draw?'

'Ah, it's difficult to explain. I suppose you had to be there.'

'Still the same old Vinnie.' She smiles at me, nudges my arm with her elbow. I smile back, like it's an in-joke. Something between us.

We look like a family. Sitting in TGI Friday's having burgers and chips. A normal family.

That's what we are. Except I don't feel the same. I don't feel like the same old Vinnie.

'You know we need to talk, Vince.' She whispers it, glancing at Finn. He's drawing pictures of Captain Underpants on the notebook Paula bought him at the zoo. He's not listening to us.

I nod. I know.

'Are you working tonight?'

'Yeah.'

'Could you swap shifts? We could stay in. Talk when the kids go to bed. It's time we did.'

'I'll see if Kenny will cover for me.'

I ring Ma when I get home. Haven't seen much of her this past week. I hope she's been taking it easy.

'I can't talk to you, Vincent. I'm on my way out the door. I'm already running late for the "Safety in the Garden" lecture that the Green-Fingered Grannies are holding in the parish hall.'

'I didn't know you were a member.' Anything with the word 'granny' in it is usually a no-no.

'I'm not, I offered to take the minutes.'

'How come?'

'The secretary, Carmel, pulled a muscle in her back. Weeding.'

'You should be taking it easy.'

'Ah, would you stop. I'm fine.'

'I could drive you over. Pick you up.'

'Do I sound like someone who needs an escort?'

'No.'

'Well, then, I'll drive myself.'

'Take care, Ma.'

'You're a good boy, Vincent.' She hangs up.

We sit on the couch after dinner, me and Paula. Kerry comes downstairs for a glass of water. Makes a great show of ignoring us.

'She'll come round,' I tell Paula, when Kerry retreats to her room.

Paula nods. 'I feel hopeful, Vince.' This catches me unawares. A new development. She tended more towards the glass half empty side of things before.

We're sitting on the couch when the phone call comes through.

Paula does most of the talking. 'I want us to try again, Vinnie. I want to make a go of things.' She reaches for my hand. I'd forgotten how cold her fingers are.

'What about your . . . how you're feeling . . . in your head, like?'

'Can we at least call it by its name? Bipolar disorder. That's what it's called.' She pulls her hand away. Rubs it up and down her leg. A pulse jumps in her neck.

'I'm sorry, Paula, I didn't mean to . . .'

She looks at me again. 'I haven't had an episode for six months. Longer, even. Yes, I have to take the medication.

338

Maybe I always will, I don't know. But I feel better. Stronger, you know?' Her tone is pleading and I nod a bit too vigorously, in the absence of a response.

'I've missed the kids,' she says.

'They've missed you.'

'Kerry hasn't.'

'She has. She's just . . . she's not great at expressing herself. It's her age, you know?'

'I've missed you, Vinnie.' She whispers it, her face suddenly still.

Silence then. I could say lots of things. I could say, 'I've missed you too.' Because I have. There have been times when I've missed her like a limb. Like when Ma found the lump that time. I sorted her out as best I could but Paula would have known what to say to her. How to jolly her along for that week we were waiting for the results. Benign it was in the end, thank God.

And not just big things like that. Small things. Things you'd barely notice ordinarily. The quietness of the house after the kids went to bed. The parent–teacher meetings. The first one I went to was a month after Paula left. A wreck, I was. Bleary-eyed. Going day to day, back then. Just about getting by. The sympathy was awful. I could see it in the teachers' eyes.

While I'm sitting there, casting around for something to say, she shuffles across the space between us on the couch and kisses me.

The familiarity of her kiss is shocking. It's the same. The exact same. The smell of her. The taste. The way she slides her hands up my arms, around my shoulders, down my back. The same. Like she never went away. Like she's been here all this time.

That's when the phone call comes through.

'Don't answer it,' Paula whispers against my mouth. Her fingers pull gently at my earlobes. I used to love that. When she touched my ears.

I pull away. 'I'd better get it. It'll wake the kids.'

She releases me, moves back. 'Go on, then' she says. 'Get rid of whoever it is.'

I run down the hall. It's late for a call.

'Is that you, Vincent?' An elderly voice. High and shaky.

'Yeah. Who's this?'

'It's Margo here.'

'Margo?'

'Margo O'Reilly. From the Green-Fingered Grannies.'

'Oh. Right. Is everything OK?' I look at my watch. Nearly ten o'clock at night. Good news usually waits til morning.

'Is everything OK?' I say again.

'I'm afraid it's your mother. Mrs Boland. She's—'

I should never have let her go out tonight. I should have insisted she stay in. Or gone with her. But there's no talking to Ma when she's made up her mind. She's a stubborn old goat. She'd tell you that herself.

'Is she alright? I can come and pick her up. Does she need me to come and pick her up?'

Later, I'll wonder why I kept talking. Interrupting. Not letting the woman get a word in. Perhaps I already knew. Some part of me already knew.

'No, no, there's no need to do that, the ambulance man said—'

'Ambulance?'

'He thought it was a heart attack. He said she wouldn't have felt a thing, it was very sudden. Very quick.'

'Is she at the hospital? Which hospital did they take her to?'

The woman at the other end of the phone starts to cry. A small, withered cry. The kind with no hope in it.

'I'm so sorry, Vincent. You shouldn't have to hear this on the phone but I just . . . everything happened so fast and they've already taken her away and I thought it would be best for you to know as soon as possible and—'

'Where is she? I'll come right away.'

'She's . . . she had a heart attack, they think. We thought she was asleep on the chair at first. She looked so peaceful. You wouldn't believe how peaceful she looked. I've never seen her so still.'

'What do you mean? What are you saying?'

'I'm so sorry, Vincent.'

Forty Eight

My mother is eighty-two. Was eighty-two. Eighty-two years old.

Now I know. A nurse at the hospital told me. It was in Ma's file.

Eighty-two. A good innings, Da would have called that. Mad about the cricket, he was. Played for Rush, where he lived before he met Ma and moved to North Strand. No way was she moving out to Rush. The sticks, she called it. He settled in well enough, Da. Apart from the cricket and his north county accent, he was nearly as good as a local, Ma said. She was well in her thirties by the time they met. Thirty-five, maybe. 'I turned down many an offer,' she told me, more than once. 'But I was waiting for your da. I knew he'd be along.'

'I'll come with you, Vinnie,' says Paula. 'You can't go on your own.'

'No.' It comes out sharper than I intended. 'I mean, would you stay here? Keep an ear out for the kids.'

'Sure Kerry is grand being left with Finn now, isn't she?' She's on her feet, looking around for her bag. I'm desperate to leave. To be on my own.

'I'd say she's asleep and I don't like leaving the house without letting her know. And I don't want to tell her about Ma. Not tonight. I just . . . I can't.'

She sighs. 'Alright, then. I'll stay. If that's what you really want.'

'Thanks.'

'What'll I say if they wake up?' There's worry on her face. Fear, almost. Like some part of her has forgotten. How to be a mother.

'Just . . . tell them I had to do a limo run.'

I can't find the car keys. My jacket. My wallet. Paula finds them in the end. Hands them to me. She steers me towards the door. It's like a bit of me isn't working. Isn't operational.

'You're in shock,' Paula says.

Eighty-two. You'd think I'd be more prepared.

The lights of the city are a comfort. Everywhere, I see the ghost of myself and Ma. There we are at the door of the credit union on North William Street. I'm seven. She's got my hand, leading me in. My first account. 'Once you're with the credit union, son, you'll never go without.' Five pounds, she gave me. That was a lot of money in those days. My first deposit. Five old Irish pounds.

The two of us outside the Ambassador. Queuing at the box office for one of the *Star Wars* films. *Return of the Jedi*, I think. I'm twelve and don't hold her hand any more. She takes a hanky out of her pocket, hands it to me. I blow my nose. In the plastic bag she's carrying, there's toffee popcorn and a can of Coke.

There we are outside the graveyard where the old man is buried. I'm seventeen. Burying my father. This time, it's me who's holding her hand. She leans on me. I am shocked at her grief. The force of it. For the first time, Ma seems vulnerable. I remember feeling afraid.

I see us outside St Mary's. I'm twenty-seven. Ma says it's normal for the bride to be late. It's nothing to worry about. She tightens my tie. Nearly chokes me. Tells me never to go to sleep on an argument. 'And a cup of tea goes a long way, Vincent. Especially if it's brought up to you in the bed. Never underestimate the little things, Vincent. It's the little things that matter.'

I drive on through the night. The roads are deserted. It's like the world is standing still. Paying its respects.

I have to identify her. Identify the body. That's how they put it.

Her hair is set in lines of rigid curls, more grey than blue under the fluorescent lights. She managed to get them in, the curlers. She wasn't well and still, she managed.

I force myself to touch her. I worry that she will be cold. She, who has never been cold a day in her life. Too busy to be cold. Too active. Too full of life. No time for being cold.

She is warm still. Warm and soft. Pliable. She's wearing her favourite blouse with the matching cardigan over it. A twinset, I think you call that. She was delighted when it was all the rage again a few years ago. She still had a few sets from the first time around, she told me, thrilled with her foresight and thriftiness. I stand beside her, watch my tears fall onto her twinset, try to make myself believe that she'll never open her eyes, never sit up, never tell me to stop the whingeing.

There's no point crying over spilled milk, Vincent. That's what she'd say.

They take her away. They tell me why but I don't remember. I take out my phone. I have to ring Joey. It'll be . . . I look at my watch, but I can't remember what time it is in Sydney.

In the end, I don't ring Joey. Not right away.

I open my contacts. Touch the name.

She answers on the third ring.

'Vinnie?'

'I'm sorry to call so late.'

'I'm glad you called.'

'Did I wake you?'

'I wasn't asleep. Is everything alright?' The concern in her voice is tangible, like arms around me.

'It's Ma.' It sounds so childish. Ma. But I've never called her anything else. I'm not going to change now. Ellen waits. I like that about her. The way she can leave a space be.

'She died tonight.'

'Oh, no.'

'She was eighty-two. I didn't know that. I could have worked it out, I suppose. Never really thought about it. Her age.'

'She seemed a lot younger than that,' Ellen says.

For a moment, neither of us say anything. I'm in a corridor. There's no sound other than the faint crackle of static down the line and Ellen on the other end, quiet and careful. I picture her, standing in her apartment. The kitchen, maybe. In her bare feet. With the phone in her hand, hearing the faint crackle too. It's a comfort. I don't know why.

'Where are you?' she says finally.

'In Beaumont. They have to do an autopsy. I don't know why.'

'That's standard procedure. When someone dies suddenly.'

'They won't release her til tomorrow. Or maybe the day after. I hate the thought of leaving her here. On her own.'

'Do you want me to come? To the hospital?'

I realise I'd like that. For her to be here, to be with me.

'No,' I say eventually. 'I just . . . I wanted to talk to you.'

'Have you seen her?'

'Yeah.'

'That's good. I . . . I didn't see Neil afterwards. I couldn't face it. I wish I had now. I think it's a good thing to do.'

'She looked like she was asleep.'

'She was proud of you.'

'Was she?'

'She told me. At the Communion. She said you'd done a fine job with the kids. She had worried about that at the beginning. You on your own with them. She said you were like your dad. A strong man. She said she couldn't have been prouder.'

There's a chair in the corridor and I sit on it.

She never said that. Ma. That she was proud of me. We're not that sort of family, I suppose. The realisation settles someplace deep inside.

Warms me.

Then Ellen says, 'I'm so sorry, Vinnie. For everything.'

I nod. So am I. Sorry about Ma. Sorry about Neil. Sorry that things didn't work out between me and Ellen. Sorry that doing the right thing turns out to be the hard thing.

It's four o'clock in the morning by the time I make it home. Paula is awake. Watching the shopping channel, I think. An ad for gym equipment. A rowing machine, as far as I can make out.

'You should have slept in my room.'

'Used to be our room. Remember?' She's sitting on the couch, her legs folded underneath her. The same place she always sat. The same position.

'Yeah.' I rub my eyes. They're gritty. I need to get some kip. Get my head together before the kids wake up. The idea of telling them is something I don't want to think about. Not yet.

'I couldn't sleep anyway. Worrying about you.' Her eyes are glittery, almost black with pupil.

I notice the bottle then. On the mantelpiece. Nearly empty. 'You been drinking?'

She glances at the wine, dismisses it with a flick of her hand. 'I just had a couple. Take the edge off, y'know?'

'I didn't think you were supposed to drink. With the medication. You said—'

'Jaysus, Vinnie, I had a couple of glasses of wine! I came home and you're hardly rolling out the red carpet and Kerry doesn't want to know, and now your mother's gone and died. It's like I'm cursed. Like everything I touch turns to shit. So I had a few drinks. So what? God knows, nobody would blame me.' She drops her head, grabs fistfuls of hair with her hands.

'Sorry,' I say.

I pick her coat off the couch. 'Here, put this on you. I'll walk you over the road. You should get some sleep.'

She looks up. 'I'm not tired.'

'You should be.'

'I could stay.' She whispers it. Her tone is suggestive.

I shake my head. 'I'm tired, Paula. I need to sleep. Get my head together. Before I tell the kids in the morning.'

She folds her arms across her chest. 'I should be here when you tell them, Vinnie. I'm still their mother.'

'I'll call you in the morning, alright?' I don't have the stomach for any more talking. Not tonight.

We walk across the road. There's no sound other than the clip of her flip-flops against her heels. I wait at Trish's gate. She twists the key in the lock, then she turns, looks at me. I will her inside, the door closed and her on the other side of it. I feel bad, thinking that about her. The mother of my children.

But I think it, all the same.

If Ma were here, she'd say, *Go to bed, Vincent. Things will seem better in the morning.*

Forty Nine

I pick Joey up from the airport. He says he'll get a taxi but I insist. Glad of a chance to get away, bein' honest. The house is bedlam, people coming and going, all hours of the day. The fridge will barely close now, with the casseroles. They're all at it. Bringing casseroles. As soon as someone dies, people start making casseroles. I can't work it out.

He's arriving into the new terminal. My first time there. Inside it, I mean. Snazzy. You could be anywhere. London. New York, even. Impressive, it is. Busy too. Good to see. Two fingers up to the recession. Although maybe they're all emigrating.

I check the information screen. Joey's flight is due to land in five minutes. I get an espresso, a newspaper, find an empty chair in the arrivals area.

I wait.

Two years. That's how long it's been since he's been home. Ma kept talking about making the journey down under. That's what she called it. She never said Australia. 'I'm thinking about going down under,' she'd say. But there was always some event she had to organise, a fundraiser she had to oversee, a committee she had to chair, an outing she had to arrange.

The Nifty Fifties.

The Swinging Sixties.

Eighty-two.

'Next year, please God,' she'd say, when Joey mentioned her coming over to visit. 'I'll make it down under next year.'

The flight has landed. Could be a while yet, though. Getting through customs and that.

I found the instructions this morning. In the blue woolly hat in the top drawer of her bedside locker. I didn't find it, exactly. She told me, months ago. Maybe a year ago. 'If anything happens to me, Vincent, you're to go to the top drawer of the locker in my bedroom. There's a blue woolly hat in there. You remember it. The one I used to wear before I got the snazzy red one? Remember?'

'No.'

'You do, Vincent, you know it. It's got a bobble on the top and flaps that come down and cover your ears. I always said it was too itchy to wear. Remember, Vincent? Of course you do.'

'Yeah.' I hadn't got a clue.

'Well, everything you need's in there, son. Just in case anything ever happens to me.'

'Would you stop.' I loved the way she said, 'if'. And 'just in case'. *If* anything happens to me. Like it mightn't. Like there was a chance it mightn't.

I look at my watch. Joey's been on the ground now for fifteen minutes. I make my way over to the doors, so he'll see me when he steps through them.

She was right. Everything was in the blue woolly hat, and the hat was in the top drawer of the locker in her bedroom. An envelope stuffed with money. On the front of the envelope, she'd written 'funeral money'. I thought about her then, sitting in this room on her own one night and writing those words in her big, illegible scrawl on the envelope. Stuffing it with money. Perhaps putting a little by every week. Or maybe taking a chunk out of her savings account. Putting it in the envelope. A note inside the elastic band holding the wad together. *I want a decent coffin (oak, maybe – your father always said it was the best of the woods). The plot is paid for. Put me in beside your dad.*

Instructions. Lots of them. The readings. The gospel. Who was to read what. No eulogies. She underlined the word *No* three times. A list of acceptable hymns. She wanted the local choir, the North Strand Singers. 'Be Not Afraid.' 'Ave Maria.' 'How Great Thou Art'. And then, at the bottom of the list, 'Fire and Rain'. James Taylor. She was mad about him. And that song in particular. I remember her and Da, years ago, dancing in the kitchen, that song on the radio. Me standing at the door, still as a statue, watching them. I couldn't have been more than eight or nine. I remember them still, clear as day. One of those memories that doesn't fade, despite the flow of time across it. Her apron over her good clothes. Must have been a Sunday. The needle and thread on the table, where she'd stitched the cavity closed, once she'd stuffed the chicken. The bowl of marrowfat peas, covered with water on the counter. His hand on the small of her back. Her fingers draped over his shoulder. The sound of their shoes shuffling against the linoleum. The way they looked at each other. Like there was no one else but them.

But I always thought that I'd see you again.

The outfit is specified with much attention to detail. *The pink dress with the white roses. It's on a hanger on the right-hand side of the wardrobe. With the cardigan on top of it. The white one. Put that on me but don't button it up unless it's really cold.*

Her navy shoes. Her 'good' ones, she calls them.

The silver chain with the cross. The one her mother gave her. On her wedding day. *I'll leave everything else to Kerry but I want this one around me, when my time comes.*

There was no letter to me or Joey in the blue woolly hat and for this, I am grateful. Might have been difficult to read a letter like that. No, the blue woolly hat is about practicalities. Arrangements. Instructions. Useful telephone numbers.

I can almost hear her say, *Don't you go blubbering, when there's work to be done.*

Joey looks different from last time. Older, I suppose. You don't get to the age of forty-six without a few scratches and dents. He's put up a bit of weight too. The good life, Ma would have called that. It suits him, though, with his height. He's tanned. He always picked up the sun dead easy, even back in Dublin years ago. People used to say they couldn't tell one of us from the other but it was easy, really; I was the skinnier, paler version.

'Joey!' The white shirt and black slacks are pristine. Like he hasn't just flown halfway across the world. Not a crease anywhere. He was always particular about his image. We were like chalk and cheese that way. Most ways, I suppose.

He smiles when he sees me and then it's like he hasn't changed a day. He's still Joey. The big brother who told me about sex in such detail, I swore I'd never do it. The one who explained the offside rule. Who searched for dock leaves after I fell into the bank of nettles in Fairview Park. Who ironed my shirt the day of Da's funeral.

I hold my hand out and he grips it and we shake and then he pulls me towards him, hugs me briefly, claps me on the back, releases me, looks me up and down. 'Good to see you, Vinnie.'

I pick up his bag. Nod towards the exit and we start walking. On the way to the car park, we engage in that idle chit-chat that people who haven't seen each other for ages do.

'How was the flight?'

'Grand, yeah.'

'Did you manage to get any kip?'

'A bit. After Hong Kong. Couple of hours.'

Neither of us mentions Ma.

It's a bit easier in the car. Like old times, Joey in the passenger seat and me behind the wheel. He taught me how to drive. A month before he left. 'A man has to know his way round a car,' he told me, when I asked him why he was so keen to show me. He probably wouldn't have bothered so much if Da had been around. 'You're the man of the house now, Vinnie.' That's what he said when he left. I was fifteen years old.

'Nice motor,' he says, when I pop the boot. 'Is it an automatic?' I nod, close the boot, get in. He runs his hand along the dashboard. 'Walnut?' he says.

'Yeah.'

'Lovely finish.'

When Joey's in the car, I find myself driving the way he taught me. Both hands on the wheel, the ten to two position. Putting the handbrake on any time we stop. Checking my rear-view mirror.

'Will we swing by McCarthy's?'

I shake my head. 'Better not.' I told the kids I'd be straight back.

'Just for the one?'

Joey's never been great at having just the one.

I indicate, drive into the car park at the front of the pub. 'Just the one, then,' I say, stepping out of the car.

The bar is pretty empty, which is fair enough, since it's only half three in the afternoon on a weekday. The Stowe brothers are there, stooped over a deck of cards near the back, and a huge man with a purple face stands in front of the flat screen filled with horses thundering around a racecourse. He grips a betting slip, his eyes full of desperate hope. I find myself wishing his horse comes in.

'Well, if it isn't handsome and handsomer,' Mary says, winking at Joey as he strides towards the bar. Her face sobers when Joey reaches her and she puts her hand over his. 'I'm sorry for your loss, love. She was some woman for one woman, your ma.'

'Thanks Mary. It's good to see you. You haven't changed a day.'

'Go on, you charmer. What'll it be? The usual? It's on the house.'

Joey smiles and nods. I settle myself at a table, my back to proceedings. I don't want to see the man's disappointment at the end of the race and if I catch either of the Stowe brothers' eyes, even by accident, they'll be over in a flash and we'll never get out of here.

'Cheers,' Joey says, handing me a pint and lifting his towards my glass.

'Welcome home,' I say, and we reach for the drinks with our mouths.

Joey sets his drink on the table, sits back in the chair, pushes both hands through his hair, then down his face. 'I should have come home at Christmas.'

'You weren't to know.'

'Still.'

'You thought she was coming out for a visit. Later on this year, she said.'

'Down under.' He sniggers then and so do I and we start laughing, the pair of us. Any time there's a chance of one of us stopping, the other says *down under*, the way she used to, and we're off again, fit to burst. *Down fucken under*.

My stomach hurts when I manage to stop. I know it's not all that funny but still, the muscles there ache, all the same. And it's sort of broken the ice a bit. Not that there's anything to break, exactly. It's just . . . it feels like old times when we laugh like that. At stupid stuff that doesn't make sense to anyone else.

'So? What happened?' Joey takes another drink, puts his glass back on the table, burps discreetly into his cupped hand.

'Just what I said on the phone. Heart attack. She was sitting in the chair at the back of the parish hall. She was supposed to be taking the minutes. But she ended up sitting in the audience. She was a bit tired, she said.'

'That's not like her.'

'No,' I say. I don't tell him about her having a cold the few days before, going to bed in the middle of the day. I should have taken her to the doctor that day. Insisted.

'Go on.'

'That's it, really. They found her. On the chair. Thought she'd nodded off.'

'They couldn't have thought that.'

'That's what they said. She was still warm when I got there.'

'Fuck sake, Vinnie.'

'I mean, she wasn't long gone. And it was quick. She probably didn't realise.'

'Maybe.'

'It's not a bad way to go.'

'I suppose.'

'She's laid out. At the house.' I've been wondering how to tell him since he came through the doors at the airport. It's not the kind of thing that comes up naturally in a conversation.

'You're havin' a fuckin' wake?'

'It's what she wanted.' I tell him about the blue woolly hat.

'Still, though. A wake.'

'I know.'

'The last time I saw her, she was giving me her fruit cake at the airport. Wrapped in a piece of newspaper. The weight of the thing. Like a boulder, it was.'

'She was no Delia, that's for sure.'

'And now she's in a coffin in the front room. I presume she's in the front room, yeah?'

I nod.

'The "good" room. Remember?'

'Yeah.'

'Fuck sake.'

'She looks . . . she doesn't look too bad, really. She looks like herself. Like she's asleep.'

'In a fuckin' box. In the good room.'

'Yeah.'

'Sorry, it's just—'

'I know. It's weird. I've had more time to get used to the idea.'

'Just you and me now, Vinnie.'

'Yeah.' I hadn't thought about it like that.

'I suppose it's different for you. With the kids an' all.'

'Ah, here, you're not going to have a midlife crisis on me now, are you?' I say, smiling. 'I've enough stuff going on without that.'

He grins then. Shakes his head, picks up his pint. 'Been a long flight.'

'You can get some kip at my house. You're in Finn's room. He's sleeping in with me.'

'How are the kids?'

'Alright, yeah.' I don't tell him. About Finn, crying in his sleep last night. So loud he woke us all up. Saying the same thing over and over. 'I don't want Granny to be dead.' Half asleep, he was. Didn't know what he was saying. But still. The insistence of it. Like if he insisted long enough, she mightn't be dead. Kerry rocking him in her arms when I went downstairs to get him a glass of milk. Singing to him the song Ma used to sing. *'We'll gather lilacs in the spring again.'* Something like that. A desperate dirge of a song, the way Ma sang it. It sounded different last night, coming from Kerry. She sang it into his hair, rocked him til he was nearly asleep, her arms wrapped around him, her voice sweet and true. She could have been Paula, sitting there on Finn's bed. Except that Paula never sang a lullaby. Or rocked the children in her arms, if they woke up in the night, crying. *What's wrong with him?* She'd wake me up. Shake me if she had to. I was a heavy sleeper back then. *What's the matter with her?* She'd be confused. Scared.

Go back to sleep. I'd get up. Heat the bottle of milk. Feed them. Sit on the floor beside the cot. Then on the edge of the bed when they got a bit older. I wouldn't sing. Wake the dead, I would. I'd sit there. Tell them a story, maybe. They liked hearing about themselves when they were babies – the first words they said, the stuff they liked to eat. Mashed up bananas. 'But I hate bananas,' Kerry used to say. 'You loved them when you were a baby,' I'd tell her. 'What else?' she'd whisper, lying down and putting the thumb in.

I don't say any of that to Joey. Why would I? It's just stuff that happens in a house. Nothing that anyone else would be interested in.

'When's the funeral?'

'Tomorrow. Ten o'clock. The removal is tonight. Six o'clock from the house. We better make a move.'

'You've let everyone know?'

'There'll be a good crowd, I'd say.'

'What about Paula? She and Ma were thick as thieves back in the day.'

'Yeah.'

'Does she know?'

'She's here.' It still sounds strange. Saying that.

Joey leans forward. Eyeballs me. 'When did she come back?'

I shrug. ''Bout a week ago.' So much going on. It's hard to keep track.

Joey catches Mary's eye behind the bar. Indicates a chaser with his thumb and forefinger.

I pick up the keys of the motor.

'I'll be quick,' he says, standing up and moving towards the bar.

I put the keys on the table. The bottle of pills is in my pocket. Dr McDaid brought it when he came to pay his respects yesterday. I haven't taken one. I've been too busy, getting stuff organised. It's only when you sit down, stop for a bit, that you remember things. Like the notice in the shop earlier. About the bingo being cancelled. A mark of respect. Something small like that. Would have meant a lot to Ma.

Joey picks the tumbler off the bar counter. Tosses the whiskey into his mouth. Then drinks the glass of water Mary's poured for him. She still remembers how he likes it. That's probably why she's been in business so long.

'Is Paula back for good?' Joey says, reaching for his jacket draped across a bar stool.

I stand up.

'Is she?' Joey was always persistent.

I shrug. 'I dunno. Maybe. She says she wants to try again.'

'What about you?'

'What about me?'

'What do *you* want?'

'It's not that simple.'

'It is.'

'It isn't. I've got the kids to consider.'

I think about Kerry then. About her face, when I told her about Ma. The way it fell. I could see it falling, right in front of me. The wail of her. I hadn't expected that. Hadn't thought she'd cry. Not in front of us. Thought she'd go to her room. Close the door. Slam it, maybe. But she stood there, in the kitchen, right in front of us, crying with her whole body, shaking with the force of it. I took a step towards her but it was Paula she turned to. Paula who held her in her arms. 'My girl,' she kept saying. 'Mygirlmygirlmygirl,' her voice soft and rhythmic. I stood beside them, not really knowing what to do. But a part of me was glad, that her mam was here.

I look at Joey. 'You don't have kids. You don't have a clue. No offence.'

He shrugs then. 'Still,' he says, 'you should at least know what you want. That way, you'll know what you're missing when you don't get it.'

Ellen's face appears then. In my head. The image is sudden. Sharp. I shake my head, dislodge it.

Joey puts the empties on the counter, nods at Mary with the smile that earned him the nickname Joey-the-boyband-Boland.

He had a reputation. Back in the day.

'We'll go,' Joey says. 'Face the music.'

'Yeah.'

'See yiz after the removal later, boys,' Mary calls after us. 'I'll have the trays of sandwiches at the ready. Egg and onion. Her favourites.'

Joey opens the door, holds it for me as I walk through. He puts his hand on my shoulder. Briefly. Enough for me to feel the warm weight of it. His hand falls away and we're heading now.

Heading home.

Fifty

We waked Da too. I remember him in the coffin in our front room. In his good suit. Ma had put a carnation through the lapel of his jacket. A white one. 'He loved carnations,' she said. She slid the stem of it through the buttonhole, touched his cheek.

Janine has set up a sort of a deli in Ma's kitchen and she's handing out plates of casserole, glasses of sherry, slices of Ma's fruit cake, spread with butter. Janine found it in the bread bin, wrapped in Monday's newspaper. She needed both hands to haul it out.

The last one.

In spite of the glut of casseroles, I don't think I've eaten today. Not really. I keep meaning to and then the doorbell goes or the phone rings or someone taps me on the shoulder to tell me something about Ma.

Everyone's got something to say about Ma.

'You wouldn't give her eighty-two,' says Mrs Finnegan, shaking her head at Ma in the coffin.

'No,' I say, nodding.

'A great head of hair, your mother had. Always did.'

'She did,' I say.

'And good teeth. You can't beat a decent set of choppers, all the same.' She puts her hand on the cross of the rosary beads wrapped around Ma's fingers. Mouths a prayer with her eyes closed. Then she opens one eye, touches Ma's hair. 'Still so shiny,' she says. 'You'd never take her for dead.'

359

Any time I spot Kenny, it hits me that Ma is dead. It's his clobber. Nothing flamboyant about him today. A regular black suit. A grey shirt. Ordinary leather black shoes. Even his moustache is sober, no telltale curl at the ends where he teases it with a comb.

When Kenny senses an audience, he starts to sing. He prefaces each song with a 'Mrs Boland loved this one, God rest her soul,' whether she did or not.

'Will you put a bloody sock in it and help me with the food,' Janine hisses at him through the side of her mouth. 'It's like a fecking soup kitchen back there. You'd think half of them hadn't been fed in days.' Janine takes Kenny by the elbow and steers him away from his audience, who make up most of the residents of the old folks' home where Ma said I could put her out to pasture when she was an auldone.

The house is full of oxygen tanks, Zimmer frames, hearing aids, blue rinses, long-handled shopping bags on wheels, quivering voices. Old people.

I never thought of Ma as an old woman. She had none of that delicate frailty you associate with old age. Maybe it was her voice, the confident belt of it. Or the height of her. Her size eight shoes. Or maybe it was because she knew what she wanted. There was a certainty about her. A sureness.

Paula and Trish sit at the table in the back garden. They're sharing a bottle of wine. Their second one, as far as I can make out. 'Everyone has a few jars at a wake, Vinnie,' Trish says, when I ask her if Paula is alright. 'She's just letting off a bit of steam, go easy on her, would you?'

Worry squirms like a worm inside my belly, blatant in its familiarity. The same thoughts. The same fears. Going around and around my head. One thought, really. One fear.

Paula.

Is Paula alright?

'Stop nagging,' she used to say when I asked her if she was alright. If she'd taken her tablets. 'You're like a warden, with your questions.'

It was only after the attempt – the genuine attempt – that I realised she hadn't been taking her pills. Found them – what was left of them – when I went home to pack an overnight bag for her, in the zip section of her make-up bag. Mother's little helpers, she called them, her laugh brittle and dry.

And the drinking. I'd read loads of stuff about bipolar over the years and the general consensus was not to drink. Or maybe just the odd one. Certainly no binge drinking. Even if you don't have bipolar, binge drinking can make a meal out of you. Leave you down.

'How many drinks has she had?' I ask Joey when he comes in from the garden to get another bottle.

'She's just having a few scoops,' he says. 'Take it easy.'

Joey never saw her when she was bad.

Paula grabs his arm when he returns to the garden. 'Dance with me Jo-Jo,' she says, arranging his arms around her waist, tucking her head under the awning of his chin. He glances towards the house, sees me looking. He arranges his face into a question and I shrug because I have no answers and he dances with her, perhaps because he feels he should. Because she asked him. Because his mother is dead. Because his brother won't.

Kerry has gone to Mark's house. She refused to stay at the wake, declaring the process 'macabre'. She agreed to be at the church in time for the removal this evening. And the funeral tomorrow morning.

Finn, by turns, is fascinated and distraught. He likes the fact that there is a dead body in his granny's house. It's the fact that the dead body is his granny he's destroyed about.

Janine says I shouldn't have him in the house at all. 'The poor lad'll be haunted.' Maybe she's right. Earlier I thought he should see Ma like this. He'll accept it better, once he sees her.

'Am I going to die?' he asks me later, whispers it.

'Not for a very long time,' I tell him, lifting him up in a way I haven't done in ages. I hold him close, inhale him. The warm, soapy smell of him. Kerry bathed him this morning. Put him into his Holy Communion get-up.

'But I am going to die, amn't I?' he says, holding my face between his hands so I have to look straight at him. 'Someday.'

I nod. What else can I do? He cries then, the small, helpless cry of a boy who's becoming aware of the world and how forever might not last as long as he'd thought.

Later, he touches her. Leans in and kisses her. Not a bother to him. 'She's very cold, so she is,' he tells me afterwards. 'Is it because there's no oxygen inside her?'

'I'd say so,' I tell him.

The hearse arrives on time. Closing the lid is hard. I put a photograph of the four of us in beside her. Me and Ma and the kids. Don't know why. Just seems like the right thing to do. Something Ma would like. Me and Joey close the lid together. I wonder then if there's such a thing as heaven. I wouldn't say so, but if there is, that's where she is now, organising the Apostles into a committee, with herself as chairperson.

They take the coffin away and Joey throws his arm across my shoulders. 'You OK?'

I shrug. 'Yeah.'

'You hungry?'

'Not really.'

'I could do you a lovely bowl of casserole, if you like.' He winks at me, nodding towards the line of casseroles on the counter in the kitchen.

'You're alright.'

'Come on. We'd better get in the car. I'll get Finn and Paula.'

'Does Paula seem . . . do you think she's alright?'

'Yeah. Grand. A bit hyper, maybe.'

'Hyper?'

'Just with the few drinks, I'd say.'

'Yeah.'

'She was talking about your lady friend.'

'What?'

'You never said you were seeing someone.'

'I'm not.'

'Well, Paula seemed fairly worked up about it.'

'Fuck sake.'

'Come on, Vinnie, it hasn't been easy for her. Coming back after all this time. You with someone else. And now Ma.'

'I'm not with anyone else.'

'Well, then, she's got it wrong, hasn't she?'

Joey looks at me.

'What?' I ask.

'Remember when we used to go fishing, up in the Strawberry Beds, in the summertime?'

'What about it?'

Joey shrugs. 'Nothing, really. Just . . . it was great, wasn't it?'

'We never caught any fish,' I remind him.

'I know. We didn't give a fuck, though, did we? The pair of us, sitting there. On the bank. It was so quiet. And sunny. Do you ever wonder about that? How it was always sunny back then?'

'You're losing it, Joey.'

He grins and punches my arm. I punch him back. We move on, out of the house, towards the next part of the day.

I do remember, though. Those afternoons, on the bank, with the fishing rods in our hands and the lines that rarely twitched. The endless sky and the high arc of the sun and the certainty of youth.

That things would always be like this.

That nothing would ever change.

Fifty One

The church is packed at the funeral mass at ten o'clock the next morning. Ma would have been pleased, I think, with the send-off. They're all here. The Nifty Fifties. The Swinging Sixties. The Green-Fingered Grannies. Even Carmel, the secretary. Her back must be better now.

The Bingo Club. The hangers-on from the hospice. What's left of the residents from the old folks' home. The staff from the credit union. The cranky auldfella from the post office. Mary from the pub. Dr McDaid. The staff from the hairdresser's. The cashiers from the Centra. The butcher from Brady's. The woman who looks like Dot Cotton from the launderette. Even the hardware shop is represented. She was one of his regulars, the fella from Edges tells me. Forever putting up shelves, taking them down, putting them up again some-place else. Filling them with spider plants and well-thumbed copies of *Reader's Digest*. She loved *Reader's Digest*. And spider plants.

They last for ever, spider plants, she said.

That's how I thought of her, mostly. That she'd last forever. Stupid, I know. I thought she'd always be there, telling me what to do and how to do it. Giving me coupons for groceries I would never buy. Getting me to complete slogans for competitions. '*I like "You've got to be joking, of course it's butter" because . . .* Ten words or less, Vincent. Vincent? Did you hear me? Well?'

She would have been pleased at the turnout, I think.

Finn puts his hand in mine, and Kerry, on the other side, leans her head against my shoulder and I put my arm around her and hold her tight and let her know that I'm here. That I'm not going anywhere. I decide, all of a sudden, that I'm never going to smoke again. I feel the packet of cigarettes in my trouser pocket, the rectangle of it against my leg, and the urge to take it out and fling it far away is nearly overwhelming. Both of them, gone. Matching heart attacks. And Da only fifty-nine when his claimed him.

I don't notice how bad Paula is until the mass is over, when me and Joey and Kenny and Fr Murphy lift the coffin and carry Ma down the aisle on our shoulders. Paula is behind us, Kerry and Finn on one side of her and Trish on the other. I hear wailing, a jagged sound that cuts through the dense smell of incense. I look around, see if the kids are OK. Trish has both arms around Paula. As if she's holding her up. If she lets go, Paula will collapse like a house of cards. That's what it looks like to me.

Finn puts his hand in Kerry's. 'Is Mam alright?' he asks, his huge dark eyes full of the kind of worry and anxiety that seven-year-olds should not be familiar with.

Kerry squeezes his hand. 'She's fine, Finn. Just a bit sad.'

He nods. 'Will there be cake at the bingo?' he asks then.

The bingo. That was another thing on the list of instructions in the blue woolly hat. A game of bingo at the party afterwards. That's what she called it. A party.

When life gives you lemons, Vincent, might as well make lemonade.

A party. In the parish hall. A game of bingo. She even had prizes. *They're in the cupboard under the stairs, Vincent.*

Boxes of jellies. A tea cosy. Tins of biscuits. A snow globe from Lourdes. A brooch. Turkish delight. The top prize was the recipe for her famous fruit cake. She called it that. Famous. And in a way it was. Everyone in the neighbourhood had been force-fed it at one time or another.

Bingo. I suppose there are worse ways to bow out. And she was fond of the game and had won her fair share of biscuits and tins of fruit cocktail over the years.

We slide the coffin into the back of the hearse. The undertaker says we'll head for the graveyard in five minutes. I nod and move away from the crowd. I need a few minutes. I feel like I've been saying the same things over and over again, nodding and shaking people's hands for days.

I see a woman walking out through the gates of the church car park. Walking fairly fast in spite of a crutch. She's wearing a black dress that reaches past her knee. The nails of her toes sticking out of the top of her black sandals are painted a traditional red. A short black jacket over the dress, with a few red roses on long green stems sewn into the fabric. I think Ma would have approved. Respectful with a touch of snazzy, she would have said.

I walk quickly, catch up with her.

'Ellen?'

She turns around, sees me and raises one hand in a stationary wave, the other resting on her crutch.

When I look at her, I feel calm for the first time today. For the first time in ages. Like when you step inside your house and close the door and the noise of the world falls away.

I look at her face. The bright amber eyes and the paleness of her skin except where it gathers and puckers around the scar that I hardly notice any more. The way her dark hair frames her face. The curve of her mouth.

I miss you. That's what I'm thinking. I'm burying my poor mother and trying to make things right for me and Paula and the kids, and that's what I end up thinking.

Ellen looks worried. 'I didn't mean for anyone to see me. I don't want to intrude.'

'Don't be daft.'

'I just wanted to pay my respects.'

I nod. 'Ma would have appreciated that.'

I want to see her smile. I think I'll be fine if I can make her smile. I tell her about the instructions in the blue woolly hat. And about the bingo. The prizes under the stairs.

Ellen smiles.

'What the hell is she doing here?' The words are loud. Not quite a shout but enough volume to get people's attention.

I know it's her before I turn. It's Paula. She wrestles herself out of Trish's arms and storms towards us.

'I'm sorry,' says Ellen, looking at Paula. 'I shouldn't have come.'

'Too fuckin' right, you shouldn't have come.'

'Mam!'

Kerry appears, dragging Finn along behind her, his hand still in hers. 'What are you doing?' Kerry sounds frightened. Finn is crying. I move towards them, pick Finn up. He buries his face into my neck and I hold him tight.

'See?' Paula points at the children, looks at Ellen. 'Look what you've done.'

'Paula, come on,' I say. I keep my voice low. Calm. That used to help. Sometimes. 'It's time to go to the graveyard.'

Paula glares at me before she turns back to Ellen, pointing at her, stabbing the air with her finger. 'This is a family occasion.' She's shouting now and when I look at her face, I see the signs. They're all there. The flushed cheeks and her pupils dilated, the shake in her voice that's climbing higher and higher and the white flecks of spit on her mouth in her effort to get the words out.

'Take it easy, Paula.' I hand Finn, still crying, to Kenny, who has pushed his way through the crowd to reach us. I move until I'm standing in front of Paula. Between her and Ellen. I put my hand on her arm, try to pull her towards me.

She shakes me off with a jerk. '*Take it easy, Paula,*' she sneers at me, her voice sharp and high. '*Take your tablets, Paula. Be a good girl, Paula.* That's all you want, isn't it? Me taking my pills, keeping quiet, staying away.'

'I never told you to stay away.' I know I shouldn't rise to her but I go ahead and do it anyway. Maybe it's the day that's in it. I'm not quite myself.

'Well, you didn't exactly waste a lot of time finding a new model, did you?' she says, pointing at Ellen.

'I'll go,' says Ellen, her face flushed now.

'Yes, why don't you do that,' Paula spits at her. 'And leave my family the fuck alone while you're at it.'

'This is not the time or the place.' My voice is low and rigid. My throat hurts with the effort of not shouting. Ellen walks up the road. Kenny and Janine walk towards the church, taking the children with them.

Paula looks at me. 'When is the time, Vinnie? Where is the bloody place? You tell me that. I'm just trying to get my family back. I just want to . . .' She's crying now, bent double with the force of it. I reach for her, hold her against me.

I see Ellen, getting smaller as she walks farther away.

Once Paula starts crying, I know what to do.

'Ssshhh,' I say.

'It'll be alright,' I say.

'Don't cry,' I say.

I keep holding her.

After a while, her crying slows and quietens and her body stops shaking and she lifts her head and looks at me and I take a tissue out of my pocket and wipe her face like I do with Finn after he's had an ice cream.

'I'm sorry, Vinnie.'

'It's alright.' Like if I say it enough times, it might be alright.

'I keep making the same mistakes over and over again.'

'It's a hard day. For all of us. Let's just get through it, OK?'

She nods and tucks her hand into the pocket of my jacket the way she used to do, back when we were young and happy and neither of us imagined that life could be this hard.

Fifty Two

Things are OK after that. Not fantastic or anything but ...
we're doing OK. Getting through the day. It's not until the
bingo is nearly over that I realise.

Joey volunteers to call the numbers. No choice, really. The
auldones have him hemmed in, throwing questions at him,
rubbing him, smiling their huge denture smiles. Telling him
stories about his mother, how he's cut out of his father and
wondering at the height of him.

'It's all that sunshine down there,' Mrs Finnegan concludes.
'Down under. That's what it is. The heat. Everything grows tall
down there.'

He's giving it everything, Joey, calling out the numbers, winking at the ladies in their Sunday best, making them wait before
he announces the next number. And the next.

Nelson's Pillar; number one.

Baby's done it; number two.

Cup of tea; number three.

Shut the door; number four.

Man alive; number five.

Kenny and Janine are in the kitchenette at the back of the hall,
Kenny barely visible behind platters of sandwiches. The good thing
about him and Carol splitting up is that Carol's not here, as his
plus-one. He broke up with her a couple of days ago, Janine told
me. The last straw for Kenny was the discovery of Carol's 'stash' in
a cupboard in her kitchen. Sachets of coffee, sugar and teabags,

filched from every self-service coffee dock she'd accepted a coffee from. 'I haven't bought a bag of sugar since June 2004,' she bragged to Kenny at her apartment, handing him a cup of tea and a digestive.

'The biscuit was from the tin at work,' Kenny told Janine. 'She told me. Wasn't even embarrassed.' He shook his head. 'I have my limits, you know.'

'Very few, mind,' Janine said, but she smiled, all the same.

Janine is making pots and pots of tea, barely able to keep up with the demand of the meals on wheels women, filling their trolleys and pushing them into the hall. Kenny is washing cups and saucers and spoons. 'There's a bit of lipstick still on the rim of that one,' Janine tells him, glancing at the draining board.

'I've been at it with a Brillo pad, there's no shifting it.'

'Wonder what brand it is?'

'You don't need lipstick, Janine, you've lovely pink lips, so you do.'

'That's because I'm wearing lipstick, you thick.'

'Oh.'

She puts the knife down on the table, looks at him. 'Sorry.'

'For what?'

'For callin' you a thick.'

'You always call me names.'

'I don't mean it. It's just a habit.'

'I know.' Kenny grins at her, and she smiles at him before picking up the knife, her hands a blur as she butters more bread.

I'm at the door of the kitchenette, looking at the pair of them, working away. Ma always said that good friends were better than money in the credit union. Janine asked her sister to man the phones at the depot. Kenny's taken the entire day off even though it's the Friday of the bank holiday and he could make a good bit of rent on a day like today.

'Thanks, lads,' I say, and they look up and Janine blushes.

'How long have you been standing there?'

'Just arrived,' I tell her, and she nods, relieved that I haven't overheard her conversation with Kenny. Soft as a pat of butter in the sun, Janine. But she'd kill anyone who spread that around.

'Have you seen Finn and Kerry?' I ask.

Kenny nods towards the door. 'They're out there, playing bingo. They're at a table with Paula and Trish.'

'I couldn't see them.'

'The place is jammers,' Janine says. 'Here, bring these sambos out for the vultures, will you?'

'The far right corner, Vinnie,' Kenny says. 'That's where they are. Near the emergency exit.'

I pick up the platter of sandwiches. Have to hold it with both hands, the weight of it.

They're on me like a pack of wolves. 'Over here, Vincent!'

'Don't forget us, Vincent!'

'There's something about a funeral that gives me a powerful appetite.'

'Tuna fish is the devil's work, the stink off it.'

'Is there an eggy one? I'm partial to a hard-boiled egg, even though it doesn't agree with me. Gives me terrible heartburn, so it does.'

'I'll take a few, save you coming back.'

The platter is nothing but crumbs now. I set it on a table just as someone – Mrs Waters, I think – leaps off her chair and shouts, 'BINGO!', her arms raised as high as her tightly buttoned coat will allow.

I look at the table on the far right of the hall. Trish is there, alright, but she's on her own. The emergency exit door is open, swaying and squawking on rusty hinges. In my temple, a pulse begins to thump.

I walk over. 'Trish?'

She looks up with the glazed expression that tells tales of a bottle of wine. 'Howeya holding up, gorgeous?' she says.

'Grand, yeah. Where's Paula?'

She looks at the chair beside her, then back at me.

'She was right there,' she says, surprised.

'What about the kids? Where are they?'

'The kids?'

'Finn and Kerry. Have you seen them?'

'They were there too.'

'Did they go out that door?' I nod towards the emergency exit.

Trish looks at it. 'I was wondering why there was such a draught,' she says, smiling at me.

I scan the room again. Slowly this time. Examine every table. Every chair. Joey kisses Mrs Waters' cheek at the top of the room. Gives her one of the prizes. A bag of Liquorice Allsorts. Everyone claps and cheers, eats their sandwiches, drains their teacups.

No sign of them.

'Sit down here and talk to me, Vinnie Boland,' Trish says, patting the empty chair beside her.

'Sorry, Trish, I have to go,' I say. The door opens on to a lane, which is deserted. To my left is the car park and down to the right is a recycling area. Bottles and cans, mostly. A clothes bin, maybe. I run to the car park. A few people standing at the front door of the hall, smoking. One old man with a pipe, the sweet, earthy smell of the smouldering tobacco throwing up a memory of my grandad, leaning against a bale of hay in the field at the back of his house in Rush, on a summer's evening, heavy with heat.

I scan the car park. No sign of them. I hear a shake in my breath on the exhale and I tell myself not to panic because there's no need to panic. She's brought them to the shop. For an ice cream. Or back home. Maybe Finn had an accident. Wet his pants. He doesn't do that as a rule. Not in the daytime. But maybe he did today. The day that's in it. Kerry has a key. They've gone to the house is all.

I take my phone out of my pocket. Ring Kerry's mobile. It's turned off. The battery could be dead. She was looking for her charger this morning.

I ring Paula's phone. Goes straight to voicemail. 'Hi, this is Paula. Leave a message.' A high, chirpy tone. Like everything's fine. Nothing could be wrong.

I hang up. Dial the landline at home. It rings and rings.

I ring Ma's house then. Habit, I suppose. But Kerry has a key of that house too and maybe one of them left something there yesterday and they've gone to get it. Paula's handbag, perhaps.

I'm pretty sure they're not there but I ring anyway. Something to do. I'm trying not to panic. There's a simple explanation. I'm sure of it.

I'm just about to turn and go back inside when I see it. The motor. Or rather, the space where my motor should be.

The space is empty.

The car is gone.

I'm running now. Back inside the hall. My jacket is hanging on the back of the chair beside Trish. I pick it up. Shake it. There's no jangling of keys. No sound at all. Still, I reach into every pocket, to be sure, but they're gone, the car keys. They're not there.

I drag my hands down my face. 'Here, my love,' says Trish, putting her hand in her bag and lifting out a naggin of vodka. 'Have a sup. You look like you need it.'

'Was Paula drinking?'

She looks at me, blinking, like she's just woken up. 'She had a few, alright. Nothing major.'

I'm running again, into the kitchen this time. Close the door behind me. Lean against it. 'Kenny. Janine.'

'Jesus, Vinnie, what's wrong? You're as pale as a ghost.' Janine drops the butter knife and Kenny puts the teapot down. They come out from behind the table and hurry over to me.

'She's taken the car.'

'Calm down, comrade. Who's taken the car?' Kenny puts his hand on my shoulder.

'Paula. She's got the kids with her.' I see them look at each other. Trying to look like they're not worried.

Janine turns back to me. 'Are you sure, Vinnie?'

I nod. 'My car keys are gone, the car's gone and I can't find them anywhere. Paula. Or the kids. They're gone.' Now my breath is like a rag and it feels like there's a hand around my throat and I can't get enough air in. Black dots appear on the edges of my vision and it's like I can feel the world turning, and I'm struggling to keep my footing.

Janine pushes me into a chair. Shoves my head in between my legs. 'Breathe,' she tells me, before sending Kenny out into the hall to look again. 'They're not there,' I tell her, and my voice is muffled but she hears me because she says, 'Shuddup and breathe.'

I come up for air. 'Where are your tablets?' Janine asks. 'Your Valium.'

I shake my head. 'I don't know.'

I close my eyes and breathe. In for five. Hold for five. Out for five. I try to visualise something nice, like Dr McDaid suggested. A beach, he said. Or a river. Somewhere lovely. Someplace you like to go. All I can see is Kerry and Finn, getting into the car with her. She's never been a good driver. Nervous on the road. Beeping the horn. Cursing at the other drivers. Someone's always cutting her off, not giving her the nod when she lets them out, not indicating soon enough, someone driving too slow, too fast, someone tailgating her.

Distracted. She's a distracted driver. And she's been drinking. Trish said she'd had a few, which could mean a lot more than a few. And she's volatile. The way she erupted with Ellen at the graveyard. Irrational. I've seen her like that before. Lots of times. When she just explodes and she doesn't care who's there. She lets herself go. She lets go of herself.

She's in my car with my kids and she's let go of herself.

Janine rubs my back. 'It'll be alright, Vinnie, love. We'll find them. They'll be grand. Keep breathing.'

I squeeze my eyes shut and breathe for five, hold for five, release for five.

Fifty Three

Janine and I get into Kenny's car. Joey borrows Trish's. He goes to my house and Ma's house, to make sure. Then he trawls the narrow streets and lanes around North Strand, looking for them.

Kenny drives us back to the graveyard. 'They might have wanted to spend some time with your Ma,' he says, and the way he says it, it doesn't sound unreasonable.

They're not there.

I ring her mobile again and again. Each time the same, straight to voicemail. Finally, I leave a message. I try to keep my tone neutral. 'Where are you? Are the kids with you? I . . . Could you ring me back? As soon as you get this message? Please, Paula?'

Joey rings. 'No sign,' he says. I tell him to go back to the parish hall in case she's brought them back.

We go to the house where Paula's parents used to live. We go to the house where Maureen used to live. We go to a café Paula used to like. We go to Fairview Park, where she walked in the evenings before she got sick and lost interest in parks and walking and life in general.

We go to St Anne's Park. The playground where she took Finn only last week. It seems so long ago now. We drive to the hairdresser's where Paula used to work. Maybe she wanted to catch up with Camilla, who still works there, as far as I know. Show the kids what she did before she got sick and had to give it up.

So many things she gave up. It hasn't been easy for her, I know that. But it's hard to think like that when she's driving around the city in a state with my kids. That's how I think of them as we turn the city upside down. My kids. I know I shouldn't but I do, all the same. I can't help it.

We go to the pubs she used to frequent. Some kips she drank in when she was bad. Places where there was little chance she'd run into anyone she knew.

'Kerry is with them. Kerry will mind them,' Janine keeps saying. And a part of me thinks it's true. But Kerry is only fourteen. I think about her crying the other day when I told her about Ma. And her, looking for her mother then. She's still a kid, Kerry. In lots of ways. She just thinks she's not and that's where the difficulty is.

We're in rush-hour traffic now and I can't think of anywhere else to go. I ring Paula's number again. 'Where are you? Where have you taken my kids? If anything happens to them—'

Janine grabs the phone off me before I can finish the sentence. 'Vinnie, that's not helping. Calm down and think, would ya? Where else could they be?'

I push my face into my hands, close my eyes, try to come up with something. Anything. Nothing occurs. Part of me knows it'll be fine. There'll be some innocent explanation. A plausible reason. Something we should have thought of ages ago but maybe slipped our minds, with the day that's in it. We'll all have a laugh about it later. They'll call me a dope for worrying.

Then there's the other part of me. The one who's heard the stories on the news. The headlines in the paper. The things people do. When they're not well. The people they take with them. The kids they bring along for the ride. That's the part of me who's pushing his face into his hands, closing his eyes, coming up with nothing.

'FUCK!' I roar it, so loud Janine and Kenny jump in the front seats. Kenny pulls over into a loading bay. Puts his hazards on. Hands me a cigarette. I forget I'm never smoking again. My fingers holding the lighter shake and the flame goes out. Kenny takes the cigarette, lights it, hands it to me again.

'Think, Vinnie,' he says.

I get out of the car. Pace the footpath for a bit. Smoke. Breathe. In for five. Hold for five. Out for five. I can barely get to two now. I put my hands on the boot of the car. The metal is warm from the heat of the day.

Ellen. The thought floats to the surface of my mind. Paula doesn't know where she lives. I'm pretty sure she doesn't. I could have mentioned Clontarf, couldn't I? That she lives there. It's a possibility. Or maybe someone told her.

I take my phone out of my pocket again. Ring Ellen. It's the only thing I can think of. The only thing that's left to do. She answers on the first ring.

'Vinnie?'

'She's gone. Paula's gone. And she's taken the kids. She's in my car. I don't even know if she has a licence. Her licence was suspended, years ago, when she'd been drinking that time and the guards pulled her over. She might have applied for a new licence in Spain, I don't know. She's been drinking. And she's not right. You saw her yourself at the church. She's in a state.'

'OK, listen, take a breath. Try and calm yourself.'

'What am I going to do?'

'You're going to find her, that's what.'

'I've looked everywhere.'

'You haven't. You've missed a place. Someplace important to her. Or important to the kids, maybe.'

'I can't think. I'm going out of my mind.'

'Vinnie? Vinnie, listen to me now.'

I grip the phone, try to control my breath. Try to calm down. I'm no good to anyone like this, I know I'm not.

'I'd say she's gone somewhere where she can talk to the children. Maybe someplace that means a lot to her. Maybe she wants to explain things to them. She's their mother, after all. She wants them to understand.'

I nod. That makes sense, I suppose. It's my fault, maybe. I haven't given her enough time on her own with the kids. Haven't trusted her enough. Things have been crazy, with Ma, and Joey coming back and all the arrangements to be made. I haven't given the situation with Paula enough attention. I was just, I dunno, winging it, I suppose. The usual.

I keep thinking about Maureen. Her sister. Walking into the sea at Dollymount that night. The stones in the pockets of her coat. The tag still on the cuff of her jacket and her hair cut. Like she wanted to look nice when she was found. Presentable.

Dollymount Strand. I proposed to her there. Slid the ring up her finger. Ma gave me the ring. Her mother's ring. I worried that Paula mightn't like that. The idea of another woman's ring. I remember the way the stone sparkled in the last of the sun and Paula laughing and crying at the same time. 'It's beautiful, Vinnie,' she said. 'You're beautiful, Vinnie,' she said. She ran at me, flung herself into my arms, her legs wrapped tight around my waist. The hot taste of her mouth when I kissed her. The happiness I felt. A bright heat inside me, spreading and surging like the tide coming in over warm sand.

'Dollymount Strand,' I say.

'Is that where you think she might be?'

'Maybe.'

'Go on, then. Go and find them.'

'OK.'

'Ring me later. Let me know.'

'I will.' I hang up, get into the car. Janine and Kenny exchange a glance when I tell them about Dollymount Strand. How I think Paula might be there. And the kids. I know they're thinking about Maureen and what she did there, and maybe I'm wrong, but the closer we get to the strand, the more convinced I become that that's where I'll find her. And the children too.

Fifty Four

The tide is coming in.

We drive down the North Wall. Park on the beach.

Out to sea, the sun glances against the white walls of the Baily lighthouse at Howth. The sky is blue, interrupted by occasional clouds, small and white, like cotton wool. The strand is busy enough. The weather, and the promise of the bank holiday, I suppose. There are the usual kitesurfers, joggers, strollers, couples holding hands, a woman barefoot at the water's edge. She cries out as a wave reaches up her legs. She gathers her skirt in her hands, runs backwards and the sound of her laughter carries on the breeze. It's an innocent sound. A sound that suggests nothing bad could happen here. Not today.

'There's the car!' Janine points to a space on the other side of the car park and I follow the line of her finger and I see it. I start to run. My shoes crunch against the stones underfoot, and I concentrate on the rhythm of the sound and try not to think about anything else. I hear the squawk of a seagull, the relentless murmur of the tide coming in.

I reach the car first. There's no one inside. The driver's door hangs open and creaks in the wind that's getting up now. It looks abandoned. Not parked. Finn's jacket is flung across the back seat. I pick it up, tuck it under my arm. He should be wearing it. It's nippy now, with that wind.

I look around me, up the beach, then in, towards the sand

dunes. I can't see them. Behind me is the water. I can hear it, coming and coming.

Janine sits inside the car. Takes the keys out of the ignition and puts the handbrake on. Steps out of the car, closes the door, locks it. Anyone looking at us would think we're three ordinary people. Three friends. Out for a drive. A stroll. An ice cream, maybe.

I force myself to turn around. Examine the water. Even now, with the sun flashing against the surface, the water looks grey. Murky. There's a windsurfer out there, the wind punching a dent in the sail. I call out to him but he's flying along and doesn't hear me.

'Well,' Janine says, bending and taking off her shoes, because of the heels and the way they sink into the sand. 'At least we know they're here.' Without the shoes, she looks different. Smaller. Her feet are tiny. I've never noticed that before.

'KERRY! FINN!' I roar their names with my hands cupped around my mouth.

Nothing. The tide runs towards us, stops, pulls away. I try to think.

'Maybe they went up there,' Kenny says, pointing at the mounds of sand behind us, covered in the sharp marram grass that makes ribbons of your legs. 'To get some shelter from this gale.'

We make our way towards the dunes, our faces bent against the grains of sand carried by the wind. Underfoot, I see crisp packets, a flattened can of Coke, cigarette butts, the tail of a kite, withered by the elements. Why did she bring them here? What's her plan? Does she have a plan? Or is she like me, going from day to day, making it up as she goes along? Is there a purpose? Some reason she came back. Something she wants to do.

The thoughts come at me now, hit me and scatter like confetti caught on a breeze, airborne and swirling, no order to them, impossible to pin down.

Janine slips her hand through mine. Squeezes. When I look at her, she smiles and nods. 'It'll be alright, Vinnie.'

Kenny nods, agreeing. 'She probably just wanted to see them on their own. Chat to them and that.'

'It's just . . .' But there are too many thoughts, hard to put words on any of them. Taking the kids. Taking the car. Not saying a word. And today. Doing it today. Ma's funeral.

'Come on,' Janine says, taking my hand and pulling me along. 'We'll find them.'

I stop when I reach the edge of the dunes. Their slightly elevated position affords a better view of the beach. The water. My eyes are attracted by movement on the North Wall. The steps leading down to the water are on the other side of the wall. Maureen walked to the bottom of those steps and kept on going. From here, I can only see the top of the steps. Nearby is a figure, as still as the statue of Mary on the plinth at the end of the wall. Janine is looking too, looking at this figure.

'Is that . . .?' she says, squinting towards the wall.

I force myself to wait. To be sure. The figure – the woman – is dressed in black. Wide-legged black trousers billow from her legs like sheets on a line, in the grip of the wind. But it's the scarf that gives her away. Pink and green. *Your Ma's favourite colours, remember?* That's what Paula said this morning. When I picked her up on the way to the church.

I run, my feet sinking into the soft sand, slowing me down. Up the bank, onto the pier. I see her. It's definitely her.

'PAULA!' I'm shouting now. Running and shouting.

The woman turns. It's her. She smiles when she sees me. Smiles and waves.

'Where are they? Where are the kids?'

'The kids?' She looks at me and her eyes are wide and staring as if a piece of her is missing. I put my hands on her arms and shake her. In that moment, I hate her and my hate is pure and white and hot and it's the only thing I see, the only thing I feel.

'Stoppit, Vinnie!' Kenny shouts at me. He wraps his arms around my chest. Pulls me away. Steps between me and Paula. Looks at her. 'Listen, Paula, love, we're looking for the children. You took them, didn't you?'

She looks at him. 'I . . . I didn't take them. I just . . . I wanted to talk to them. Tell them why I can't stay. Here. In Dublin. How terrible things happen when I'm around. Like Mrs Boland. She was fine before I got here. Vinnie said she was right as rain.'

'She was an old woman,' Kenny says. 'It was her time, that's all.'

Paula shakes her head. 'I brought them to a café. I just wanted to talk to them. Get them to understand.' She puts her hand on Kenny's shoulder. 'I love them, Kenny. You believe me, don't you?'

He nods, and when he speaks again, he speaks slower, like she's someone who doesn't speak his language. 'Where did they go, Paula? The kids. Where are they?'

She looks around, helpless, like she's lost something but can't remember what it is. 'I put them back.'

'What do you mean, put them back? Where are they?' I'm shouting now, lunging forward, trying to get past Kenny, trying to reach her. People are staring. Stopping and staring.

'I just . . . Finn started crying and I couldn't make him stop and Kerry said Vinnie'd be worried so I . . . I brought them back to the parish hall. And then I decided to come down here. Say a prayer for Maureen.' Paula looks past Kenny, right at me. The sun is on her face but she doesn't blink. She stares at me.

I take a step back. Take out my phone. No signal. Three missed calls from Joey. Two texts. One from Joey:

The kids are here. At the hall. They're fine.

The other from Ellen:

Did you find them?

When I put the phone back in my pocket, Paula's looking at me, like she knows. She knows what I was thinking.

'I'd never hurt them, Vinnie, how could you think that?' Her voice is a whisper now, hard to hear in the wind.

I shake my head. Stuff my hands into my pockets. 'I was out of my head. I didn't know where they were. You just left. In my car. I don't know what I thought.'

'You did, though. Didn't you? You thought I was going to hurt myself. Hurt them as well.'

I shake my head again but the thought persists. *I did, though. I did think that.* I close my eyes and pull my hand down my face.

'Come on,' Kenny says, and he puts his arm around Paula and leads her away and she leans her head against his shoulder and lets him. Janine tugs my sleeve, gives me a small smile. She walks away and I follow after, back along the wall.

I did, though. I did think that.

Didn't I?

The past is hard to let go of.

It stays with you, long after it's done.

Fifty Five

'Mam told us that she's going back to live with Papa Spain,' Finn says, after I close his curtains and choose a book from the shelf. I sit on the edge of his bed and smile down at him, the messy head of him.

'Yeah,' I say. No point in saying anything else.

'Kerry says that Mam isn't well.'

I nod again. 'Sometimes, she's not well.'

'Is that why she had to go into hospital that time?'

'You remember that?'

'Yeah, Uncle Kenny made a fried egg and the wind blew the curtain into the frying pan and it went on fire.'

I laugh then. Six months, it was. Before I realised that the kitchen curtains weren't there. I presumed Paula had taken them down. To wash them, maybe. Before.

'Is it?' Finn asks again and I say, 'Yes, that's why she had to go to hospital.'

'She was sad. In the car today.'

'She'll miss you. You and your sister. When she goes back to Spain.'

'Callam was real sad when he had the chickenpox that time. He missed the school tour.'

I pick a book. *Fantastic Mr Fox*. I've read it to him a hundred times. Doesn't matter. He gets me to read it again.

I knock on Kerry's bedroom door but there's no answer. I open it. Poke my head 'round the door. She's lying on her bed, the earphones in. She doesn't turn around. I knock again, on the wall this time, the mural, and she turns her head, sees me, sits up. I walk to the window, lean against the sill. She reaches for the iPod, switches it off, takes off the earphones.

'I just wanted to say thanks,' I say.

'For what?'

'You minded your little brother today.'

She shrugs. 'Someone had to.'

'Well, I'm glad it was you.'

Another shrug. Smaller this time.

'Dad?'

'Yeah?'

A pause. She catches her hair in her hands, pushes it behind her shoulders. She looks at me then. 'Do you think I'll get what Mam has? I'll get bipolar?'

I suppose I knew she'd ask that question someday. I wish it didn't have to be today. It's been a long day. But I suppose today's as good as any other for a question like that.

I take a breath. I have to say something. It's hard. Having kids is hard. It's hard because you want only good things to happen to them.

'It's possible,' I say.

She nods. 'I knew that. We did it in Biology. DNA, genetics, all that kind of stuff.'

'Why'd you ask me, then?'

'I just . . . I wanted to see what you'd say. If you'd tell me the truth.' She smiles, and I'm glad I was honest with her. Glad I didn't dodge it.

'Well, you're not a kid any more, you know. You're nearly fifteen.'

'Finally. He notices.'

I walk over to her and she moves a little, makes a space for me. I sit beside her. I think about putting my arm around her, giving her a hug, maybe. Then I don't. Things are going OK. Don't want to wreck it.

'It doesn't mean you'll get it, though,' I say. 'It's just . . . it's a possibility.'

She nods. 'I don't think I'll get it. I feel pretty happy, most of the time.' This is news. Good news. My daughter feels happy.

Downstairs, I open a bottle of beer and sit in the garden. My phone beeps and I check the screen. It's Ellen, responding to the text I sent her when I got home.

Glad everything turned out OK. E

I think about Ma then. *All's well that end's well*, she might have said, after a day like today.

'The kids are safe as houses,' Joey said, when I got through to him on the way back to the parish hall.

'Good.' That's all I managed to say.

'I'll start clearing them out, will I? The old dears?'

'Ah, no, let them play on for a bit longer.' That's what Ma would have said.

Play on.

Paula's asleep in Trish's spare room. I told her she could stay here tonight. I wouldn't have minded the couch. She said no. There was something final in the way she said it.

I look at the text again. Did things turn out OK? I suppose they did. Just not the way I had planned.

I text Ellen back.

So am I.

I do one of those smiley, winky faces with the semi-colon and the bracket. Ma would get a kick out of that.

Fifty Six

Turns out Ma had a few quid in the bank. Not a fortune, by any means. But some put by, all the same. My half of that, together with the proceeds from the sale of her house, will be more than enough. To buy Paula's share of the house. With a few quid for Paula. A bit of a nest egg.

'Are you paying me off?' she asks when I tell her.

'No, it's what Ma would have wanted. She was always fond of you. Said you were the daughter she never had, remember?'

'That was a long time ago.'

We're in Trish's house. It's Wednesday morning. Her flight leaves at four. I'm watching her pack. The two suitcases are on the bed, already overflowing. She sits on one, tries to close it.

'Here,' I say, walking over. I take a pile of clothes out, fold them, put them back in the case. I stuff underwear and jewellery into the shoes, inspect the toiletry bag, take out two empty bottles of shampoo and a tub of body butter with only a knob left in the bottom. 'Rub that into your arms. You might as well use it up and then you can throw the empty tub away. Make a bit more room.'

The smell of vanilla spreads through the room. Sweet. Innocent, somehow. I know that if I smell it again, it'll take me back here. To this moment. Me and Paula in a room. Packing up. Saying goodbye.

I close the case but I have to get her to sit on it again so I can pull the zip around. We manage in the end. Paula sits on the edge of the bed, looks at the suitcase. 'You always were a better packer than me,' she says.

I shake my head. Sit beside her. 'There's no skill to it. It's just a question of reorganising things. Making them fit.'

'I was never very good at making things fit.'

'Would you stop. You just needed a bit of help. Look, it's grand now. It's done.' I tackle the second suitcase. It takes a while. I set it on the floor beside the other one and we look at them for a moment, the two cases, packed and ready to go.

Paula lifts her bottle of pills from the bedside table, shakes it so the sound cuts through the space between us, then slips it into her handbag.

'I thought I was better, you know. I could come back and . . . I dunno, things would be better.'

I spot a pair of her shoes, under the bed. Pick them up. Open the suitcase again. Try to stuff them in. 'How many pairs of shoes did you bring, in the name of God?'

She shakes her head. 'I shouldn't have come back.' Her hair falls across her face and I reach across, lift it, tuck it behind her ear.

'I'm glad you came back.'

She looks at me. 'Are you?'

I nod, surprised by the truth of it. 'I suppose I was always waiting for you. Waiting for you to come back. Every time the doorbell went, the phone, I always thought it might be you. It was like a kind of limbo in a way.'

'I'm sorry, Vinnie.'

'No, don't be. You came back. It's like we've jumped a hurdle. Got it out of the way. We can move on now. Both of us.'

'I wish I never got sick.'

'Me too.'

She puts her hand out, palm up, and I take it and we sit there for a while, on the edge of the bed, not speaking.

We walk to the school to collect Finn. She wants to do it. Wants me to go with her. 'For old times' sake,' she says.

We walk through the streets and in a way, it feels like old times.

Vinnie and Paula. Paula and Vinnie. People used to say it like it was one word. Run it together. VinnieandPaula. Like we were a unit. And we were, I suppose. For years.

We meet Jonathon, yer man from *Fair City*. He's a face as long as November. 'Just found out today,' he says, when Paula asks him what ails him, 'my character's getting murdered next month. A stabbing. In Howth. Like that's realistic. I get to linger in hospital for a few days after, but then it's curtains.'

'*Fair City*'s shite,' Paula tells him. 'You're better off out of it.'

The news that the soap opera he's been in for the best part of ten years is shite doesn't lighten Jonathon's mood and he moves away, his hands thrust deep in his pockets.

It's a beautiful day in Dublin, one of those days that looks like it might just last forever. The heat shimmers in front of us, making everything hazy, and Mrs Finnegan's apple blossom clusters along the branches that reach over her garden wall, into the street so we have to stoop, walking past.

We pass McCarthy's and there's Jimmy and Jackie Stowe, billowing like chimneys at the front door, touching the tips of their caps in greeting as we pass. One of them – I can never tell which one is which – winks at Paula and she ignores him and hurries on.

'I made a holy show of myself in there,' she says.

I don't say anything because, sometimes, there's nothing to say. Mary, ringing me. 'You'll have to come and take her home, Vinnie, she's out of control.' One night, I carried her out. Across my shoulder, like I was a fireman and the pub was on fire. Her kicking and roaring. 'I haven't finished my drink!'

We walk on. Here and there, the tarmac is sticky from the heat of the sun. 'You could be anywhere,' people tell each other. 'In Spain, even.' But there's no place like Dublin when she puts her lights on. No place I'd rather be and that's a fact.

'I love them, you know.'

I nod. 'I know.'

'It's just . . . coming back here . . . I don't know. Everything that's happened. I can't . . . I can't be with them. Day in, day out. Not like you can. I just . . . I can't, I'm not able for it. I thought I was.'

'You can come and visit. Any time. And they can come out to you. Summer holidays. Midterms. We can organise something.'

'You'd let them?'

'Of course.' A part of me tightens when I say that. I suppose I'll always worry about them. Maybe that's just part of it. Of being a parent. It comes with the job.

We round the corner and the school is visible now. Knots of parents gathered at the gates.

'What about you?' she asks.

'What about me?'

'What would you do with yourself if the kids came over to me for the midterm?'

I shrug. 'Haven't given it much thought.'

'You could spend time with Ellen.'

I stop. Look at her. 'I wasn't . . . I didn't go out of my way, you know. I wasn't looking for anything.'

She smiles at me and it's sad, the smile. It pulls at something inside me. 'I know, Vinnie. You don't have to explain.'

'Sometimes, I think . . .' I'm struggling here, struggling to find the right words. 'I think I didn't do enough. When you got sick. I didn't . . . I should have done more.'

She shakes her head. 'You did what you could, Vinnie. You did your best.'

I don't know if that's true but it's like Ma says. *You'll only get a creak in your neck, lookin' back.*

'We had a good run, you and me,' she says, touching my arm, and the touch is light. Faint, somehow. Like the memory of a touch. Of a hundred different ways we ever touched each other. A thousand. 'You deserve to be happy, Vince.'

'Everyone deserves to be happy.'

She stops walking then, moves towards me, pushes her face into my neck and I put my arms around her, hold her there. 'Are we going to be friends?' she whispers, and I feel the heat of her breath against my skin.

I nod. 'We *are* friends.' I let her go and we walk the rest of the way, without saying anything.

'Mam!' Finn rushes through the gates with his face split into a smile and it's only then I notice his adult teeth. Two of them, the front ones, coming down through the pink of his gums. He looks older all of a sudden. There's nothing babyish about his face any more. The notion sends a pang through me and in my head, Ma says, *'Would you ever cop on to yourself, Vincent.'*

Finn flings himself into Paula's arms and just as quickly disentangles himself before any of his classmates spot him. 'I scored two goals today!' he tells her, handing me his schoolbag and tucking his hand into hers.

'Papa Spain was a good keeper in his time. Did a trial once. In Manchester,' Paula tells him.

'Manchester United?' Finn's eyes widen.

'Manchester City.'

'Oh.'

'He still has a few tricks up his sleeve, you know. He'll show you when you come over in the summer.'

'Is Dad coming too?'

She looks at me and I feel it again. That pull, deep inside. It's hard to let go, I suppose. Hard to say goodbye.

'Dad might have other plans. Besides, it'll be nice, for a change, the three of us. You, me and Kerry. And Papa Spain. He can't wait to see you.'

Finn smiles and nods and launches into a plan he and Callam have to set up a circus, with Archibald as one of the star attractions. 'We're going to teach him how to roll over and play dead and maybe even jump through a hoop, but don't worry, we won't set it on fire or anything.'

Maybe you *can* teach an old dog new tricks.

Kerry's home from school when we get back. Her bag's in the hall. Half-day on Wednesdays.

'I'll go up and say goodbye to her,' Paula says.

'Me and Finn will be in the garden,' I tell her. She nods and walks up the stairs, moving slower now. I feel for her. Perhaps it was easier the last time. When there were no goodbyes.

We sit on the garden wall, out the front.

'Granny will never see me playing for Cardiff.'

I put my hand on his head, tousle his hair, warm from the sun.

'Do you think she can see us? From her cloud?' I don't know where he got the idea that she's on a cloud but he seems pretty positive about it.

'You were her favourite grandson,' I tell him.

'She didn't have any other grandsons.'

'Yes, but if she did, you'd still have been her favourite one.'

Paula walks out of the house alone. She nods at me, kisses the top of Finn's head. 'I'm going to go,' she says, and her voice is quiet and I wonder what went on inside.

'I'll give you a lift to the airport,' I say, getting off the wall. She shakes her head.

'I've asked Kenny to take me. I just . . . I'd prefer that.'

I nod. I get it. Better for the kids too. Hard to watch her walking away.

Goodbyes. There've been a few lately.

Joey. I dropped him last night. 'You'll have to come and visit now,' he said. 'That chunk of change Ma left, burning a hole in your pocket.'

'Down under?' I say, grinning.

'Yeah,' he says. 'Down under.'

And the pair of us are laughing as the doors slide open and he walks into Departures and disappears into the crowd. I think about the kids then. With ice cream cones, on Bondi Beach. And it doesn't seem mad or anything. It feels like something that might happen. Something we could manage.

Goodbye to Ma. I still can't get my head around it. I keep expecting to hear the peal of the doorbell. Three rings, she gave it. One was never enough. Always getting ready for the next thing. And the next. It seems impossible to think about all that energy. All her energy. Gone.

It'll take a while, I suppose. To get used to it.

Some things do.

We stand on the footpath, me, Finn and Paula. Kerry must be staying in her room. Kenny arrives wearing a shirt the same colour as Kermit the Frog, and a massive pair of sunglasses. He waves to us from the car, the engine idling away, waiting. I collect the cases from Trish's house, put them in the boot and Paula hugs Trish at her front door before she waves and turns, walks towards Kenny's car.

She throws her handbag in the front passenger seat and looks at us. Finn, suddenly shy, slips his hand into mine. She bends so her face is level with his. 'Have you got a kiss and a hug for your mam?'

He lets go of my hand then, wraps his arms around her neck, hugs her tight.

'That's my handsome boy,' she says, and I look at her and she's breathing him in, inhaling him and her eyes are closed but she doesn't cry and I'm glad about that, glad for Finn, for all of us.

She pulls him away from her, holds him at arm's length. 'You be a good boy for your daddy, won't you?'

He nods. 'I'm usually good,' he tells her, serious as a penalty shoot-out. He turns to me. 'Amn't I, Dad?'

I nod. 'You are.'

Paula bends and kisses him. 'I'm not going to say goodbye,' she says.

Finn looks confused. 'Why not?'

'Because I'll see you soon, won't I?'

'Do they have milkshakes in Spain?' he asks, and she laughs and says, 'Yes,' and he says, 'Adios. That's what they say in Spain you know. Teacher told me.'

'Adios, then,' Paula says, smiling.

Kenny calls Finn over to show him a new football app he got on his phone. Paula looks at me. Touches the side of my face.

'Goodbye, Vinnie.' She whispers it. I pull her in close to me, and in that moment she is the slip of the girl I once knew. The girl with the green eyes and the long hair and the plans.

All the plans we had.

She pulls away from me, turns quickly and reaches for the handle of the car door and that's when Kerry runs out of the house, holding something in her hands.

'Mam!' She shouts it and Paula turns.

'This is for you.'

It's a painting. Watercolours, I think. On a small square of canvas. Paula takes it, studies it and when she looks up she is smiling.

'It's beautiful,' she says. 'Look.' She hands it to me. It's a painting of a photograph taken when Kerry was a baby. I remember the photograph but I haven't seen it in years. Ma took the picture, far as I remember. Paula on the armchair in the front room, her hair covering half her face as she looks down at the baby in her arms. The baby's hand reaches out of the bundle of blankets, the tiny hand wrapped around Paula's little finger. Kerry has captured the image perfectly.

The quietness of it.

The beauty.

It's like all the beauty of the world is right there, on the canvas.

Dear Neil,

It's been a while. But this is it. This is the last letter.

One for the road, you would have said.

High time, I suppose. Even Dr Deery said YES with out-of-character emphasis when I broached the idea of not writing to you any more. She says it can become a crutch. Writing letters to people who have passed, she says. She never says 'dead'. Too negative, probably.

I had my last physio check-up yesterday. Duncan said I'd always have a limp but because he's so cheerful, it doesn't sound that bad. When you compare it to the original prognosis of never walking again, it seems like fantastic news. I am grateful to my limp for being a limp.

A limp and a scar. I got off lightly, when you think about it.

I saw an ad for Grey's Anatomy *the other day and I remembered how you used to watch it in secret. On your iPad in your study, with the sound down low so I wouldn't know. You didn't want me to think of you as someone who watched melodramatic medical dramas on the telly. I liked that you watched it. I liked that you didn't want me to know that you watched it.*

I should have said no, that third time, in the restaurant. I should have told you to get up off the floor and sit down and put the ring away and be my friend. I suppose this is what people mean when they talk about the benefit of hindsight.

Me and Faye are 'back together'. That's how she puts it, like we broke up for a while. I suppose we did, in a way. I did. We're going out tonight. After our yoga class. As a group, we make up about 50% of the class: me, Mum, Vinnie, Kenny, Janine, Faye and Barry. Week six. Janine is the best. She can do the splits.

Kenny's always bragging about how bendy she is. Vinnie still can't get over them. I don't know why. They're one of those couples who look like they've been together for years. But in a good way.

Vinnie is pretty terrible at yoga. His balance is awful, he falls over a lot. But he gets up, tries again. I like that about him. Makes me think that I can do that too. Try again. You're gone and I'm here and life goes on and on, whether you like it or not and I didn't like it. Not for a long time. The yoga class is on during EastEnders. *I record it but I don't always get time to watch the recordings any more. Not with college. The Fine Arts course is full-on. I should be a qualified art teacher just before it's time for me to retire! When Mum visits me now, she says, 'Are you not watching* EastEnders?' *She'd deny it, but she was as addicted as me in the end.*

We're all going to Vinnie's house after class today. He's cooking. Won't say what. Something French, I think. He bought a lot of garlic at the farmers' market yesterday. His kids are in Spain for the midterm, visiting their mum and grandfather. I know Vinnie misses them when they're not there. Worries about them. Kerry texted me a photograph of the sunset she's painting on the beach beside her mum's apartment. She says she's going to do the same course as me when she leaves school. Orna said she was a natural, when Kerry did her work experience at the studio.

Finn reckons you're sitting on a cloud, beside his granny. He's positive about this. I'm pretty sure you're not, but some days I think about you sitting there, with our baby girl in your hands. I worry about things then, what you might think about everything.

Dr Deery said this was normal. She said I have to be honest.

I haven't seen her for a good while now. She asked me, at our last session, how I felt about Vinnie.

I told her I love spending time with him.

'Yes, but how does he make you feel?' She sits back in her chair, like she's prepared to wait for however long it will take for me to answer.

'He makes me feel glad to be alive.'

That's what I say, in the end.

Ellen

Acknowledgements

If it takes a village to raise a child, then I think it's fair to say that it takes many villagers to write a book. And being a writer who is in the throes of raising three children, I think there are comparisons to be made between both ventures. Often, one is not just 'raising children' or 'writing books', but cajoling, persuading, pushing, pulling, yanking, roaring, patting, mauling, manipulating, crying, laughing, shrugging, smiling, hoping, trusting, fearing, loving . . . The whole gamut of the human experience is involved in both enterprises which, I suppose, is what makes such projects so compelling.

So, to the villagers who helped with this particular project, you know who you are but just in case you've forgotten, here you are again:

Thank you to Vanessa Dowling, one of the many dedicated nurses at St Patrick's University Hospital in Dublin 8, who took time out to show me around the fantastic facilities at the hospital and familiarised me with the mental health services offered to their service users.

Thank you to Declan Grant, who patiently answered my enquiries about the taxi business.

Thank you to Rob Scanlan, a GP who is always on the other end of the phone for my many medical-related enquiries.

Cathal Martin, my family doctor for many years, was charged with that role from when I began writing books until 2012, when he died by suicide. I take this opportunity to thank Dr

Martin for helping me realise how precious our mental health is, how easily eroded it can become, how jealously we should guard it.

Thanks as always to my agent, Ger Nichol, my editors, Ciara Doorley and Francesca Best and all the great people at Hachette Books Ireland and Hodder & Stoughton. Thanks also to Aonghus Meaney for his thorough copyediting, Jacqui Lewis for her meticulous proofreading, and to Sarah Christie for the lovely cover design.

Thank you to Bernie Furlong who is my 'go-to' person for information on a wide-ranging set of subjects, and who is also my friend.

Thank you to Niamh Cronin who helped me push the idea for this book down the runway until it took off, and for always making me laugh out loud.

And to Eamon MacLochlainn (junior) for the supply of answers to questions about things like golf and Luke Kelly.

Thanks also to Stan Erraught, for information about Dalymount Park, Bohemians, Shamrock Rovers . . . and a simile.

To Frank MacLochlainn, for the supply of football-related information. Any mistakes made are probably yours . . . but thank you all the same. For everything.

For my sister, Niamh, who is my lighthouse in stormy seas. Thank you seems too small for someone as important as you. But thank you all the same.

To the readers, as always. There would be no point without you. Thank you, thank you, thank you.

And finally, thank you to my three children, Sadhbh, Neil and Grace. When my sister, Niamh, first read this manuscript, she said there was a very definite theme, and that theme was parenting. I was impressed. A theme! I never set out to write about 'themes'. I write stories. But it's true to say that parenting is something I have become familiar with over the past sixteen years. On that note, I want to say a huge thank you to my own parents, Breda and Don Geraghty, for their years in the trenches.

Perhaps parenting is one of those things that you have to do yourself, before you can truly appreciate the work that goes into it. It is always interesting, sometimes terrifying, often amusing, occasionally mystifying. I want to thank my children, for giving me that theme. Their stories. This life.

About the author

Ciara Geraghty lives in Dublin with one husband, three children and an adopted dog called Heidi who is a King Charles Spaniel and the poshest member of their group.

Ciara's hobbies include giving up cigarettes, looking at pictures in recipe books and reading great books, mostly because they're great but also because they make her want to be a better writer.

She began writing when she was thirty-four years old and hasn't been able to stop since. She is the author of five novels, *Saving Grace, Becoming Scarlett, Finding Mr Flood, Lifesaving for Beginners* and *Now That I've Found You*.

Because writing is a fairly quiet, solitary activity, Ciara loves to hear from readers.

Join her on Twitter
@ciarageraghty

or on Facebook
www.facebook.com/CiaraGeraghtyBooks.

Drop in to her website to say hello and have a cup of tea* at
www.ciarageraghty.com.

* tea not provided.

Ciara Geraghty

LIFESAVING FOR BEGINNERS

Kat Kavanagh is not in love. She has lots of friends, an
ordinary job, and she never ever thinks about her past.
This is Kat's story. None of it is true.

Milo McIntyre loves his mam, the peanut-butter-and-banana
muffins at the Funky Banana café, and the lifesaving class he
does after school. He never thinks about his future, until the
day it changes forever.
This is Milo's story. All of it is true.

And then there is the other story. The one with a twist of fate
that somehow brings together a boy from Brighton and a
woman in Dublin, and uncovers the truth once and for all.

This is the story that's just about to begin . . .

**Read on for an extract from *Lifesaving for Beginners*,
out now in paperback and ebook.**

HACHETTE
BOOKS
IRELAND

PROLOGUE

1 June 2011; Dublin

He knows he is driving too fast. Not over the speed limit. Never over the speed limit. But too fast for the way he feels. The tiredness. It's in his bones. It has seeped into his blood. It's in his fingers that are wrapped round the steering wheel of the truck. It's in the weight of his head on his neck. He feels himself sagging. He straightens and slaps his face. He blinks, over and over, training his eyes on the road ahead.

He'll be home soon.

He turns on the radio and takes a long drink from the can of Red Bull on the dashboard. The sun has warmed it but he finishes it anyway. 'A Pair of Brown Eyes'. He turns up the volume and thinks about Brigitta.

The truck roars down the motorway.

Later, he will deny that he fell asleep at the wheel. But afterwards, in the stillness of night, when he sits up in bed and wonders why he is shaking, he will concede that it's possible – just possible – that he closed his eyes. Briefly. Just for a moment. A second. Perhaps two. Sometimes that's all it takes.

He can't remember how long he'd been driving when it happened. Too long. He should have pulled over. Climbed into the back of the cab for a rest. Splashed cold water on his face in a worn-out toilet cubicle at the back of a petrol station. He should have done a lot of things, he admits to himself when he sits up in bed in the middle of the night and wonders why he is shaking.

Instead, he drives on. The conditions are near perfect. The road is dry, the sun, a perfect circle of light against the innocent blue of the sky. It looks like a picture Ania draws for him with her crayons. She folds the pictures inside his lunchbox. 'So you won't miss us when you're far away, Papa.' A yellow sun. A blue sky. Four matchstick people. His face relaxes into a smile. He thinks perhaps this is when it happened. This is when he might have closed his eyes. Briefly. Just for a moment. A second. Perhaps two.

When he sees it, the deer is already in the middle of the road.

Some things are cemented in his memory. He remembers the beauty of the thing, the sun glancing against its dappled side as it runs its last run. The fear in the liquid brown eyes. Human almost, the fear. He's never seen a deer on the road before. He's seen the signs. The warning signs. But this is the first time he's seen one on the road. He knows he shouldn't try to avoid it. Shouldn't swerve. He wouldn't have, if he hadn't been so tired. He wouldn't have, if he hadn't taken on the extra shift. The Christmas-fund shift. He started it last January. Julija needs a new bike. And then Ania will want one. She always wants what her big sister has.

He grabs the steering wheel and swerves, glancing in the mirror only afterwards to check the lane is clear.

The lane is not clear.

The thud as the front of the truck hits the animal. Hits it anyway. The sound of his brakes, screeching, the crash of the gears as he wrestles them down. He remembers the car. A bright yellow car. There's a suitcase on the back seat. Held together with a leather belt.

The truck gaining on the car.

The sound when he hits it.

The sound.

His body shoots forward but is wrenched back by the seatbelt. Later, there will be a line of bruises from his shoulder to his hip. The airbag explodes in his face and he will have to admit to the judge that he doesn't know what happened next.

The witness will know. He will describe how the car, the bright yellow car, is tossed in the air like a bag of feathers, rolling and turning until it lands in the shallow ditch the workmen have been excavating.

The technical expert will know. He will talk about the truck. How it jackknives as it swerves, hitting two cars, causing one to roll and turn and end up in a ditch and embedding the other against the crash barrier, like a nut caught in the steely grip of pliers. The technical expert will present these facts with the calm monotone of a man who never wakes in the darkest part of the night and wonders why he is shaking.

The judge will say it's a miracle. That more people weren't killed. That woman in the Mazda, for example. The thirty-nine-year-old woman. A hairline fracture on one rib after being cut out of the car embedded against the crash barrier. That she will live to tell another tale is nothing short of a miracle. That's what the judge will say.

And Brigitta. His beautiful Brigitta. She will be in the courtroom. Somewhere behind him. She will have asked Petra to mind the children for the day. When they lead him away, he won't look for her. His eyes, open now, will be trained on the floor.

He will be a long time getting home.

1 June 2011: Brighton

Mam says, 'Milo, you gave me a fright. What are you doing up at this hour?'

I say, 'I set my alarm.'

'Ah love, you shouldn't have. It's five o'clock in the morning. You'll be falling asleep in Miss Williams's class.'

'No way. We're making papier-mâché masks. If everyone knows their spellings.'

'And do you know your spellings?'

'Course.'

'Sorry for asking, Einstein.'

The kitchen is colder than usual. Probably because the sun's not properly up yet. Mam stands at the counter, with her hands wrapped round the mug I got her last Christmas. It says 'World's Best Mum'. I tried to find one that said 'Mam' but I couldn't. They probably sell them in Ireland, where Mam is from. Still, she drinks out of it all the time. She says she doesn't mind about the Mum bit.

'What time is the ferry?'

Mam looks at her watch. 'I'd better go if I'm going to catch it.' Her suitcase is on the floor beside the table. It's still got Dad's old leather belt tied round it. She was supposed to get a new case ages ago. She must have forgotton. The sticker on it says 'Elizabeth McIntyre' but everyone calls her Beth.

'I'll put your suitcase in the boot.'

She smiles. 'Don't worry, love, I'll do it. Besides, the boot is full. I

4

forgot to take out the boxes of flyers I got for the café the other day. I'll put the case on the back seat. It'll be grand.'

I hand her the car keys and look out the window. There have been a few car robberies lately but Mam's car is still there. I don't think anyone would steal it. We call it the bananamobile. It's bright yellow. The writing is pink. Shocking pink, Mam calls it. It says 'The Funky Banana', which happens to be the name of Mam's café.

'So when are you coming home?'

'I've told you a million times already. I'll be home on Sunday.'

'I wish I could come to Auntie May's with you.'

'There's the small matter of school, remember. Anyway, you'll have a great time with your sister.'

That's true. Faith doesn't know how to cook so we won't have to eat vegetables and things like that. And Rob always gives me money to get DVDs and sweets when they have to go to Faith's room to talk. They're always going to Faith's room to talk.

Mam puts on her coat and hat. It's a beret, which is a French word and that's why you can't pronounce the t at the end. Her lips are red on account of the lipstick. She doesn't wear half as much make-up as Faith but she still looks nice. For an adult, I mean. She puts her hand on my head. 'Don't forget to brush that mop before you go to school, mister.'

I say, 'I won't,' even though I probably will forget.

'And you've got lifesaving class after school today, remember?'

'My bag's in the hall.' As if anyone would ever forget about that. I'm still in the beginners' class but Coach says if I keep on doing well, she'll move me up to intermediate next year.

'OK, so, see ya Sunday.'

'Yeah, see ya Sunday.'

'Are you gettin' too big to give yer auld mam a kiss?'

Mam's mad about kissing. So is Damo. He says he's done it loads of times with girls but I don't believe him. I mean, he's my best friend and everything, but sometimes he makes stuff up. His mam says she wouldn't believe him if he told her the time. And last summer, he said he climbed Mount Everest but when I asked him where it was, he said it was in Spain. Near Santa Ponza.

Mam holds out her arms. Before I can duck, she squeezes me so tightly I can barely move. Her hair tickles my face. She smells like soap and toothpaste. She'll probably tell me not to forget to brush my teeth. She kisses me on the cheek and I rub it away with the back of my hand.

'Be good.'

'I'll try.'

'I mean it, Milo. No messin' with Damien Sullivan, OK?'

She's only saying that because of what happened the last time she went to Ireland. And that was only an accident. Damo's eyebrows have nearly grown back now.

'And make sure you brush your teeth.'

'I will.'

'I'll ring you tonight, OK?'

'Promise?'

She presses the palm of her hand against her heart. 'Cross my heart and hope to die.' She picks up her suitcase with the leather belt wrapped round it and that's when I have the idea. About buying her a new case for Christmas. I still have most of my First Holy Communion money in the post office. I'll buy her a green one. Green is her favourite colour.

I stay at the window until she drives up the road and I can't see her anymore.

2 June 2011: Dublin

'She's coming round.'

'Thank Christ.'

'Kat?'

'Katherine?'

'Can you hear me?'

'Come on now. Wake up.'

'Don't crowd her.'

'Kat?'

'Easy now. Take it easy.'

'Thomas?' My voice sounds strange. Rusted. Like I haven't used it in a long time.

'Give her some space.'

'Am I in a hospital?'

'Get her some water.'

'What happened?'

'It's all right. You were in an accident but you're all right. You're all right now.'

'Tell me what happened.'

'Calm down, Kat. Take it easy.'

My breath is quick and shallow. Panic isn't far away. I move my legs to see if I can move my legs. They move. I can move my legs. I try to calm down, to beat panic back with both hands.

Someone puts a hand under my head. Puts a glass against my mouth. I think it's Thomas. 'Here, take a drink of water.' That's definitely him. The soft, low voice. It would make you think of Wispa bars, whether you wanted to or not.

The water goes down, cold and pure. Panic falters. Takes a step back. Thomas's hand is solid against the back of my head. I keep my eyes closed, in case he's looking at me. In case he sees the panic. And the gratitude. I am weak with gratitude all of a sudden.

When I open my eyes, I say, 'I'm not forty yet, am I?' so that we can have a laugh and everything can go back to normal. It works because everyone has a bit of a laugh and the atmosphere in the room slackens and there's a chance that things can get back to normal.

Thomas says, 'You've still a bit to go.'

The light grates against my eyes as I look around the room. The hospital room. I'm in a hospital. I hate hospitals. I haven't been in a hospital bed since I was fifteen.

I do a headcount. Four people. They look tired, like they haven't slept, or, if they have, they've slept badly. My parents. My oldest friend, Minnie. And Thomas. Almost everyone.

I say, 'Where's Ed?'

My mother says, 'I had to send him home. He was too emotional. You know how he gets.'

'He's not on his own, is he?'

Dad steps forward. 'Your brother's fine, Kat. Don't worry. I brought him to Sophie's house and Sophie's parents are there. They'll look after him. You need to worry about yourself for now.'

'What's wrong with me?' I feel far away, like I have to shout to make them hear me.

Dad says, 'You got a bump on your head. The doctor says it'll hurt for a while.'

Mum says, 'And you've got a fractured rib. You either got

it in the accident or afterwards, when they cut you out of the car.'

'Jesus.' I curl my hands into fists so no one can see the shake in them.

Minnie says, 'It's not even a proper fracture. It's just a hairline one.'

Thomas says, 'You were lucky, Kat.'

I don't feel lucky. I feel far away.

Minnie looks at her watch. 'Well, now that I know you're not going to cark it, I suppose I should go back to work.' She sounds annoyed but when I look at her, she's got that pained expression on her face that she gets when she's trying not to smile.

It's only when Mum puts her hand on my forehead that I realise how hot I am. Her hand is cool and soft. I'd forgotten how soft her hands are. Her eyes are puffy, like she's been crying. But she never cries. The last time I saw her crying was in 1989, when Samuel Beckett died.

She says, 'We'll go too. We'd better pick Edward up.' She pulls at some strands of my hair that are caught in the corner of my mouth. I try to sit up but I'm like a dead weight so I stop trying and lie there and try to make sense of things.

The room smells of heat and bleach. The sheets are stiff and make a scratching sound when I move. There's a deep crack zigzagging along the ceiling. Like the whole place is going to come tumbling down. Right down on top of me.

Dad says, 'Get some rest, Kat. I'll call you later, OK?'

'Will you tell Ed I'm fine? Tell him I'll see him soon. Tomorrow.'

'Of course.' Dad bends, kisses the corner of my eye. I'd say he was going for my forehead but he's a little short-sighted.

Minnie says, 'The next time you're going to have a near-death experience, could you do it on a Friday? Get me out of the weekly meeting with the Pillock.' Pillock is what Minnie calls her boss, and the funny thing is that they get on quite well. She picks up her handbag and coat and is gone in a cloud of Chanel Coco Mademoiselle.

Now it's just Thomas and me and, all of a sudden, I feel sort of shy, like I've been doing the tango in my bedroom with an imaginary partner before noticing that the blinds are up and the neighbours are gawking. I grab the sharp edge of the sheet and pull it to my neck.

I say, 'Shouldn't you be spreading dung on some poor unfortunate turnips?' If you ask Thomas what he does, he'll say he's a farmer, even though he's a freelance journalist who happens to have inherited a smallholding in Monaghan where he grows impractical things like grapes that are never anything but sour, and sunflowers that, as soon as their heads poke above the earth, get eaten by his one goat, two pigs, three hens, a garrulous goose and a lamb-bearing ewe.

He doesn't answer immediately. Instead, he sits on the edge of the bed. Carefully, like he's afraid he might break something. I want to punch his arm and tell him he's a big eejit but I can't because of the wires attached to my wrist. I don't think I can laugh out loud either. My head feels funny: heavy and dense. When I touch it, there's a bandage, wrapped round and round.

I say, 'This is a bit *Grey's Anatomy*, isn't it?' My voice sounds nearer now but there's a shake in it. I clear my throat.

He smiles but only briefly. Then he puts his hand on mine. His hands are huge. Like shovels, they are. I pull my hand away. 'What?'

He says, 'What do you mean?'

'You look kind of . . . appalled. Is it my hair?'

He smiles a bit longer this time.

He says, 'I'm just . . . I'm glad you're OK. When they said the car was a write-off, I thought . . .'

'The car's a write-off?'

'Yeah. Sorry.'

'I love that Mazda.'

'I know, but it's replaceable.' He looks at me when he says that. A really intense look like he's cramming me for an exam. For a terrible moment, I think he's going to say something horrendous. About me. Not being replaceable. Something heinous like that.

But he doesn't say that. Instead, he says this:

'I thought you were dead.'

'Jesus, this is actually cheesier than *Grey's Anatomy*.'

'Can't you be serious for a moment?'

'I'm as serious as a car crash.'

'That's not funny.'

'It's a little bit funny.'

Thomas nods, thank Christ. He's not usually like this. He's usually got quite a good SOH, as Minnie calls it. Even though she's got Maurice and they've been smugly coupled up for years, she still reads the ads. For me, she says. I don't know if she does it anymore. The Thomas situation has been going on a fair while now. Maybe a year and a half.

Although I think Thomas said, 'Twenty-two months, actually,' when I mentioned it the other day.

Thomas says, 'Do you remember the accident?'

I nod. 'Sort of.'

'What do you remember?' He can be such a journalist sometimes.

'There was a deer on the road.' What the hell was a deer doing on the road? 'There was a truck. It swerved. Really suddenly. And there was a car. In front of me, I think. A yellow one. Really bright yellow. Something about a banana written on it. Then the airbag exploded in my face and then . . . I don't know . . . I don't think I remember anything else.'

'You could have died.'

'Are you going to keep on saying that?'

'That woman . . . the one in the yellow car. She . . . she died.'

'You're not going to cry, are you?'

'No.'

'Thank Christ.'

Thomas stands up. Walks to the door. Pauses. Looks back at me.

I say, 'Can you get the doctor?'

'Are you feeling OK?' He looks worried, like maybe I've got a brain tumour or something.

'I want to know when I can get out of here.'

'I'm sure they'll want to monitor you for another while. You've been out cold.'

'I just want everything to get back to normal.'

He looks at me then. Says, 'No.' Like we're in the middle of an argument.

'What do you mean, no?'

'I mean no. Things are different now. You could have died.'

'Can you stop saying that?'

'We've wasted enough time.'

I manage to prop myself up on my elbows. I ignore the pain in my head. My body. I need to nip this in the bud. I say, 'Look, there's no need for all this. I didn't die. I'm fine.'

'I don't care.' Thomas closes the door. Puts his back against

12

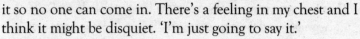

it so no one can come in. There's a feeling in my chest and I think it might be disquiet. 'I'm just going to say it.'

'I wish you wouldn't.'

'I know. But I'm going to say it anyway. I love you.'

'Where are my clothes? I need to get out of here.'

'I want to get married.'

'Congratulations. Who's the lucky lady?'

'And I'd love to have a baby.'

'Good for you. They're making huge leaps in human biology these days so I'm thinking, any day now.'

'Can you stop joking around, just for a minute?'

'How about a peace settlement in the Middle East while we're at it?'

He sighs then. 'I'm going to get the doctor.'

'Good idea. See how she's getting on with that cure for pancreatic cancer.'

It's only when Thomas leaves the room that I notice how quiet everything is. Quiet as a grave, Thomas would probably say in his current maudlin form. There's pain down my right side. But other than that and the dull throb in my head, everything feels the same as usual. I'd love a cigarette. I don't know where my bag is. I need my phone. I need to phone Ed – he'll be worried – and tell him not to worry. Tell him that everything is the same as usual.

Nothing has changed.

Even Thomas, when he returns, seems to have gone back to his usual self. He couldn't find the doctor but he has somehow discovered that one of the nurses keeps hens in her back garden and they've been discussing feeds and eggs and coops and what have you.

It's only when Thomas is leaving – I have to stay another night for 'observation'– that he goes all funny again. He says, 'I want you to think about what I've said.'

I say, 'Can you put the telly on before you leave?'

Thomas hands me the remote. 'Here.' His tone is brusque but then he bends down from his great height and kisses me. Right on the mouth. As if I'm not lying defenceless in a hospital bed, with no access to a toothbrush or toothpaste or mouthwash or anything. He just kisses me like he always does. No lead-up. No warning. Just his mouth on top of mine. It always gets me. How soft his mouth is. He's so big and farmer-ish, you'd be expecting dry, chapped lips from being out in all sorts of weather. He kisses me for longer than would be considered appropriate in a hospital visit sort of scenario. I don't tell him to stop.

'I'll pick you up tomorrow. Take you home.'

I think the accident has had some effect on me after all because, all of a sudden, there's a chance I might cry. I'd say it's the medication they have me on. Because of the shattered ribs. Well, OK then, a hairline fracture on one rib.

I nod and close my eyes as if I'm going to have a nap.

When he leaves, I open my eyes and – this is the strange part – I do cry. Not loud enough for anyone to hear. But still. There are tears. I'm crying all right. They gave me something for the pain and they said it was strong. I'd say it's that. I blow my nose and lie down and close my eyes. I want to go to sleep as quickly as I can so it'll be tomorrow as soon as possible then I can go home and everything can get back to normal.

Ciara Geraghty

FINDING MR FLOOD

Dara Flood always says the most interesting thing about her life happened before she was born. Thirteen days before she came into the world, her father walked up the road and never came back.

Now in her twenties, she lives a quiet life with her mother and sister, Angel, and works at the local dog pound – she finds dogs much easier to understand than people.

But when Angel gets sick and neither Dara nor her mother is a match for the kidney she desperately needs, Dara knows she will do anything to save Angel – even track down the man who left them behind.

So with the help of a scruffily handsome private investigator with a few secrets of his own, Dara steps anxiously into the big wide world with a dream of finding Mr Flood.

But as you know, following your dreams can lead you to unexpected places . . .

Out now in paperback and ebook

HACHETTE
BOOKS
IRELAND

Ciara Geraghty

BECOMING SCARLETT

Meet Scarlett O'Hara – wedding planner extraordinaire –
who's famous for making dreams come true.

From scuba-diving ceremonies to flamingos at the reception,
her colour-coded checklists make everything look simple.

Scarlett's personal life ran just as smoothly. Until now.

Her dependable boyfriend has moved to Brazil.

She's had to give up her Dublin flat and move back home.

And she's pregnant.

Worse still, she doesn't know who the father of the baby is . . .
even though she's slept with exactly 4 ½ men in her entire 35
years.

How will Scarlett cope now all her best laid plans have gone
with the wind?

Out now in paperback and ebook

HACHETTE
BOOKS
IRELAND

Ciara Geraghty

SAVING GRACE

*It all started with a bottle of Baileys that was a year out of date but
I drank it anyway . . .*

One minute, well, Friday night, you're in a long-term if long-
distance relationship with the perfect Shane. The next,
Saturday morning, you're waking up in bed with the mother of
all hangovers . . . and Bernard O'Malley, newest member of the
I.T. department.

Another entry on the list of things you can't forgive herself for.
The worst is Spain. What you did there. And what happened
to your brother. Ever since then, your life has slowly spiralled
out of control . . .

You dust yourself down, have a cigarette and pull on your
stiletto boots. But you know that something's got to give. You
just hope it's not the zip on your skinny jeans . . .

Out now in paperback and ebook

HACHETTE
BOOKS
IRELAND

Reading is so much more than the act of moving from page to page. It's the exploration of new worlds; the pursuit of adventure; the forging of friendships; the breaking of hearts; and the chance to begin to live through a new story each time the first sentence is devoured.

We at Hachette Ireland are very passionate about what we read, and what we publish. And we'd love to hear what you think about our books.

If you'd like to let us know, or to find out more about us and our titles, please visit www.hachette.ie or our Facebook page www.facebook.com/hachetteireland, or follow us on Twitter @HachetteIre